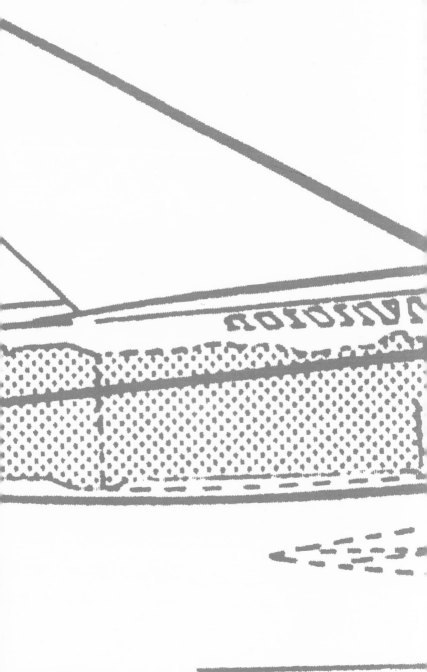

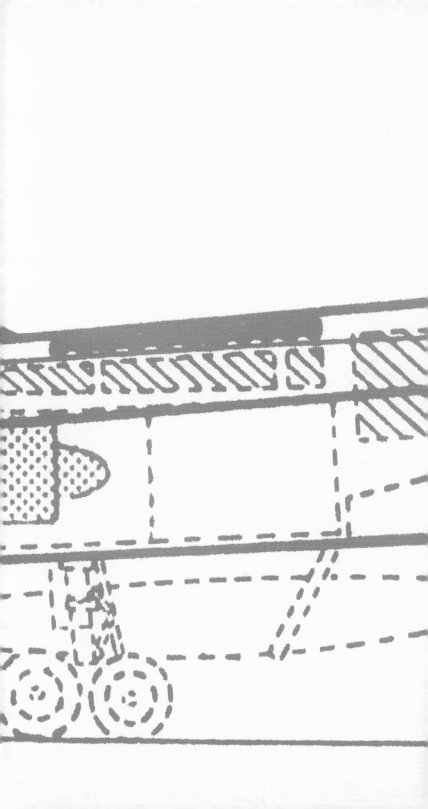

THE LIGHTNING FIELD

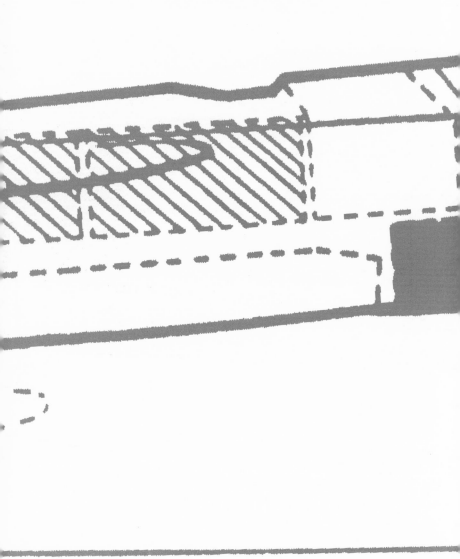

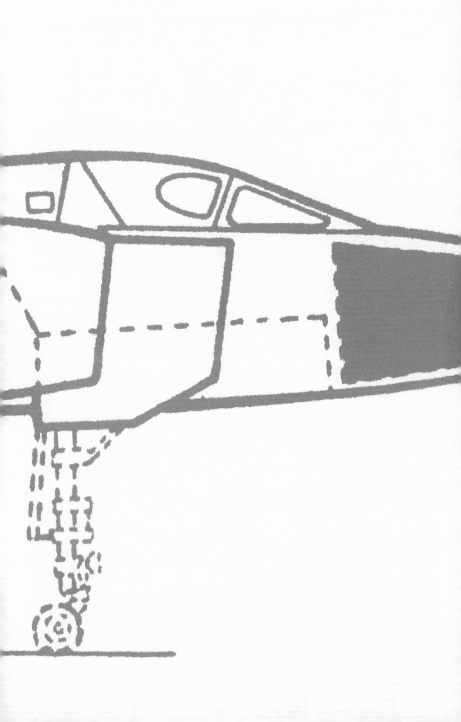

THE LIGHTNING FIELD

A novel by Heather Jessup

GASPEREAU PRESS · PRINTERS & PUBLISHERS
KENTVILLE, NOVA SCOTIA
MMXI

This book is for you, Mum and Dad
Sincerely, Yours Truly, Love

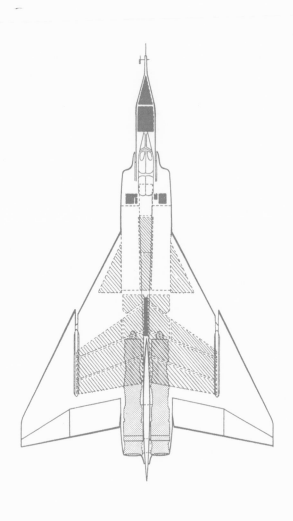

THE GOLDEN SWAN

When her father whistled, the entire world was the length of one sidewalk crack to the next sidewalk crack. If he whistled while they walked this meant he was thinking. (Most likely it meant he was thinking about fishing and when he could next get up to Lake Simcoe.) Lucy's father could whistle entire symphonies, entire operas. He could whistle the high soprano notes of flutes and the low sadness of the oboe. Lucy looked in all of the shop windows that hadn't closed their dark velvet curtains—silverware, fabric, jars of candies—and made song requests to her father. On Sundays he would only whistle hymns.

"All things bright and beautiful," Lucy shouted, and Simon Ainsworth would start up like a marching band. "Go tell it on the mountain." He would switch scores once they'd reached the next block. Mavis, Lucy's mother, would hum the descants at Lucy's side, her voice unfurling like the long lavender ribbon tied into Lucy's freshly brushed red hair. It was as if her father's whistling created a room for them. No, not a room, but a silk brocade sedan-chair carried on the shoulders to cross streams and swamps and deserts in faraway lands. That's how Lucy felt when her father whistled. That she was being taken somewhere softly, wearing silk pyjamas, and given the perfect weight of an orange to hold in her hand.

¶ This is where Lucy goes now when she can't fall asleep. She goes to Sunday mornings when the shops were closed. She goes to the quiet of streets with very few cars. She has been moving slowly lately from room to room in the house on Maple Avenue, resting on top of the children's beds with a worn quilt she brings along with her after a long morning of packing up boxes with Kier, her first-born. They have cleaned out the basement. All of her records are packed. The plates with the windmills are wrapped in newspaper. In the afternoon, Lucy tells Kier she thinks she will lie down for a moment, although she never gets under the bedcovers—that would dirty the sheets and feel like defeat—instead she sleeps as a cat sleeps, not asleep but in a lesser layer of awake.

Sometimes, to wake her, Kier will bring her a tray of tea, carrying it up to Rose's room, the milk in a creamer, the sugar in a matching china sugar bowl, the tea made properly; not with a tea bag thrown into a mug, but in a teapot big enough for two with a cosy and her favourite cup, printed with lilies of the valley. "Tea, of all things, must remain elegant, Lucille, even if everything else is in decline." This is Lucy's mother speaking in a British lilt, although her mother Mavis is now long dead. Lucy is glad she taught her boys how to make tea properly. Peter had never really known how. But that didn't matter now, did it?

¶ When she was a girl, from the window of a streetcar, Lucy had seen men cutting and rolling out long strips of sod for a lawn-bowling green. She pictured her bare feet against the green grass and knew that it was this aisle that she wanted to walk along when she got married. This kind of a carpet wouldn't be allowed at her family's parish of Saint James. The church had a red wedding carpet that the Altar Guild kept rolled up in a dusty closet in the basement. "Think of the dirt," the altar ladies would say.

Lucy had learned in English class that if a play ended in a marriage it was a comedy, and if a play ended with someone dying it was a tragedy. But what Lucy didn't know was if a wedding or a death happened at the beginning of a play, how could you tell which one it would be?

"I think about my funeral more often," Lucy's friend Claire France had told her.

Lucy loved her friend's name, Claire France. Just talking with her made Lucy think of baguettes, and bicycles, and Picasso in his polka-dotted neckerchief (she had seen his portrait in her father's copy of *Life* magazine), and of sipping champagne at the top of the Eiffel Tower. Lucy wasn't sure if they even served champagne at the top of the Eiffel Tower, but sipping champagne is what she imagined one should do.

Lucy and Claire sat together in the bleachers after school and played Spit or Spite and Malice with a deck of cards that Claire had stolen from her brother's room. A picture of a dark-haired girl in a red bikini on the back. Lucy had never seen a real bikini.

"I think about all the girls in our grade who've been cruel to me. I picture them all crying and feeling oppressed by guilt at the fact that I'm dead and they'll never be able to apologize."

"You never imagine your dress?"

"God no."

Lucy looked at the boys' rugby team practising on the field.

"Have you ever heard of Beryl Markham, Lu?"

Lucy looked down at the queen Claire had just played. "Huh?"

"She was a writer and a pilot. Hemingway admired her prose. I always thought of you sort of like Beryl Markham. Like Amelia Earhart, except you don't die in a plane crash, you die on an exotic beach somewhere holding one of those drinks with a pineapple wedge and a tiny paper umbrella."

"Which one was Hemingway again?"

Claire hit Lucy on the arm. "God, champ, don't you know anything?"

Lucy hit her back. "I read. I'm the one who told you what pathetic fallacy means, remember? I'm the one who got a copy of the *Kinsey Report*. That took me convincing Cheryl's cousin to carry it over the border back from Buffalo, and now, thank god, we finally know what a wet dream is."

"Yes. We're enlightened."

This was before Lucy had met Peter, a time that is difficult for Lucy to fully comprehend from her distant perspective as an old woman napping on a bed. Although, of course, inside that old woman she feels precisely seventeen. It's the playing cards on the bleachers she can hardly believe. Game after game of casual chatting with hearts and spades. That particular type of nothing that one does when one is young. When exactly did she stop doing nothing?

When did the world flood in and take over those long afternoons without requirements? And yet, the whole time one is doing nothing, there is this peculiar desire for something to begin. When Lucy met Peter, she thought that her life had begun. How little she knew back then.

¶ The first month Peter started work at Avro Aircraft, the fields and runways were white. A line of boot prints marked the path from the parking lot to the hangar door in the freshly fallen snow. Peter drove to work while it was still dark, teeth brushed, car radio on to the news. This was before Highway 427 was built. This was before Toronto had an international airport. This was back before Finch Avenue was named after the famous hotelier and was still called, in these parts, Peel Regional Road 2: a concession road, with churches, schoolhouse and cemeteries lining either side. These were the mornings when Peter imagined Lucy lingering lazily in their apartment on College Street, before any of the children were born; before the accident; before the endings began because everything was busy beginning. She was tidying the morning newspaper perhaps. Maybe she was jotting down things to get at the grocers that afternoon. Peter wasn't actually sure what she did when he wasn't home. They had recently been married.

Before Avro Aircraft took over, the hangar where Peter worked was called Victory Headquarters and supplied planes and ammunition to the front lines. Peter hadn't been at the front lines. He'd never stood in muddy rivers hoisting out dead bodies. He'd never swum through the currents of those rivers leaving the dead behind. Peter was stationed in Cornwall, England, as an aviation mechanic patching-up Allied planes. Lancasters mostly. He was chosen by a Lieutenant Harvey Briggs to join the Mechanics Corps when they'd landed in London the spring Peter was to graduate from high school.

"What's thirteen eights?" The officer barked out to the lot of them.

Peter stepped forward, "One hundred and four, Sir," then stepped back in line.

"Nineteen twelves."

"Two hundred and twenty-eight, Sir."

The other soldiers looked at him.

"Thirty-seven times ninety-one."

"Three thousand three hundred and sixty-seven," Peter said.

"Sir," the officer said.

"Three thousand three hundred and sixty-seven, Sir," Peter said.

"I'll have to trust you on that one."

¶ Peter felt, when he returned home from England, that he'd spent the war listening to the war on the crackling shortwave radio bracketed to his metal tool cart. The war was the program that was on when *Best of the Big Bands* wasn't playing. His corps was relatively safe, stationed as they were in Cornwall. They saw more cows in the abandoned rye fields than Nazis. Peter cautiously repaired gauges and throttles. He carefully soldered radio wires. He was seen by his comrades to be slightly inhuman. Even with hammers, welding torches and the occasional bomb-siren wailing through the hangar around him, Peter was able to calculate, without a figuring pad or a slide rule, the exact weight that should be patched onto a wing so a shot-up Lanc could fly straight again.

Halfway through the war, Peter gripped three small wires: green and black in one hand, white in the other, like a garter snake uncoiling from its skin. His foot tapped to Jelly Roll Morton. He stood by the back wall beneath the posters of pin-up girls that the other mechanics had plastered around the workshop. He looked up at his favourite one. He'd had the time to pick out a favourite, he realized: the girl on ice skates that had taken a tumble and was looking behind her, down past her short tartan skating-skirt to her back thighs already starting to bruise. Standing there like that, with the three wires in his hands, and the pouting pin-up girl staring down at him in her tartan, it occurred to Peter that what he was doing in England was insignificant. He was a mechanic. All he'd done was dirty his fingernails with grease. The pilots came in from dogfights. He heard them by the canteen talking about aerial combat manoeuvres as if speaking another language: the Scissors; the Split-S; the Chandelle, invented by the French, Peter learned, during the First World War.

"Come on, that's the basics, Mac," he heard one pilot say to another, "You roll her, right? And then take her up a steep bank." The pilot poured himself a fresh cup of coffee from his Thermos. "As she begins the turn, you pitch the nose up well above a power-on stall. But before the stall takes and you lose speed, level the wing and drop the nose. Then," he dunked a rarely rationed shortbread into his mug, "you're right as rain, straightened-out just above stall speed."

Peter had no idea what the hell they were talking about, but knew, sitting silently at the far end of the lunch tables eating a sandwich, that he was not a pilot. He was a mechanic. Even if there was a small part of him that wished to shoot enemy planes out of German skies like a kid hitting can after can off a fence with a slingshot, he was scared shitless at the thought of going up in one of those flying tanks. Peter had realized early in his life that he would never make a daring rescue. He was scared to fly. The only thing that Peter could envisage rescuing from that Air Force hangar in Cornwall was a shorted-out electrical system, and so the pilots remained another species to Peter, although a kind species, like a dog, a rarely bred dog, like one of those lanky hounds, or a whippet. The well-bred pilots asked him questions courteously, knowing he was the man who could give them a new altimeter if need be. Peter, in turn, tried to remember their names when they spoke with him. Some he recognized from regular fuel-ups: the young one from Great Village, Nova Scotia, who had given him a candy bar; the one with a punched-out hockey-player's smile. But Peter never really got to know the men who flew off again from the runway; he was needed at the back of the hangar to figure out another calculation, to solder a fuse, to rewire.

Peter never would have said it was God. Why do we always need something else besides the facts in front of us to explain the world? It wasn't that he didn't believe in miracles. He vaguely felt that his life being spared during the war was a miracle—but a miracle in the sense of statistics: a miracle in the way cars stopping at a four-way intersection is a miracle, or the Brooklyn Bridge is a miracle.

¶ Peter met another mechanic in the infirmary on the boat home that said they'd be able to find work at any of the aeronautical engineering companies across North America. There was a market for skilled trades.

"I don't have high school." Peter leaned over a bucket. "Didn't finish English."

The mechanic had gotten the hook of a trout fly caught in his hand trying to fish off the boat. "English? They don't care, mate."

Peter looked over at the man's hand. "You know there's no trout in salt water, right?"

"Do now."

When Peter's boat sailed into the harbour in Montreal, he was greeted with tickertape. Girls who spoke French blew kisses at him and his fellow soldiers walking up Rue Mansfield to the Gare Centrale to catch their trains. By the time Peter had returned to Toronto he had seen virtually nothing of Europe and knew he was not fit to be in either the Air Force or the Navy. Peter also knew, however, that he could fix any wire on a plane in the beat of a moth's wing. He could patch pneumatically controlled air-pressurized valves. He knew how to repair hydraulic actuating subsystems for both braking and fuel injection. And he learned, from an article on defence mechanics in the September 1945 issue of *Aircraft Magazine,* that he purchased for fifteen cents at a Café Figaro and then proceeded to read on the train-ride home, that "Combat warfare is over" and that after the U.S. attack on Japan, "It is simply a matter of who has the bomb."

Lockheed Martin out in California had wanted him. Grumman Engineering Corp in New York had wanted him. The Dallas offices of Pratt and Whitney had offered to have Peter flown down for a tour of their facilities. Peter had walked carefully from booth to booth at the aeronautical job recruitment fair held in the Horse Palace of the Canadian National Exhibition when he had arrived home. Each aeronautical company had their own glossy pamphlets and posters of smiling men holding briefcases, walking down Madison Avenue. Or of planes flying over palm trees with the thin blue line of the Pacific in the distance. Businessmen with thick hands and American accents manned the tables and smoked cigars. Peter remembered Grumman's poster particularly: an image of a neighbourhood where all the houses were made out of Bibles. *Knowledge* the poster read, *is the ultimate defence if kept free to repel the evils that besiege mankind. To give knowledge the time to win, it must be protected on its outer perimeter by weapons.* Peter stared at the poster. At all the miniature Bible houses in a straight Bible row.

"In'erested in protec'n the free world, son?" A broad man wearing a grey suit huffed toward Peter.

"Just looking," Peter said, and turned around.

Peter had imagined going back over to England to work. He'd liked the rhythms of the days. How at five o'clock, if it was possible, the mechanics broke for tea. England was bucolic. He had learned that word over there. Lieutenant Briggs had uttered the word "bucolic" while talking about the mist settling over the Cornwall pastures. At first Peter thought it was a disease that had broken out amongst the cattle. "No, Jacobs, and pass that strawberry jam your mother's sent you. It means rustic, idyllically rural." Briggs started reciting poetry. He was always surprising Peter. *Come live with me and be my love, and we will all the pleasures prove that valleys, groves, hills, and fields, woods, or steepy mountain yields. And we will sit upon the rocks, seeing the shepherds feed their flocks, by shallow rivers to whose falls, melodious birds sing madrigals.*

And then, as Peter tells it, he met Lucy Ainsworth at a young people's church bingo game and as suddenly as his commanding officer had broken into the iambic tetrameter of Christopher Marlowe, Peter didn't want to go back to England anymore.

¶ The stone church with its dark wooden rafters and wide wooden pews was a boat to Lucy. An ark. An ancient underwater diving discovery. The church smelled like pine trees and something else, amber maybe, something old and clear like a crystal. In the church, Lucy lived in the hollows of her throat and mouth and ears. She shut her eyes and held onto the wooden pew beneath her, anticipating the music.

The church was silent except for faint coughing and the certain collective breath of the choir. The opening G minor chord of Allegri's *Miserere Mei*: their voices turning quarter notes to song; their bodies the instrument. The hymn rose into plainchant as sure and even as the vertebrae up Lucy's spine. The movement into the simple chorus was a window, a measured amount of sky, and then the soprano's voice rising like Lucy imagined the sun rose over a desert, the waves of heat and light reverberating over great distances, over dunes and vanished gardens. Lucy felt the highest note at her throat and she took a breath, the music pulling her upward. She imagined her body rising up and out of her seat, hovering above the other parishioners in shocking ascension.

When the music ended, as suddenly as it had started, opening the latch that let Lucy into her mind's room, she opened her eyes. Nave, Lucy saw with her opened eyes, transept-crossing, gothic arch. For her confirmation she had chosen to study the architecture of the church. Nave was named for the keel shape of its vaulting, like an upturned ship. The sacristy was the secret wooden door to Lucy's left, where the chalice and linens were kept. The vestry was behind another secret wooden door to Lucy's right, the place where the priests and attendants dressed in their liturgical vestments, where they prepared for service and vested. Lucy had learned the verb *vested* so she could be confirmed. And after she had worn her white dress and her father had knelt down and held her against his chest, he stopped climbing trees with her in the yard like he used to, stopped giving her good-night kisses altogether, and Lucy didn't entirely understand why, but knew it had to do with the white dress, and with her beginning to know the words for things hidden behind secret doors.

Lucy had learned that the spire of Saint James was used as a landmark by ships entering Toronto Harbour. She knew the clock tower held the largest chiming public clock in Canada, and that when the face of the clock was lit at night, sometimes people mistook it for the moon. Lucy knew each of the six works of mercy depicted in the stained glass window of the same name: tend the sick, shelter the homeless, feed the hungry, visit the imprisoned, clothe the naked, give drink to the thirsty. She looked at the six works while the priest droned out the service in his reverberating buzz. She prayed for mercy that she would never get the blood again that came to her in the Canadian Tire washroom while her father shopped for winter tires. Since her confirmation, since learning the precise words for things, Lucy felt different about the church. Now it was like entering a forest where she could identify the names of trees: *oak, birch, hackmatack*. Before, the church was a simple calming place. Before the church was shade.

¶ At the end of Peter's first day at the career fair, he'd gone over to Chuck's with a case of beer. These were the last warm days of autumn. They were drinking on the front lawn. The same front lawn that, during the winter they were twelve, the two boys fortified with the largest snow-fort on the block. They would run to the fort as soon as the school bell rang and bombard all the other kids walking home with snowballs. Now they were old enough that Chuck's mom couldn't take away their beer. Still, Peter instinctively hid his up the sleeve of his jacket when he wasn't drinking.

"But it's all the way over on Church, Chuck. The Danforth's great tonight. Couldn't we go to a movie or something?"

"There'll be fine ladies there, I'm telling you."

"But it's church."

"It's bingo."

"Look, let me get this out on the table." Peter took a long swig of his beer, tucked the bottle back into his shirt sleeve. "I'm just tired of the sermonizing and justifying of good and evil when both are actually the direct result of human action, and of physics, and are not connected in any way to this comforting lie of a God we have created for ourselves."

Chuck just looked at him. "It's bingo, Pete. Seriously. Bingo."

"Driscoll, it's like this. It's like we've hidden a rock behind a bush and then later we come by the bush again and pull out the rock and say 'Look, look at this rock that I've found!' all pleased with ourselves."

Chuck shrugged. "You spend too much time reading books. You know that, right?"

Peter had another sip of beer. He looked at his friend. He'd had one or two friends in all his life so far. "Don't I hate bingo?"

¶ Peter stood next to the plates of cheese straws and cherry squares with a name tag pinned to his sweater. He had not been in a church since before he'd left for the war. Since his father's funeral. His mother had died while he was overseas, in the last few months of the war, and he hadn't heard until a family friend had met him at the train station in Toronto with his mother's bank book and a death announcement clipped from a newspaper. There was part of him that had wanted to write something stupid under the printed "HELLO I'M" of his blue and white name tag. Hello I'm: John Jacob Jingleheimer Schmitt. Hello I'm: with Chuck. Hello I'm: slightly drunk from the four beers I drank before I got here. Hello I'm: lonely. But, in the end, Peter wrote Peter.

"How would you say you sleep at night?"

"I beg your pardon?" he turned.

A girl with hair the colour of copper took out a pen and a small notepad from her purse, and held the book closed, in one hand. Yes, like copper, Peter noted, before oxidization sets in.

"Do you dream?"

"Sure I dream."

"What would you say you dream about?"

Peter looked at her. She had a pretty mouth. "Mostly I'm being chased, but I can't see my assailants' faces." He reached for one of the small triangles of egg-salad sandwiches that had been laid out next to the punch. "Either that, or fire."

The girl opened the notepad and clicked her pen. "Do you mind if I write that down. I'm sort of taking a survey. Well, really I'm a telephone operator."

"I guess not," Peter said, wondering about the connections between dreams and misdirected numbers. From behind them the bingo caller's voice announced, "Under the G. Fifty-Nine. That's Brighton Line Fifty-Nine."

"I'm reading Freud," the girl went on to say, by way of further explanation.

"Okay." Peter didn't know much about psychology.

"Sorry, I'm Lucy." She clicked her pen again and held out her hand.

"Yes, I can see that from your name tag. A derivative of light." They shook hands. Someone shouted Bingo.

"Pardon?"

"Your name. It's from the Latin for light."

"Sure." She looked at Peter's chest. "And you're an apostle."

He snorted.

"Okay, not an apostle."

Peter poured Lucy a glass of pink punch with a lemon floating at the top like a life preserver.

"Alright. You're Peter Pan and you know how to fly with fairy dust and you never want to grow up." Lucy absent-mindedly dunked the lemon down into her drink with her pinkie finger and took a sip.

¶ That night they left bingo early and went for a soda. He liked Lucy because she wasn't afraid to read her book out loud to him in the café, something he never would have done. While she read, he watched her. Expressions moved across her face with each line, with each character, like private systems of weather.

"'To be loved by Susan would be to be impaled by a bird's sharp beak, to be nailed to a barnyard door'."

He fidgeted with a sugar dispenser.

"'Yet there are moments when I could wish to be speared by a beak, to be nailed to a barnyard door, positively, once and for all.' That's Neville speaking."

"Is he the one from Australia?"

"No, that's Louis. Neville's the writer, like Bernard. And like Virginia Woolf too, I suppose. I bet she's been in love as sharply as a bird's beak."

Peter nodded. He wondered if loving someone as sharply as a bird's beak was a good idea.

¶ The second day of the job fair, Peter decided he wanted to stay in Canada. He walked toward the table of A.V. Roe and Company where the man standing behind the table looked nothing like the Grumman guy. He wasn't even wearing a tie with his suit. The man told Peter that they'd started work on a plane that every other NATO country had said was impossible.

"Supersonic. Turns on a dime. Can withstand sub-zero weather conditions. Can intercept a fleet of Soviet bombers over the Arctic Ocean. The British said no. The Americans said it was impossible.

We looked at the specs and said, yes, we can do this." The man shrugged. "The entire world is waiting for us to fail."

"Can supersonic even do that?"

"What, protect us from the Russians?"

"No, turn on a dime."

"We think we've come up with something, yes."

¶ To Peter, the jet hangar was like a giant heart; a huge chamber, pulmonary in its production, red and rosy in the morning light. He hurried through the hangar's corridors with draftsmen, engineers and machinists: measurers of things, fools for the accuracy of a line. They held clipboards and blueprints. They wore white lab coats with golden-winged insignia on their backs. On their lunch hours, they talked about creating an oblique shock wave at supersonic speeds to allow optimum pressure recovery. The hangar was a pumping, moving, palpable place where orthographic, auxiliary and isometric projections were drafted, edited and redrawn before final whistle and punch out occurred. A place where Peter's fear of flight did not prevent him from briefly voyaging beyond culs-de-sacs, news reports, and tuna casseroles; a plane, an air-going vessel, that, even in the most simplistic terms, could voyage mankind beyond the rain cloud.

At night, in their first apartment, Peter dreamt, lying in Lucy's arms, about avionics, wing-span and vortex patterning. He woke up at 3:00 a.m., turned on his bedside lamp, and jotted down notes about aero-elastic efficiency and the effects of downwash on the wing region. Lucy would find receipts and movie ticket stubs riddled with Peter's notes. Reading the words in his tiny draftsman's script was to discover another language: *Different ratio at wing root than wing tip?* Wing roots, Lucy knew, were nothing like the crocus roots she was forcing on the window ledge in old jam jars.

In the beginning days, Peter arrived early at work so he could stand at the entrance of the hangar and watch the sun rise pink through the lead-paned windows over desks and drafting tables, over plane parts and test-models and long rolls of blue prints. The new cockpit was mounted on a trolley for simulated pilot visibility tests through the arctic corridor. Peter stood and looked across the workshop floor. He listened to the hollow windy sound of the hangar before everyone else arrived at work. He stood for a moment in silence before the drills and riveters started up and then he climbed the stairs to the second level offices and put on a pot of coffee so it was ready for Robert.

In the pale pink light, Peter unrolled a long line of white paper across his desk. He took out the slide rule with his name on it that the Avro Company had given to him upon signing his contract. He clicked open its black velvet case, like a jeweller's necklace box, and delicately placed the rule on his drafting table. He did the same with his other tools: his pencils, protractors, compasses, his set of bevelled Burmester French curves. He lined them up at the top of his desk, all their edges and points in a row, and began his work where he'd left off the evening before. He calculated and modified and sketched out the spans of wings in light blue pencil like veins. Flutter, lift, drag: Peter's hands smoothed over the paper anatomies of flight. While the wind—the real wind, not the wind they made in their laboratories and tunnels—pushed against the metal and glass of the hangar and creaked.

¶ Drifting in and out of sleep on the islands of her grown-children's beds, Lucy found herself wondering at the wisdom of Claire France at the age of sixteen. Why did Lucy spend more time meditating on the detailed architecture of her life—a Gothic-Revival spire, a five-toned chiming clock-tower, the length of a hem for a dress she would wear once in her entire life—than she did giving a thought to the qualities and possible beauties of the person she might want to marry, or to giving a thought about what else she might do with her life? If Lucy had not married Peter, would she have flown over Africa? If Lucy had been less concerned with hemlines, would she have written her own book?

I magine their first real date. Lucy would have said that the soda was technically their first date, but Peter felt more nervous the next time he saw her. Peter had calculated that time increased the remembered enjoyment of Lucy's company. The first snow had fallen. Even though it had only been a few weeks since he'd met her in the basement of Saint James, it was a new season. He couldn't tell at first whether it was the remembering her that caused his excitement, or her actual company. But then being with her again was like an explosion. A minor chemical explosion where no one got all that hurt. He saw Lucy again and she led him up a set of stairs off a street downtown he'd never even seen before, and he knew then that calculations wouldn't work on her.

Lucy gave two kisses on either cheek to the girl working the coat check of The Golden Swan. "This is Peter," Lucy said, unbuttoning her winter coat. "Peter, this is Claire."

Claire gave him two tickets for their coats, which Lucy would later tuck into the pages of her diary: COAT CHECK 51, COAT CHECK 52, each with a picture of a man in a top hat wearing a monocle over an eye.

"You'll come in and sit with us?" Lucy asked Claire.

"On my break."

The room had high ceilings and high brick walls. Tall industrial windows, like the ones in Peter's hangar, faced the harbour. Old red velvet theatre curtains were hung on pulleys beside a small wooden stage. At the back of the room was a car from an old passenger train with candles and bowls of olives set on mahogany dining-car tables. Peter tried to deduce by the entrances how the train could have gotten into the room. Perhaps it was hoisted in with a crane before the windows were in place. Peter absently followed Lucy while picturing a train car hanging from a dolly, swivelling in from the sky. The bar itself was made of cherry wood, and behind the bar were mirrored shelves lined with shining bottles. Lucy led Peter to a table next to the train with two mismatched wing-backed chairs and a good view of the stage.

"How do you know about this place?"

"The Swan? Claire's dad owns it. He used to be a musician in New Orleans."

A waiter came over and Lucy stood and kissed him on both cheeks too. "Charlie, this is Peter. Peter, this is Claire's brother."

Peter stood up, formally, awkwardly, not sure if he should be kissing Charlie too, or shaking his hand.

Charlie proceeded to do neither, and Peter sat down again.

"What'll it be?"

"Gin julep," Lucy said without hesitation.

Peter looked at her across the table and then up at Charlie. "Beer?"

"Pop's made a batch of his Christmas coffee porter. That's all we got."

"Sounds good."

Lucy waved across the room to a blonde girl wearing a blue dress, and before Peter could ask Lucy anything else, stage lights came up and three musicians ambled out, one taking a seat at a beat-up piano, one standing behind a base, and the other at the microphone with a harmonica. Lucy held Peter's arm. "This guy's amazing," she whispered. "He sings *Muddy Water* better than Bessie Smith." The room filled with belting-out blues and all of the small insecure questions that Peter carried along with him like folded handkerchiefs—Should I hold her hand now? Should I have shaken hands with the waiter? If the density of a solution is the sum of mass concentrations of the components of that solution, then the density of air ought to be calculated with a partial density of the mass concentration of a given component Pi. But would that mean that

$$\rho = \sum_i \rho i$$

is the correct formula? Should we order food?—all unnecessary thoughts slowly fell away and the notes of the music stood out in a new kind of sky like starlings sitting on a string of telephone wire.

After five or six more rounds of coffee porters and gin juleps, after a killer last set where the singer surprised the crowd by bringing out a horn, and the room got up dancing to *When the Saints Go Marching In*, when the last of the men had left with the last of the women, Lucy and Peter helped Claire tidy the coat racks and arrange the forgotten hats. Claire said "one second," and came back from the kitchen with a paper bag filled with breaded crawdaddies, and she

26

and Lucy and Peter meandered through the downtown streets, west toward Trinity Bellwoods Park, eating as they walked.

"Do your parents know you're up this late?" Peter asked Lucy.

"I'm sleeping over at Claire's."

"Okay?"

"So technically I'm already asleep."

"I see."

"This is a dream," Lucy said. "Tomorrow you'll wake up too. You'll shake your head and ask yourself, 'Did that redhead really take me to a bar with a train inside?' You'll think, 'Could Claire's daddy's crawdaddies really taste so good?'"

"They only taste this good late at night," Claire said. "Although in a pinch they'll do for breakfast."

When they got to the park, Lucy went off into the trees and threw herself down in a thin snowbank in her winter coat to make snow angels. Peter watched her from a bench.

"She's gold," Claire said after a moment.

"I know," Peter said.

Claire looked over at Peter. "You've never heard live blues before, have you?"

"Well, not like the ..."

"That was the first time you've been in a club, wasn't it?" Claire said.

Peter paused. This was a test. "In Cornwall there was this one place.... The Crown and Thistle?"

"The Crown and Thistle? No, my friend, I mean have you heard any real jazz?"

Peter knew a test when one was posed to him. "I used to listen to *Best of the Big Bands*," Peter tried. "While I worked on the airplanes."

"What, like Benny Goodman or something?" Claire leaned back against the bench with a vague look of disgust.

Peter looked at Claire. He hadn't passed. And even though Peter did not have much experience with these sorts of things, he knew that the approval of the best friend was an important test to pass.

Peter and Claire both watched while Lucy brushed snow off her coat sleeves and then flopped down to make another angel. "I keep telling Lu that I'm gonna take her down to New Orleans with me," Claire said. "And that Lu and I are gonna go to Mardi Gras and wear a hundred beaded necklaces, and then the next morning, after our feet are plain sore from dancing, we're gonna eat bourbon-and-banana-flapjacks instead of going to church."

"Do you play an instrument?" Peter said.

Claire ignored him. "I know it won't happen."

The conversation was confusing Peter. He looked out at the snow and mentally began to revolve an octahedron to regain composure.

"Lucy and I have known each other since we were seven. She has the sweetest handmade nightgowns."

Peter sat up and began riffling through his jacket pockets. During the war, a French pilot who'd spent time in northern Africa taught Peter a trick he knew. Much depended on the mind of the subject. Peter wasn't sure the trick would work, but he knew that he was failing with Claire, and that if he failed with Clare he would fail with Lucy, and so Peter determined it was worth a shot.

Claire looked over. "Forget something?" Claire was used to forgotten things working the coat check.

Peter turned to Claire. He was holding out a deck of cards. The pilot had taught Peter that he must relax. He must feel as though his limbs were as hot and as heavy as vines in the sun. He must see into his subject as if gazing through a crystal glass.

"I can guess what card you've chosen," he told Claire.

"What?" Claire said.

"Here," Peter began to shuffle the deck. "I can guess what card you've chosen."

"You do magic tricks?"

"Telepathy. Extrasensory perception. I learned during the war. A measure taken to protect the Allies against spies."

Peter fanned out the deck of cards.

Claire stared at him.

Peter asked her to choose a card from the fanned out arc in front of him and to tap the card she had chosen. "Don't pick it out and hold onto it or anything. Just tap it and then think about it. Remember it while I shuffle." He bridged the cards against his lap and told her that he would read her mind, so she needed to think carefully of the suit and number of the card she had chosen.

Claire tapped on her chosen card and Peter squared the deck and held it in his hands. He stared at Claire's face for nearly a minute in the almost-dark.

Claire stared back at him.

"The card you tapped in the deck is this one," Peter said, holding up the stack of cards so that the eight of clubs faced her.

"But the card you were thinking of was the queen of diamonds." This part intimidated Peter, but he was pretty sure.

Claire's gaze moved between the eight of clubs and Peter's face above his worn, turned-up coat collar. She didn't say anything.

Peter returned the cards to his pocket. "I thought so."

Peter and Claire sat in silence on the bench with the empty greasy crawdad bag between them. Claire shook her head in quiet disbelief. Peter tried not to smile. They both watched as Lucy fell backwards into a deeper snowbank made by the ploughs. "Look!" Lucy stood and ran back to Claire and Peter. "The angels. They're all holding wings."

T he wedding was on a Saturday morning. Lucy had made her dress from a swath of elegant white silk she'd bought half-price from one of the textile merchants along Queen Street. Her hem was finished with a frill of remnants from the gauzy pink curtains of her childhood bedroom. There were small pink roses at her hem. She carried a bouquet of flowers, although Peter wouldn't be able to tell you what kind.

Lucy had persuaded Peter into having the ceremony at Saint James.

"As long as you know it means nothing to me."

"The wedding?"

"No, of course not the wedding, darling. The place."

"What's wrong with the place?"

"The Golden Swan, that's a place. I fell in love with you at The Swan."

"Don't be ridiculous, Peter. I'm not getting married in a bar."

¶ For an engagement present, Claire France gave Lucy a copy of Beryl Markham's *West With the Night*. They were lying on Lucy's bed flipping through bridal catalogues. With each new page of dresses and cakes and flowers and table favours, Lucy could feel Claire against her shoulder making a face.

"Mum's already planned the menu."

"Yes, your mummy? Has she?"

"She's making tea cakes with strawberries and Devonshire cream. She said it was a morning wedding, so there should be canapés to start, with smoked salmon and watercress. Cold roast-beef sandwiches, potato salad and devilled eggs after that. Oh, and fresh greens. Perhaps a little trifle to go with the cake."

"You hate devilled eggs."

"Yes, but the guests might not."

Lucy shut the catalogue and turned to Claire. "Do you think it matters that he's an atheist?"

"Well, champ, how does it make you feel that he's an atheist?"

"He said getting married in the church meant nothing."

"How did you feel when Peter said that?"

"What are you doing?"

"What do you mean?"

"You keep asking the same question after everything I say."

"Oh. That. Well, Charlie said that if ever a girl asks him how a dress looks on her, he always says, 'How does that dress make you feel?' I'm applying the same principles."

"Why do you need to apply principles to have a conversation with me?"

Claire picked at a fuzz on the chenille blanket. "What exactly is watercress? Is it like a chive?"

Lucy looked back down at the floral bouquets in the catalogue.

¶ Lucy asked her father to pick out the hymns.

"For your wedding? Doesn't Peter want to pick?"

"No. We want you to pick."

Simon Ainsworth sucked the tips of his moustache.

"If it were just me, Papa, I'd want you to whistle all the hymns. I'd want all the favourites and I'd want you to whistle me up the aisle."

"Oh, I don't think so," Simon said, "we'll hire the organist."

¶ By the morning of her wedding, Lucy couldn't help but feel that others had orchestrated the entire day. Lucy's mother had made Claire a lavender dress rather than the midnight-blue satin that Lucy had fingered in the fabric store, as light and liquid as ink. "You do not wear midnight-blue satin to a wedding, Lucille, let alone a daytime wedding," Mavis Ainsworth had said. "Dark blue satin in the Church of England at eleven o'clock in the morning. Honestly. Do you want me rolling in my grave?"

And the cake. Peter and Lucy couldn't even cut through it.

Friends and family all held up their cameras. Peter and Lucy clasped the sharp knife. They cut together into the hard fondant icing of the traditional wedding cake made by a well-meaning aunt but the surface had hardened like an ice rink. Lucy smiled for the cameras. She and Peter bent toward the cake. Their grip on the knife reddened their knuckles. Lucy's hand was crushed beneath Peter's grip. Lucy's ring made a sharp diamond indent into Peter's palm. "What's so wrong with chocolate?" Peter asked under his breath as the room was suddenly lit up with the smoke and flare of a dozen flashbulbs. "It was made by my aunt," Lucy whispered back. Peter smiled and tried a gouging method at the icing instead. "A good Devil's Food. Now that's a cake." Lucy half-smiled and half-grimaced while she posed again for photographs, touching her hands to Peter's shoulders while he sawed back and forth into the cake. "Lemon," Lucy said from behind her teeth, "now that's a cake." Finally, when the flesh of the fruitcake was revealed, Peter fed Lucy a forkful of marzipan and brittled candied peel like cough syrup as the guests let out a final barrage of flash and smoke from their Kodak Brownies.

¶ At four o'clock, after the luncheon was over, after hands were shaken and the cheeks of uncles were kissed, after Lucy and Peter had their photograph taken in the church gardens and by the wedding car, Claire, still in her lilac bridesmaid dress, rode with Lucy in the backseat to the club while Peter and Chuck smoked cigars up front. All four were drunk from champagne, as half the guests who'd been invited to the luncheon, it had turned out, were elderly or expecting or didn't drink. They still had two cases left over in the trunk.

Claire had spread the train of Lucy's wedding dress over her and was slouched beneath so it looked as if they'd both been put to bed.

"Whose bed is this?" Claire asked.

"Goldilocks' bed," Lucy said.

"No," Claire said.

"It is," Lucy said.

"Goldilocks was a thief," Claire said.

"She was a little girl," Lucy said.

"She stole porridge," Claire said, "from helpless bears."

"Bears aren't helpless," Lucy protested.

"Neither are girls," Claire said.

"What those two say makes no sense to me, Pete," Chuck said from the front seat.

¶ The four of them climbed into the train car at the back of the empty Golden Swan. They could hear the kitchen staff slowly starting for the night, the click of the gas stoves, pots and pans being taken off the shelves in the otherwise silent club. They each opened a bottle of champagne and poured from it into each other's cups. "We shall toast to the good on every fourth sip," Chuck said.

"To watermelon," Lucy toasted.

"To hand-knit socks," Chuck said.

"To sequins," Claire added.

"To volcanic rock," Peter said.

They looked at Peter.

"What?" he said, "I've always liked rocks."

"To rocks," Claire affirmed.

With the appearance of a proper piece of chocolate cake and four forks, their voices rose to the empty warehouse walls unlike any prayer uttered in the nave of Saint James' church. "To Lake Huron at sunset. To chandeliers. To ice-skating. To tango-dancing. To crawdaddies. To Canada's largest chiming public clock." The sunlight sliding down the bottles behind the cherry-wood bar. "To my new wife's soft neck."

¶ Lucy undressed that night in a room Peter had booked at the Royal York. She found a piece of rice embedded in the skin against her collarbone. "To rice!" she yelled, and held it up, but Peter was busy being sick.

Their first apartment was on College Street. Peter had wanted to move Lucy right into their very own home, but there was a housing shortage in Toronto after the war. All the armament factories were being changed over to lumber and drywall. The apartment on College was temporary while their house out in Malton was slowly framed and the bricks were laid down. Peter and Lucy were waiting for their house, but Lucy hated waiting. She never wanted to feel as if she wasn't home. So she hung a bit of lace in the windows of their apartment. She found a table and two matching chairs at a buy-and-sell. The rest of their belongings—the wedding presents and hand-me-downs—were being stored in her parent's attic and would be moved to Lucy and Peter's new house when it was done.

Lucy didn't mind the apartment. She loved the thin walls; her three keys that let her in: one for the silver mailbox, one for the front door, one for their two rooms on the third floor.

¶ Two weeks after Peter and Lucy had put the down payment on the Malton house, the Ainsworths had the young couple over for dinner.

After eating her mother's roast, Lucy sat on the chesterfield next to Peter.

"When you're all settled in, we'll be moving back to England, Pumpkin," Simon Ainsworth said softly from beneath his moustache.

"What?" Lucy said.

"Pardon," Mavis Ainsworth corrected.

Lucy looked at her mother who had laid out the Mah-Jong set and four glass tumblers on the coffee table. She was swizzling a pitcher of cocktails.

"Say 'pardon,' Lucille."

"The village where Mavis and I grew up is being rebuilt," Lucy's father remarked to Peter.

Peter nodded.

"There's going to be a war museum," Lucy's mother said. "Built by the Ladies Auxiliary. Martha wrote about it. You remember your Great Aunt Martha, don't you Lucille? The one who keeps those parakeets?"

"No, Mother, I meant, you are doing what?"

"Martha always was such a pioneer," Mavis said, ignoring her daughter's tone.

"Daddy. She can't be serious." Lucy looked down at her stockinged toes. Red polish beneath white silk. She pushed them hard into the carpet until it hurt. "What about grandchildren?" Lucy asked.

"Oh, darling, not to worry about that," Simon said. "Plenty of time before that, isn't there?" He paused. "Anyone else for a Tom Collins?"

"Precisely the point," Mavis offered. "Let's not get into the details of this all now, shall we? We just wanted to inform you of the matter, that's all. Peter, help me twitter the sparrows."

"Sorry?" Peter said.

"In Mah-Jong that's the expression for shuffling the game tiles," Mavis instructed.

"Mother, you're expecting Peter and I to sit here and play Mah-Jong after you've dropped this little piece of information as if nothing is happening?"

"Lucille. There is no need to be dramatic."

"In this case, grammatically speaking, it would be 'me and Peter'," Simon said absent-mindedly, "not 'Peter and I'."

Lucy looked back and forth at her parents distantly, as if from a cliff or a tall unstable building. "I'm not feeling well," Lucy said. "It must be something I ate." She stood up and smoothed down the fabric of her skirt.

Peter looked up at Lucy, his fingers moving the Mah-Jong tiles in tiny circles like Mavis Ainsworth had directed.

"Pete. Stop twittering. Please would you get my coat?"

¶ The day after the dinner at her parents' place, Lucy walked aimlessly downtown. She looked at posters for musicals; took *Anna*

34

Karenina out of the library even though she knew she wouldn't finish it. She'd already tried to get through the novel twice before and stopped each time at the steeplechase scene when Vronsky's mare Frou Frou breaks her back. Lucy could never stand to read about animals in distress. She hadn't cared that Anna was pregnant with Vronsky's child and that Karenin would soon find out; the shooting of the horse had haunted her. Still, she took the book out again because she was curious as to how Anna's predicament would turn out, and she shopped for groceries in Chinatown, and when she came back to College Street in the late afternoon other people's laundry greeted her, drying out on the balconies and over the banisters in the halls. Some of the apartments in their building had two or three families living together: immigrants from Italy, Poland, Ukraine; soldiers and their new brides. First key: an electric bill. Second key: the corridors, always smelling of two things at once—boiling potatoes and musky men's cologne; spaghetti sauce and children's wet boots. Lucy took the stairs instead of the great iron elevator in the centre of the building that rose and lowered itself like a claustrophobic lung. She passed door after door as she rounded the spiralling stairs, carrying the groceries up in her arms. Sometimes the doors she passed opened and she could peer for a moment into someone else's life. Today she saw an old man sitting by a rickety card table, gently playing a song on a worn violin; she saw pierogies and onions in a deep cast-iron pan stirred by a woman with bright red cheeks and dark hair; a handsome man smoking in his undershirt at the opened door. Lucy smiled. The man nodded. Third key: groceries down.

Even inside the apartment, after Lucy had shut the door, there were more families. The windows of Lucy and Peter's apartment faced windows—a twin brick apartment across the alley. Holding her coffee cup, a chicken pot pie baking in the oven, an unread magazine open at the kitchen table as she waited for Peter to come home from his game of squash with Chuck, Lucy saw the tenants' lives like newsreels: the man who lived alone and hid his bottle of sherry from himself. The sharply dressed blonde woman who lived in the apartment next to him, who smoked and paced across her living room floor as if waiting for someone. Or the family with what

35

seemed like eleven boys, constantly with diapers and tiny pairs of pants hanging on a line from their window. When Peter got home he commented on the proximity. "We'll have trees and yards where we're moving to, Lu."

But Lucy liked knowing she was never alone. After dinner, Lucy stood listening at the sink. She could hear radio programs and vacuum cleaners. She could hear the shouts of cribbage games and records being put on. She could hear the woman who practised opera each night: Mimì's aria from Puccini's *La Bohème*, coughs and creaks playing counterpoint while Mimì lit her candle, fell in love with Rodolfo, and died in her garret night after night.

Peter put his hand on Lucy's shoulder. "Wing root" he whispered, sliding down her shirt sleeves over her freckled arms past the soap-suds to her wet fingers in the sink. "Wing tip."

The distance of Lucy's arms and shoulders, fingertip to fingertip, naked, closing the blinds, reckless of the neighbours.

The models they started with were no bigger than the ones Peter would build with Andy and Kier once they'd been born; tiny planes housed in wind-tunnel boxes like relics in a church. If everyone in the free world thought this plane would fail, there was only one option for Peter: not just to succeed, not just to make the Arrow seriously high speed, but to make her elegant. Lucy's red toe polish, the arches of her feet hanging off the bedspread. "Sexy," as the pilots called a new plane they liked the look of. "That's one sexy beast." Peter nudged a pair of safety goggles up the bridge of his nose. Robert hunched down to watch the model through the glass.

Peter Jacobs and Robert Lambert had their names, along with Wing Development, inked onto their door. Robert had graduated from the École Polytechnique in Montréal and Peter pronounced his name Ro-bare, even though the other engineers called him Robert with hard English consonants. Peter attempted to speak to Robert in the awkward high-school French he'd learned before going overseas. They listened to Radio Canada while they worked so that Peter might learn more. Peter caught parts of the weather report "froi ... neige ... tempet ..." or an occasional part of the news, but usually it was just a rhythm to work by, the newscaster's inflections keeping time to the calculations and measurements in Peter's head.

Robert had taped photos to his drafting table of his mother's house in Trois-Rivières. "T'ree Rivers" Robert had said in English once to Peter, and they'd both laughed at how wrong a place name could sound out of its mother tongue. Robert had been the one to scrounge an electric coffee percolator from a storage closet in the hall, fix a broken wire and set it up near their drawing boards. Peter usually arrived first in the mornings, so he was the one to put the coffee on. When Robert arrived, Peter poured some into his Noorduyn Aviation mug from the percolated pot. He took out a small container of cream Lucy packed in his lunch and tipped a little into their cups.

They spoke most intimately of their lives first thing in the mornings.

"Pouvez-vous me passer la règle, s'il vous plait?"

"Bien. Et la famille, ca va aujourd 'hui?"

"Oui, ils vont bien, merci." A pause. "Et vous?"

"Pierre, you no longer must use the form 'vous' with me. We are friends. Please refer to me as tu. Est-ce que tu comprends?"

"Oui, excuse-moi, Robert. Tu it will be."

Then, after a few sips of their coffee, they bent their heads to the lines of their work or to the models they flew in fabricated currents of air.

"Prêt?"

"Prêt."

"Okay Pierre, turn it on."

Avro was following a new method of aero development. The Cook-Craigie plan. Cook and Craigie had gotten rid of the prototype phase of aerospace design all together and went straight from blueprints to models to planes. This meant that Peter and Robert's lines directly translated into the machine that the pilot would fly. Their drafted lines had to speak the plane's mother tongue.

Peter turned the black knob on the control panel slowly, listening, like he was tuning-in to a station on his shortwave.

"Again."

Peter turned the knob a quarter inch.

"Encore."

Quarter inch by quarter inch, Peter turned up the dial.

Robert took notes on a clipboard. "We 'ave skin friction." He pointed at the model plane with his pencil. "The metal is still 'eating up."

Peter and Robert leaned toward the wind-window and watched. They watched and turned the dial until smoke rose off the wings like a miniature storm cloud. Streaks of wind whipped over the fuselage in a tidy arc but then became caught in a whirlpool of air at the wing tips, vortexing, churning into a maelstrom, heating up the metal until, poof, in flames, "Comme une guimauve," Robert said. Like a marshmallow at a campfire.

Peter noted down the final speed.

Robert got the fire extinguisher.

"I bet we could get her to Mach 1 if the wind tunnels were bigger. All we need is a different combination of alloy for the wing skins.

"But the vortexing, Pierre."

Peter looked at the growing list of instability factors they'd tacked onto the wall. Robert was right. They were getting pitch-up because of the vortexing. It was causing an abrupt change in the movement curve and serious tightening in the turn. This could kill a pilot. This was the small hitch with Cook and Craigie's plan. Robert and Peter could kill a pilot. If the draftsmen were off by one eighth of an inch in a calculation, if they couldn't stop the tightening in the turn, in-flight would be like a race-car driver pulling a wrong turn at 230 mph and running into the guardrail; but with the plane the speed was more like 770 mph, and the guardrail was the entire sky. Peter unrolled an earlier diagram they'd drawn onto Robert's drafting table and compared it to a flutter model.

"Mais, not tonight, Pierre. Je rentre chez moi."

Robert gave Peter a lift to the new subway stop because Lucy had the car. Below ground a woman with a flowered handkerchief over her hair was selling tulips from ice-cream buckets. Peter bought three bunches of orange and red ones for Lucy. They looked like bobbing runway lights resting on the subway seat beside him, like tiny flames blazing instability.

¶ That afternoon, Lucy drove her parents down Avenue Road to Union Station. The Ainsworths had decided that they needn't wait any longer to return to Berkshire. Their house at High Park had sold to a young expectant couple who, quite frankly, Lucy's mother had said, paid too much.

"What if we'd wanted the house, Mother?" Lucy had asked over tea in the Eaton's department store luncheonette.

"Who?"

"Peter and I?"

"Darling, I didn't even think of it. You have a house."

"Or what if I'd wanted to come with you?"

"Where?"

"To England."

Mavis straightened her gloves. "You are married, Lucille."

Lucy looked down at the butterscotch pudding Lucy's mother had ordered for her without asking before she'd arrived. A perfect rosette of whipped cream topped with a maraschino cherry that was bleeding pink syrup into the cream. Lucy had loved butterscotch pudding when she was a child. She had always eaten around the cream until it was an island, saving the cherry until very last. Tea with her mother at the Eaton's luncheonette had, in Lucy's mind, been the height of sophistication when she was a girl.

"Lucille, it is unbecoming to frown." Mavis took a sip of her tea. "You will get wrinkles."

"Yes, Mother," Lucy said. She took her spoon and mashed the cream and pudding and cherry all together and then pushed the glass parfait dish away from her.

¶ The Ainsworths hired a team of men to load all of the belongings that Lucy had wanted to keep from the childhood house into a warehouse, where the dining room sets and dressing-tables would be stored until Peter and Lucy's house was finished and they could move to Malton. Her parents wouldn't see Lucy's first home. Lucy's father wouldn't be there to whistle. Lucy's parents wouldn't find out until they were on the other side of the Atlantic Ocean what Lucy already somehow knew as she drove them to the station.

Lucy drove and her mother and father nattered at each other about luggage tags and seasickness tablets. Lucy thought that perhaps she was like a lantern. Perhaps inside of herself the wall of her belly was papery and warm like her favourite antiquarian bookshop on Yonge Street with the creaky wooden staircase and the shelf with hinges that she swore was a door. At Queen's Park Circle Lucy stopped at the whistle of a traffic policeman and she wondered instead whether she was a kaleidoscope beneath her flower-printed dress. By Dundas, Lucy imagined her child's face: the face of the centre angel in Saint James' King Alfred window: a child-philosopher, severe and quizzical with hair in locks like a lion.

That morning, as she had waited for her mother's call, Lucy sat on the window ledge of the College Street apartment, her feet on the cool metal of the radiator, looking down the alley, watching a girl build a kite. Peter had told Lucy a few days ago that scientists believed that the same molecules found in meteors were also in humans and she wondered how exactly that worked. Where did the molecules come from? How far back had they travelled? Would that mean that before a baby was a baby, a baby was a supernova? The girl had pulled the triangle of fabric over two sticks and was wrapping string around the ends to hold it tight against the wind. Were children already in the air surrounding their parents? Was this child that Lucy had just begun to feel already there in the charge of air surrounding her and Peter? There, in that moment, when he had handed her a glass of punch?

"There's a parking spot, right there," Mavis said, tapping Lucy on the shoulder.

Lucy pulled in behind a line of taxis idling in front of the white columns of Union Station.

Before Lucy had walked around the car, her father had hailed a Red Cap with a dolly to carry the Ainsworths' luggage to the ticket booth.

"I can help, Daddy," Lucy said.

"Nonsense," her father said, taking out a dime from his pocket to tip the man.

Lucy walked into the large atrium of Union Station holding onto the fur sleeve of her mother's coat. It was nearly summer and yet

40

Mavis Ainsworth, because she was travelling, had insisted on wearing the fox fur over her yellow dress, with her matching purse, gloves and shoes the glossy shine of Sunlight dish detergent.

"The boat leaves tomorrow morning from Montréal."

"I know, Mother. You've said."

"We're staying at the Queen Elizabeth if you need to reach us by telegram."

"Why would I need to telegram?"

"I don't know, Lucille. In case your father has forgotten our passports?"

"I'm sure Daddy's remembered."

Lucy stood on the platform while her mother and father boarded the day car that would take them through Guildwood, Kingston and Dorval into the central station in Montréal.

"Please take care of the china, Lucille," her mother said as the porter helped Mavis Ainsworth up the metal stairs. "Keep the silver polished," she said and turned around to face her daughter. "It was my mother's, you know. I brought it over with me wrapped in bath towels." A line was beginning to form. Lucy's mother stood her ground at the door to the day car. "I'll stitch another nightgown for you on the boat ride over and put it in the mail when we arrive. You'll have it in no time, Lucille." The porter was about to gently shoo Mavis inside when she abruptly pulled out a handkerchief, mumbled "Goodbye to Peter," and turned toward the darker recesses of the train where Lucy could no longer see her.

Goodbye, Mother.

¶ The tulips were in a vase on the kitchen table when Lucy got home with the car.

"I started making eggs for dinner."

"Thanks, Pete," Lucy put her keys in a glass dish on the kitchen counter. "The flowers are lovely."

"Eggs in a hole. You know, with the circle cut out of the toast and the whole thing fried up in bacon fat."

"Hmm," Lucy said and kicked off her shoes. "Sorry I didn't have a chance to get anything on the table."

"How were your father and mother? Get off okay?"

41

Lucy poured herself a glass of red wine. "They say goodbye."

Peter put two plates of runny fried eggs nestled in fat-soaked bread-slices with sides of bacon down onto the table. "Robert and I hypothetically killed another pilot today," he took a sip from her wineglass.

Lucy pushed her plate of eggs away. "Peter?"

"We have skin friction."

"You know those molecules you were talking about the other day?"

"It's causing this pitch-up," Peter said with a mouthful of dinner and demonstrated the movement with his knife.

"Pete," Lucy said, trying to get his attention.

"Unhuh?"

There was no real way to say it. "I think that we may be having a baby."

Peter paced and drank four cups of coffee from a paper cup. He was supposed to be at the high school doing his equivalency. All he'd needed was to take Senior English that summer before he went overseas and he would have been done: graduation, mortarboards, drinks of snuck rum with girls in the backseat of Chuck's car. But then Peter's father had died, and Peter signed up for the war, an act his father had forbidden.

Now Avro and the Air Force were making Peter finish his high-school diploma. Every Monday and Wednesday afternoons he left the office early and stood at the lockers outside Mrs. Robertson's English classroom waiting for the bell, feeling tall and ridiculous in his good grey hat. The boys in the halls of Parkdale Collegiate weren't even shaving yet.

And now this: a waiting room wallpapered with storks carrying blue and pink bundles in the shapes of teardrops. A flock of expectant fathers milling about the coffee cart. The four cups—black, no sugar—making him need to piss, and Peter arriving late for his mid-term.

At the squeaking sound of the classroom door, Mrs. Robertson swivelled her wooden pointer toward Peter. "Hello my brave new world. The funeral baked meats did coldly furnish forth the marriage tables."

Peter took his seat.

Her pointer swivelled again to the chalkboard and she tapped at it. *How did Hamlet hoist his own petard?* "Take out a blank sheet, Mr. Jacobs."

The class was silent, hunched over their in-class exams. The unified terror of scritching pencils across lined paper. Peter looked at the rounded shoulders of the girl sitting in front of him. She wore her hair in curls and her sweater was fuzzy. She always knew the answers. Genevieve, Peter thought her name was. Peter wanted to lean forward and whisper in Genevieve's ear, "My wife. She just had a baby." His face flushed. Nobody talked like that. What was he thinking? Peter wrote his name at the top of his sheet. He could still picture his tiny red son, Kier Cunningham Jacobs, wide-eyed, constantly amazed, wrapping his small fingers around Peter's thumb. Peter wrote out the test question and underlined it. He looked at his sheet. What the hell was a petard?

¶ "Little Bean," Lucy called Kier and held him swaddled against her chest in blankets. She walked up and down beside her bed at the hospital, and then back and forth across the hardwood floors of the apartment, her body rocking slightly on her heels as she roamed from bedroom to living room as the movers packed up Peter and Lucy's belongings, the weekend arriving for them to move to the suburbs. Lucy would catch herself walking in this rocking gait years after the children were grown, when she stood talking on the phone, or in the line at the grocers, her arms crossed at her chest, rocking and bobbing as if she were carrying a baby.

Lucy ventured out only once that first week home from the hospital. As far as the corner store and back again; and only because she'd had a craving for grilled cheese sandwiches and tomato soup for dinner and there were no tins of soup left in the cupboards, and the movers had all gone home.

Coming back into the apartment was more difficult with Kier

43

Jacobs in her arms. She didn't even bother with the mail. She barely noticed the neighbours. Perhaps Peter had been right that they would need their own home.

Door number nine was open again with the stern handsome man smoking in the doorway. Lucy expected him to nod and for her to move on, but he stubbed out his cigarette in a glass ashtray he was holding and called over his shoulder. The woman and old man Lucy had seen before came out of their apartment and all three spoke a language to one another that Lucy didn't understand, smiling and shushing the whole time at Kier.

"Name?" The woman with dark hair pointed to the baby.

"Kier." Lucy said, holding out his face to them.

"Care." Nodding.

The old man said something to Lucy and went back into the apartment. He began to play, the music of the violin reaching Lucy softly before he was even back beside her in the hallway. The woman began to sing a lullaby to the baby, the song sounding to Lucy of grapevines and garden trellises, laburnum arches and pots of cyclamen. The stern man joined in, his voice as thick and sweet as the smell of his tobacco.

Peter heard the violin, soft at first, the bow across the strings like a scratchy whisper. The old metal elevator heaved itself up and amidst the elevator's rattle Peter could hear the singing, the tune swelling between the iron bars. The numbers of the floors advanced slowly. As Peter approached the third, he saw Lucy's shoes through the metal bars, standing on the meadow of the faded floral carpeting in the hall. Surrounding her shoes, other shoes he didn't recognize. Feet stomping out a rhythm. Legs, hips, torsos, swaying in time to the music. Hands clapping, and faces singing. An old man with his eyes closed playing the fiddle. A woman with black curls serenading Peter's child. A younger man accompanying her, stern in the shoulders but joyful in the face. This is how Peter found his family the first week home from the hospital as he slowly rose floor to floor in the iron elevator. Lucy swaying, almost dancing, holding on tight to the baby and her tin of tomato soup.

"They're all beige."

"What?"

"The houses, they're all this same shade of beige brick." Lucy held Kier to her chest in the passenger seat of the car. "I didn't know they would be beige. When the builders said brick, I thought, you know, brick-coloured."

Peter turned onto their street. "It's the quarry." He parked the DeSoto at the curb by the moving van and pulled on the parking brake. "Don Valley Brickworks. Same bricks as Casa Loma. Same bricks as Massey Hall. Good solid bricks."

"Even the doors are beige."

"Good solid Ontarian bricks," Peter said again. He squeezed her knee and got out. Through the half-opened windows: "Lu, take a look at this lawn. You could golf on this lawn."

She looked at the manicured grass. She stayed in the car. "We don't golf, Peter." She paused, looked at the house again. "People like my mother golf."

¶ On Monday, Peter went to work. Lucy put Kier in a playpen on the lawn beneath the scrawny shade of the newly planted maple. In a pair of Peter's old overalls, Lucy opened the sticky lid of paint she'd bought that weekend at the hardware store. She kneeled down and began to paint the beige door cherry red.

¶ When they'd left the apartment for their house in Malton, driving out of the city, Lucy had seen the girl with her kite again. Was that even possible? Could it be the same girl standing in Harbord Park with the line tangled in a poplar tree? It had been almost a year ago that Lucy had seen the girl beneath her window. But there the girl stood, on her tiptoes, tugging and tugging at the line, the pink paper bows dancing up and down. Lucy had wanted to stay and help that girl with the untangling. She hadn't cared if they'd met the moving van on time.

¶ After the door had been painted and she'd drunk a cup of tea, Lucy stood in each room looking at the empty walls. She had never lived in a new house before. Everything felt blank compared to her house in Toronto where generations of people had lived before the Ainsworths had even arrived, spilling drinks on the floors, measuring their children's heights and ages in pencil on a door frame in the pantry, smoking, cooking, bathing; infusing the walls with their smells. In comparison, the house in Malton smelled as unsmudged as a sheet of new glass. Not a single cobweb. The spiders hadn't even had time to settle in.

Lucy started unpacking the kitchen, opening boxes with her house key until she found the pair of kitchen shears. Kier asleep now in a bassinet on the floor. The kitchen smelled of store-bought pineapple upside-down cake that Lucy had sliced that morning and put into Peter's lunch. The newness of everything was catching in Lucy's throat. "Woven silk pyjamas exchanged for blue quartz," Lucy said into the empty house. She was unpacking the dishes they had received at their wedding. Plates with a tiny blue girl and a tiny blue boy standing on a hillside of flowering bluebells underneath a lazy blue windmill. Lucy wanted to walk right into the plate. To spend the afternoon in Norway or Switzerland, and roll down hills like she was a child. When Peter got home he wouldn't even know what had happened to her. "I'm in here," she would say. "I'm in this plate!" But maybe he would never find her. "The quick red fox jumps over a lazy brown dog," Lucy said to her reflection in the kitchen window, louder, just to hear another voice. "Pack my box with five dozen liquor jugs." Pangrams. Old phrases from typing tests. A single sentence using every letter of the alphabet. The strange satisfying compactness Lucy felt in that compared to the plain openness of this new house. "Waltz, bad nymph, for quick jigs vex!" Lucy stacked the plates one on top of the next, hill after hill, girl after boy after girl. Despite herself, Lucy started crying. God, what was wrong with her? Hadn't this been what she had waited for her entire life? This was her own house. This was her own first house. "Sphinx of black quartz, judge my vow."

Lucy set down one of the windmill plates with a ham and tomato sandwich on her mother's turquoise Formica kitchen table with the four matching chairs. She polished an apple and poured herself a glass of milk. She folded a paper towel for a napkin and sat down.

The house was so quiet all Lucy could hear was the sound of herself chewing the thick slice of Black Forest ham, the meat squeaking beneath her molars. There were no taxi horns. There were no arguments on the sidewalk outside her door. There were no Chinese grocers with their stacks of eggplants. Purple eggplants. The fresh white heads of leeks. The concrete and rain smells of Dundas Street. She swallowed the damp clot of bakery bread down her throat with a gulp of milk. There were no coughs through the walls. Lucy had lived in the city her entire life. Lucy tried another bite of the ham sandwich but her throat constricted at the back of her throat and the tears came again. Her mouth hung open with each teary gulp of air, the ham sandwich half-chewed. Lucy cried the great heaving sobs of a child. What on earth is wrong with me? She looked down at Kier still asleep in his bassinet. She softened herself into her shoulders a little and blew her nose. Then she stood, threw her lunch napkin into the garbage, and focused on her posture. She walked in a tiny circle around the boxes in the kitchen minding her posture. "Stop being hysterical, Lucille," she said to the empty house. "Pull yourself together." The words her mother would have said, had she been there.

All Lucy wanted was to call Claire. The phone wasn't even hooked up. Were there pay phones in suburbia? Lucy found a nickel for the pay phone in her change purse. She put Kier in the pram and walked to the end of Maple Avenue. Now what? She turned left and walked three blocks down Rhododendron Row. No pay phone. When Lucy reached the end of a cul-de-sac she turned around. She hadn't even changed into a skirt. She was still wearing Peter's overalls. There was cherry red paint dried in a line on her forearm. She leaned down to tuck the blanket up around Kier's chin. What was she doing out here? Her face wasn't even on. Lucy turned back onto her street again. She wouldn't call Claire. She couldn't hear her say I told you so. Go back to the house Lucille Jacobs, she told herself. Find the radio. Hope to god they've got some Hank Williams on.

I n mid-January of the following year, Peter and Lucy were invited to a Hawaiian luau held at the Stewanakies' place. Peter wrapped an extra coat around Lucy to get her from the car. She insisted on wearing a grass skirt over a flowered dress she'd found half-off in the Eaton's catalogue even though she was expecting again and was starting to show. The magenta hibiscus pattern stretched slightly across Lucy's middle.

The neighbourhood women sat together in the living room wearing leis and holding fruity drinks with umbrellas while outside it snowed. The men smoked in the front parlour. The two Stewanakie boys ran up and down the stairs shooting toy guns at one another and riding the banister as if it were a horse. It was when Peter stood alone in the kitchen staring intently at the Shirley Temple he was mixing for Lucy, that he figured out the problem of the wings.

The red grenadine swirled round and round the glass like the sunsets from the boat when he was coming home from the war. His face was so close to the tumbler he could smell the tang of the orange juice. The carbonation from the club soda hit him in the face like a summer rain. Peter stood at the counter, unaware of the noises of the party: the record being changed, the women howling in laughter from the other side of the wall. Peter stood among the liquor bottles, the flicked caps of Coke and 7-Up, the sticky countertop, the bronze bucket of ice and the opened cupboards filled with wine glasses and martini glasses and juice glasses, all lined up in tidy rows, and he watched intently as the spoon pulled the pomegranate syrup in tiny whirlpools through the orange juice until the drink became a solid hue of pink.

The women from the block talked non-stop about babies. Lucy wished they could talk about something else sometimes. Books, maybe. Or even movies. She'd rather talk about movies than babies. It was bad enough not fitting into any of her clothes. Or the hemorrhoids, the swollen ankles, the varicose veins. Her recently and acutely developed nauseous sensitivity to certain smells: garlic, for instance, Lucy had banned from the house. Women loved to talk about babies, Lucy had noticed, but they never talked about vomiting every morning before noon.

"Some babies are born with infant sets of teeth that fall out before their baby teeth come in," Connie Romano said. The Romanos lived next door.

"That's not true!" Linda Stewanakie said.

Connie nodded. "And some babies are born with hair, kind of like fur, all over their bodies."

"What?" Lucy said, drawn in despite herself, "Fur? Where did you read that?"

"Seriously. *Reader's Digest*. It was an article about preparing mothers for the unexpected." Connie took a deep sip of her piña colada. "Eventually it stops."

"The unexpected?" Lucy asked.

"No. The fur-growth. It falls off."

The women laughed and laughed. Lucy excused herself to find Peter.

¶ "What are you doing?"

Lucy watched as her husband stood hunched over the countertop staring at a glass full of pink liquid. He was stirring. With a fork. A tablespoon, a teaspoon and a butter knife lay beside her drink in messy pools.

"Vortexing."

"What?"

"Your drink is vortexing."

"The juice has gone off?"

"No. The fork. Your drink is the wind."

"Did you have all that?" She pointed to a half-empty bottle of Gordon's gin in front of him.

He looked up at her. Then at the bottle. "Haven't had a spot. I've been stirring your drink this entire time." He handed Lucy the Shirley Temple, kissed her deeply on the mouth and turned toward the front room. "Has anyone seen Robert Lambert? From the hangar? The French guy? He here?"

¶ What Shirley Temple taught Peter was that the fork, out of all household cutleries, held the least resistance in water. This, and that the wings of the plane needed a notch cut into them so that the wind could flow freely, past the wing tips, past the danger of fire, and into the pink mixed-drink sunset of the sky.

¶ "Une fourchette?"

Peter tried to explain to Robert that Monday at work.

"Yes. The fork."

Robert watched as Peter stirred cream into their cups of coffee.

"Look, when the coffee goes through the tines there aren't the whirlpools, like with the spoon. Less displacement."

"Tines? What is tines?"

¶ Peter and Robert worked together steadily on new drafts of the wings all through the beginning of the new year and into the spring. They added the notch. They did more wind testing on the models. More planes caught on fire. Nothing was repeatable. Then Robert thought of adding an extended leading edge droop. That's where the computer came in. An International Business Machine, Model 704, was installed at the hangar. The 704 was the most powerful IBM digital computer of its time. It took up a whole room and had the computational capacity of a team of thirty mathematicians. It cost the same as the annual salaries of thirty mathematicians. Avro rented it month to month. It would have been too expensive otherwise.

¶ During her second pregnancy, Lucy walked the outskirts of the outskirts of town with Kier in his pram. She walked past the finished houses to the unfinished ones. She walked past construction sites and unpaved culs-de-sacs to smaller dirt farming roads. She walked along a small riverbank, a gully that had no water. Lucy thought of a town she'd heard of once that had been deliberately flooded under to make way for a dam. Houses and schools and graveyards stood beneath the surface of the water. Some with their furniture still inside. She imagined brooches in jewellery cases and rocking chairs. She imagined sailing a boat over top, looking down from the surface of water to what used to be the surface of land as if she were flying.

Lucy wandered to the edge of other townships. In the distance she could see a water tower painted the blue of a robin's egg with a peeling slogan, *A Nice Place To Live*. She walked by marshland with ducks and wayward herons. She walked even in the face of rain, through puddles that, by the time she returned home, were forming under the elm tree, in the bottom well of the tire-swing

Peter had recently hung up for Kier. She walked past forgotten pastures, barns standing decrepit and beautiful in their tilt. And then she returned home by the same route so she wouldn't get herself lost. She put Kier down for bed, made dinner and read from Ovid's *Metamorphoses* so she didn't feel she was waiting for Peter who was often late coming home. Sometimes after dinner, Peter put on a classical record. Good for the baby's development, he said, patting Lucy's growing belly. Lucy would have preferred listening to a little Lena Horne.

¶ Peter and Robert had come up with eight different notches and three extended leading edges in various combinations. The depth of the notch was the most critical parameter. They'd found that if the notch was too deep the wing tips could fracture completely from wind and altitude pressure and break off in the sky.

The computer worked. They found their ideal combination. New models were drafted. New wing skin alloys had been applied. The model tests were working. Repeatable. Repeatable. They took the models to Lake Erie. Shot them into the sky. Still not enough data. More mugs of coffee. More months of pacing. The planes were operating consistently just under Mach 1 and above that they had no idea. Their wind tunnels weren't powerful enough to get the proper data. Not even the ones in Ottawa. Avro had asked the Royal Canadian Air Force to make an official request to the United States Air Force so that they could take the model planes to the Cornell Transonic Wind Tunnel Laboratories in Buffalo. "We need complete sting mounted tests," Peter and Robert had written in their request. A month later, Cornell agreed. Official military permission was granted for only a narrow swath of time: twenty-four hours. *The Canadians will have free range of the laboratories from eleven-hundred hours, August 27, 1953, to eleven-hundred hours August 28, 1953, but that is the very limit of what we can afford.* A single day to conduct hundreds of wind tests on all of the various component parts. The guys from Engine Intake would come down along with Rueben from Marketing and Development. Marty from Fins and Fuselage, and Simon from Acoustic Analysis would be there. Fatigue and Thermal Stress would be working through the night.

¶ On August 27, 1953, at 09:00 hours, Lucy was laughing and drinking lemonade in the backyard with Connie Romano and Patricia Schwartz from down the block. Connie Romano was a short Italian woman with tight black curls who smoked menthols and lived next door. Trish practised her oboe when her husband was at work. The weather had turned hot late-August and the sunflowers were already fully blossomed in the yard. Lucy was glad she had come to know the neighbours, but they were nothing like her friends in the city. They were mousy women, Lucy thought, who always commented on her outfits. "You wear such outrageous things, Lucille. I wish I could pull that colour off."

"You can!" Lucy would insist, "you'd look magnificent," and lent Connie a gold belt or Patricia a turquoise sundress.

Her friends in Malton still called her Lucille. They were at the full-name stage of friendship. Lucy missed being Lu.

Peter sat reading at the kitchen table while Kier coloured. The flight to Buffalo was in less than an hour. Despite having worked on planes since he was a teenager, this was Peter's first flight. He had taken a book out of the library entitled *Conquering Aerophobia*. The book began by telling Peter a number of supposedly reassuring statistics. *Air travel is the second-safest mode of transportation in the world. The most dangerous part of your flight is the drive to the airport. Ninety-nine percent of turbulence injuries are from unfastened seat belts, or falling luggage. You have more of a chance of dying from the food being served onboard than being involved in an aeroplane accident.* The taxi would be arriving soon. From the swinging chaise the women's voices floated through the open kitchen window, an occasional shushing and chattering like wind through the lilac bush. Lucy was the size of a barn. Like the globe Kier sometimes spun around when Peter took him to the library. Peter was glad Connie and Trish were around to keep an eye on her this late in the pregnancy. Lucy had hoped her mother would come over from England, but Mavis had written to say that a transcontinental voyage was not possible as she was in the midst of redecorating the old house, and that she hoped Lucy would send photographs of the christening. At night, Peter helped to hoist Lucy up from the bed every time she needed the washroom, which at this stage was sometimes four or five times before breakfast. He held a hot water bottle to her lower back and spelled out baby names between her shoulder blades.

A–R–T–H–U–R, he drew with his finger.

She laughed. "No way."

S–E–Y–M–O–U–R.

She laughed again. "Seriously? Seymour? Besides, what if it's a girl?"

R–O–S–E, he spelled out quickly.

She nodded. "I like that one."

¶ Peter stood up from his book. *Treat the turbulence like bumps in the road. Don't tense up or fight it, but instead, let your body sway with the movements of the aircraft.* The movements of the aircraft. Who were they kidding? The movements of the aircraft were happening 30,000 feet above the earth. He leaned over the sink to speak to Lucy out the kitchen window. "I've got to get going," he said.

"Okay then," she waved. "Come give me a kiss and bring me that boy."

Kier was mad about something. "No, Dad." He shook his head and the green line he was colouring also shook.

"No what, Bean? I'll be coming home."

"No baby." Kier had been saying it all week.

"A little late for that," Peter said, and scooped Kier up into his arms, pulled up his striped t-shirt and blew against his tummy. Just then the taxi pulled up. Peter heard the blaring of the horn. He grabbed the handle of his suitcase. He heard a squeal from the ladies in the backyard.

Connie and Trish stood up abruptly so as not to get their dresses wet. Lucy called into the kitchen where Peter was putting on his suit jacket. "We're going to need a towel out here." Lucy's water had broken. The beginnings of Andrew Seymour Jacobs' birth pooled onto the violet flowers and plastic stitching of the chaise and dripped onto the lawn.

"Oh Lord." Peter said when he saw her. He came outside holding Kier and his suitcase with a flowered tea towel thrown over one shoulder.

"Go, Peter."

"But ..."

"No," she said. "You're getting on that plane."

"For crying out loud. You're giving birth."

"You are needed in Buffalo."

"I can't go while you're having ..." he looked at her. "Seriously, Lu."

"Look, I've already done this before. All you'll be doing is standing in the waiting room. I'll ask for the Demerol."

"I'll go with her," Connie said. "Tell the cabbie to call another one."

"Connie will come. Trish will take Kier." Patricia took Kier from Peter's arms. Lucy took the tea towel. Peter looked at Lucy. "Go, Peter. It will be alright."

Peter kissed her. He hesitated. He didn't know if he should go.

She hit him with the towel. "For the love of god get on that plane."

He kissed her hard on the mouth and got into the taxi that would take him to the wind in Buffalo. "I love you, Lucy Jacobs," he called from the car.

Peter and Robert had waited months for the okay to fly down. Only twenty-four hours. And then Lucy in the yard giving birth. Lucy holding the tea towel in the backyard. Peter's hadn't accounted for that. *Breathe deeply as often as you can, and remember that the sick bag in front of you can be used as an anti-hyperventilating device.* Peter thought about Lucy and the new baby as he gripped both armrests for the duration of the flight. He phoned home from the hotel on a break from the wind tunnels. No answer. He tried to focus on the gauge of the testing box. No answer. He and Robert pushed her up past Mach 1, past Mach 2. The Americans were floored. Finally a message posted in the lobby with Peter's name. "It's a boy!" That night all the men drank too much bourbon and Engine Intake bought Peter a box of Cuban cigars.

¶ It took Claire a year and a half to come visit the house in Malton. It took Lucy calling Claire after Andy was born during a long stretch when Peter was swamped at work. It took Lucy explicitly saying the word *help*. It took Claire finally getting on the subway to the last westbound stop, riding the long circuitous route on the bus, and walking the nine and a half blocks in her kitten heels. And then she was in Malton, smoking a cigarette, pacing in front of the settee with a look on her face that Lucy assumed to be the certain brand of judgement city people reserve for those lost forever to the vast noth-ingness of suburbia, and then Lucy wished Claire had never come.

Lucy had tried to have lunch with Claire in the city a few times, but Claire's favourite restaurants didn't accommodate children, and when they finally settled on a dinerette on College, Kier had tossed so many pieces of hamburger meat, sesame-seed bun, and French-fried potatoes at patrons eating at the surrounding tables that Lucy had sworn never to return to Mars Food again.

"What is this?" Claire asked.

"What?" The babies were in a playpen on the living-room floor. Kier was pulling out the red woollen hair of a Raggedy-Andy Doll, while the real Andy was on his back, gurgling to himself.

"This colour." Claire pointed a bangled arm toward the living-room wall.

"You hate it," Lucy replied without looking up from the vegeta-bles and yogurt-dill dip she was putting out on the coffee table.

"It's just very ..."

"... Orange," Lucy said. "I know," and she crunched down on a cucumber slice without offering them first to Claire.

Lucy was tired. But not the tired of dancing. Not the tired of late-night talks at the Vesta Lunch. Root tired. The tired of bones with-out enough milk. "It was supposed to be coral."

"No, you know," Claire said, looking back at the wall with a scep-tical appreciation, "It's actually quite bright."

"It's called Florida Keys." Lucy ate another piece of cucumber, this time held the bowl up toward Claire who took a slice.

"Coral," Claire said, "I can see it,"

"You hate it," Lucy said again.

"No. I like it."

Lucy leaned back against the settee. "At least I know it's orange. At least I can admit that I painted my own living-room wall a hide-ous shade of orange."

Claire sat down next to Lucy and leaned her head against her friend's orange wall. She ashed her cigarette. "What did Peter say?" Claire asked.

"He said it reminded him of Cheese Whiz."

Claire burst out laughing.

"I know," Lucy said.

"Come on. Cheese Whiz isn't so bad," Claire said. "On broccoli. It doesn't get better than that. Or celery sticks. Or that spray cheese that comes in a can? I could eat that on Ritz crackers all day."

"You're disgusting," Lucy said. No. She was glad Claire had come.

"Okay champ," Claire said, "where do you keep your milk and vodka? What we need here to go with this wall are not these waist-line minding cucumber slices, but a few White Russians."

¶ By the time Peter got back, the two women were upstairs in bed laughing so hard Peter couldn't understand a word they said. Kier was bouncing in Claire's arms and Andy was asleep in Lucy's, oblivious to the women's howling and the silver Hershey's Kisses wrappers thrown like confetti over the bedcovers. Open on the floor was a large flat cardboard box, with a round piece of bread covered in what looked like tomato sauce, pepperoni, and cheese.

"I made dinner!" Claire finally said coherently to Peter, pointing to the meal she had gotten an Italian friend to make them and deliver in his car.

"What is it? Bread?" Peter said. He'd never seen a bread pie before, certainly not one in a box on his bedroom floor.

"Peter. Get with the times. It's pizza."

"You shouldn't have, Claire."

"Get in!" Lucy said, and opened the covers.

"No, thanks," Peter said, "I'll eat my dinner elsewhere."

"Oh, don't be like that," Lucy said.

"Be downstairs. Give you two hysterics time to recover."

¶ Lucy walked her bobbing walk up and down the bedroom with Andy on her shoulder, rubbing his back and shushing until he was asleep again, heavy in her arms. Claire sat at the foot of Kier's small bed holding an ashtray while she smoked and listened to Lucy read

Goodnight Moon with the red balloon and the old woman who was whispering hush. Lucy's face was lit only by a triangle of light coming in from the hall. Kier was already asleep before the last page. Lucy shut the cover and sat for a moment with the book in her lap looking over at her friend. Claire's expression had this strange astonishment to it. Lucy understood. After all, they were girls. They were both just girls, always pretending they were older than they were, but now with Lucy the pretending had caught up with her real life.

Lucy suddenly remembered doubling Claire along Dundas street on her bicycle, drunkenly avoiding the streetcar rails, as they headed home from a hotel bar where they had drunk their first sip of whiskey after seeing *Guys and Dolls*. Lucy had hated it. Not *Guys and Dolls*. Claire had hated *Guys and Dolls*. Lucy had hated the whiskey. Lucy had leaned her bicycle against a tree on the short promenade to the hotel and a doorman had bothered them about cluttering up the entrance. "Well sir, we've been waiting for the valet for half an hour," Claire had responded, and had led Lucy into the lobby by the elbow, the bicycle still comfortably resting against a dwarfish poplar. They had giggled in the powder room for twenty minutes before heading into the bar. And what of that now? Now Lucy was a mother.

¶ "I'm moving to Paris."

"What?" Lucy asked. They had come downstairs with the cold pizza and the three of them were drinking at the kitchen table. Claire had brought a bottle of coffee porter for Peter who had poured it carefully into a tall glass and was taking measured sips to maximize the pleasure. Lucy and Claire had moved onto champagne—Peter and Lucy still had half a case in the basement left over from the wedding.

"I've met someone."

"Claire. That's wonderful."

"He lives in an apartment where the bedroom window looks over Notre Dame Cathedral and he can hear the organist practise in the mornings while she paints."

"While she paints?"

"His wife."

Lucy looked at Peter. "Wait, sorry, I don't understand."

"He's blind."

"And married?"

"He's a cellist. He played a show at the club with this quartet—they just yanked him up on stage—and I'd never heard anything like it. He plucked the strings like a base at first, but then pulled out his bow and the whole place went silent. I've never heard the Swan so quiet. It was completely his show."

"And he's married?" Lucy asked again.

"His wife asked me to come back with them. I met her the first night I heard him play. Apparently she was watching me listen to the music. She wants to paint me listening. It's a new series she's doing—painting the sense of hearing—synesthesia she called it—a visual representation of an aural phenomenon. You know. Like Edvard Munch's *The Scream*. They are paying for my boat over."

"But ..."

Peter stayed quiet. He knew anything he said at this moment would be the wrong thing to say. He looked back and forth between Lucy and her best friend and noticed that they'd been holding onto each other's hands across the table, like the snow angel wings.

"So you're living with them?" Lucy asked.

"Yes."

"And posing for the wife while listening to the husband play music?"

"Yes."

"Is this actually a life?" Lucy said. Not as an insult, but as a question.

¶ That night Lucy wanted Claire to sleep over like they used to when they were in high school. But how could that work? Peter sleeping on the fold-out bed in the spare room? Claire insisted that she had to catch the last subway, that she had an appointment at the photographers in the morning to get her passport photos taken.

"Claire, can't we play cards and then go out walking? I need to show you something."

"I'm going to bed," Peter said, and kissed Claire on either cheek and held Lucy against his chest for a moment, kissing the top of her head before going up the stairs. "If Andy wakes up I'll give him a bottle," he said from the landing, "just in case you two decide to paint Malton red."

"Please, Claire. Stay until the morning."

Claire touched one of Lucy's red curls. "Your hair has gotten long."

"That's a yes!" Lucy said, "you're staying."

"What would a no have been?"

"Putting on your shoes."

¶ The women played rounds of Spite and Malice until the bottle of champagne was finished. They shut the front door quietly behind them at the first sign of morning. "Sometimes if I'm up early I mistake the city for the sun," Lucy said as they walked arm in arm down the empty streets. Dogwood Lane. Cherry Terrace. Rhododendron Row. Streets named after blossoms that couldn't survive an Ontario winter. "I hadn't noticed before, but the city gives off this light like a planet. This red glow from far away." They passed the neighbourhood park. A slide and a swing set. A set of three ducks on springs with handles at the sides of their smiling beaks. "I want to take you to this place that looks like the end of the earth."

¶ In the early hours of the morning the construction site looked more eerie than when Lucy passed in the daytime. The unfinished houses she had first seen when they'd moved were finished now, the sod of the lawns laid down. Families were already living there, balls and hockey nets on the driveways. But beyond the new houses were more empty lots and trucks and piles of sand and brick and mud, followed by more concrete foundations with the ribs of the houses and nothing more. "Come in here," Lucy said, and pulled Claire into one of the unfinished houses. "Look out the window." Through one unfinished window, Claire could see through window after window after window. The houses were identically built and identically positioned on the lots. "It's like the mirrors in the Eaton's change room," Lucy said. "Remember? The ones where you stand in the middle and your reflection goes on forever?"

It was dark and they were both shivering. Lucy's voice had a strained quaver. Claire took out her cigarettes and tried to imagine what Montréal would look like from the steamship.

"There was this one day," Lucy said, "when Peter was at work."

Claire would leave Canada and all of its newness. She would walk down streets with cobblestones older than this country. She would have conversations about Manet's *Olympia* and Kadinsky's paintings of jazz.

"I was standing at the picture window holding back the curtain, waiting for Peter. I remember I was at the front door even before he'd gotten out of the car. 'I've put a flashlight and an extra can opener and some tinned food in the basement in case there's an attack while you're at work,' I said to him. And he was so confused. 'An attack?' he asked. 'And clean drinking water,' I said. 'What attack is this?' Peter kept asking. He hadn't even gotten his arms free from the sleeves of his coat."

Claire stared ahead through the windows to the end of the earth. She would learn the accordion and take up smoking a pipe.

"I told him that I'd practised shutting the blinds to shield Kier and myself from the light of the bombs, and how I'd learned that we were to go down to the basement and wait until he came home or until I heard the All Clear siren." Lucy spoke quickly into the beginning of the morning. "I remember Peter asking 'Bombs?' as if the idea had never even occurred to him. He fixed me a drink as if there was nothing to worry about. A Pink Lady." Lucy kicked at a jagged edge of the concrete foundation. "'You know what I'm talking about, Peter.' I said to him. Poor Kier. He was just looking back and forth at us from his highchair and this bowl of mushy peas I'd made for him. I could smell the pasty smell of the warm peas and the syrupy pink of the drink. 'No one's dropping nuclear bombs,' Peter said nonchalantly. 'It's Canada. Who wants to bomb Canada?' He was laughing at me for putting away tins of soup."

Claire stood with her cigarette unlit. She would become obsessed with a rare breed of Russian dog. She would read *The Autobiography of Alice B. Toklas* in cafés. Anything not to live in this shortbread cookie cut-out of matching bedroom furniture and manicured lawns. "You two are just tired, Lu."

"I was pregnant again," Lucy said, "with Andy. I'd just found out and hadn't told Peter yet. I was suddenly afraid of the baby being born."

"You must be so tired." Finally Claire clicked her lighter making a small circle of light at her face. She exhaled slowly through the glassless window.

"But then I thought of Peter's plane. Of course he's not afraid. The plane is ..." Lucy trailed off. "His plane can ..." The sun had risen. The street lights at the edge of the construction site had gone off. "I was so busy being in love with Peter that I didn't really think what he does."

"Kills people."

Lucy looked over at her friend. She could see the red of Claire's wool coat now in the grey frame of the empty house. "What?" Lucy said.

"The plane. It kills people." Claire turned her wrist slightly to look at the face of her watch as if she hadn't said anything at all.

"Well, it doesn't exactly kill people. It intercepts."

"What's the difference?"

¶ When they arrived back at the house, Claire picked up her big shoulder bag from the hall and came over to where Lucy was sitting in an armchair. Lucy kissed her friend by the ear and squeezed her. "Thanks for coming." Claire blew Lucy a kiss, "See ya, pal," and walked out the front door. Her friend was gone and Lucy could already feel the hangover coming on. She knew she should get up for some Alka-Seltzer but couldn't bring herself to move.

Lucy was sitting as she had been, still wearing her coat, when she heard the soft knocking at the door.

"Claire!"

"I nearly forgot," Claire whispered, "this is for Andy and Kier." She held out a record of Louis Armstrong and his Hot Five. "This is *West End Blues*," Claire said. "The best piece of jazz ever recorded. I expect the boys to know the introduction by heart when I come home." She passed Lucy the record. "And this is for you and Peter." It was a greasy paper bag. "I'm sorry. I know I said they weren't the best for breakfast. But maybe if you heat them up a bit, with a little hot sauce."

Lucy stood holding open the front door and kissed Claire. "Good bye, Claire France."

"Good bye, Lu," Claire said. She kissed Lucy back. Then she ran off this time, her heels clacking down the quiet street, past the paper boy.

THE LIGHTNING FIELD

"Okay, pretend you're a giraffe and I'm on Safari," Kier said. Andy said "No."

They were at the grocery store. The most boring place in the world.

"Okay," Kier thought for a second, "pretend you're a horse and I'm a cowboy and I'll ride you over there to the cereal boxes and the porridge will be our ranch and you can eat oats out of my hands and we'll sleep under the stars."

Especially when their Mama kept stopping to talk to everyone.

"No." Andy held the sticky shell of a walnut in his hand. He tried to chew at it.

"Okay," Kier said, "pretend you are a shark and I'm an underwater sea diver and you're the biggest shark ever in the whole world, yeah, say you're the biggest shark, and then I discover you with the beam of my underwater flashlight and you try to eat me and then I escape but I take your picture with a camera and become really famous and rich and you get to stay underwater and I get to be a famous diver and we never meet again, ever."

"No," Andy said again, and stuck the walnut in his mouth.

It was no fun having a brother. He was too little to want to pretend anything properly. And Kier had been building his first model plane with his dad, and Andy had flushed down the toilet one of its fins. He couldn't even colour.

¶ Noreen Leavis shook a bunch of parsley at Lucy. "I just don't think they should roll out the plane."

"Andy, put that down." Lucy sighed. "Kier, please take that walnut away from your brother."

"I want it!" Andy yelled.

"I know it will be a big to-do. And they've been working so hard. I know all of us could use a to-do."

"Andy. No. You can't eat those like that. You'll chip a tooth." Lucy was trying to put rutabagas into a plastic bag. Mrs. Leavis was talking to her from across a display of Florida oranges.

"Remember the Rosenbergs?"

Lucy nodded. Mrs. Leavis had obviously listened to the same radio program that she had yesterday afternoon. A five-year retrospective of the trials of Ethel and Julius.

"Ethel's brother, Greenglass somebody, testified that she'd typed up notes containing U.S. secrets in her apartment."

Lucy nodded again and kept an eye on Andy. Kier had gotten the walnut out of his brother's hands and was kicking it around the produce bins, shouting out indecipherable hockey commentary. Andy was sitting on the floor, sucking on the edge of his coat.

"And her husband, Julius. He supposedly supplied the Soviets with documents from the National Aeronautic Advisory Committee, you know NACA or whatever it's called."

"The Lockheed's Shooting Star." Yes, it was the exact same radio program. Lucy knew everything Mrs. Leavis was telling her.

"Exactly! I mean what if all those newsmen with their cameras and tape recorders at the rollout aren't all newsmen, you see what I mean, Lucille?"

"I'm sure they'll be careful." Lucy said. "It is the Air Force."

"You can't be too careful these days," Mrs. Leavis said.

"From what I've heard, the plane doesn't even have its engine yet, Noreen. It's just a full-scale prototype."

"Still, you can't trust anyone. I mean Ethel Rosenberg. She looked like a lovely woman. She wore such respectable coats."

¶ Lucy was to bring the cake. She was to pick it up from the city baker's that morning. She left ahead of Pete and the boys, laid out their clothes on the beds, left them Monte Cristo sandwiches warming in the oven for lunch, and blew them kisses from the stairs. She said she would meet them at the tea tent after the rollout.

¶ Peter and the boys arrived at Avro headquarters with the Romanos in their station wagon. Earlier that morning a storm had blown through and the tarmac looked black and clean. The faint scent of roads and wet dust rose from the concrete as families got out of their cars in the parking lots, slamming their doors and calling to one another amongst the patchwork of Studebakers and Chrysler Plymouths.

A small bandstand had been erected on the Avro runway. Pale blue and yellow bunting hung over a collapsible wooden stage. The entrance to the experimental hangar—Peter and Robert's hangar— was curtained off with a large white banner printed with the golden image of a triangle with wings. A cargo van with the Royal Canadian Air Force insignia on its passenger door drove past Peter and the boys as they walked toward a tower of bleachers that was already looking to be full. The van stopped next to a diamond of runway cordoned off with a braided silk rope. Two soldiers exited the back doors and began efficiently setting up extra rows of folding chairs.

Air Force officers, reporters, engineers, mechanics, pilots, politicians, employees and their families milled about the runway dressed in their finest afternoon attire. Peter could hardly move closer through the crowd to that triangle of tarmac with the boys. He assumed that's where the plane would stand. Peter scooped Andy up to ride on his shoulders. "See any spots in the bleachers, Ando?"

"Over there, Dad," Andy lurched forward against Peter's neck and almost kicked a riveter in the head.

"Sorry about that, Frank."

Peter turned sideways, holding tight to Andy's wiggling legs, and squeezed the three of them forwards between people's coats. His crooked elbow slammed into a woman's sweatered chest. "Oh Ma'am, so sorry." He turned to find Kier. "This way."

They slowly neared the front of the crowd. The bandleader was warming up the Air Force orchestra. Peter noticed that beside the stage a row of chairs decorated with ribbons was already filled with people he'd seen walking through the plant but never spoken to, investors and military personnel. To his left Peter caught site of Robert's brown hat with the quail feather.

"Robert," he shouted into the growing crowd.

Robert turned. "Pierre." He pushed between the shoulders of two men, "Je m'excuse."

"You remember my boys? Andrew," Peter pointed up, "and Kier. Say bonjour to Monsieur Lambert."

Kier kicked at the pavement. "Bonjour Monsieur Lambert."

"Ton français est très bon!" Robert winked at Peter. "He's better than you, non?" He laughed his wheezing motor laugh. "And she? Where is Lucille?"

"She should be here somewhere." Peter turned toward the tea tent stationed at the back of the tarmac. "She went to get the gâteau for everyone."

"Bien sûr. I hope for vanilla."

The crowd quieted. The orchestra sat with trumpets and trombones held in their laps. The flags snapped in the wind. Peter and the boys were so close to the rope now they could hear the well-ironed squish of uniforms as the musicians stood and moved their instruments to their lips, inhaling together like a sea. The conductor held up his baton and brought it down. *The Maple Leaf Forever* blared out of their brass horns. The bass drum reverberated through Peter's chest.

Official-looking men in grey flannel suits were announced to the crowd as they mounted the stage. Sir Roy Dobson, one of Avro's international officers, had been flown in from London and was wearing a bowler hat which made him look like a salesman. Either a salesman, Peter thought, or Scotland Yard. Crawford Gordon, the chief Canadian officer, by contrast, wore a grey fedora, dark glasses, and a pointy handkerchief in his breast pocket and looked as though he needed a drink. Gordon often looked a bit haggard as he toured the hangars on his rounds, like a chief surgeon who had just come from performing complicated and potentially fatal surgery on a stabbing-wound victim. He was the type of boss to have clean pressed shirts in one of his desk drawers in case of unforeseen circumstances. Peter could respect that. The token politician flown down from Ottawa for the day, Defence Minister Major-General George Pearkes, stood next to Gordon and read over the text of his speech, occasionally glancing up to look out over the crowd through his circular thick-rimmed glasses as the orchestra played *God Save The Queen* and he mouthed the words. There were then further introductions by a competent Master of Ceremonies and Pearkes moved to the microphone to give the governmental address.

"Much has been said of late about the coming missile age." A slight delay between his voice and the transmission, like the crack of a baseball being hit out of the park. "There have been suggestions from well-intentioned people that the era of the manned airplane is over." Andy squirmed against Peter's shoulders to be let down. "However, the aircraft has this one advantage over the missile. It can bring the judgement of a man into battle." Pearkes adjusted his glasses. Andy sat down on the concrete at Peter's feet and began to untie and tie his shoelaces. A skill he had recently mastered with the trick of a rhyme. "And the Arrow, with its complexity and performance," Pearkes continued, "combined with a man, with his good sense and human judgement, will provide the most sophisticated and effective defence that human ingenuity can devise." Pearkes lowered his glasses and pulled on a tasselled rope hanging next to the podium like a magician performing a carefully choreographed trick.

Flashes of camera bulbs and plumes of smoke. Andy wanting to be let back up again. Kier wanting to be let up too. The Avro banner parted slowly to reveal the darkness of the hangar. People stood on their chairs. Men took off their hats. A white runway tractor, no bigger than a golf cart, was driven out by a man in a white jumpsuit. He towed the plane slowly into the light. The sun hit the nose first: a pointed radar-rod nose. The clamshell cockpit and the fuselage's new paint shone so brightly it was like a movie was being shot. The wide white triangular delta wings—notch, leading edge, Mach 2 capabilities—towered over the crowd. Even now, it surprised Peter how big the plane was, how enormous the length of the wings that had come from the blue lines and compass spans, how high above them the two red maple leaves were emblazoned port and starboard. The white-jumpsuited man on the tractor brought the plane to a halt. Peter and the boys stood closest to the twin exhaust cones. They were so close they looked up at the undercarriage. They could almost touch the landing gear past the ropes. The crowd burst into applause. Whistles. The Arrow revealed. Peter's paper airplane brought to life.

Reporters jotted down their first impressions on pocket-sized pads. *Twice the Power of the Queen Mary. Deadly.* The Arrow was scheduled to be the headline for October 5, 1957—all the newspapers had men there; Peter was told that even June Caldwell was there, Canada's top female reporter—but the plane was outdone news-wise, and therefore bumped to second byline, by an unexpected event.

That same afternoon, as the Earth circled the Sun in its perpetual orbit—while the ladies served sandwiches without crusts and waited for Lucy to appear with the cake; while Peter wandered the entire length of the parking lot looking for the car; while Kier and Andy went to Mrs. Leavis' house and Peter borrowed Robert's car to search the road on the way home to call the bakery; while the Arrow was celebrated sans gâteau, the old war men shaking hands and raising hats to one another, posing for photographs by the plane— Soviet scientists launched the first satellite into space from the Baikonur Cosmodrome. Sputnik. October 4, 1957. The Earth circling the Sun. Sputnik circling the Earth. The Missile Age.

"It is now unquestionably possible for a nuclear bomb to be launched to any place on Earth from Space. With calculated accuracy it is likely the Soviets could even target a single building." Peter turned the radio of Robert's car up as he sped home. "You, the average listener, will be able to see Sputnik tonight, with your very own naked eye. This new moon of Earth's will orbit over Toronto just after midnight. Turn off your lights and look toward the northern horizon." Peter came to a stop, signalled and turned onto their street. The radio was now casting Sputnik's telemetry signal into the contained space of the car ... *beep beep* pause *beep beep* pause *beep beep*. Peter parked in the driveway and listened for a moment to the rhythmic blips of the satellite's voice before he turned off the dial and opened the front door to the house. The phone was ringing.

¶ The details of someone being struck by lightning are different in every case. Research is scant and subject to a number of shortcomings including heterogeneity, longitudinal or prospective evaluation and pre-morbid factors not indicated in concurrent psychopathology. This is what the textbooks say, the clinicians' manuals that Peter will take out of the Banting and Fitzgerald medical libraries at the University of Toronto trying to understand what is happening to his wife beneath the bandages and shrouds. What Peter can make of all these words later, late at night, sitting alone in the kitchen with the boys asleep upstairs, seems irrelevant to the facts of their specific case: he left the rollout ceremony of the plane whose wings he'd drafted. In the car the radio announcer reported on a satellite shot into orbit. Then, when Peter arrived home, the phone. A nurse from the general hospital. Lucy was there. She had been struck by an electrical current of over a million volts. From a bolt of lightning coming down from the sky. A priest had found her, the nurse had told him. A priest who drove a blue pickup truck. The priest had left Lucy's body at the emergency room without leaving his name. Peter tries to imagine this man, looking out the rain-splattered windshield of his pickup with Lucy slumped against the window in the seat beside him. The words must be especially incomprehensible at the age of five, or eight, Peter thinks. To be taken to a neighbour's. To have fish sticks for dinner. To hear your dad on the phone saying he won't be picking you up until late that night, because your mama's in the hospital, and won't wake up, even if you were there to secretly pinch her palm.

The textbooks conclude that there is numbness. Sleep disturbance. Confusion and weakness. Random fears. Peter will wonder whether lightning has any effect at all. Don't we all fear randomly now and again? Isn't our sleep sometimes disturbed? Occasionally, aren't we all numb and weak and confused? Aren't pre-morbid factors, factors that happen before we all die, a constant and unknowable problem?

The one thing unaccounted for in the research is the lightning itself. Doctors have analyzed the effects of lightning, the ringing in the ears, the agoraphobia, the nightmares and what they call the deficits of memory and attention; but they have missed the fact that lightning remains inside its victims, is still there, jazzing its way through vein and vessel like a trapped bird.

¶ The hospital corridor was pale blue. Peter sat with his hands on his knees. The hallway smelled viral with a patina of antiseptic: like lemons mouldering. It was just before the dinner hour. Peter took off his hat and put it down on the chair next to him. The sunlight shone in through the hallway of windows. He could see a short bit of lawn and then beyond, the parking lot. Through an open window the faint scent of dried seeds and disintegrating leaves, but the mouldering lemons were stronger. He held his hands up to his face and smelled his skin. Better. Sweat and pencil shavings and the faint leather of Robert's steering wheel.

Peter sat in a trance. He went to the cafeteria for a coffee. He sat down again and tried to read an article in the *National Geographic* about the tides in the Bay of Fundy. He ate an egg sandwich from a candy-striper's cart. He paced. He deliberated about buying a package of cigarettes. He sat. He did a lot of sitting. It was after dark when the doctor came over to speak with him and Peter stood up.

"Doctor Sousa," Doctor Sousa said.

"Peter Jacobs," Peter Jacobs said.

"Jacobs, I'll jump right in. Your wife is in a coma because of severe electrical shock. We won't know more until tests are complete. She's under constant monitoring, and I've scheduled a number of preliminary appointments with specialists for tomorrow. I won't lie to you. Her condition is far from stable at this point."

"Am I able to see her?"

"I'll send a nurse to fetch you when they've finished wrapping the burns." The doctor looked down at his clipboard. "There is some good news, though." He looked at the clipboard a second time. "Good news. Despite possibility for tremendous muscular damage, Mrs. Jacobs' heart didn't stop. At this point in time, your wife and the baby are managing to pull through."

"The baby?" Peter recited square roots to focus himself (square root of one is one, square root of four is two, square root of nine is three, square root of sixteen is four, square root of twenty-five is five, square root of thirty-six is six ...).

"Oh, I see. You didn't know."

Peter shook his head.

"Your wife is in her first trimester. Week eleven, approximately."

Peter was up to sixty-four. "And the baby? The baby will be okay? ... in the ... um ... uterus?"

"We have them on a drip. As I said, we'll know more tomorrow after the tests."

Peter nodded (square root of one-twenty-one is eleven, square root of one-forty-four is twelve, square root of one-sixty-nine is thirteen ...).

"Do you have any questions?"

Peter shook his head.

"Alright then. Someone will let you know when you can go in." The doctor walked down the long hallway to triage.

When Peter went in to see Lucy, the room was lit by a single reading lamp. The bed with its curtains reminded him of the netting a beekeeper wears.

"Lu," he said softly. "Lucy." He took her hand, the one without the bandages, and drew along the lines of her palm with the tip of his finger.

¶ Peter picked up the boys from Mrs. Leavis' house just before eleven that evening. He still had Robert's car. He'd called Robert from the hospital.

"Don't worry, Pierre."

"But work tomorrow."

Robert asked tentatively, gently, "Where is your car?"

"They found her on a secondary highway, near an interchange."

"We will go get it together."

"Robert. I couldn't ask you ..."

"Pick me up demain and we will go."

"Thank you, Robert."

"Pas de problème."

"Thank you."

71

The boys were standing at Mrs. Leavis' door, ready in the peacoats Lucy had laid out for them that morning. "Daddy!" they said, as they usually did when Peter got home from work. Peter knelt down. He squeezed them both and leaned forward to tighten one of Andy's loose shoelaces. "Come on boys. Back home."

They walked to the car in the path of the porch light with Mrs. Leavis watching from the front door.

Peter tucked Andy into the backseat and made sure Kier was okay in front. "Thank you, Noreen," Peter said, as he came around to the driver's side.

"Anytime." She waved at the boys as Peter started the engine and reversed out the drive.

It wasn't until he was on the road home again, the headlights casting ahead of them into the dark, that Peter started to tell the boys.

"Your mama was meant to get the cake."

Kier looked over.

"And on the way there she had to stop the car on the side of the road and get out."

"Maybe for a stretch?" Andy asked from the backseat.

"Yes, Ando. Maybe for a stretch."

Kier was quiet in the front.

"There was an accident. She was in a field. During a storm. Lightning hit a tree near your mom, and then jumped from the tree branch to her shoulder."

Kier looked out the window.

"She has burns on her arms and neck. And she's asleep. She's going to be asleep for a while."

The boys were quiet.

Peter looked in the rear-view mirror at Andy. "What do you think, Boo?"

"But why did the lightning go to Mama?"

Peter paused for a moment. "Because we're made out of water. Sixty-percent water, Ando. And electricity is attracted to water. Especially lightning bolts."

Peter pulled into their driveway and turned off the ignition. He took a deep breath. The three of them sat quietly without opening the doors. Peter wasn't sure what else he was meant to say. "Do you have any questions?"

Silence. Then Kier's voice.

"Like when I touched the kettle?" Kier turned toward his dad. "Those kinds of burns?"

"Sort of like that."

Then Andy. "Does it come out if you get a hole?"

Kier looked at his brother. "What?" he asked. "Does what come out?"

"The water. Can it leak out?"

Kier looked over at Peter.

"No," he looked at the two of them in their matching coats. "No, the water can't spill out. It's in your muscles and tissue. In your blood."

"Oh," Andy said.

The three of them were quiet again. Peter got out of the car and came around to the passenger side to help the kids.

"Dad, can we look at the new moon?" Kier asked.

Peter looked at him.

"Sputnik," Kier said. "Mrs. Leavis was watching about it on the television."

"Right." Peter had completely forgotten. He looked up at the sky and then back in at Andy. "Andrew?"

Andy nodded.

"Okay, but pyjamas must be on."

¶ Peter and the boys sat on the porch steps with all of the house lights off, and all down the street there were shadows of other families, also up late, looking toward the sky. One woman held an empty baking dish and a tea towel, as if the collective beeps of everyone's radios had called her out of her kitchen into the night air. *Beep beep* pause *beep beep* pause *beep beep*. Sputnik's thin telemetry signal was broadcasting live. Transistor radios leaned up against porch railings, on window sills, resting on the hoods of cars. A few of the neighbourhood men were still in their good suits from the rollout, their smooth drunken voices floating into the street with the smoke of their cigarettes. Andy and Kier took sips of hot Ovaltine that Peter had made for them, and then ran out into the yard with their pyjamas on beneath their coats, their necks craning up to the sky. They couldn't see anything at first. Stars. Dark. Then Andy caught sight of it and shouted, "Look! Like a balloon!"

Peter stood up. "Good eye, Ando." And sure enough, there it was like a lost birthday decoration. As if it had been let go by a Russian kid somewhere on the other side of the world. The spherical light drifting over Moscow, over the pointed Easter-egg domes of St. Basil's Cathedral. Further, orbiting over Toronto, the house on Maple Avenue, the hospital where Lucy had begun to dream. Sputnik: travelling companion. A Russian mirrored ball over the dance-floor of the planet. A whiskery silver moon circling the Earth. One-hundred-and-eighy-four pounds and the shape of a basketball. Nothing like a grapefruit, as Khrushchev called the United States' attempt at a satellite months later. A serious accident. The Soviets were first.

"It's gone," Kier said. He and Andy held their hands over their eyes and looked back and forth across the sky.

Sixteen minutes. Sputnik was overhead and visible for sixteen minutes. Peter felt cold. He had not quite realized until that moment how vast was space. We were nothing. The Earth itself, which Peter had seen so little of in retrospect, was a dime. A cat's eye marble. A pistachio in its shell. The thought paralyzed him open-jawed on the lawn. The boys went back to their mugs of Ovaltine, sat on the front steps. Peter stayed staring at the sky.

"If Mama's not out of the hospital in time for Thanksgiving, who's going to make us a turkey?" Andy's voice in the darkness.

"Dad'll make the turkey," Kier said.

"He will?"

"Sure."

"He knows how to make turkey?"

Peter leaned against the maple tree in the front yard. The entire street had one on each front lawn. They had been planted when the houses were built. Peter looked down the block at the rows of lights coming back on in the windows, the slick black street.

"It's gone, Dad."

Peter felt as though there was no border between the edges of the landscape he could see and the reflection of the sun's light off of that man-made ball of metal in space. It was as if everything he knew was extending upward and outward in all directions into the universe. Yes, that. But what he didn't know was collapsing around him at the same time. It was the strangest sensation. Like the expression, "in the dark." Peter felt, standing on the lawn of his house, as though he were in the dark.

"Dad, it's gone."

Lucy was by a lake. A bright blue lake, so blue it was as if there was hardly any atmosphere between the water and the sky. Lucy was at a great altitude so that it was hard to breathe. There were mountains in the distance, at the farthest edge of the lake, jagged and covered in ice. The sun was shining, but, because Lucy was so far up, she felt cold and shivered in spasms. Then she was carrying a glass of milk in her hand. She walked along the shore of the blue lake, and she dropped the glass on a rock and it shattered everywhere, and her hand bled and there was glass at her feet. Above, a falcon was circling. The falcon circled in great arcs over the water, its reflection also circling. She saw that bird flying in the sky for days, for weeks maybe. It simply swooped and glided and drifted on the currents of air, never once touching its talons to the earth. And then, just as suddenly as it had arrived, the bird flew off again, up high beyond the peaks of the mountains, and Lucy felt lonely. Then the slow flicker of waking up.

It was the voices at first. As if they were calling to her from the other shore of the lake. "Lucy," "Mama," words so faint in the distance she could hardly make them out. What season was it? Were those falling leaves or snow? She couldn't recall how long she'd been at the shore. Then there was a smoothness, an ease. The nurses' hands while they changed her dressings. Lucy also began to detect the different qualities of light, as if the great blue sky over the lake had opened up and was changing colours. Soft roses brushing against the window hanging at the horizon, blooms of light shifting from pink to yellow, dawn opening at the glass.

The yellow light honeyed slowly about her bed and brightened to white. Long shadow people at her side: their silhouettes stretching out over the sand, then over her bed. And more shadow people, coming and going over the rocks and driftwood, over the pebbles and dried reeds, coming to her and standing over her, until her bed was covered in shadows, and it was night. She moved her shoulder. She cried out.

She began to smell flowers. Chrysanthemums. Delphiniums. Silence. She could hear a billowing sail. A page from Andy's colouring book pinned on the wall nearest the window's cool breeze. Rescue.

Lucy crouched down at the shore to spell HELP with the rocks.

The neighbours gave Peter so many casseroles that the freezer was full and he had to keep some in the crisper drawers at the bottom of the fridge. Lasagnes and cabbage rolls and bangers with gravy were stacked and frozen in tinfoil. There were even Yorkshire puddings in there. It had come to that. Even Yorkshire puddings were in their freezer. And still, Peter had to work. Lucy in the hospital, two small boys at home, Yorkshire puddings in the freezer, and the same drive at seven in the morning with the radio on to the news.

While Peter had been away the memo had come. The suite of weaponry was to be housed in the fuselage below the wing. When Peter returned to work, Robert had sketches and specs of missile prototypes spread across their drafting tables. From the memo Peter learned that with missiles it was the opposite of birds, the Sparrow was bigger than the Falcon. Four Sparrow 2s could sit partly in and partly out of the belly of the aircraft. The eight smaller Falcons could fit fully inside, which meant heightened agility and less drag. But with the Sparrows there was possibility for development. The Sparrow x was being designed with the capability to carry nuclear warheads. All this Peter knew from the memo, from these newly delivered specs across his desk. But when the evaluators with their bright white coats and clicking clipboards came around the hangar on that Friday after the accident, Peter thought they were talking about music at first when they began to ask questions about the suites.

76

¶ On weekends the boys sat side by side on the carpet watching acrobatic cowboys doing flips on horses while ballerina cowgirls stood on their shoulders. *Acrobat Ranch*. It was Andy's favourite show. On the carpet in front of the boys were two toy fire trucks, a stack of comic books, a spill of crushed up Sugar Smacks and two bowls of sugary milk. Peter slept in on Saturday mornings, one lovely singular morning, his arm covering his face from the light. He slept while the boys snuck downstairs early, turned on the television, and waited until the buzzing black and white Indian-head test card disappeared and the Saturday morning programming began.

Peter came down from his bedroom tying the belt of his flannel robe around his pyjamas. He stopped in the living room. Andy was sitting cross-legged close up to the television. Kier was lying on his belly, glancing between a comic book and the TV. Peter stepped over their bowls of milk.

"Hey Dad," Kier said.

"Hi Daddy," Andy said.

Neither took their eyes from the TV.

Peter made himself a pot of coffee in the kitchen and sat at the table. Two articles had come in from the Banting library on the effects of lightning strikes on unborn children. The articles were from Europe. It appeared that no research had been completed in North America on this particular medical situation, and so Peter, with the help of the medical librarian, had begun to mail article request cards to the European journals. One of the articles was written in German, and so after stopping at Banting, Peter had made his way to the Trinity library to take out a German dictionary to see what he might be able to decipher. All he could guess at in the title was *Kind*: child, it meant, not kind, as in English. But Peter was tired, and so he only managed to glance at the articles before his gaze wandered around the kitchen.

Cutting boards hung from hooks on the wall. One of Lucy's aprons hung over the handle of the oven door alongside a tea towel commemorating Queen Elizabeth's coronation. A Howdy Doody egg timer that the boys had given Lucy last mother's day sat on top of the stove beside a bottle of HP sauce and the wooden coffee grinder with the little drawer. On top of the refrigerator was a bag of salt and vinegar potato chips and a fruit bowl, empty save for a few browning bananas and a shrivelled orange. Everything seemed slightly unreal with Lucy gone from the house. Slightly Technicolor. Peter stood up and leaned against the stove to get a different perspective of the room. Beside the medical articles, the turquoise Formica table was stacked with bills and unopened get-well cards. Peter took a swig of his coffee and put the mug down next to the sink. The table. It fit awkwardly between the side kitchen entrance into the house and the swinging doors to the living room. Even sitting down at the table, Andy had nearly hit Peter in the head barrelling through the swinging doors because the end chair jutted out precariously into the pathways of the kitchen; the chair continually got thwacked with the door ricocheting back. Something must be done about the table. Peter sat down again and dug through the piles of mail. He found a pad of graph paper and a pencil and he began to draw.

¶ Telemann, Peter had wanted to tell the external evaluators, had written over two hundred suites. Handel wrote twenty-two suites for the keyboard alone. And Bach. Peter had played Bach's cello suites on the record player when Lucy was pregnant with Andrew. He'd read somewhere that babies could hear in utero during the third trimester, and that listening to classical music at a young age made children more likely to excel at math or art.

¶ Peter made another pot of coffee and headed down the basement steps to his workbench. He sat on a stool beneath the one window that offered any light: jagged ground light, broken up by the thistles and long grasses growing in front of the window in the backyard. He turned on the hanging lamp that was hooked over a basement pipe. Trouble Lamp it was called in the Canadian Tire catalogue. His tools hung in rows. A neat stack of lumber leaned against the wall. The smell of pine resin.

Peter sat and stared at the drawings he'd made upstairs. He climbed back upstairs and moved the record player into the basement so he could listen to the album Lucy had bought him for an anniversary gift that year: Glenn Gould playing Bach's *Goldberg Variations*. It was Lucy's favourite Bach. Although she always seemed to prefer Duke Ellington. "He's like the Bach of jazz," she told Peter as she switched records.

Peter put on his safety goggles and sawed a large oval out of a piece of plywood. He sanded the edges until it was a smooth shape. He drilled holes into the panel and screwed in three supporting doweling pieces, one at the top of the oval, two at the broader end. The record ended and he switched sides. Peter made more coffee, came down the stairs again, and looked once more at his drawings. He thought about whether he could find a guy to do some chrome plating. Chrome like on the Avrocar that John Frost was working on in hangar five. The flying saucer Avro was building for the U.S. Army. Peter hadn't worked on the saucer, but he'd been there for the hover trials. A wobbling flying silver space car, zipping down the runway, straight out of *The Day The Earth Stood Still* with Patricia Neal. He wanted Lucy's gift to look as sleek as that space car.

¶ After the evaluators had left, Robert quietly humming at his desk, Peter kept thinking of music instead of bombs. He looked at the specs and saw loudspeakers strapped under the Arrow's wings. The planes flying out over frozen fields of ice, over the ocean, over vast fields of Russian wheat, gliding and dipping over the year's harvest, blasting the Reds with the music of cellos, violins, and flutes. The speakers rigged to play Tchaikovsky for those Russians. *Swan Lake*, *The Sleeping Beauty*, *Marche Slave*.

Peter looked at Robert, bent over his drafting table. Looked back at the specs.

"Robert?"

"Ça va, Pierre?"

"Have you seen these specs?"

Robert put down his rule. "Specs?"

"These falcons or whatever they want to call them," Peter said.

"The bombs?"

Peter nodded.

"Mais, Pierre, tu as travaillé à Lancasters pendent la guerre, non?"

"It's just different."

"Oui. Mais, Pierre, on n'est pas les seules à posseder les bombes. "

"No, I know that."

79

Peter turned back to his desk, which had become cluttered with papers, clipboards and instruments. The bombs had been abstractions. Peter had been thinking in abstractions; and not even in large abstractions, but in insignificant detail. It was like during the war. He was a mechanic. Peter had thought of his time in the Service as nothing more than the component parts he had added and adjusted on each of the planes: altimeters, pressure valves, gauges, throttles, fuel caps. But with these falcons on his desk, it was as though this animal, which had been in the distance, killing things, had returned to his wrist.

"Do you need to go home?"

"No, no. I'm fine," Peter lied.

The men worked again in silence.

¶ The turntable had finished playing Glenn Gould and was making a soft click click noise. Zoinks and boffs and ahoogas from the cartoons echoed down the basement steps and mingled with Peter's sanding.

"Do you think Mama could have super powers?" Andy asked Kier.

"Huh?"

"Mama. Could she have super powers, you know, like The Human Torch."

Kier looked up from the Superman comic he was reading. "Did you spill more cereal?"

"Like when Professor Horton made an android. But he burst into flames when the newspaper people were all there for photographs and they laughed at him."

"Ando. The cereal. It's all over the carpet."

Andy's hair was still messy from sleep. The buttons of his pyjama top were misbuttoned. "But the android wasn't hurt," Andy went on. "He could control his own flames. But Professor Horton got mad at The Torch and put him back inside his tube so he could figure out how to use his powers nicely."

Kier began scooping cereal crumbs into one of the bowls. There was cereal in the fibres of the carpet.

"Maybe Mama's coma is like The Torch learning how to use his powers."

"Ando, Mama's not The Torch. Come on, help me clean this up."

Andy stood watching, thinking, as Kier picked up the carpety Sugar Smacks. "But she could be. She could be developing her super powers while she's sleeping and we won't know until she wakes up."

Kier looked up. "She's not The Torch and this is a stupid conversation. Do you want me to tell Dad that you spilled?"

Andy was quiet. He shifted his weight from one foot to the other foot and then hunched down to help Kier with the cereal. He waited a moment before asking his brother the question. "Can we go back to the Field?"

Kier looked at him and then looked back down at the carpet. "It's just about Howdy Doody."

"Please?" Andy asked.

Kier thought about it. "Okay," he said, "Go tell Dad we're gonna play in the backyard."

¶ In the Field it went like this: first, the boys pretended that they had bikes. Then they pretended that they parked these bikes on the gravel-edge of the secondary road, kicking down their kickstands. They'd pedalled their way along the back roads all morning until they'd seen the back bumper of the DeSoto in the ditch with its fins and shiny hubcaps, its slick white stripe down the side.

In the Field, the elm tree didn't exist, and the tire-swing didn't exist, and their mama's strawberry patch didn't exist. In the Field the driver's side door of the DeSoto was open like a wing and no one was in the car. The road ahead of the DeSoto stretched off toward the horizon, toward what they couldn't see. The road behind led back to the house. In the Field the weather was bright and clear. No cloud-gatherings. No storms. The leaves of the Field's birches were golden in the sun.

The boys carried notebooks and magnifying glasses. They pretended they were in their dress clothes: brown and white saddle shoes and matching argyle socks that Lucy had laid out for them on their beds. Standing at the side of the road they did not know why their mama would ever have stopped here, but they were keen detectives, and they would figure out the mystery. Maybe she pulled the car over because she wanted to stretch her legs, Andy suggested.

Either she had wanted to stretch her legs or she had wanted to dance to a good song playing on the radio. Or maybe, Kier wondered, she'd pulled over so she could turn the car around because she'd forgotten something: that powder she used for dusting her nose, or her autograph book, or the cheque she was supposed to bring for the baker that morning. Instead of no reason, they decided on a simple item, forgotten on the kitchen table when it should have been in her purse. Yes, something forgotten, or a good song.

There, Andy pointed, and Lucy stood with a hand over her eyes, their mama. She wore a crisply ironed dress and a matching autumn coat that was navy blue with small white polka dots. Her red hair was up in a chignon, which she wore for special occasions, and red lipstick was painted in a heart on her lips. And oh, her freckles! Andy imagined her freckles, scattered like constellations across the slope of her nose. Oh her scent! Kier imagined her scent, Chanel No. 5., like a secret door.

The boys moved closer to the car and looked at the dashboard clock. Its tiny metal hands had stopped ticking down time, which Andy took note of in his notebook. *Clock. Stopped.* They circled the car, investigating the details. Kier saw a map flung into the backseat. *Toronto and Townships.* She was often getting herself lost driving from Malton into the city for an afternoon of shopping at Eaton's. For a moment, Kier remembered how they would hide in the coat racks while their mama tried on shoes. (Fortress of coat racks! King of the coat racks! "Boys! Come over here. You'll knock that down!")

Kier looked at the passenger seat and saw, resting there, an unopened umbrella, Lucy's favourite navy purse with the thick gold clasp, a piece of notepaper in her handwriting that read *Hawthorn's Fine Cakes and Pastries. Queen Street West. Near Dovercourt, North Side,* and a blue chiffon scarf that sat on the white vinyl seat like a pool of water.

The radio was on. But to what sort of station? Andy imagined jazz. Kier agreed. She often listened to jazz when she took the DeSoto for drives, a station she picked up from over the border in New York somewhere. Andy thought it might have been *Take the A Train* she was listening to when she pulled over to the side of the road that day. Kier suggested *Salt Peanuts,* but Andy said "Definitely

not *Salt Peanuts*," and so they agreed on an instrumental piece that
she would have hummed along to: *Ornithology* by Charlie Parker.
"Good ol' Bird" they imaged her saying.

Kier imagined how Charlie Parker's saxophone would have
sounded with the rain falling. Andy thought about the birch leaves,
brittle and rattling. Yes, the saxophone and the rain and the wail of
the wind through the autumn leaves.

Andy and Kier stood side by side by the open driver's-side door
looking toward the Field. Their eyes scanned past the wildflowers
in the ditch: the last of the fireweed, purple aster and goldenrod.
They couldn't see her footprints because the rain had washed them
away. The long grasses were bent heavy with water. They looked at
the open field and climbed down the ditch, careful not to get their
shoes dirty in the gully's fresh mud. They walked farther in, and
eventually spotted the tree in the distance with its black bark. But
first they almost stepped in something.

"What is it?" Andy asked.

Kier looked closer. "Puke."

"Eww." Andy moved his toes away. Fresh puke. Had Mama been
carsick? Kier didn't think so. Was she allergic to something? No.
Shellfish? No. When was she sick? In the mornings. Oh. They both
realized now. Sick in the mornings. Woman things. She was pregnant. With a baby. A baby was making her sick. They both took
note of this in their notebooks: *Mama sick. The baby's fault.* Andy
wanted to use his magnifying glass to figure out what their mama
had eaten for breakfast but Kier said, "That's disgusting. Look up
ahead," and he pointed his finger at the tree, still smoking slightly,
poised like a charcoal hand.

In the long grasses they saw her body. Her milky limbs burnt with
river lines. Ashes from the fruit tree floated down beside her and she
was a map, like the soft folded paper of *Toronto and Townships* in
the back seat. There were a series of roadways and byways on her,
tributaries where the lightning had been. Beneath the crinoline of
her dress, which was crushed now and singed, was a journey. Her
hair had come undone and her cheeks were pale as Ivory soap.

The boys stood and looked at their mama in that field. Was she
breathing? Had her heart stopped? Andy wanted to go to her body.

He wanted to find her pulse like he'd been shown how to do at Cub Scout camp. Andy wanted to find the convergence of veins under his mama's thin pale skin and press his fingers softly to her wrist to feel that her heart would be okay. But then Kier remembered that they had to get out of the Field, because the real-life priest would be coming down the highway any moment in his beat-up blue truck to really find their mama, and to take her to the hospital where their dad would bring Kier and Andy to visit, and where, eventually, their dad had told them, she would wake up. The boys stood and looked and took in every last detail. They heard the truck coming. Kier tugged on Andy's shirt. "Come on. We have to go."

The boys took one last look at her thoughtful sleepy face, and turned, and ran back through the grasses, up the slippery bank of the gully, out of the Field and back along the shoulder of the road to where their bikes stood. They kicked their kickstands hard and pushed off, leaning firmly into their handlebars, pedalling fiercely into the long stretch of road ahead. It wasn't until they both looked back over their shoulders that they realized they had lost one another. Kier was pedalling hard toward the distance and Andy was pedalling equally hard back in the direction of home.

The room was brighter than Lucy remembered rooms ever being. And white. Entirely white. She might have thought she was dead, except when she moved her head a pain skewered her left side, probing her flesh like a meat thermometer and she could feel the baby inside her, bobbing in her body like a pickle in a jar. She was thirsty. She could not imagine ever drinking enough water to quench this thirst. And she couldn't see out of her left eye. There were objects glinting around her. Things flashing from the corner of her vision that she couldn't concentrate her sight upon. And beeping, strange ringing and beeping in her ears like sparks of sound. Lucy slowly tried to push herself up in the bed but again the pain, slicing itself through her left back, shoulder and arm. She grit her teeth and pushed up with a wrist she thought belonged to her and was unbandaged. Her head hung at her chest and she could see her green gown, the tail of a wound skirting out from white gauze plastered to her chest. The wound was white and looked as though it was shining. The sky's handwriting. A tattoo of pale ink, like the diary entries she wrote in lemon juice as a girl and then held up to sunlight to reveal the hidden script.

She wanted a glass of water but couldn't remember how to say it, how to put thoughts back into words. Water. A glass of water. She said it over and over in her mind, and finally, as if a film was being shown to her, a nurse pulled back the clouds of white and stood there in a pressed cotton dress saying, "good morning," and "you're alright," and "let's get this tube out of your throat."

It is after this that Lucy fell back asleep and woke up to find the lightning in the room with her.

¶ The team of hospital physicians stood in a horseshoe around the foot of her bed, all the luck falling out, and asked whether Lucy could remember the day she was struck. "I see ..." she said, and the day came to her the same way the nurse had, pulling back a curtain, Lucy from a distance watching a film stutter onto a screen: the nurse in her white dress; the sky darkening; Kier's first cry as he was born; her father whistling the hallelujah chorus of Handel's *Messiah* as they walked down Queen Street to church; the blue of the great lake that met the horizon as Lucy dreamed: all were dilated open so that they were one thing, or closed tight as Tupperware, as if they happened within the same sealed second. Time had suddenly become vertical when asked to remember "when," not the vast horizontal of days and weeks.

The film was damaged, so that all of the frames didn't come through. There were gaps where Lucy could see only the projector's sharp light. A leaf in the glove compartment, she told them. The ironed creases of a fresh handkerchief in her purse. The worn corners of a street map. The perfect arc of a blade of grass. Lying down, or falling maybe, into the field. Hundreds of bent blades moving together like a sea. A flame in the apple tree. Then absence. Flickered light.

¶ Lucy noticed the lightning first in the simplest objects. An orange. An orange was brought to her on a tin meal tray and Lucy knew immediately that the lightning was with her. She reached out her good arm, the one without bandages, and slowly pulled the tray closer to her. She nodded at the orange, addressed the lightning there, and paused in recognition of its presence in her room. The orange sat silently in a divot of the tray.

Lucy looked at the orange. The dents and discolorations of its flesh. The way it tipped to its right side. Its scarred knot at the top, a cut umbilical as it was pulled from its leaves and the branches of a tree in Florida.

Lucy pushed her thumb into the peel and the smell of the citrus enveloped the room. A sea-mist of orange. A waterfall mist of orange. A Niagara in the room.

The peel revealed a perfect sphere of segments, the chiming clock tower of the Saint James cathedral aglow in her hand. Each segment a purse of juice. Each purse a perfect crescent moon. Lucy ripped through the pith and pocket of the inner orange with her teeth. She took on her index finger one single piece of pulp. One raindrop of juice. She placed it on her tongue and squeezed her tongue to the roof of her mouth. A corolla. A firework. The orange rings of Saturn in her mouth.

¶ And then, for a while, it was as if the lightning had left her and Lucy saw herself in a mirror. After a few weeks, the nurse had allowed Lucy to wheel by herself down a stretch of corridor into the female patient's washroom on her ward. To see the container of herself like that, after so many weeks of looking out. The tap had been dripping, causing the ringing to start in Lucy's ears again, but Lucy held onto the wheels of her chair and stared at her reflection. Her lips were chapped and she had white paste in the corners of a crooked smile. Her eyes were dark. Dark circles. Dark irises. They didn't look like her eyes. Her hair was long and unkempt and stringy with soap that had not been rinsed properly. Bandages covered her whole left side like an extra layer of white cotton skin from just above her clavicle down to where a belt buckle might rest. A slight bump where the baby was. A set of Russian Dolls. A self inside itself and a different self inside that. She had no cover-up at the hospital. Nothing to cover herself. Peel away the wallpaper and she was cracked plaster. No, she couldn't have the children see her like this. She would ask Peter for a little more time. She would ask for them not to visit just yet.

¶ "Mummy!"

"Mama!"

Kier stood at a distance. Peter was helping Andy out of his coat. "Mama!" Andy said again when he was free from his scarf and boots. He ran forward and reached his hands up to the bed by her waist.

"Hey there, Boo," Lucy managed.

Kier watched her carefully.

"I thought this would be a nice pick-me-up," Peter said to Lucy.

Lucy couldn't look at him.

She put her unbandaged hand into Andy's. He held her fingers in his fists and rubbed the back of her hand gently against his cheek.

"Want me to crank you up?" Peter turned the metal-handled dial on the foot of Lucy's bed so that she was seated and looking at her family.

Kier was standing by the door to her room. He still had his coat on. "What is it, Love?" She looked at Kier standing straight and rigid. This is why she hadn't wanted them to come. That look on her son's face.

"What is it, Kier?" Lucy said again.

"I thought you might be dead."

Lucy paused. "No," she said, "I wasn't dead. I was just asleep."

"You looked dead," Kier said.

"Kier," Peter said.

"Well, you were asleep for a really long time."

"I'm sorry," she said. "Come over here. Tell me what you've been up to."

Kier stood where he was.

"We missed you!" Andy said.

"I missed you both too," she winked at Kier and gestured for him to come closer.

"So, what have you been doing this whole time?" She looked down at Andy. "I want to hear everything."

Peter poured Lucy a glass of water and brought it to her.

"Thanks," she said, mesmerized for a brief moment by the clinking sound of the ice before she held the glass to her lips.

"We-ell," Andy started and trailed off. Kier stepped closer. They both watched her drink. Her hand bringing the glass to her mouth. Her dry lips pressed to the edge of the glass. Like a kiss. The small gulp gulp movements of her throat. Her eyebrows, how they rose up a bit. And her arm, straightening slowly, her shoulder, turning to place the glass on the side table. Small drop of water glinting from her lower lip. Mama-Lazarus. Like in the picture Bible.

"We've been doing lots," Andy finally said. "Sometimes we go to Mrs. Leavis' after school, and sometimes we go to Mrs. Romano's, and sometimes Mrs. Schwartz has us to her house and plays us her oboe."

"Mrs. Schwartz always has Oreos," Kier added from the corner.

"Oboe Oreos," Andy said and laughed to himself.

"And?" There was that ringing in her ears. "What else?" Tinnitus, Doctor Sousa had called it. Always a student doctor in tow while making his rounds. "Common in lightning patients." And the student writing everything down on a pad of paper, Lucy a specimen who heard ringing.

"Mrs. Leavis' dog JoJo wants to eat what the people are eating and Mrs. Leavis lets him, lets JoJo jump at the table and beg." Andy told her.

"Really?" She hadn't thought about dogs, had forgotten about them really. "We don't have a dog, do we?" She tried to picture a dog they might have. Black and white? With a spot over one eye? Or was that dog from a television show?

"No, but we could get one if you wanted to."

Peter interrupted. "No, Ando. Nice try."

Lucy closed her eyes for a second. She couldn't focus. The room was spinning, tiny trails of light moving out from behind objects: the vase of irises at her beside, the ice cubes in the glass, her sons.

"Peter, could I have more water?"

"For someone who's been asleep so long you look tired," Kier said.

"Kier," Peter scolded, "only say nice things to your mother." Peter refilled the glass from a tall pitcher.

"What about you, Bean?" She tried to focus on Kier's face. To pretend she wasn't nauseous, that they weren't all spinning, that the light wasn't refracting like a crystal in the room. "Dad tells me you're still taking Saturday art classes."

"We drew trees last week," Kier said. "With pastels." Finally her son stepped closer.

Lucy nodded.

"And I tried to draw a bird, but halfway through it flew away."

"Yes," Lucy said. The room was moving now in circles, traces of colour extending from each object. She shut her eyes. The boys would need to go home now. How could she tell Peter she would need them to go home? "I bet birds are hard to draw."

"Daaa-aad," Andy yelled from the kitchen.

"Shhhhh," Kier said, and held his hand over Andy's mouth. "Dad's trying to sleep."

"Stop holding my arm."

"You're not allowed four scoops."

"Why not? You can have this much too," Andy said and stirred his fourth spoonful of powdered Quick into his glass of milk. A foam of chocolate bubbles formed at the top.

Kier let go of Andy's arm. "We're not allowed," Kier said.

"Why?" Andy said.

"We're supposed to use two spoons and that's it."

"Who said?"

"Mama said, remember?"

Andy stopped stirring for a second and looked up at his brother. Remembering what Mama did or did not say was a way of having her authority present even while she was still in the hospital. "She let me have four, Kier, she did," Andy said.

"No, she never let us."

"I remember," Andy said, uncertain. It had been three months without her, the shape of his mama's face had become more of a mystery without her in the house; without her voice reading to him about that boy and his purple crayon, or the ducklings and that big unfriendly swan and the policemen that helped them get back to the garden; but now she was awake again, and her authority was real, sitting, drinking water, in a room only a car-ride away from their house. Their mama could come home at any minute. Well, once she had the baby, Dad had said. But, Andy supposed, she could have the baby any minute.

"You have it," Andy pushed the chocolate milk toward his brother.

"I don't want it," Kier said.

"You can have it," Andy tried again. He didn't want Kier to tell Mama. He didn't want her to be mad when she came back home.

"Ando. I don't want it."

Andy looked at the glass of milk. The opened canister of chocolate powder. "I don't want it either." He was almost in tears, now. "I don't want it."

"Fine," Kier said, "I'll drink it." He took the glass with him into the living room and Andy could hear cartoon voices from the television.

Andy stood looking at the empty chocolatey ring the glass had left on the counter.

O*ur newly-elected Canadian government seems to be giving the aviation industry a hard time. Now that Sputnik has caused fear of the bomb, questions are beginning to rise as to whether Dief's government will cut work orders on Avro's new CF-105 Arrow.* Peter was kneeling in a snowbank in the front yard reading the business section of the newspaper. *Despite the fear of Intercontinental Ballistic Missiles, NATO countries still have an outstanding need for Air Defence.* Peter had opened the door for the paper that morning and seen a scarlet tanager dead beneath the picture window. He'd put his boots on and picked up the paper from his doorstep.

He had noticed the tanager earlier that week, pecking at the suet ball. Its red breast standing out against the leafless trees. He'd never seen one in the yard this late in the year. That bird should have known to fly south and now it was dead, its claws—was that what they were called?—arched as if grasping at a branch. And now Peter out in the snow with the porridge not even on. He'd be late for work. The kids needed to eat and get dressed. And this news in the paper. *Britain itself has indicated a call for Avro's latest interceptor. But will Dief back-off and unemploy 10,000 capable Canadians? Defence with Dief: Wonderful!* Peter had come to hate news reporters. He was always reading things in the paper about his job that Gordon and the other bosses hadn't bothered to tell them. What did they know? Newspaper reporters were like weathermen. Half the time they got the facts wrong and they still got to keep their jobs. If people like Peter got facts wrong bridges collapsed and planes fell from the sky.

Peter made the newspaper into a little shovel and scooped the tanager out of the snow bank. He threw the dead bird and the newspaper into the garbage pail and went back into the house.

"The phone rang." Andy was already standing on the landing in front of the bathroom door. "I tried to wake up Kier, but he's still sleeping."

"How many times did it ring?"

"Seven?"

"Alright, Boo. Thanks. Wash your face and get into your school clothes, okay?"

Peter put the porridge on, walked up the stairs, and leaned into the boys' bedroom where Kier was sprawled like a starfish on the bed. He'd kicked the covers onto the floor. Peter stood for a moment and watched his son sleep. Kier normally had a serious and determined countenance to his face. But not when he slept. Somehow when he slept all that slipped away. Peter was loath to wake him. The day had already gotten off to a bad start. He felt like retreating back to bed himself, but they needed to get a move on. Peter reached out and tousled Kier's hair until his son moved his hands to his face and rolled away from Peter's touch.

"Do-on't," Keir said in a sleepy voice.

"Time to get up. Porridge's on."

Peter went back downstairs and stirred the porridge. He began to flip through the notepad by the phone for the hospital's number. There was a knock. It was Connie Romano from next door. She was standing at the kitchen door in her winter boots and her housecoat.

"Peter ..."

"Come in."

"... the hospital called." Connie kicked the snow from her boots. He shut the door behind her. "What?"

"The baby's here."

"The baby's what?"

"Apparently they tried to telephone you, but there was no answer."

"Merde." Peter clapped his hands together. "The baby's *here?* As in already born? But the due date. Two months."

"That's what the lady on the phone said." Connie shook her head. "I don't understand it myself." She put her hands in the pockets of her housecoat as if looking for her pack of cigarettes. "My Beatrice took eleven hours. Eleven solid hours. And yet with Lucille they seem to just slip out."

Peter stood, staring at her.

Connie looked at him, "Well, go on Pete. This is the second one you've managed to miss. Get down there. Quick."

"Boys," Peter yelled up the stairs. He moved through the kitchen to turn off the porridge pot and put on his coat. "Your mom's had the baby." He looked for his car keys. "Put on your coats."

The drive to the hospital was familiar now. The curves of the highway and the sharp corners, the boys' sleepy heads keeling left and right like drifting boats. Andy rested his head on the back of his seat and looked over at Peter.

"Hey, Dad?"

"Yes, Ando."

"Do we start at zero?"

"Do we start at zero." They were almost there.

"If the baby's not going to have a birthday until next year, does that mean it's going to be zero all year?" Andy had just learned the number line in math class.

Kier opened his sleepy eyes and looked out the window.

"Well. That's a good question."

"Dad?" Andy tried again.

"Yes?"

"Where does zero come from?"

"We forgot to brush our teeth." Keir announced from the back.

The DeSoto wheeled into the parking lot marked *Emergency Entrance* behind a car that was moving at a remarkably slow pace.

"Goes back to the Babylonians. But they didn't use it as a number, more of a placeholder. The absence of something." Peter leaned forward to see what was going on with the car ahead of them. Why weren't they moving forward? "They didn't put it at the end of numbers, say like zero after a one makes a ten." He withheld the urge to honk the horn. "I think the Greeks first used zero as a numeral. Although then they philosophically questioned that, I think. How can something be nothing and all that. Basically we all needed a word for whatever wasn't one." Peter slid the car into a parking spot. "We'll look it up in the encyclopædia when we get home. And we'll brush our teeth real soon, Kier. I promise."

Car parked. Kids out.

When they got to the hospital suite they couldn't see past the door. The room was full of men in suits holding notepads and cameras. It was like the rollout in there. A woman was bent down at an electrical outlet testing the heat of a curling iron against the back of her hand. Peter looked at the room number beside the door again. He stopped a nurse in the hallway. "Where would I find Lucille Jacobs?"

"You've found her. That's her room."

"But why are all those people ...?"

The nurse looked into the room. "Taking pictures, I would guess."

"Lu?" Peter pushed passed the reporters. "We're here, Lu."

¶ Lucy was propped up in bed with cushions. In her arms was a tiny bundle of blankets. "Boys," Lucy gestured them over. Kier and Andy were unbuttoning their coats. Andy's mittens dragged on the floor from a string hung in his sleeves. "Come say hi to her."

"A girl," Peter said. He'd forgotten to ask Connie Romano whether it was a boy or a girl. It hadn't even occurred to him. For the entire car ride it was still just a baby.

"What are they doing here?" Peter pointed to the reporters. "And why didn't anyone call earlier?"

"Look at her," Lucy passed the baby to Peter. She was tiny, breathing and kicking in Peter's arms. Perfectly healthy. A perfectly healthy baby girl.

He sat down in the chair next to Lucy's bed, cradling his daughter's body against his chest. The boys leaned on either arm of the chair and watched their new sister. "She looks smushed," Andy declared. "She's red and funny looking." Looking at her, Andy's posture changed. His authority over small things had just gotten bigger. Not just bird's eggs and marbles. He had a sister. A person he got to be older than.

Kier looked at the baby's fingernails. Had he ever seen something that small? An ant maybe. When she got home Kier wanted to look at her fingernails with his microscope. How did you even trim that sort of fingernail? Maybe with babies you don't trim.

"Why didn't they call?" Peter looked over at Lucy. "I'm so sorry I wasn't here." He looked down at the baby. She was a little-bellied sea horse. "She's beautiful, Lucille." She was a moon snail. The baby moved her legs and arms in the blanket. No. Peter remembered Andy's question in the car. When we are born, we are certainly not nothing.

"Rose," Lucy said.

"Rose," Peter said back.

¶ The reporters asked Lucy and Peter questions. And then, while Peter let each of the boys have a turn carefully holding the baby, an assistant put rouge on Lucy's cheeks so she wouldn't look so tired and curled her hair with the hot iron. A photographer placed the family around the bed, so that Andy and Kier sat on either side of Lucy, and Peter stood with his arm around Lucy's shoulders. Peter was careful not to touch the last of the bandages at the back of Lucy's neck. Rose yawned, fists reaching upwards. *MIRACLE GIRL DEFIES SCIENCE*. Headline on the front page of the *Star*, January 22, 1958. *"It's a miracle!" doctors say. Pictured here is the first Canadian mother-daughter duo to survive a lightning strike with baby still in the womb. Thanks to the kindness of an unidentified priest and the hard work of physicians, this happy family has a new member, the tiny Miss Rose Ella-Fitzgerald Jacobs, to welcome home.* This was a story in the newspaper Peter would not grudge. He would buy fifteen copies the next day.

¶ Doctor Sousa waited until after the reporters had left and Kier and Andy had gone to school for the afternoon. "There is a hole in her heart," he said. His voice was flat and plain like a piece of paper. His voice, Lucy thought, was as bleached and starched as his white coat. "When we checked her heartbeat there was a murmur, a whooshing sound." He sat down on the side of her bed, took the stethoscope from his neck and held it in his hands.

"A hole?" Lucy didn't understand. Rose was alive. Her fists were moving and she was kicking as soon as they got her out. She had cried. Wasn't that how you were supposed to tell? If they didn't cry?

Doctor Sousa cleared his throat. "The type we're looking at is an atrial septal defect, ASD it's commonly called. This means there's a hole in the top collecting chamber of the heart that is creating an irregular heartbeat, a palpitation," Doctor Sousa played with an ear-piece of his stethoscope. "This typically causes the blood to shunt, or flow, from the left to the right chamber. The right side of the heart eventually enlarges as it works to keep the extra blood flowing. The patient may experience fatigue." He put the stethoscope down in his lap. "In some cases, heart failure or stroke."

Peter reached over and held onto Lucy's hand.

"Can we fix it?" Lucy asked. "Can we sew it up?" Lucy thought of all the socks she'd darned in her life.

"A reasonable question. Yes. An operation can be done. Research so far suggests though that it may be better to wait until the patient is older. Intrusive surgery may not be our best option. Some holes in small babies close themselves."

"What can we do?" Peter asked.

"For now, we'll keep her in with you, Mrs. Jacobs, for a while longer, so our cardiologists can do more tests." He paused. "We'll need to know more about the shape and position of the hole before making a decision about surgery." Dr. Sousa put his stethoscope back around his neck. "People live with this condition well into middle-age and they're just fine. They take cooking classes, ride horses, learn how to roller skate. You know, they live. But sometimes it can prove more serious, and that's why we're doing the tests." He looked up and smiled a weary smile at Lucy.

95

Lucy looked at him. "This isn't because of the accident, is it?" She had learned, from being in the hospital for so long, to ask questions when they occurred to you. Otherwise you might not have a chance to ask them at all. "Did I do this?"

Sousa paused. "It's a possibility that the malformation of the heart is connected to early exposure to high voltage electricity, yes. Hard to say, though, as this is generally not a typical scenario experienced during foetal development. It could be genetic. It could have been unknown contact with toxoplasmosis or German measles during the pregnancy." He cleared his throat. "We can't say, Mrs. Jacobs. I wish I could tell you more."

Lucy and Peter were silent.

Lucy also knew, from being in the hospital so long, that some questions never do get answered. Doctor Sousa was a good doctor. Lucy knew that he was even a good enough doctor to lie to her.

"Alright, then." Doctor Sousa tried a supportive smile. He patted the blankets next to Lucy's leg as he stood up. "I have an ectopic pregnancy to look at. The cardiologist will be in this afternoon."

¶ They stuck needles in Rose's heart. They measured her pulse at different intervals throughout the day. They took x-rays and listened with stethoscopes to her tiny chest. If she so much as coughed, someone was in their hospital room with a new instrument. "It'll be okay Rosie," Lucy said as she bobbed up and down, walking softly around the room. Peter went to get them coffee. Lucy slowly tried to get strength back into her legs after being in hospital beds for nearly six months. Peter read *Maclean's* magazine. Lucy sang jazz tunes softly into the curve of her new baby's seashell ear, *Been away a year today to wander and to roam. I don't care it's muddy there, but see it is my home.* Rose kicked her legs.

Peter left Lucy in the afternoon to pick up the boys from school and leave them with Mrs. Leavis. He'd had a Chinese checkerboard under his arm that he'd bought for them at the hospital gift shop. Lucy sat on the white blankets of the bed. She loosened the top tie of her gown and leaned down to feed Rose. She'd bottle-fed Andy and Kier because that was what was done, but Lucy wanted to feed Rose herself this time, and so the nurse had helped to teach her.

When Lucy's gown was open and her baby was at her breast she could see the remaining scars like a script over the left side of her body, tattoos in white ink. When the nurses had finally taken Lucy's bandages off, Doctor Sousa had been there to explain the pattern of scars across her left side. When the lightning had entered her shoulder from the tree it had followed the estuaries of her body's blood and water, he had told her. The heat had evaporated the residual moisture on her skin, turning her sweat to steam and burning riddled lines across her torso. Lucy had imagined the rest from what she could faintly remember: the current travelling down along the curving bank of her hip, the silk of her leg, singeing her stockings, and out her left foot, the sole of her shoe burst and burning as the priest entered the field. Lucy looked down at Rose asleep against the scarred currents of her skin. Lucy looked into her baby's heart. Instead of a hole there was a tiny round mirror. A telescope. Lucy peered in and saw a sky full of stars.

BLACK FRIDAY

"Each house is more the same than the last one." Lucy looked out the passenger window as Peter drove. Rows of brick houses passed by in a warm undulating hue, as incessant as the wheat of a prairie field. It had snowed twice while Lucy was in the hospital but then there was a thaw revealing lost things in the gutters and on the curbs: waxed paper soda cups; melty-looking LOST DOG posters; a baby's shoe; tiny machine parts that looked as if they were from a dismantled electric can opener; three whole but rotted red apples.

The thaw had also revealed gnomes and miniature wooden windmills on select lawns distinguishing these houses from the sweep of brick. Tiny children holding umbrellas, an elf fishing, a wishing well.

"What are you thinking?" Peter asked.

"I was thinking about that weekend."

The car was silent except for the humming of the dashboard heater.

"We were taking Kier for a walk in his pram. It must have been our second spring. We were expecting Andy and I was craving chocolate halfway through our walk."

"I'd only brought nickels."

Lucy had asked Peter to stop at the corner store and pick up two Hershey's bars. She'd asked for two. Just in case. They opened one of the chocolate bars and shared it while they were walking. But then, on the way home, the neighbours were having a yard sale and there was a garden gnome for sale that Lucy wanted.

"Do you remember that?"

"I don't remember a gnome."

"He was sort of hideous, but I loved his little expression as he pushed his wheelbarrow full of flowers. They wanted a dime for the gnome, but we didn't have any more money with us. We'd spent it on the chocolate bars. So that's what I offered them, remember? The unopened Hershey's. For the gnome."

"And there was a wife," Peter said, "and she was pregnant too."

"We got the gnome because she wanted the chocolate."

Peter kept his eyes on the road as he carefully hand-over-handed the turns and waited at the stoplights.

"Where is that gnome?" Lucy asked after a pause.

"As I said, I don't remember a gnome."

For the rest of the car ride neither of them said anything. Lucy looked down at Rose sleeping in her arms and out again at the houses. Peter turned into their driveway, turned off the ignition and pulled the brake.

Lucy stared at her red door. She'd forgotten she had painted it. The cherry red she'd slicked on seven years ago was chipped in places and fading. The door looked to her now like a child who'd been allowed to wear her mother's nail polish, but who hadn't been grown-up enough to keep it neat. Even this door she'd painted to make everything seem real when she and Peter had moved there, to stop herself from feeling as if she was pretending house, she could see now was just another sort of dress-up. What was real, then? Any of it?

¶ Peter held the suitcase and Lucy carried Rose, wrapped in a nursing blanket, to the front step. The last time Lucy had stood on the step she had been rushing to get to the baker's on time. The young maple in their front yard was still in leaf and blazed red that afternoon. She had wanted to take a picture of the sunlight slanting through the leaves and the brooding yet beautiful black cloud overhead, but instead she had leaned down, careful in her high heels, picked up one of the leaves on her way to the car and put it between two manuals in the glove compartment to press. The leaf was probably still there, dried now.

Lucy's time in the hospital was like that black cloud, or a perfect black hole on a sidewalk that cartoon characters are always stepping into, falling right through the earth. Autumn was gone, she had missed the first snowfall, and already the white afternoon slant of winter made crisp lines of sky between the empty boughs of the trees. Time had continued on without her. How terrifying and comforting that was. She could slip into a black hole and everything would go along on the sidewalks up above.

"Surprise Mama! Surprise Rose!" It was Andy and Kier shouting from the staircase. Andy held a big card he'd made out of construction paper with drawings of secret agents and rocket ships in bright crayon. Kier's card had a blue and pink cake with a flaming spiral staircase of candles. *WELKOM HOme* it read, the last two letters pressed against the right side of the paper, embodying somehow to Lucy the very wonkiness of her coming home.

"What's all this?" Lucy asked.

"It's a party!" Andy exclaimed.

"A party?" Lucy tried to keep a smile on her face as she turned to look behind her into the living room for more people. Oh god, the Stewanakies? Was Connie there?

No one was in the living room.

"We thought we'd just have a small party," Peter said. "We weren't sure if your mama would want the whole neighbourhood over right away, isn't that right?"

"Just a special guest," Kier said.

"What's that, Kier?" she came out of the swinging kitchen doors, hip first, wiping her hands on one of Lucy's aprons that was stretched over her middle and embroidered with an orange L. "Welcome home, Lucille." It was her mother. Her mother was standing at the door to her kitchen. Mavis kissed Lucy on the cheek and looked down at Rose asleep in her arms. "Oh, and you. What a sweet little button she is. I've been dying to meet her. Look at that red hair. Let me take your coat." Lucy's mother took her coat as if Lucy was coming into her mother's home rather than her mother somehow standing there impossibly in Lucy's.

"Mother," Lucy said. She looked at Peter. "How long have you been here?"

"I just arrived yesterday, and we thought it would be darling if it was a surprise. A homecoming. Isn't that right, boys?"

This was the first time in their lives Kier and Andy had met their grandmother, and already it was clear that they were enamoured with her. Aside from the extravagant Christmas packages she had sent them over the years, and the fancy-looking telegrams, Mavis had brought with her over the Atlantic, Lucy was soon to find out, an entire suitcase full of sweets, and for the past eighteen hours had plied Lucy's children with Blackpool Rock Candy, Jujubes, Sherbet Twists, Rhubarb and Custards, Humbugs, and Dolly Mix.

Mavis Ainsworth hung Lucy's coat on a hanger in the hall closet.

"Would you take her a moment, Mavis?" Peter asked and nodded at Rose.

"I've been dying to ask."

Lucy passed the baby to her mother. Where was Noreen? Where was Connie? Lucy would rather have had those two women welcoming her home. With Noreen Leavis she felt both envy and gratitude. This was the woman who'd taken care of Lucy's children while she couldn't. Lucy would have no idea how to begin to thank Connie and Noreen and Trish. But her mother? Her mother had parachuted in once Lucy could again take care of things for herself. Where had her mother been through all these past months while Lucy had been in the hospital? Undoubtedly she was redecorating. Or working for the woman's league. Or arguing for the benefit of dahlia gardens on the Berkshire commons.

Mavis propped Rose on her shoulder and Rose snuggled against her grandmother's neck. "Oh. Spit up cloth." Mavis held out a hand to Lucy, who obliged her with a flannelette. "Come along, boys," Mavis steered Lucy's children into the kitchen. "Help me with the cake."

Lucy stood in her living room with the orange wall she had never bothered to repaint. The sun came in above her through the stairwell window, casting shadows on each wooden step and the banister's swirl in the hall. Lucy could smell furniture polish and grape jelly. She could hear the boys laughing with her mother through the swinging kitchen doors.

"When were you planning on telling me that she was here?" Lucy turned to Peter.

"We thought it would be a nice surprise."

"God, Peter," Lucy sat down on the settee. She hadn't even taken off her gloves.

"She'd asked me to keep it a secret. She's here to help with the baby."

"The baby?" Lucy repeated, the pitch of her voice raising.

"What?" Peter asked.

"Did it occur to you that she hasn't bothered to help with the other two babies?"

"Lu, you're not being fair. Your father paid for the airfare. It's only two weeks. I couldn't say no to your father. He called long distance from the post office over there. All of this must have cost him a fortune. I think they've been worried but haven't known what to do."

"Peter," she finally said in a firm but quiet voice. "You should have told me."

Peter nodded at Lucy.

"Promise."

"Okay, I promise you that if your mother comes to visit again from Wickershire I will tell you."

"Berkshire."

"Wherever."

"Thank you."

"But there's one thing."

Lucy looked at Peter.

"You have to close your eyes."

"Peter," she said. "Please...." She was already exhausted. Her heart felt like it was racing and she'd only walked from the car to her living room. She pictured the white curtains of the hospital and they felt, in that instant, more like home to her than her coral-coloured walls.

"It's good," Peter said, "I think."

Lucy pulled her gloves off by the fingers and stood up.

Peter placed a hand over Lucy's eyes.

She smelled the familiar scent of his skin—musky and dry like letter paper and she leaned against him as he guided her through the kitchen doors.

She could hear Andy's giggle by the sink. Someone opening a drawer and then the rattle of the cutlery. She could smell the sweet cocoa of the cake, and a pot of coffee brewing. She liked her blindness, this lack of a sense. This was better. She was going home just by sound and smell as an animal might.

She was kissed and it was Peter's kiss and he took his hands away from her eyes.

A glare of light shone at her from the corner of her kitchen. What was that shape? A kitchen table? She squinted. Her eyes hurt in the light. She wanted Peter's hand over her eyes again. A nook? What had been there before? She couldn't remember. She looked around the kitchen. The dish soap was the wrong brand. Her cutting boards had been moved. Where had the spice rack gone? No. She turned back. Her turquoise Formica table and the four matching chairs. What had happened to them? "Oh," was all she said at first. She felt slightly nauseous. As if she had swallowed a poison capsule.

"It's an intergalactic breakfast nook," Peter said.

"Uh huh," she said. She needed to sit down. The muscles in her legs felt sore, and this was all too much for her first fifteen minutes home.

"Look." Peter moved proudly toward his creation. "I took it to this guy Smitty Lebowitz's shop to be chrome plated." He rubbed the tabletop that shone under his new galactic lighting. "And," he sat down on one of the oval benches, lined with padded cushions that were plasticized in vinyl and glittering blue, "there's shelving too, for homework and the paper." At the end of the nook, against the wall, Lucy noticed condiment holders. Miniature spaceship salt and pepper shakers. A flying saucer butter dish. And the lamp above, cylindrical with cut-out star shapes, dazzled over the slippery metal rink of the tabletop.

"Okay?" Lucy still had her eyes squinted against the sharpness of the table's light. Her wallpaper. The greens and yellows of her daisy wallpaper. They didn't go with this nook at all.

"Well, hon," Peter smiled at Lucy from the bench, "what do you think? I made it in the basement while you were away."

"It took him forever," Kier added, standing next to the unserved cake.

"Isn't it quite bright, Lucille?" her mother chimed in.

"Wow ..." Lucy said.

Peter, Kier, Andy and Mavis Ainsworth all waited for her to continue.

"... I hate it."

Peter stared at her. Mavis laughed. It was a joke.

"I hate this table," Lucy said again.

It wasn't a joke.

Lucy stood staring at the table. She wanted to go back to the hospital. She wanted to get in the car and drive back to the hospital where there were oranges to eat and clean sheets. She looked over to Peter. "I mean, the fact that you made this. Wow...." A pause. Everything was in the wrong place in her kitchen. There were so many different sorts of smells in her house. She wasn't used to this many smells. And her mother was there. Mothballs and lilac talcum powder. Lucy stood staring. Peter looked crestfallen. "Peter," Lucy finally said. At the hospital she could draw the white curtain around her when she wanted to be alone. "Just so much change, Pete." Lucy moved toward him cautiously. "Maybe it just takes some getting used to." She reached her hand out for Peter's. She touched his shoulder. "Thank you, Peter. I love it ... I'm sure I'll love it."

He looked up at her, uncertain. He put his hand on top of hers and pulled it against his chest. "Did you see the butter dish?"

"Cake time," Mavis Ainsworth interrupted, putting coffee cups and cutlery on the shining tabletop. Kier and Andy helped cut the cake. Lucy sat down on the bench beside Peter. Rose began to cry and Mavis walked back and forth across the kitchen floor with her, but, in one pure moment of solace, Rose was only appeased when Lucy took her away from her grandmother.

Lucy came downstairs in the morning, bleary-eyed, holding on to Rose and a tube of ointment she had been instructed to rub into the last of the burns, to find her mother standing on a kick-stool ladder cleaning out the top shelves of Lucy's kitchen cupboards. Mavis was already showered and dressed in a sweater set and magenta silk pants. She had magenta lipstick on to match. On the countertop, in orderly lines, stood all of Lucy's baking supplies: flour, sugar, baking powder, Arm and Hammer, Bird's custard powder, and her mother's cup of tea with a magenta lip-print. Lucy could smell something baking in the oven.

"Did I wake you?"

"No, Mum," Lucy wrapped her housecoat around herself and put Rose down in the bassinet on Peter's space table. It was so early it was still dark out.

"I'm five hours ahead. It's already ten-thirty to me."

Lucy scanned the stack of dried goods on the counter for the coffee.

"This cream of tartar is out of date." Lucy's mother shook a small black and white tin at her from the height of the ladder.

There was the coffee. Behind a blue box of Crisco shortening.

"And I found a set of food colouring right at the back of the cupboard. There's a full green."

But where was the grinder? Lucy found it under the sink. She wasn't sure why the coffee grinder was under the sink.

"I thought I could make some playdough for the boys," Mavis said cheerily.

Lucy spooned two scoops of coffee beans into the grinder and turned the metal handle. "Kier's almost nine, Mum. He doesn't really play with playdough any more."

"I don't mind, Lucille. You know I'm here to help."

Lucy emptied the coffee grounds into the percolator she had managed to locate in the dry rack, tightened the steel parts in place, and put her coffee on the stove.

Mavis sprayed down the empty cupboard with vinegar-water and wiped everything down with paper towels. "One can't be too rigorous about keeping one's pantry."

Lucy watched the stove element heat slowly from black to red. Why was everyone fussing with her kitchen? And why, in rummaging around in her cupboards, did it feel like they'd actually rearranged all the contents of her stomach, heart and chest?

106

¶ Lucy and Mavis sat across the space nook from one another with Rose between them. Her mother had started dying her hair. Lucy could see an ashy line of grey at the roots that contrasted against the auburn. She'd started plucking out her eyebrows and drawing them back on again. Arched lines of brown above her mother's eyes that made her look like a doll with a porcelain head.

Lucy stood up to pour herself another cup of coffee.

"Let me do it," Lucy's mother said, standing up as well.

"Please Mum, just sit down."

Upstairs, Lucy could hear Peter in the shower and the boys getting their school clothes out of the dresser drawers. When they left she would be alone with her. What would they possibly have to say to each other? So, Mum, why does it take a near-fatal accident and my third child for you to make your royal way to the colonies?

"I've made a quiche," Mavis said as Peter came into the kitchen.

"Amazing," Peter said, as if this was a scientific discovery.

Two weeks could not pass quickly enough.

¶ As she would discover, the only moments in those two weeks where Lucy had any stretch of time to herself were during Rose's late-night feedings. Lucy sat in a rocking chair in the living room without any of the lights on and looked at the shadows of the furnishings of her house distantly, as if at objects that she contemplated purchasing from a mail-order catalogue. It surprised Lucy to realize that she had felt more currents of wonder when she'd woken up in the hospital room than she did upon returning to her actual life, to her own living room. The entire contents of Maple Avenue, rather than revealing themselves in splendour, as the oranges had at Lucy's waking, were suffused with various stages of her recovery. Were suffused with normalcy. Lucy felt cast against her life again squinting, like she was trying to read in a weak light.

The gerbera daisies that Connie Romano dropped off became unrepayable kindnesses. The grey cashmere coat that Peter had bought Lucy two years ago with the dropped hem sat by the sewing machine and became interminable chores. The sound of the wind through a neighbour's poplar tree became the knowledge that it was too late to choose a different sort of life. As Lucy put Rose back down in her crib and climbed into bed with Peter, the misaligned strip of wallpaper over the dresser became endowed with suffering. Not suffering like those in the war had suffered, like those in the camps had suffered, like the reality that Lucy was now beginning to hear about, of the Japanese whose skin had been burned off from the blast of the bombs. Yet it was some kind of mild and insidious suffering that Lucy felt amongst all of her belongings and nice things, which she knew, in context, was selfish and ridiculous. Most people would believe that she had suffered in the hospital; she had been suffering and had returned, after a long stretch, to comfort. But how could Lucy explain to any of them—to Connie, to Trish, even to Peter—that to her it was the other way around? The austerity of the white sheets of the hospital had become a comfort. The crooked vines of her wallpaper were a trap. For now the misaligned woodland birds of the wallpaper had become the late night discussions over Rose's heart, Peter asking, "Is she breathing?" and Lucy answering, "The monitor's on."

"I'm just going to check."

"You'll wake her up, Pete. I just got her down."

"I know what I'm doing."

Lucy feared that she would never see that glimmer of light around the corner of objects again; that irises, ice cubes, angora mittens, chandeliers, fish and chips from the shop on Harbord wrapped in newspaper, the lines airplanes left across the sky at sunset, fresh loaves of bread, even postcards, had ebbed into the ordinary, even into the treacherous. It was absurd of her to treasure her time in the hospital, she knew that; to feel that her life now was just an unending list of obligations and chores. But now that she was back in the world, the hospital somehow felt sacred in its clockwork against disorder, in its brief moments of miracle. The hospital had become the room of her father's whistling. The hospital—rather than Saint James' cathedral—was Lucy's church.

¶ How Lucy managed to navigate the duration of Mavis' visit came as a surprise to her. Peter was too busy preparing for the first piloted test flight to notice much of anything, let alone be much at home.

Kier was building a tree fort with Anthony Romano next door. It was Andy's scrapbook that distracted Lucy's mother from the other cupboards of Lucy's kitchen, and allowed Lucy to sit with the baby and her Mum for stretches of time without needing to actually converse with her.

"If I were a dog, if I were another space dog, I would be in love with her," Andy confessed to his Nan, as he was calling her now.

"And you would make such a handsome space dog," Mavis replied.

Muttnick, Zhuchka, Little Bug: the dog had more nicknames across continents than any other stray could. After the boys got home from school and Mavis fed them ginger snaps dipped in milky tea, Kier would run next door and Andy would sit with his Nan at the space nook and carefully cut out images of Laika that Lucy and Mavis had bought from the newspaper stands along King Street on afternoon trips into the city. Lucy leaned back in the nook with Rose in her arms and watched as her mother and her son cut out headlines and pictures and glued everything down into Andy's scrapbook with Elmer's glue and its white smell of nothing.

The scrapbook was what Andy had chosen to present for his turn at show-and-tell day to the grade one class. Andy's name had been drawn from Mrs. Penny's magician's hat on Monday and in one week's time he must present an item to his classmates that fit into one of the three categories Mrs. Penny had set for the sake of challenge: unusual, educational, or exemplary. It was a particularly daunting show-and-tell day to be chosen for, Lucy and her mother began to comprehend, because, as Andy told them repeatedly, the last girl who was chosen from Mrs. Penny's hat, Jessica Major, had brought in real porcupine quills she'd rescued from her basset hound's nose, which Mrs. Penny had deemed unusual, educational *and* exemplary for their biological curiosity and for their unparalleled indication of Jessica Major's bravery.

"Mrs. Penny will certainly see the work you've put into this, Andrew," his Nan assured him.

"But it has to be exemplary," Andy insisted, and so each day Lucy and her mother scoured for magazine covers or newspaper articles about the little Russian space dog that they might have missed the afternoon before: a *Popular Science* with Laika poised in a dog-sized astronaut's helmet; or an article from *Flight* with TOP SECRET printed in dossier type, diagonally stamped in ghostly overlay, across fuzzy 'pocket-camera' documentation of the Cosmodrome. Andy read from the articles, slowly sounding out the letters, with Mavis at the nook while Lucy put a stroganoff on.

It was on Monday that Andy was to present the Laika book. It was on Friday that Andy arrived home in tears. "Geraldine, that girl who had to do grade one twice, told me that when satellites come down from space they incinterate," Andy stood in his raincoat, his bookbag dropped at his side. Lucy was at the sink tying string around a roast. "I asked Mrs. Penny what incinterate means and she told me it meant blow up, and then I thought, what if Laika's up there and she decides she doesn't like it, how are they going to get her back down?"

Mavis had found an article in the *Sunday Times* not dissimilar to the facts that the-girl-who-had-to-do-grade-one-twice had told Andy. Lucy and her mother had debated whether or not to give the article to Andy.

"I'm sure it's fine, Mother. He should be made aware that scientific discoveries can have violent consequences."

"He's just a child, Lucille."

"It's reality."

"It's cruelty. Read this terrible thing."

Lucy gave Rose to her mother and read the article standing up at the kitchen sink. *Today, in Britain's capital, members of The National Canine Defence League called on all dog owners to observe a minute's silence for the life of Laika the dog, who, they fear, as the first live creature to orbit the earth, has passed away in her craft from heat and exhaustion. Pet owners gathered outside the Russian Embassy this rainy London afternoon, many with their own well-loved dogs in attendance, to protest the mistreatment of animals in the race for space.* In the end, Lucy admitted that her mother was right. She couldn't bear to hear Andy read out the line, in his broken learning-how-to-read voice, *has passed away in her craft from heat and exhaustion,* and Lucy had thrown the last of the Laika clippings in the garbage. This was much worse than *Anna Karenina* and the death of Vronsky's horse.

"Don't you think Laika could stay alive, Mama?" Andy said hopefully, still standing in his coat, "Like you?"

Lucy snipped the ends of the strings on the roast with the kitchen shears and rinsed her hands off in the sink. "I'm sorry, Boo," was all she could say, and knelt down with her arms open.

On the last page of Andy's scrapbook he drew Laika landing back on Earth, walking out of her spaceship like a hero-dog down a red carpet outside of the Cosmodrome. There were fireworks.

On Monday, Mrs. Penny told Andy that his show-and-tell was unusual, educational *and* exemplary.

And so, because of Andy's obsession with Laika, and the ensuing panic of his show-and-tell deadline, only three days remained in the itinerary of Mavis Ainsworth's visit, and, despite herself, Lucy discovered, for brief flickering moments at least, that she did not want her mother to go back to Berkshire.

¶ On Saturday, Lucy and the boys dropped Mavis Ainsworth off at the airport. As with most of Mavis' departures, it was swift, dramatic, and she wore a matching outfit: a red suit jacket, red and white checked capri pants, and a scarf printed with tiny images of the seven wonders of the world. "Write," she told the boys; "Goodbye, Nan," they waved; "Good bye, Lucille," she said, "Thank you for a lovely visit," and then she kissed Lucy and brisked through the gate. Lucy drove home, her mother's red lip-print on her cheek.

¶ When Lucy and the boys got through the kitchen door, Andy announced, "I want to learn Russian."

"You're six," Lucy answered. "It's not even the same alphabet." She put the car keys on the key-shaped wooden hook by the kitchen door.

"It's Cyrillic," Peter said without looking up from his newspaper. Rose was swaddled in blankets beside him on one of the sparkly vinyl benches. "The alphabet's Cyrillic."

"I want to learn Cyrillic," Andy said.

Lucy and the boys hadn't taken their coats off yet. She'd need to take the sheets off the guest bed but that could wait. They needed new vacuum bags and she'd wanted to pick up something simple for lunch. Hot dogs and Pillsbury crescent rolls.

"Stay with Rose?" Lucy said to Peter. "I'll drop the boys at the library?"

"I was going to work on that electrical panel-board for the Romanos' air conditioner."

"It's not even fifteen degrees outside yet, Peter. I'm sure they can wait for it."

Peter leaned over Rose's sleeping face.

"Or you go to the library." She put away a ketchup bottle that was still on the table from breakfast. "I don't care. Just pick up some hotdogs and my books that are on hold."

"No, no, go." Peter spoke to Rose, "It'll be you and me, Tadpole. I'll teach you about electrical boards."

"Please don't plug the soldering iron in around the baby," Lucy said.

"Kidding," Peter said. "Kidding."

Lucy grabbed her keys again. "Come on, boys."

"And, Lu."

Lucy turned around.

Peter pointed a finger to his cheek. "You've got a little something there."

¶ Lucy dropped the boys off at the entrance to the library. They pushed their way through the turnstile into alphabetical order and the dusty smell of books. Andy headed toward the looming brass-handled wooden dressers full of catalogued cards for everything under the sun (even for the sun). The drawers were like tiny doors into endless fields. Lucy had taught Kier how to flip through the cards and then Kier had taught Andy and now Andy stood in front of the drawer marked R–S in tidy librarian script.

"I'll be by the Westerns," Kier whispered. "And then in 709. Ancient Greece."

Andy and Kier understood about Dewey Decimal.

Andy flipped through S-Sa, Sh, Sn-Sp, Sw-Sz:

Sulphur

Salinity

He needed to learn Russian ...

S (unit of time): *see* second

... because he'd decided to become a spy.

Saber-toothed, Société Radio-Canada: (*see* Canadian Broadcasting Corporation), Shark (fish), Sun, Syrinx: (*see* Vocal Organs, Birds, Etcetera) ... And flip flip flip back through to R:

R (unit of radiation)

He would move to Nova Scotia and train on the submarines.

R-plane (see aircraft)

He would have gadgets below the deck, like Dad's gadgets at work, and he would sail to Russia, or submarine to Russia, or marine to Russia ...

Finally at Ru: *Russian, Beginner Lessons in* (w/ helpful illus.).

... Andy would get out of his submarine and break into the Cosmodrome and free all the dogs who wanted to go to space, and then he'd blow everything up.

Andy took a piece of scrap paper from a tiny cardboard box. He picked up the pencil attached to the card catalogue by a string and held it carefully in his hand. He focused on printing. Andy printed out his call number. He shut the drawer and looked at his piece of paper. The dogs, Andy knew, spoke Russian. He looked up at the letters and numbers on the sides of the shelves. 491.9-583.2. And off Andy went to get the book on his own.

Kier waited outside in the Su–Sv Sun while Andy checked out his book.

"You won't be able to read this." The librarian's long horse mouth drawled. "First of all son, it's not from the children's section, and second of all, it's not even English."

"I know this," Andy said to the librarian. Andy gave his library card to her like Kier had shown him. The librarian wrote down his name, card number, and book title in her great big record book. Then she stamped the due date into Andy's new book with a thud. Andy held *Beginner Lessons in Russian* to his chest and zippered his coat over top. He went outside and stood next to Kier who was already reading one of his Westerns. They were waiting for Lucy to come back with the car. Andy unzippered his coat and sat cross-legged on the ground so he could start reading. *Chapter One: Practice your pronunciation!*

¶ "They're flying her!" A man Peter had never seen before leaned into the office.

"Ç'est quoi ça?" Peter said to Robert.

"I think ..." Robert looked up at Peter. They both grabbed their coats and ran down the stairs.

¶ An Arrow was taxiing. Her sleek delta-wing triangle almost two storeys high with the red maple leaf Air Force ensign on the side. Huge white wings glowing in the sun. The weather-vein nose protruding into the air like a giant proboscis. The arched curvature of the clamshell cockpit sparkling in the early spring light. 9:52 a.m. March 25, 1958. Peter put a hand over his eyes. Bluest of blue skies. Linemen with tools still in their hands poured out of the hangars and offices onto the runways. Peter could see the Orenda engine crew jogging over from across the road, some of them still had goggles on their faces, white coats on, looking down the runway to the plane. Peter and Robert stood together and watched as Janusz "Zura" Zurakowski, Avro's chief development pilot, gave her some speed down the runway. Not even halfway to the end of the tarmac and up she rose at 45 degrees into the clouds. A CF-100 was already in the sky with Spud Potocki and a photographer. Jack Woodman took off to chase in one of the Sabres.

The wings! Peter's head was bent back, looking toward the sky. Two planes on either side of her escorting. God damn, those were beautiful wings. She was soaring beautifully. Altitude of 11,000 feet. 250 knots. 40,000 separately-crafted parts. Milled metals. Pistons. Rotaries. Rivets. Cylinders. Nine-thousand-five-hundred technicians' hands. Peter could do nothing but stand there and stare. She was in the air! And Good-Sacré-Cœur-de-l'Enfant-Jésus and Tabernac and All-Sweet-Angels-of-High-Holy-Heaven-Above did she belong there!

Peter reached over and grabbed onto both of Robert's cheeks like he was a child. "We did it!" Robert grabbed Peter's cheeks in return, "Ouais, elle est vraiment haute!" and they stood there, a slight bit of drool running down both of their chins, holding onto each other by the face and hopping in little circles like grinning idiots.

The flight lasted thirty-five minutes. Thirty-five short minutes. The plane made 250 knots before she was down again. And oh, beautiful touchdown! Parachute brakes trailing out behind her like a bride's veil. The push of the crowd rushing toward the tarmac as she pulled in snug and fit to her docking bay. The debarking ladder was wheeled toward the cockpit. The clamshell window lifted. And there he stood: Zura, Saint Zurakowski, patron saint of Malton, taking off his helmet, holding it toward the sky. And as he came down the ladder, that magical steel ladder leading to the clouds, he was taken up on the workmen's shoulders. Thronging, jubilant, hoisting him into the air. He took her almost to Mach 2 on his first run without even having a pilot's licence. His only request for modification to the cockpit on that first flight was a clock, because he didn't know what time it was while he was flying her fast and swift and sweet and gorgeous into those clouds.

The living-room carpet was covered in Tinkertoys. Because it was raining out, Kier and Andy were forced to play inside even though the weekend before they had both been given brand new bikes from their dad for Easter. Lucy and Rose had gone to church on Maundy Thursday and Peter had taken the boys to Canadian Tire. Lucy never bothered to wrestle the family into pews, but if she felt like going to church she went, and if the boys felt like going to Sunday School they went, and Peter never argued. So, while Lucy stood among other Holy Week parishioners, heard the story of the disciples getting their feet washed, looked at the hanging cross above the altar, and walked up the aisle to receive a blessing, Peter and the boys stood among the aisles of the nation's great hardware store. They stood among camping equipment, electrical components, the faint smell of grease and house paint; among scooters and pogo sticks and children's tricycles; and the boys pointed up to the bikes hanging from hooks. "That one," Andy said, pointing to the red Speedster. "The blue one," Kier said pointing at the Road Warrior. And a man with a long stick with a hook at the end brought down their bikes from above so they could ride them up the aisles and then take the same bikes home in boxes where Peter put them together in the basement while he said curse words. But today there would be no riding around the block, jumping up on curbs, slamming their feet backwards in order to skid out on patches of loose gravel and last autumn's leaves. It was raining and Lucy had asked them to look after Rose in her playpen while she made telephone calls from the kitchen.

It would be TV dinners for supper tonight, no time to cook up Cornish hens as Peter had asked. He had no idea how much time it took to defrost, stuff and bake five tiny birds filled with cranberries and bread crumbs. Peter had been fed by other people almost his entire life: first by his mother, surely; then by the cooks and quartermasters in the Air Force; then by Lucy. Even on the rare occasion that a lunch wasn't ready for him when he went out the door to work, there was the coffee cart at the hangar that sold sandwiches. So, tonight, no Cornish hens, Pete, unless you want to stuff them yourself. Lucy took five tinfoil boxes from the freezer and put them on the counter to thaw.

Lucy flipped through the telephone directory under the heading "Church Parishes" and placed a pen along the spine to mark the page. She dialled the first number and moved to the counter, pulling the phone cord taut across the kitchen. The receiver rested between her shoulder and ear. She took two apples and a jar of peanut butter from the fridge. The kids would need snacks soon. She should start teaching them how to make their own food, they were old enough now, and these boys, unlike their father, should learn how to cook a little, but Andy liked his apples peeled, and she simply did not have the energy today to deal with Andy wielding a knife.

"Yes, hello ... um, hello there ..." Lucy hadn't rehearsed what she was going to say if she got someone on the other line, and now she wasn't quite sure how to phrase the question. "This may seem strange, but I was wondering if you might know of a priest in your parish who rescued a woman from a field last autumn."

She could hear a tower of Tinkertoys fall down in the living room and she hoped this wouldn't upset Rose.

"No, no, it wasn't a farming accident."

She held the phone against her shoulder and stretched the cord toward the living room.

"Yes, I see. Well, could you maybe leave my number with a general inquiry to your clergy?"

Rose screeching out vowels, but no crying.

"Yes, that's right. Thank you."

Tinkertoy emergency averted.

"God bless you too, okay then, cheerio."

Lucy took out a cutting board and moved to the table to look up the next number in the list of churches. She moved back to the phone and dialled. While the number rang Lucy went back to the open phone book and scanned the list of churches. St. Andrew's, St. Anthony's, St. Augustine's. This would take her a while. "Good afternoon to you too. I was wondering if you'd been at your parish long ... well, I have a rather strange question to ask you.... You see, there was an accident in the fall...." She started peeling the apple.

Lucy had dialled an entire page of churches with no positive response when the mailman came to the kitchen door with a postcard of Notre Dame Cathedral.

Ma Cherie,

Pops sent the Star *article with you and the family. A miracle baby! But are you okay? I'm sorry you haven't heard from me. I've been busy at openings and in the clubs. I'm singing these days! Imagine! You have to get over here, darling. You'd love this place. It's like one hundred Torontos all in one. I'm worried about you.*

Love, Claire

No return address. The first word in seven years.

¶ "Boys, I need out of here."

Andy and Kier looked up from their massive Tinkertoy construction project. Then they looked out the window at the rain.

"Right now?" Andy asked.

"Yes," Lucy said and scooped Rose up from the playpen.

Andy and Kier stood looking at each other. Lucy was already out the back door on the way to the car. "But our coats!" Kier called after her.

¶ She took them to the most exotic place in Toronto she knew of: Allen Gardens. Broad-leafed banana plants umbrellaed over them as they entered the domed entrance to the conservatory. Birds and butterflies flitted beneath the glass. Tiny rivers and ponds ran amongst the palms and the orchids, and there was a thicket of blue flowers that looked like shooting stars by the statue of a Grecian lady. In the Arid House Lucy stood beneath a cactus that was two-storeys tall in the one-storey building. The cactus bent over in its middle at the roof and had grown itself in amongst the pipes.

"Mama, I'm hungry." Andy swung his feet at a bench by three golden barrel cacti.

"Kier?" Lucy waved her son over from the succulents. "Did you bring any allowance with you?" She'd forgotten to grab her purse as they'd run out the door. She'd even driven without her licence, she realized now.

Kier counted out quarters from his pants pocket and Lucy sent the boys to the concession in the park for three ice-cream sandwiches. By the time they came back, Rose was asleep in Lucy's arms. Lucy and the boys unwrapped the waxy paper from their Neapolitan bars and ate beneath the cereus hexagonus with the rain falling against the glass.

"Do you want to run away to Paris with me, boys?" Lucy asked them as she ate through the stripe of chocolate ice cream.

"I can't," Andy said. "Dr. Cuff and Dr. Kehrlein of Arkansas are starting a University of the Air."

Kier licked the ice cream methodically out of the middle of the sandwich part, so all that would remain was the cookie.

"What?" Lucy said.

"He's been going on about this all week," Kier said. "Mrs. Penny told the grade ones about it."

"Classes will be offered in hot-air balloons," Andy added.

"But you're not even in grade two, yet, Andy. University is a ways away."

No one was in the Arid House now except the Jacobs family and a group of German tourists.

"I know, but I don't want to miss out on the opportunity."

"I'll go to Paris with you, Mum," Kier said. "As long as we can go to the Louvre to see the archaic torso of Apollo."

Whose kids were these?

"Okay, Boo, you can start saving up for tuition, and we'll save up our allowance for Parisian air fare, how 'bout it, Bean?"

"Mum," Kier said. "I don't really like being called that."

¶ Long after the ice cream was gone, the sky remained a stubborn grey beyond the rain-splattered glass of the dome. The boys walked around the garden counting the stepping stones and then hunkered down by a tiny walking bridge in the Rainforest Room to watch for turtles. The Germans took pictures of the bananas and the lilies with fern-like leaves and wandered down the garden's flagstones.

¶ Lucy put the TV dinners on hotplates in front of the family as soon as Peter got in from the International Aviation Symposium where he and Robert had been manning a table. "I want to find the priest."

Peter salted his Swanson's beef stew. "What priest?"

"The one who found me," Lucy said. She put a bib on Rose and blew on a carrot.

"Where'd you get that idea?"

Andy and Kier looked back and forth between their parents. Kier was quiet, pushing his potatoes to one side of his tin container. Rose was spitting the carrot back onto the tray of her high chair.

"What do you mean 'Where did you get that idea'?"

"Where did you get the idea that a priest found you?"

"It was in the newspaper. The nurses told me." She thought about the fact that after they'd come home from the gardens, she'd called all the way down to F in the White Pages, to Saint Francis of Assisi, and now Peter was suggesting that it was all a mistake.

"I don't recall a priest." He chewed at a piece of roast beef.

She wanted to suffocate him. She wanted to push his face down into the tinfoil basin of stew until he said he was sorry, until he said of course there was a priest. He wasn't around. He didn't know. He didn't even know that Claire had written and that she was happy and fine in Paris after seven years of silence, and was singing in night clubs, and that she'd probably had drinks with Duke Ellington. That the city was one hundred Torontos. That here, back in the singular city of Toronto, there were still Tinkertoys all over the carpet because Lucy hadn't cared to pick them up. Lucy stood. "More milk anyone?"

"I thought we were going to have those tiny chickens," Peter said toward the refrigerator.

Peter can recall the high pitch of the loudspeaker. Years later, when he is getting the car's oil changed, and a gate lifts; or when he hears the same particular squeal in truck brakes on a highway interchange, these will bring the memory on. There was even that once, at a dentist's office, when Peter leaned in close to the chest of the dental hygienist because her perfume had the same floral and citrus scent as the degreasing hand soap that Avro had in the dispensers of the men's washroom. And then pow! There he was again, in the office hallway with Robert, the hangar's loudspeakers squealing when the mic turned on, Crawford Gordon's strained voice ringing out over Avro's internal intercom. One of the riveters in the parking lot said Gordon was already drunk. "Liquid courage. Been at the bottle all morning just to make the goddamn announcement. Coulda saved a morning's worth of titanium alloy if he'd had some goddamn balls." Peter had watched as the man took off his jacket and folded it into a square before he put it into the backseat of his Dodge. "Given us the dignity of knowing the truth he'd had in that office for an hour and forty-five minutes on his goddamn own." The jacket still had the man's Avro security identification card clipped on.

When Peter recreates the events of the cancellation, that morning appears to him with precision; laid out like the lines of a blueprint. In retrospect, the trajectory of decisions is mapped and measured;

an obvious pattern of development. But with that first crackle and reverberating squeal of the loudspeaker, Peter had no idea.

The plane was in full production. The floors of the hangar were at capacity. Riveters, machinists, men and women in white coats with safety goggles oversaw their square part of the conveyer belts and testing apparatuses, their drills and sanders. Peter saw all the men and women working from the tall plate glass window in the hall that overlooked the production floor, all of them busy just hours before, as he returned a gyroscope to Frank down the hall. It was like the Ford Motor Company down there.

But then the first announcement came on. Quarter to eleven after first coffee break. Not Crawford's voice. Crawford's announcement came later. It was one of his junior staff. A young guy. Probably had no idea himself. "Message for all staff. Message for all staff. Down tools. Return all tools to the tool crib. I repeat down tools and return all tools to the tool crib."

Peter looked up across the drafting tables at Robert. There were rarely messages for all staff, and there was never a call to down tools at quarter to eleven in the morning. That was just absurd. Why would you halt production midway through morning shift? What the hell was going on?

"What?" Peter ventured to Robert across their desks.

"Je ne sais pas." Then a moment later, Robert's head still cocked to one side as if listening for further explanation. "I 'ave no idea."

The message to down tools did not apply to the design staff in the upstairs offices, but still Peter and Robert hurried out to the hallway window to look down at the floor. The floor was a mess of workers wandering from their stations, clustered in groups of conjecture, the obedient ones already in a queue at the chain-link tool lockers to return their equipment for lockdown.

"That man just put a hacksaw into his jacket." Peter pressed his finger to the glass of the window pointing toward a corner of the production floor.

Robert looked silently down at the floor, and then, almost in a whisper, asked "Qu'est-ce qu'ils savent?"

"What do you mean?" Peter looked at Robert. Peter had never heard suspicion in Robert's voice before.

"What does that man know? Why would he steal if this loudspeak is not a lockdown régulier?"

A number of Robert and Peter's co-workers had made their way into the hall.

"It's gotta do with that meeting in Ottawa," Marty from Fins and Fuselage conjectured.

"Yeah," said Simon from Acoustics. "Gordon was meeting with the P.M. this week and I know for a fact that Dief hates our man."

"Tories been trying to get rid of this project since they took over office." Marty added.

"Bullshit," Reuben from down the hall in Marketing and Development stepped in. "I've got an order for five from Brussels and I just did a presentation to the Brits. They're gonna take twelve by the spring, I swear."

"Well then why would they order tools down?" Peter asked again. No one knew what the hell was going on.

"A security threat?" Robert asked, and that got them all silent for a second, thinking that perhaps the Soviets had got a man onto their floor.

Then, while the lot of them were standing around in the hallway the second announcement came on, Crawford Gordon's strained voice warbling with booze over the intercom. Peter later found out from the wife of a friend who knew Gordon's secretary that he was reading word for word from a telegram he'd received from Prime Minister Diefenbaker's office that morning. Word for word. Peter imagined the words of the telegram and their precise spacing. The stops registered in between each sentence. The formality of the telegram paper with its thickness and official stamps, and yet the shock of it, the informal way this change to Peter's life, to all their lives, was delivered.

Crawford Gordon read slowly. "You shall cease all work immediately. I repeat, you shall cease all work immediately. Please instruct all your subcontractors and suppliers to take similar action. You are requested to submit to the Department of Defence Production any claim which you may have as a result of this termination." The shuffle of papers in the background. "You should make your applications in writing to the Chief Settlement Officer, Department of Defence Production, Ottawa, for the requisite set of forms." A rheumy cough. "Return all tools to the correct locker and take your personal belongings. Stop work. I repeat. All contracts have been terminated. Please leave the premises immediately. This goes for all staff. You are to leave the premises immediately."

"This is a joke," Simon said. "This is an April Fool's joke."

"It's February," said Marty.

"Well it's clearly a mistake," Ruben said. "They're going to change this around by Monday. You'll see. This will just be a long weekend for us, boys. They'll be changing this faster than you can say ..." but Peter had already started toward his office leaving the chatter of the men in the hallway.

Peter stood at his office door and looked down at the blueprint half-drawn on his desk. He'd heard that the next project after the Arrow was going to be rockets to space. He'd already been thinking of modifications to the wing design. Chamberlin over in Trial Prototypes had thought that if an Arrow could fly upside down at the edge of the atmosphere, it could be used as a launching pad for space craft.

"People are stealing tools down there," Peter said to Robert who had come into the office behind him.

"It is not your matter."

"Like I said, I just saw someone put a hacksaw in his coat."

Robert began carefully to peel the tape from the family photos on his desk.

"Did you hear me Robert? A hacksaw. That's what this has all come to. A hacksaw in a coat."

"It is unquieting, yes. But it is not your worry. We must go home."

"But Ruben's right. This has gotta be a mistake. We're in mid-production."

Robert had peeled away his mother's house in Trois-Rivière and was beginning to unstick a picture of his family seated on his mother's porch.

"Stop it."

"Stop what?"

"Stop taking your photographs down, Robert. This is a mistake. We're going to be back in here by Monday."

"Pierre, you heard the message. We must go home."

"But not for good, Robert. I'm certain of it. Why would they let us go for good like that? There is no logic to this decision. This is ludicrous."

"Pierre. We are fired."

"No. That's not what the message said."

"Oui, Pierre. We are fired. We make claims to the government now."

"No." Peter began pacing from the coffee pot to the corner of his desk. "No. This doesn't make any sense."

Robert moved toward the hat stand, picked up his coat and slowly put it on. He tucked his photographs into the breast pocket. He picked up his lunch box and clicked it open. He took his stained Noorduyn Aviation coffee mug from beside the coffee maker and wrapped it in a paper napkin. He put it in his lunch box and closed the metal lid.

"No, Robert. Stop it. How can you be this calm?"

"I am not calm, Peter. Je suis furieux. Mais, pour le moment, what can I do?"

Robert then went to his desk and meticulously placed his own tools: his slide rule, his metal case of draftsmen's pencils, his French curves, and a handful of paperwork into his worn leather briefcase and clicked it all closed. "Pierre. It is over. Our jobs here are done. It is time for you to go home and tell Lucille." Robert took Peter's hand in a firm handshake. Then he clasped his shoulder and gave him a hard kiss on both cheeks. Peter could feel the rough scrape of Robert's stubbled skin.

Peter stood back and looked at Robert. They were silent for a long time. Finally Peter nodded. "A la prochaine, Robert."

"Oui. Bien sûr. A la prochaine."

¶ Peter stood alone in their office. Then he got his coat. He packed up his own coffee mug, a small tin of good coffee grounds, his brown lunch bag with a sandwich and apple still inside. He packed up his tools and took his slide rule with him. The rule had been a gift when he'd first arrived at Avro and it was something Peter didn't want to leave behind. He'd never been taken seriously enough as a mechanic

124

to receive a slide rule, but at Avro he was considered an engineer, and the slide rule was the tool of an engineer. He laid it delicately in the black box that clicked like a jeweller's necklace case, he walked down the stairs to the main hangar door and out into the sun.

As Peter adjusted to the daylight and sight came back, the planes in the field and the parking lot in the distance all looked like an overexposed photograph; something that had already happened a long time ago.

¶ "Sir, excuse me sir, please, can you tell the listeners what you think of this cancellation." A reporter was shoving her microphone into Peter's face just as he got to the fenced gate before the row of parked cars. He looked up at her polite yet persistent smile. His car keys were in his hand. Had he already taken them out of his pocket? How long had he been holding them? Did he always take them out before he got to the gate?

Maintaining her smile the reporter asked again, "Sir, did you suspect the government would cancel the Arrow project? What does this mean for you and your family?"

The reporter was asking Peter questions he hadn't considered yet. It made it seem worse. What *did* this mean for his family? What *had* exactly happened? He stood for a second at the microphone, staring at the reporter with her expectant pink lips and fierce stare and he shoved passed her, pushing her microphone back into her own face. He could hear, behind him, that the reporter kept talking, was already asking another employee the same sorts of questions: "Over thirteen thousand people are employed by this project. What does this cancellation mean for the technical workforce of our nation?"

"I think it's just terrible. Dief's treating us like trash. Just putting us out on the side of the road like this."

Peter gripped the car keys more firmly in his hand so that their metal teeth ridged into his palm. When he got inside the car he locked the door and started the ignition. He needed a drink. Or maybe he needed to play a game of squash. To hit something hard and small against the walls of a contained room. Should he phone Chuck? No. He hadn't talked to Chuck in years. He wanted to be alone. He needed to get himself to a television so he knew exactly what was going on. And then he had to figure out what to tell Lucy when he arrived home.

¶ That was Friday. By Saturday afternoon the American aircraft companies had recruiting teams in motels downtown. They got the cream of the industry. But Peter refused. He refused even to go down for an interview or to gather their glossy information packages. He even refused to see about NASA's big payment packages or to get the boys the plastic toy rocket ships they were handing out. He knew Diefenbaker had backed down because the U.S. had backed down. Peter was willing to bet that Dief would soon see his mistake. It would be cleared up by Monday. No prime minister in their right mind lets all of his country's advanced technical personnel, in one weekend, get scooped up like mice in the talons of a hawk. Dief would apologize. Dief and Gordon would work this out.

"The Yanks have convinced the sons of bitches in Ottawa that airplane warfare is obsolete," Peter ranted to Lucy that night over dinner. "Mark my words."

She thought he might be drunk.

"Canada will be buying U.S. warplanes within the year if Dief doesn't get this mess sorted out." He held a forkful of potatoes up. "Just think, for the price of firing everyone, we could have gotten the whole fleet into the air, Orenda engines and all." He put the fork and potatoes back down on his plate. "Missiles."

He was slurring. He was definitely drunk.

"I still don't understand," Lucy said. "Missiles will replace the planes?"

"Missiles ... do missiles have brains? Do missiles have judgement? Can missiles see that the target computed into them is, on the ground, actually a schoolhouse? Is a river where the people go to bathe?" He was spitting the words out. "Missiles are the death of civilians. The death of civilians is what happens when war machines cease to be flown by people with brains."

"Was this all said at work? Was this told to you?"

"Nothing," Peter pointed at them with his fork, "was told to us."

Andy and Kier sat still, their backs pressed against the glittery vinyl of the nook, and said nothing.

Peter spoke through a mouth full of potatoes. "Those U.S. bastards can go straight to hell and fuck themselves."

"Peter! Language!" Lucy looked over to the boys. "Boys, you're excused from the table." She shooed her hands at them. "Go. Play."

"But we're not finished eating," Kier said.

"Take your plates to the television."

The boys hesitated.

"Go," Lucy said and they retreated with their dinners.

"But what about the money?" Lucy asked when the boys had gone out of the kitchen. "Wasn't the project costing a lot of money? That's what Connie said. Maybe it's not anyone's fault. Maybe we just couldn't sustain such a project?"

Peter looked up at her, his body hanging heavy off his shoulders. All he could manage was a sharp sarcastic laugh. "What does Connie Romano know?"

"Well why don't you and the fellas go down there and demand to know what's happening? Why doesn't someone figure this out?"

"There's no one to ask, Lu. Everyone's gone. They fired everyone."

"But this is outrageous. They can't just let you all go. What about your families? What about our future? You have been a committed worker to that company for a decade. Companies don't do this to their employees. The company Christmas card called us *family*."

"Lucille."

Lucy looked over at Peter. Not even in the hospital had she seen this hazy greyness to Peter's gaze. The thing just didn't make sense. Sure the papers had gone on about the Tories' cuts to spending, how the plane might have to go, how that sector might feel the pinch and how this deficit would need to be met, but every government says they will make cuts to spending. It doesn't mean you lay off ten thousand young people. "What if a whole group of us families all lined up at the gate?" Lucy tried.

"Lucille. Stop trying to solve it."

Lucy looked at him.

"Lu," Peter was silent. He turned his plate slowly in a counterclockwise direction and then reached his arm across the table.

Lucy looked at the blank square of his open palm.

"Would you mind, just for a moment, holding onto my hand?"

¶ On Monday nothing had changed. The only people to stay on at the Malton Avro Experimental Hangar for the following week were the secretaries and accountants. They were the ones to type up all the white slips and place them in ordered rows to be mailed to Avro personnel and contractors. Six postal sacks full.

```
SEPARATION OF EMPLOYMENT FORM

  EMPLOYEE: Peter Jacobs
  LEAVING DATE: February 28/59
  ☐ extended leave
  ☐ end of contract
  ☑ laid off
  TERMINATION PAY: Three months plus holiday pay
  CLASSIFCATION: Draftsman/Engineer
```

February. The government had promised that the planes would be up for review in March. By May half the kids in Kier and Andy's classes were gone.

Some of Andy and Kier's schoolmates went to France so their parents could build the Concorde. Some went down to the United States so their parents could build the x-20 Dyna-Soar rocket plane. But there was still a month of school left before summer holidays, so classes carried on anyway, empty seats in the alphabetical rows, half of the children's art taken down from the walls. Only a few spring-scene tissue-paper mosaics were left on the bulletin boards above the windows, the patches of corkboard beneath looking brown and faded like dead grass. The kids that were leaving Malton signed autograph books and took pictures with their schoolmates on the front steps of the school. The girls awarded favourite postcards of movie stars to best friends, even their leftover boxes of crayons, all worn down because the year was almost done.

Then there were the gaps in the street, when people started taking their houses with them. Huge trucks came and men with hard hats ran around and measured things, and then the bulldozers and lifters drove over the garden beds and soon the houses were up on blocks and all that was left in the ground were the concrete caves of family basements with yellow caution tape pegged around, and then the houses were up on big flatbed trucks that drove the Queen Elizabeth Expressway to the I-90, down through Buffalo to Houston, where the neighbours had found jobs at NASA, or across to Seattle to start work with Boeing. "An offer we can't refuse," is what they all kept saying, and both Boeing and NASA had thought of everything, including the idea of moving entire households, so that it was all practically set up when the new families arrived. Imagine driving all the way across the country, maybe even taking an extra week to drive down the Pacific coast to Disneyland for a holiday, wearing mouseketeer ears in the back of the family station wagon, *M–I–C. See you real soon K–E–Y. Why? Because I love you. M–O–U–S–E.* Or going south, arriving to find your exact same bedroom, with your exact same sheets and spaceship wallpaper, there, in the middle of Texas.

¶ When Peter got his white slip from the company he called and made a booking for the squash court. He showed up alone.

"For 4:30," Peter told the girl at the counter.

She flipped through an appointments book. "Jacobs."

"That would be me."

"Excellent. Do you have your racket, or will you need to rent one?"

"I've got one right here." Peter held his squash racket up so that the YMCA front desk girl could see.

"Will your opponent be joining you later?"

"Yes. Maybe … I'm not exactly sure."

"Alright Mr. Jacobs. I'll tell him you're in squash court two if he asks for you."

"Sounds good."

¶ Peter changed into Converse sneakers and white basketball shorts. He opened the door to the squash court and shut it behind him. He put his towel and racket press down at the bottom of the front wall, moved to the serving square on the right and hit the ball hard. He returned his serves equally hard. He ran and ducked and backhanded and volleyed and hit the ball off all four walls until his shirt was drenched in sweat and his shoulders ached and the back of his legs were sore. He needed for his mind to be held hostage by his body. He wanted to focus on his breath and his joints and his muscles moving him across the court. He needed not to think about how that week, for the first time during their entire marriage, Lucy had purchased an inexpensive bag of powdered milk for the coffee rather than the regular glass bottles of cream. He hit the small black ball hard and then harder off the blank white walls. (Later, when Peter stood in front of a Jackson Pollock canvas for the first time in his life at the Art Gallery of Ontario, the painting would remind him of that day of squash). Peter played against himself for three quarters of an hour. He leaned over his knees to catch his breath, and then, standing up, he grabbed his towel and walked out of the court. He had a shower and went home.

¶ When the boys were smaller, Peter would lie on the living-room floor and hoist them up on the bottoms of his feet at their waists, holding their fingertips, arms out like wings. They made engine noises as he flew them in little circles with his legs. As he drove home he wanted to do this now with Lucy. He wanted to lie down on the living-room carpet, touch the bottoms of his feet to her waist and fly her over him. Then he wanted to slowly lower her down on top of him. He wanted her to be naked. He wanted to make love to her on the living-room floor. Hard. It had been a long time since he had felt this desire. Lately he watched her at night from his arm-chair after the kids were asleep. She did the crossword puzzle at the mahogany dining table, the pencil sideways between her teeth. With both hands she swept her hair up off her neck into a twist. Her whole body bent over the clues. She was utterly alone in her posture of concentration. He hated how she got her teeth marks all over his pencils.

¶ Newspapers covered the quilt and floor of the bedroom for weeks. Dishes that Lucy had brought up for Peter throughout the day sat on his bedside dresser hardly touched: gummed bowls of oatmeal, congealed plates of meatloaf, browning iceberg lettuce beneath a slick sheen of Italian dressing. He had been wearing the same green flannel pyjamas printed with flying geese all day long and then again through the night.

The newspapers had called it Black Friday. One of the papers from last week had a front page article titled *15000 Idle*. The morning's paper had an image of three of the Arrows on the Malton tarmac in the midst of being disassembled with wrecking balls and welding torches and then loaded into a truck to be taken to a scrapyard. The sight of the amputated planes got Peter out of bed and brought him down to the kitchen, still in his flying geese pyjamas, newspaper folded under his arm, to the phone with the long cord.

"Robert?"

Lucy heard Peter's voice in the kitchen and came quietly through the swinging door. Finally he was speaking to Robert. She busied herself at the stove with the coffee percolator and a pot of porridge and pretended she wasn't listening.

"Have you seen this?" Peter spread out the newspaper on the shining table of the space nook. "Yes. Exactly. With torches." ... "No." ... "You've got to be kidding." ... "No. Have you found anything?" ... "I've been sick about it." ... "Exactly, exactly." ... "No, no. That was all." ... "Alright—I will phone again bientôt." ... "Yes. A coffee and a doughnut would be nice." And then Peter hung up.

God, it was impossible to tell anything from his conversations on the phone. He spoke in single sentences. This was his best friend, and he spoke as if he was composing a memo. Lucy couldn't imagine how long a phone call to Claire in a moment like this might be.

Lucy held out a bowl to him. "Want some?"

"What is it?"

"Red River."

"Don't want any."

"The boys are doing a jigsaw puzzle in the living room."

Peter sat down at the breakfast nook.

"It has a thousand pieces."

Peter drummed his fingers rhythmically against the polished surface of his table and stared at the image of the planes on the cover of the *Globe & Mail*.

"They're having some trouble now that they've got the edge pieces in."

"I don't want to see them right now."

Parts of the plane were strewn over the concrete like a dissection. And now, the article had said, the government had decided that instead of a plane, erecting a string of nukes in Canada was a better idea. Nuclear towers in all of the provinces. Guns pointed to space. But why destroy the planes? That's what Peter didn't understand. Why destroy something that exists and functions? It was foolhardy. And the blueprints. Robert had said that they were burning the blueprints. Those were his blueprints. His fine blue lines, curling and disappearing until nothing was left but ash.

"Honey, the kids'll understand if you're upset. They just want to play."

"Lu," he looked up at her. "I don't want to see them, okay?" He put his hand to his face and felt the grubbiness of days of stubble. He hadn't shaved for quite some time. His hair hadn't been washed since he'd last been to the gym. He couldn't remember when he'd put this pair of pyjamas on, but realized that beneath the flannel he was beginning to smell unbathed. In the next room something crashed and Rose started crying.

¶ Lucy phoned an old boss at the telephone company where she'd worked during the war. She was given a part-time job, starting in two weeks. All she had to do was take the bus into the city every morning and back every afternoon. They'd traded the DeSoto in at the car lot for a 1953 used economy model Chev One-Fifty. Rose was almost two and Peter could look after her during the day while he began to look for other work. He could schedule interviews for the afternoons. Three months of termination pay. They'd be fine. If only she could get him to stop reading the papers. Lucy imagined briefly sending a letter to her mother and father asking for their help, but Lucy would rather have her entire family living on the streets of Detroit before allowing Mavis Ainsworth to gush about Maple Avenue with her feather duster and her pity.

¶ "I'm going to the gym." The screen door slammed behind Peter. He had been to the gym five times since the cancellation. Five days of squash in two weeks when before Peter might play once or twice a year with one of the guys from work. He was not applying for jobs. He was not playing with his children. He was leaving abruptly, his face still unshaven, and doing god knows what.

"We'll be here," Lucy said to no one. Andy and Kier were playing at a neighbour's. Rose was down for her nap. Lucy sat at the breakfast nook with the electric sewing machine plugged into the wall. She was mending some of her old work clothes to wear when she started back at Northern Telecom the next day. A nice linen suit jacket and skirt she'd forgotten about, the lilac lining ripped at the hem.

Lucy fixed dinner that night while Rose sat in her high chair with a tin of crayons and scribbled in the pages of a Snoopy colouring book. Andy, Kier and Peter were still not home. She made spaghetti and meatballs. A spinach salad with hard-boiled eggs and bacon. When they were still not home by seven, she made vanilla pudding for dessert. She sat down at the table. Still no one. Stood up, made egg salad sandwiches for the boys' school lunches. Cut up carrot sticks. Put an apple and a miniature Tootsie Roll in each of their bags. Andy. Kier. She wrote their names on the brown paper and put the lunches back into the fridge for tomorrow.

"Mama. Kier pushed me."

"I didn't push you, Andy. You fell."

"You pushed me into the bushes."

"No I didn't."

"I have a bruise, Mama. Look."

Well. The kids were home. Still no sign of Peter. Lucy ate with the boys and kept a serving of pasta warm on the stove.

The kids watched TV after dinner. Lucy sat at the kitchen table alone, the dishes cleaned and drying in the rack, sorting through the bills. She could hear the voices from the television. "Come on Lassie. Here girl." Then she put Andy and Rose into the bath, their faces shining like moons from the basin and bubbles of the tub.

"Where's Dad?" Andy asked. He had his swimming goggles on.

Rose splashed her hands against the surface of the water. "No," Rose said. "Ki. Ki." It was her name for Kier.

Andy dipped his elbow in the bathwater to get the bubbles off and inspected his skin.

"He's just at the gym. He'll be home soon, Boo."

"I do have a bruise," Andy said, pointing.

¶ Lucy turned out the light in Andy and Kier's room. Kier was getting old enough that he would need his own room soon. They might need to build an addition, another expense they couldn't afford. She put Rose down in her crib and sat on the settee knitting to *Alfred Hitchcock Presents*. The story was something about a wife secretly poisoning her in-laws, but Lucy fell asleep before the end. She woke up. What time was it? Just after eleven. The television was static. A low buzz. The evening programming was over. She had to work tomorrow. She went to the kitchen, turned the element from low to off, took the pot of dried-up spaghetti from the burner and put it in the sink to soak. Lucy undressed and put on her nightgown. She tidied newspapers to clear a space for herself in the bed. He hadn't even called.

Peter, Lucy knew, wasn't the type to have an affair. He'd rather be alone. He'd rather be somewhere quiet and clean with very few things on the walls. Her escape would likely be similar. A soft room all in white. Cushions on the floor. A cup of tea and stacks and piles and towers of books. And one wall, one stone wall, with the stained glassed windows of her youth.

Lucy woke up to find her nightgown halfway up her thighs. Peter smelled like the pine scent of the gym's shampoo. And of whiskey. Lucy pretended to sleep. He fumbled with the lace ties of her night dress at the waist. He worked his clumsy fingers up to the neck and tried to unhook the small eyelet clasps. She lay still and kept her eyes closed.

Peter had thought about Lucy's body the whole way home in the car. He shouldn't even have been driving. He'd taken it slow. After going to the gym, he hadn't wanted to go home. He'd driven from the Y to the Legion. Some of the men from the hangar were there. They were talking about interviews they'd had with other plane companies down in the States.

"What are you doing going down there?" Peter asked.

"Working. That's what." The man in the checked shirt said. He was already down into his third or fourth beer.

"Don't you care about staying in the country? You're going to become a Yank?"

"What country? The one that just fired my ass?" The other men around him chuckled. "You're all red, my friend," the checked-shirt man said to Peter, pointing towards his face.

"Yeah. I was playing squash."

"Squash, eh?" Checked-shirt guy didn't seem to have much to say about that. "Whatever floats your boat."

Peter moved away from the men to the bar. He ordered a whiskey and drank it down. He ordered a second. There was a hockey game on TV. A small set resting by a collection of beer steins on a shelf above the bar. The Leafs were playing the Black Hawks. Bobby Hull was on fire. Taking it straight up the middle. Peter slugged back his second whiskey and ordered another. He wanted so badly to touch Lucy's body. He wanted to look down, to watch, as he slid into her. He wanted to disappear.

Lucy opened her eyes. She looked down at Peter's hands on her neck. His fingers paused, finally unclasped the hook of her nightgown. He passed his fingers over her collarbone where the lightning had burned a fern across her chest. Peter's face was twisted up. He wasn't looking at her. His half-open eyes were focused on the wall. No, they were focused past the wall, to something farther away. His fingertips pressed hard against Lucy's skin and she felt like he wanted to erase part of her. Like all he wanted was a clean sheet of paper.

She had been asleep. She hadn't heard him come in. And now his hand was rough against her nipple, rubbing it hard. His other hand pushed against the pillow by her head, tendrils of her hair were caught beneath his palm. He moved his hand away from her breast, cupped his palm and spat. Then he pushed this hand between her thighs.

"What are you doing?" she said into his collarbone.

His eyes were still focused far away.

"Peter."

His palm kept pushing, hot and sticky against her flesh, up her thighs so that the butt of his hand pressed down now against her pubic bone.

"Stop it." She put her hands up. She shoved Peter hard on the chest. "Enough." She said it as though speaking to one of the children. "That is enough."

He moved off her, disoriented somehow. He stood, looked at her, and stumbled toward the doorway. Then he went into the bathroom and threw up.

¶ Lucy had done up the buttons of her nightgown by the time Peter came back into the room, she had straightened the hem back down to her knees, and lay very still near her edge of the bed. His bedside lamp had been turned on.

"Peter."

"Yes," he slowly unbuckled his pants, pulled off his shirt and got beneath the covers in his underwear.

"Did you hear me?"

"Yes," he mumbled, "enough."

Lucy lay still, staring at the ceiling. Peter rolled onto his side, facing away from her. She could hear from his breathing that he was already falling asleep. She sat up and reached across his body to turn off the lamp. His back was hot and clammy. She could smell the tang of alcohol in his sweat: like a lime that had been left too long, like seaweed. She lay back down in the darkness. Peter rolled over to face her. He moved himself closer. She looked down at him. He was asleep. Lucy lay there in the stillness, not moving. She felt the rhythm of Peter's breath against her neck. Outside their bedroom window the sky turned lighter. She curled her arm across her husband's neck and slowly began to stroke his hair, softly attending to each strand. She paid careful attention, as she would give to the children. She lay awake for a long time.

¶ When Lucy woke up, Peter wasn't in bed. The dishes and newspapers had been cleared up. Light shone in at her over the covers. She got up and went to the bathroom. She drank mouthfuls of water from the tap at the bathroom sink. After she had a shower she put on her makeup and a slip and the lilac linen dress she had hemmed the night before. She found Peter and the boys in the kitchen making pancakes.

"Morning, Love Bug." Peter said moving towards her. "You look great. All spiffed up."

"I start work," she said stiffly.

He leaned over, spatula still in hand, and gave her a soft kiss on the cheek. "Right, I'd forgotten." He'd shaved. His hair didn't smell like gym shampoo anymore, but the plain Pears from the edge of their shower railing.

"Dad's making me Mickey Mouse ones," Andy said.

"Good to hear."

"You look pretty, Mum." Kier carried the tin of maple syrup to the nook.

Lucy moved toward the coffee percolator and poured herself a mug of coffee. She sat down next to Rose who was playing with a handful of Cheerios in her high chair. "Shoo," Rose said, "Shoo." Lucy leaned back. She wrapped both hands around her mug of coffee. Lucy shut her eyes. She could hear Peter clatter cutlery into the sink; the soft mumble of Rose clumsily gumming a handful of cereal against her cheek; the boys, having given up on helping now, shouting kung-fu 'hi-yah!'s from the corner of the kitchen. Momentarily, a calm patch of sea. But the pancakes would have to be an exception. They couldn't afford a regular luxury of buttermilk and eggs.

The watery taste of powdered milk on Rice Krispies. This is what Andy hated about the cancellation. This noticeable decline in breakfast foods.

Kier, being so busy as grade six captain of the school safety patrol, had no time to notice the quality of his Krispies. Kier arranged the timetable to help the little kids across the street. The patrols wore raincoats with bright arm bands. They held STOP signs out. "Walk your bikes," Kier was supposed to say. That was part of his job now. Sometimes the police officers would come by in the patrol car and say, "Good job. Excellent work," and give them Dad's Oatmeal Cookies out of a bright yellow box.

Rose's first full sentence was "Happy Birthday Uncle George!" They didn't have an Uncle George in the family. No one had any idea where she'd got it from. Curious George? Uncle Curious George goes to the hospital? The X-ray picture of a puzzle-piece in the monkey's stomach?

Lucy found a cantaloupe on sale. They'd been eating apples for weeks, some strawberries she'd frozen from last summer's garden. But a melon! She stood in front of it at her kitchen counter as if it were a secret, held the knife in her hand for a long while looking at its rough skin, like the craters of the moon, and then held the melon down against the cutting board and opened its flesh. Shocking orange. Like Florida Keys in her living room. This melon matched her walls. She scooped out the seeds and put them into the garbage. She sliced each piece into an exact moon and set them quietly onto a china plate. She hardly ever used the china, but for the melon, for this melon, Lucy would do almost anything.

Andy won "Best Electrical Mechanism" at the school science fair. A robotic arm that could squeeze toothpaste out of the tube and also turn on light switches. Andy had worked on it after school with his dad in the basement for over a month. They sat together at the shop desk after Peter had dropped off another round of resumes, had answered the daily newspaper ads and the jobs for engineers within driving distance got sparser and sparser. Everyone from Avro who'd stayed in the city was now competing for the same work.

"What about radio controlled, Dad?"

"Well, we'd need to wire it all up with a different voltage."

"And re-solder?"

"Ohms. We'll have to think in ohms."

Blueprints were the only kind of love letters Peter knew how to write.

At work the telephone wires sometimes got caught in Lucy's hairpins. "Hold on. Let me verify the number." Lucy's operator's voice wasn't entirely her own. She sounded like a theatrical rendition of herself. Lucy Jacobs cast in the role of herself, she thought, and pictured her operator's desk in a spotlight on a stage, a tangle of plugs and wires, cords and buttons; her station a prop, her own clothes a costume and beyond her the darkened theatre-house filled with rustling people far away on the phone.

"Thank you, Operator," the callers sometimes said from their far away velvet theatre chairs. She found it vaguely endearing that they called her by her profession. It was sort of like being called Mama at work. *The Overheard Conversations of Operator Lucille*, starring Operator Lucille:

"Aunt Min's in jail again."

"Twins!"

"I just don't think Mary Greene's porch is fitting."

"Sheila's selling for Williams Beauty Supplies."

"And I kept shouting, 'Listen to the wind! Listen to the wind!'"

Lucy's throat hurt at the end of each performance. She took the wires from her hair, tucked her chair in beneath her desk, and sucked a lemon lozenge on the bus ride home.

Kier and Andy took Rose to the library. She was just learning to read and took a long time walking. Her little legs could hardly keep up.

"This is the card catalogue," Kier explained, "but you won't need that until you're older."

Rose stared up at her two brothers and the many wooden drawers.

"And that's the librarian I told you about," Andy said. The librarian with the horse face was still there. She waved at the boys.

"Dobroe utro!" horseface whispered to Andy.

"Privet. Kak vy pozhivaete?" Andy replied.

"Horosho Spasibo, a vy?"

"Neploho."

"Poka." She waved again and wheeled a cart of books behind the circulation desk.

"Poka." Andy waved back.

Rose looked back and forth. "Poka," she said too and also waved.

"Her first word in Russian!"

"What does it mean?" Kier asked.

"So long."

¶ Lucy sat in the bleachers with Rose and Andy. Peter was at another interview. It must have been his thirtieth in half a year. Kier had never been on a baseball team before. Out in the field he'd moved as though he was afraid of the ball. Now he was up to bat. The pitcher pitched. Kier closed his eyes and hit. He opened his eyes and stood at the plate staring in disbelief. A home run. The fielders ran frantically back toward the fence. Lucy stood up. She clutched her flowered sun hat in her fist. "Run! Run!" Kier sprinting from first to second, second to third. The ball still nowhere near the plates, Kier running toward home, and oh! Peter missing this!

¶ After eight months of interviews, Peter found himself sitting in a dimly-lit office building in Scarborough monitoring an electric map of Toronto that lit up in red diodes when a street-light outage occurred. He flipped through an index, found the exact street name where the blackout had taken place and phoned in to repairs so that a truck went to the darkened street and fixed the failed lamps. Monotonous, sleep-inducing work; and, because the street lights were only ever on from dusk to dawn, Peter's shift was at night. Although, for the same amount of pay, in the summer his hours were shorter as the days grew long.

He had begun work with the Toronto Electric Street Lighting Company in mid-1960. "Don't take it, Pete." Lucy had said. "We can get by for a little longer." They had been lying in bed, Peter looking at her over the new bifocals they'd had to afford. Open books like tents on their chests. "This is it, Lu. This is what's out there. I've been applying everywhere I can think of for almost a year."

"We could move."

He shook his head.

"I wouldn't mind going somewhere new."

"As I've already told you Lucille, it's out of the question."

She sat up a little. She hated when he called her Lucille. "You could go back to school. You could become a professor."

Peter turned his book over in his lap and dog-eared the page he was on.

"Or Mother could come over again," Lucy offered reluctantly, "at least so I could work full time."

"For the love of God, Lu, it's embarrassing enough that you're working at all."

"Oh don't be so backward, Peter. Lots of women work."

"Unmarried women."

Lucy sighed.

Peter shut his book. "Look, just stop trying to solve the world's problems and actually listen to me for a moment."

She smoothed the bedspread.

"For now, no arguments. I'm taking the job with Toronto Electric and we'll think of it as temporary."

Eight months of interviews and the best they had was graveyard and temporary.

¶ When the nights were slow and hardly any diodes had lit up, Peter took out his sketchbook to draw. When he began drawing on the job in those first few months he had set objects in front of himself under a fluorescent desk lamp. A mug, a banana he'd forgotten from an earlier lunch with bruises over the skin. He'd once heard a woman at the grocery store call them "sugar spots." Sugar spots. What a bizarre euphemism, Peter had thought, for old banged-up fruit. When he'd drawn all of the objects in his office—and there weren't really all that many: a stapler, an empty filing cabinet, a handful of paper clips—he began to draw things from memory.

A time would come to him from the past; driving through the prairies once as a child with his uncle and remembering the bow of the wheat on either side of the road. They'd passed a split-rail fence and he saw, flickering between the posts like a film reel, a dead bull half-covered beneath a bleached canvas tarpaulin, the horns holding up the sheet like a tent, condensation collecting in rivulets and the shadows of flies swarming beneath the covering, crawling over the bull's head, his hide, his island-body in the sea of wheat. The first time Peter had seen something dead. He'd drawn that.

He'd drawn a chest of drawers he remembered of his mother's, and a gold cardboard box he'd found there with a matching gold scarf inside. It was one of the few luxurious items of clothing she had allowed herself. She wore it to the symphony once a year near Christmas, carefully folding it afterwards, still smelling of her perfume.

While Peter drew he sometimes thought of Robert. His jaunty hat with the quail feather and his laugh like a motor turning over. All of those airplane models they had set on fire. Working in the hangar at Avro didn't feel like a job now at all, it felt as if they'd been boys sent out to play (he pictured this like a dream: his mother dressed in the gold scarf instructing him from a pantry doorway, "Go out to play, Peter. Go out to play," and out back a huge field without any sign of a fence, and he and Robert standing there like children, pails and buckets, model airplanes, a red wagon with *Radio Flyer* written in white cursive along the side), whereas this night-work felt like a nightmare's cold sweat.

When Peter had first poured himself a coffee from the large industrial metal machine in the hall, and had poured milk into his cup, he recalled Robert's Noorduyn Aviation with its worn silhouette of the float plane.

The interviewers had felt sorry for Peter, he could tell. "Oh, the Arrow, such a shame that was. Out of nowhere too. And you with a young family," a secretary at Hydro had said to Peter on the phone, and had slipped him into the interviewing schedule, even though earlier she had said the interviews were all full. The new neighbours that had taken over the empty houses and lots on Cherry Terrace and Rhododendron Row would stop Peter in the grocers or at the gas pump and talk a blue streak about the shame of it all. Shame. That was the word most people used, the shame of it. But what did shame have to do with this? Peter wondered, as he sharpened his pencil, dusted the shavings into the wastepaper basket and began to draw a landscape he once remembered from a place far away from here.

He and Robert had met for breakfast a few times after the cancellation.

"Remember the day they flew her, Robert? God that was gorgeous. They couldn't have cancelled her if they'd seen her flown."

"I remember the mornings most."

"Yes, that quiet to the hangar."

A waitress with a pencil stuck into her black curls leaned over the counter and poured a fresh shot of coffee into their mugs.

"Excuse me for the poetics: but like the day is rolling out in front of us like our papers. Comprends-tu? Like each day there was a sheet of the nothing that we are given."

Robert had not found work. He was living off an inheritance left him by an aunt.

142

While Peter liked seeing his old friend at the diner counters of the Lakeview or the Senator, the reminiscing began to feel funereal amidst corned-beef hash and eggs over-easy, and with Peter's new work schedule breakfasts with Robert eventually stopped. He put off returning Robert's calls because he couldn't bear to describe the monotony of his new work. Eventually the time between the two men's visits stretched to months. Perhaps shame was the right word.

On this slow diode night Peter drew a landscape he'd passed on a train through the Rocky Mountains, working the mines along the Alberta-British-Columbia border the summer he'd turned sixteen, two years before his father died and Peter would leave for the war. He still remembered the shapes of the Rockies' peaks as the train flew by. "Coral," the man sitting across from him in the coach had said.

"I beg your pardon."

"Coral. On the tallest peaks are beds of oceanic coral."

This was something Peter did not know.

"It was pushed to the top when the earth's crust was formed. A slow pressure of things." The man slowly drew his hands together to form a triangle. "The oldest of ocean floors are on those peaks," the man said.

Peter drew what he had seen out the train window—Mount Rundle, Sulphur Mountain, Cascade—he drew his train-car view of the Rocky Mountains from his office that had no windows.

¶ Street-light work made Peter's body tender and watery. He felt as though there was water behind every joint, his kneecaps became the curved rudders of his carved wooden-boat legs. His arms were weighty bags of water that he had to carry home each morning, slung heavy through the sleeves of his sweater, the sleeves of his coat. His eyes felt as though he was underwater, rheumy, leaving the heavy steel office doors, walking toward the car, adjusting to the light rippling around him like he was a stone dropped into a lake of day and nothing could stay in focus. His legs ached as he got into the car, his hand ached as he turned on the radio, his arm ached as he slung it onto the empty passenger seat to look backward as he reversed the car out of his parking spot and began to navigate his bleary way back toward the house. His tongue even ached, the taste of stale coffee in his mouth acidic as a dissolving tablet of Aspirin.

At home, in the kitchen, the children had pinned a map of Toronto to the wall. Lucy would be scrambling his eggs for him, lowering the lever for the toast, heating up some milk on the stove so he could sleep through the afternoon. The children would be dressed in their school clothes. Even Rosie now, half a day at kindergarten, her sweet purple satchel for her crayons and snack. She could print her name and knew how to spell Mama, Dad, Andy, Kier and Love. Yesterday she'd drawn a picture for him and left it on the floor outside the closed bedroom door where he slept. *dAd*, her scrawl across the top of the page. A funny face with glasses and a shock of blue hair. His shirt had what looked like an elephant on it.

"Streets!" Rose shouted as Peter came in the kitchen door and put down his briefcase. All that was in Peter's briefcase was a bunched-up paper dinner bag and a sketchbook tied together with one of the boys' broken shoelaces. Only twenty minutes with them before they ran for the school bus.

Rose slipped off her booster seat and came over to Peter. He was crouched down untying his shoes. She wrapped her arms around his neck and kissed him on his cheek. "Bristly!"

"Sorry, sweetheart." He scooped her up in his watery arms.

Peter sat down in the nook with Rose on his lap and Lucy brought him the warm milk he'd imagined on the car ride home. He pulled a little white piece of paper from his breast pocket and smoothed it out on the shiny surface of the tabletop.

"Dorothy?" Kier asked, looking over his dad's shoulder. Kier was already as tall as Peter was, his arms and legs long and gangly. He knocked things over frequently these days because he wasn't used to his size. "Never heard of that one before."

"'Who rang that bell?' and behind the curtain the scarecrow and the tin man gets his heart," Rose explained to Peter from his lap.

The Wizard of Oz had played at the Rialto last week. Lucy had taken them to see it while Peter caught up on his sleep.

"McKenzie," Peter said. "Why don't you find us McKenzie, Ando?"

144

"I'm sick of this game," Andy said.

Peter watched as his son pushed around the egg on his plate.

"Kier?"

Kier stood at the map and scanned the legend with the list of street names.

"There's also a Martha."

Kier scoured the map.

"Hemlock."

"Dad, slow down," Andy said. "If you're going to make us do this at least give Kier enough time to find a single street."

"And the flying monkeys and the ruby slippers. I'll get you my pretty! Mwaa-ha-ha ha!" Rose cackled to herself.

Kier had made flags from coloured construction paper, Scotch tape and Lucy's mending pins. He tipped a few out of an old film canister into his palm and searched the map for the burnt-out streets. Lucy set down a plate of scrambled eggs and toast in front of Peter. From their flags the children and Peter had discovered that Clinton street went out particularly often. Eight flags. Andy loved this game. He'd been the one to put up the map. What had gotten into him? He'd been the one to notice that they were never to count a lamppost on Yonge Street. Peter had learned during his first week at the Lightning Company that, if hit hard at exactly the right height, this particular lamppost would turn off and then, twenty seconds later, turn itself back on again. When Peter had called it into the repair man, he'd laughed at him. "You must be new. When those university students let loose from the bars that lamp goes out ten, twenty times a night. "

Also taped to the kitchen wall beside the map was a set of guidelines Peter found in his desk drawer that the previous employee had left for him: *Street Type Designations*. Peter illicitly made a photostat to bring home.

1. Street type designations, depending on roadway function, length and configuration exist to define the character of a street. The following designations should be consulted:

STREET, AVENUE, ROAD, BOULEVARD: for major thorough-
    fares or streets of several blocks in length
DRIVE, TRAIL, WAY: for streets which are winding or
    curved
TERRACE, GARDENS, GROVE, PATHWAY, HEIGHTS: for minor
    or short streets
LANE, MEWS, CLOSE: for narrow streets generally used
    for service
CRESCENT: for streets which form a crescent
COURT, PLACE: for culs-de-sacs
CIRCLE: for streets that are circular
GATE: for a short street that provides an entrance to a
    subdivision
SQUARE: for streets that form part of a square

"Dorothy's a crescent," Kier said, looking at the latest street-light flags. "She's never burnt out."

"Ruby slippers," Rose said again, by way of explanation. She slid off Peter's lap and got her shoes on for kindergarten.

Peter kissed Rose on the top of her head and chucked the boys on the shoulder. When the kids were out the door, Peter walked up the stairs so he could fall asleep.

¶ Lucy watched the school bus pick her children up at the corner. She went to work, taking calls, transferring lines, wires and plugs in front of her that she unwound and webbed. Another performance of *Operator Lucille* to a house full of strangers she would never see. Or perhaps she would see, had seen, in lineups, shovelling walks, walking down the street. Her interactions each day with people were so brief and distant it was as if she was talking to phantoms. How could she be sure these people existed? Were the voices really attached to faces? She had stopped bothering to conjure an image of the people she spoke with. Voices. That's all she was connecting. A cacophony of voices perched like a flock of crows.

In the afternoon Lucy picked up Rose from kindergarten. They played together on the living-room floor. Dolls, Meccano, a made-up game Rose had come up with herself where Lucy was Alice in

Wonderland with a make-believe flamingo croquet mallet in hand, and Rose was a porcupine croquet ball that had to somersault and crawl through various circuitous routes of the living-room furniture. Then, when Rose stood up, that meant she wasn't a porcupine anymore, she was the Queen of Hearts and got to shout "Off with her head! Off with her head!" at Lucy, but not too loud, because Daddy was sleeping.

¶ At six o'clock in the evening, Peter stood, still wet and wrapped in his towel from the shower. He could smell chili cooking. He could smell Lucy's cornbread baking downstairs. He could already picture himself inside that tiny dark room with those red beady indicator lights indicating to him, constantly indicating to him.

TOASTERS &
LAKE CRUISING BOATS

S lam of the screen door, thump of shoes along the driveway pavement. "Don't forget to give the consent form ..." Lucy's voice trailing off like a kite. Between the broken slats of the neighbour's back gate and down the alleyway, ruts in the road, wild rhubarb just beginning to jut out from the fence lines. A diagonal through the uncut grass in the empty lot, still wet from morning. Kier in the lead, his backpack over his shoulders, a wavering sheet of study notes in his hand. Andy after him, looking backward to Rose, the grass almost up to her waist, her pink and orange striped gloves that Peter had bought her last Christmas flashing through the grasses as she ran faster and faster toward where the school bus would pull up next. Out onto Willow Drive, a collective breath, but the bus had already gone down the street, the yellow CAUTION: FREQUENT STOPS sign along the back, the tail pipe spewing its cloud of black exhaust. Kier leaning over his knees, trying to catch his breath. Andy skidding to a halt at the sight of it. Rose already turning around to walk back and beg Dad for a ride for the three of them.

¶ "Get in." Peter's lips tight across his face.

"Sorry," Rose said again.

"Dad, can you drop me off first?" Kier had to get to the high school which was the furthest away.

Peter grunted.

Kier wasn't sure whether that was a yes or a no.

The car was silent.

Peter looked in the rear-view mirror, "Andy, is your math home-work done?"

Andy sat in the back seat and stared out the window.

"Dad," Kier said again. "It's really important. I have a biology test first period."

"Andy, I'm speaking to you."

Andy looked at his father's eyes in the mirror. "As if you even have the right to ask me about my homework."

"I beg your pardon?"

"I said, as if you even have the right to ask me about my homework."

"I heard what you said."

"You aren't even around to know if it gets done or not. You aren't even around enough to know whether I've done my math home-work, or my English homework, or my French homework for that matter." He rolled and unrolled the window as he spoke. "I don't see why you get to ask. You wouldn't even have time to ask, except that we missed the school bus, so now here you are, concerned."

Peter's hands gripped the steering wheel tightly. The turn signal was on making an insistent clicking noise. "I work in a dark office every night so that you have the luxury of even *having* homework, Andrew. The secretary at work doesn't even know who I am because she has gone home before my shift begins." He looked at Andy again in the rear-view trying to get his attention. "You could be working in a soap factory, Andrew. You could be all alone working in a soap factory and no one would even ask you about quadratic equations." They were stopped at a street light, almost at the high school. "Quadratic equations are a luxury, Andrew."

"Daddy ..." Rose tried.

Peter went on. "You would be mixing lye and charcoal and toxic chemicals in a vat, and you wouldn't have gotten past your three times tables if it wasn't for me working in that goddamn office. Do you understand?"

Andy looked sullenly out his window.

"Can you even begin to comprehend the sacrifices I have made?"

Andy said nothing.

"That's it, Andrew. Out."

Both Kier and Rose looked at Peter. The middle school was at least eight blocks away. He would have to walk along the overpass.

"Andy, get out of the car."

¶ Peter had come in slamming the car keys onto the kitchen counter. Lucy had just gotten out of the shower for work. "You did what?"

"He has never spoken to me with that kind of disrespect."

"He's a teenager," Lucy said. She was quickly towelling her hair.

"I have never been spoken to so rudely."

Lucy shrugged. She wasn't sure what to say. Andy had a point. She looked at the clock on the bedside table. "Thank you for driving them."

Peter looked at Lucy standing naked in their bedroom, the towel flung over a chair, her hands on her hips as she chose what to wear. Not that long ago he would have pinned her down against the bed and she would have laughed and said, "I'll be late for work" and he would have kissed her and said, "call in sick." He would have rested his head on her naked belly and looked up at her while she held the bedside phone to her ear and made her voice sound scratchy for her boss, Janine. "I just woke up with it. Yes, like laryngitis." A pause, Peter would start kissing her pubic hair, her navel, moving up to her breasts, "Lemon and honey, yes, yes, thank you for that suggestion." She would push him away a little, trying to concentrate, "No, I won't get out of bed." But now he looked at her, undid his pants, and got beneath the covers alone. He watched her step into a yellow skirt, put her bra on, a camisole, a white shirt. He wouldn't attempt to masturbate after she left. Even for that he was too tired.

Lucy was blow-drying her hair at the bureau. "Don't forget that Monday is Rosie's fly-up," she shouted over the noise.

Peter had his eyes closed. He was pinching the bridge of his nose between his eyes. He had a headache coming on. "Yes. I know," he shouted back. "I've taken it off. You've only told me twenty times."

"I'll pick up some dolly squares. We're supposed to bring something."

"What is this ceremony again?"

"Rose gets her wings," Lucy shouted again, looking at Peter in the bureau mirror.

"What?"

"She gets wings."

"What does that mean?"

Lucy turned the hair dryer off. "She flies up to Girl Guides."

"This concept may be beyond me," Peter said and rolled onto his side.

"Did you remember to ask for Thursday too? The thirtieth?"

"I told you, Lu, not sure if I can make that one a go. Weston's been on about us trading nights."

"There's this new restaurant. Indian."

"I just said, Weston hasn't let me know. Couldn't we do it on a weekend?"

"Peter."

He looked up from the bed.

"It's our twentieth."

"I'll try. I've said I'll try."

"I've already booked a babysitter for Rose."

The phone rang downstairs. Lucy had to be at the bus in half an hour and she hadn't eaten breakfast. "That better not be about Andy," she went down the stairs. "Some sort of pedestrian accident on the highway," she shouted over her shoulder. She'd said it and then wished she hadn't.

"May I please speak to Mrs. Jacobs?"

Lucy pulled a coil of the phone chord taut in her hand. Oh god. Something *had* happened to Andy. "Speaking."

"This is Jeremiah Bulmer. Reverend Jeremiah Bulmer. From Saint Mary's Church."

"I beg your pardon?"

"I have been away from the parish on leave, and then there was a confusion of paperwork." Lucy could hear the faint click of the man's pen in the background. "My secretary had written the telephone message of your request down on the back of a typed sermon, for Palm Sunday, and we hadn't noticed the error until I was looking over some old notes." The pen clicking evenly like a metronome. "I know it's most unusual to return a call like this after so many years. The secretary did say you called. But ... well, I'd had to think deeply about what I was going to say to you. I had to determine God's will ..."

Lucy was confused. "Is this about Andrew?"

Jeremiah spoke again. "About the accident?"

"Oh my god, there's been an accident?" Lucy sat down in the nook.

"You were the one who phoned," the priest said, somewhat confused. "There was an accident a number of years ago? You called the secretary a number of years ago? I'm sorry ... you see I've been away and I wasn't quite sure how to respond."

So this wasn't about Andy? Lucy rested her head back against the vinyl seat. What *was* this man calling about? She glanced at the black cat clock on the kitchen wall. The tail ticked away the seconds. She realized she was almost late for work. "Look, I'm sorry, sir. I think you must have the wrong number." Lucy stood to put the receiver back on its cradle.

"Wait, Ma'am. I'm sorry if I've been unclear."

Lucy paused.

"An accident in a field? During a rain storm?"

Lucy stood in her stockinged feet with her breath held in. It wasn't about Andy. This was about her accident. This man was calling about her accident in the field.

"... at least that's what the secretary's note said?"

"Yes," Lucy managed to say.

"Look," a pause, "Maybe it'd be best if you could just tell me again what it is you're looking for," Jeremiah said more evenly.

Lucy sat down. She had called down to Saint Xavier in the telephone directory three separate times and found nothing. No response. This was the only priest in all of Toronto who had called her back in eight years. "Sorry. I'm sorry. The accident. It's just no one had called me ..." Lucy laughed inadvertently, nervously. "Look, it's such a long story."

"Well, I have as much time as you please, ma'am," he said, flat, calm. He had a slight Southern lilt, as though all of his words were soft, leaning slightly, like italics, like an afternoon shadow on a wall.

"I'm on my way to work." Lucy looked at the clock. She could bring a banana for breakfast. "I've got to get out the door in five minutes."

"Well," he said, "if now is not a good time, we could always grab a cup of coffee."

"I couldn't possibly," Lucy said. "After work I come home to pick up my daughter and then Peter, my husband, well, he goes to work an evening shift and I have to get him his dinner." She was babbling. This man didn't need to hear about dinner. She certainly didn't want to sound like she was complaining. "It's just I'm looking to find this priest that took a woman to the hospital. From an accident in a field." Lucy paused. "It was a long time ago. I hardly know if you could begin to help me."

"May I ask what it is that you are looking for, ma'am?" Jeremiah Bulmer said again.

"I just told you," Lucy said. "I'm looking to find that priest."

"But spiritually speaking ma'am. What is it you hope to find by finding that priest?"

Lucy sat silent, staring at her warped reflection in the kitchen table, holding onto the phone.

"Mrs. Jacobs, are you there?"

"I ... I ..." Lucy stammered, "Spiritually ... I don't know."

"Well, I'm not certain if I'll be able to help you find that particular man, I'm afraid. You seem to be doing all you can on that front. But if you would like to talk about your experience, I would be happy to assist you. We're located downtown. Across the street from Allen Gardens."

She knew the church. Red brick and small. They served sandwiches to homeless people out of a hatch at the side of the building. "I have to go to work now."

"Alright ma'am. I'd love it if you came down in person. I'll make as much time as you'd like in my schedule. And of course we have services every Sunday morning. Nine-thirty and eleven. I hope to see you here sometime."

"Okay then," Lucy said.

"Good luck," Jeremiah said.

"Okay," Lucy said again. "Goodbye." Lucy grabbed her purse and overcoat and ran for the bus. It wasn't until she was standing at the bus stop that Lucy realized she had forgotten to take the banana for breakfast. All day at work she was hungry.

B y the weekend Peter and Andy had made a truce over the quadratic equations argument, and Peter managed to convince the boys to come with him to a model and hobby store to look at trains for the old HO set. Rose sometimes still set the train up in looping contortions on the living-room carpet, lining up the various train cars, tiny metal passengers and mossy trees. Peter thought a new car might be right up her alley as a fly-up gift. If he caught her on the right day, when he wasn't sleeping and she wasn't at Brownies or swimming lessons, Peter and Rose sometimes walked down to the gully by the tracks and trainspotted together. Rose had a list of car numbers she checked off. They would go down the rail lines and sit silently, eat tuna fish sandwiches and carrot sticks that Lucy packed for them, and watch for car numbers as the trains clanked by on their way to the sidings. Peter was looking for a model Pioneer Zephyr Shovelnose Original. He'd been looking for the Shovelnose for a while, but during a particularly long night at work where he'd actually read through the telephone directory, he found a hobby store that he'd never been into before on the east side of Toronto, practically at the Beaches.

The shop was small and badly lit. It was dusty and smelled of old carpeting and faintly of cigarette smoke. There were model kits stacked to the ceiling. Trains along one wall: *The Orient Express* and *The Flying Scotsman* (the first train to boast a cinema and a hair salon), along with tiny cast-iron people waiting for loved ones or waving goodbye. Boats along another wall: *The Bluenose, The Cutty Sark, The HMS Victory*. Airplanes all along the wall behind the shopkeeper's head: *The Spruce Goose, The Wright Flyer I*, complete with figurined Wright Brothers, Orville and Wilbur.

The shopkeeper was helping another customer, and Peter stood with his back to him, hands at his hips, staring at the boxes of trains looking for the Zephyr Shovelnose. Kier was turning a squeaking magazine stand and Andy leaned against the glass counter, scanning the model airplane boxes. The door chimed as the other customer left and Peter could hear Andy asking, "Can I see that?" and the shopkeeper handing a box to Andy, "Look Dad, CF-105 Arrow."

"I had work on that plane," the shopkeeper said.

Peter turned around then at the sound of the man's voice. "Robert?"

Robert slid a pair of glasses down from the top of his head until they rested gently at the end of his nose. "Pierre?" Robert's hair had gone quite grey since Peter and he had last breakfasted over eggs and potato puffs at the Café Diplomatico. "Mon Dieu! These are your boys?" He looked at Andy and then at Kier. "They are grown."

Peter stepped toward the counter, reaching across to clasp Robert's hand.

"Pierre, what pleasure to see you."

"Toi aussi, mon ami."

"And see! Since we last meet, you 'ave even been practising the tu form."

¶ Peter had made calculations on the afternoons that he couldn't sleep after street lighting, when the furnace kept kicking on or when light skulked in through the blinds. He had calculated the dates during his last bout of insomnia. Gone over February, and that day, mid-month, when Robert and he had sat at the A.V. Roe booth at the Aviation Symposium with that blessed poster above their heads of the new postage stamp. A sky-blue five-cent stamp with the McCurdy Silver Dart of Baddeck, Nova Scotia, and three blue Arrows shooting straight up across the sky. A commemorative stamp for the fiftieth anniversary of powered flight in Canada: February 23, 1959.

Canada Post had released the stamp in anticipation of the celebrations and there were those sky-blue posters up all over the walls of that Symposium. Peter remembers feeling proud about it all back then. But at the anniversary ceremony in Ottawa, on February 23, Diefenbaker made no mention of the CF-105 Arrow. In subsequent interviews, representatives of Canada Post denied that the image on their commemorative stamp was the Arrow at all.

But Peter knew those wings. The sleek white deltas rocketed across the country on the envelopes of love letters, business contracts, birth announcements, condolence cards. The Arrows flew more as postage than they did as planes. And this is what Peter had wanted to talk about with Robert over the years: the barefaced inelegance of the dates. Thursday February 19, 1959: last flight of the Arrow, model RL 201. Friday February 20: Black Friday, most of Malton without a job. Monday February 23: the fiftieth anniversary celebrations of Canadian powered flight, just three days after the layoffs and no mention by Diefenbaker about what he'd done, calling in the ground military to keep out the Air Force while they blowtorched, bulldozed and wrecking-balled the planes; selling the metal to a Hamilton scrapyard for six and a half cents per pound.

"Know what Avro's up to now, don't you, Robert?"

"What is that, Pierre?"

"Twenty-sixth largest producer of toasters and lake-cruising boats."

And there it was again in the room. Robert's perfect wheezing laugh.

Peter chuckled. "Twenty-sixth for god's sake." He slapped his hand against the counter. "I mean, for crying out loud ..." Peter clutched his stomach. He looked up toward Robert, "... even Andy could make a toaster."

Robert had tears in his eyes and a huge grin on his face. "Les enfants could faire the toasters."

They were doubled over laughing, both men leaning against the glass-topped counter for support.

Kier and Andy just stared.

¶ "I must show you something." Robert turned the lock on the front door of his shop and put a sign in the door, BACK IN FIVE MINUTES / JE REVIENS DANS CINQUE MINUTES. He led Peter, Kier and Andy into the back of the shop. They passed through a thick flannel curtain made of old Mighty Mouse bedsheets into a storeroom. There were more boxes of models stacked to the ceiling and a small table with a Thermos and a bowl of Robert's half-eaten lunch of beef stew. Various model parts, tiny tools, and bottles of glue and paint were spread out on workbenches. At the very back of the room next to two steel roll-up loading doors was a shape slightly larger than a Volkswagen Beetle. What appeared to be a sports car, or a large mechanical engine, resting on top of three sawhorses. It was covered over in another bedsheet, this one delicate floral. Robert gestured Peter and the boys toward the back doors. When they stood around the strange commanding shape, Robert tugged the sheet off, and there, standing before them, was the nose of one of the Arrows.

"How did you ...? What ..." Peter couldn't speak.

"We secreted it."

"I can't believe ..."

Robert moved to his workbench and took a hacksaw off a hook on the wall and returned to the remains of the plane. At the back of the pointed hulk of metal was a melted seam from the flames of the blowtorches. The torch cut had severed the nose behind the cockpit. This one was white. It hadn't even been painted in its Maple Red topcoat. White primer on the nose along with the model number, 206, and then black where the radar equipment was housed. Robert took the front nose needle and with swift sure movements he began to saw. "Don't," Peter said. "Stop. What are you ...?" Robert's arm moved back and forth with force until the metal point extending out from the radar nose broke off in his hand.

"Here." Robert held out the piece of metal. "I want your boys to have this," he said, and gave it to Andy, who was standing closest. Kier came and stood behind his brother. Peter stood beside the boys and they all looked down at the slip of metal that looked a little like a stolen car antenna in Andy's hand.

"B ut the Converse sneakers are new."

"You are supposed to wear dress shoes, Rose Ella."

Peter awoke to Rose and Lucy arguing from the bathroom.

"These *are* dress shoes. They're red. That's dressy."

"Rose. This is the only time you will ever fly up from Brownies to Girl Guides. Do you want to fly up all alone in red shoes, or nice black shoes like the other little girls?"

"Red."

Peter walked into the hall wearing his robe.

Lucy stood at the bathroom mirror. She was braiding Rose's hair into two French braids.

"Mama, that hurts."

"What's going on here?" Peter asked.

Lucy looked at him. "The fly-up, remember?"

"I remember," Peter said.

"Dinner is taco-bake."

Peter went back to the bedroom and knelt down on the floor by the bed. He pulled out the Zephyr Shovelnose Original that Robert also had tucked away in the back room of his shop. He rested his cheek against the bedroom floor and raked his arm in an arc beneath the bed until he pulled out a roll of birthday wrapping. It would do. Peter went downstairs and got shears and scotch tape from the junk drawer in the kitchen. On the wrapped present he put a card. *Congratulations, Rose, on your fly-up. We are so proud of your wings.— Love, Dad, Kier and Andy.*

¶ Rose was the only girl without patent dress shoes on. She couldn't pretend to tap dance on the gymnasium floor, but she could climb the trees in the front yard during the picnic afterward and the other girls weren't allowed because they'd get scuffs.

"Do you promise to do your best, to do your duty to God, the Queen and the country, and to help other people every day, especially those at home?" The lanky lady Commissioner asked Rose from way above her, all the while giving her the Girl Guide handshake— shaking with the wrong hand and holding up her regular-shaking hand with three fingers pointing up like a trident. She looked like a bluebell on a stalk, her long stockinged legs and then everything else about her blue. She even had a blue beret blossoming on her hair. "I do," Rose said solemnly.

Peter, Kier, and Andy—the boys had been made to come too— stood awkwardly against a wall of the gym surrounded by little girls in brown uniforms. It was straight out of *Gulliver's Travels*: the three men had travelled for months on a ship with no sight of land, and now found themselves suddenly in the company of a previously undiscovered tribespeople with their own unique language, rituals and games. A group of six who called themselves the gnomes kept looking over at Kier and Andy and giggling.

"Twit twit twoo!"

Kier jumped.

The entire gaggle of girls screamed and leapt up high in the air in their matching brown knee socks, clapping their hands above their heads.

"What the hell was that?" Kier asked under his breath.

"Just wait, I've been told there will be skipping," Peter said, and sure enough each group of six girls, including the gnome group, joined hands and skipped around the rest of the pack. "We're the Brownies, here's our aim, lend a hand and play the game."

The Jacobs men tried to make themselves as inconspicuous as possible, and moved in a little huddle into the circle of the basketball key on the gym floor while Lucy leaned in close to the skipping girls to take photos. Andy stood slightly shorter next to Kier, whose limbs had become gangly in that teenage-boy kind of way. Andy wore a red plaid lumberman's hat of Peter's that was generally kept hung on a nail in the garage for when Peter raked leaves from the lawn, and now Andy's wavy hair stuck out from beneath the brim, almost in his eyes. The hat's fur-lined ear-flaps were worn, and it smelled faintly as if it were mouldering. But when Peter had asked Andy why he'd taken to wearing it, he'd just said, "It's cool, Dad." Peter knew cool, but could not figure out the mouldering hunter's cap's appeal. And then there was Kier wearing those strange pants all the kids had on these days. Bell-bottoms they were called, Peter knew. And his hair growing long at the ears with sideburns, his shoulders stooped as if protesting his new height. Peter had read an article in *National Geographic* about the new social culture of the "teenager in America" but he swore Lucy and he were never as strange or difficult as the children he'd produced. When he was Kier's age he'd fought with his father about going to war, for Chrissakes. Not whether he could have money to sign up for guitar lessons out of some café down on Yorkville. But then there was Rose and her sparkling green eyes. The freckled slope of her nose, just like her mother's. Rose was the tallest girl in the Brownie troupe, and so proper-looking in her neat brown uniform. At least if the boys refused to amount to anything, Rose would. Peter could see it in the determined set of her eight-year-old smile.

When all the girls had "flown up"—a pair of cardboard wings decorated with sequins and gossamer tulle strapped to their backs, and a shiny set of brass wings pinned to their collars by their scarves—each one ran toward her family for photographs before the picnic began.

"Way to go, Rosie," Andy said encouragingly.

"Groovy new pin, girl," Kier said.

"So proud of you." Peter gave her a hug around the shoulders and gave Rose the present. "From me and the boys."

Rose ripped open the wrapping paper to reveal the Shovelnose. "Awesome, Dad," she said and then handed the train car and the tattered wrapping back to him. "Guess what? In Girl Guides there's camping in real tents, not just in cabins, and we learn knots, and what berries to eat, and which way north is because of how moss grows, and how to make pineapple upside-down cake in a rinsed-out tuna can." And then she was off again playing tag with some gnomes.

"That wasn't much of a hit, was it?"

"How can you compete with all this?" Kier gestured toward a red and white wooden toadstool sitting on a circle of green felt.

Peter shrugged.

"It was more a present for you anyway, wasn't it." Andy said.

Peter wondered if Rose would notice if he opened the packaging.

"No, but seriously," Kier asked "what just happened here? What does Twit-twit mean? What is with the circle-dancing?"

"I've no idea," Peter said.

Peter and Lucy sat across from each other at the *The Great Taj Mahal of Agra Indian Restaurant* three days after their twentieth wedding anniversary. The restaurant was lit by hanging candelabras and tiny lanterns on each table. It smelled of beeswax and butter chicken. Their table was at the back of the restaurant overlooking a small garden planted with both real and plastic flowers and a three-foot plaster mosaic replica of the Taj Mahal.

"Is there mini golf?" Peter asked as they sat down.

"Pete. It's their garden."

Plastic coloured lanterns hung outside on strings but hadn't been plugged in.

Lucy wore a dress that Peter remembered seeing her wear before, but not for a number of years; turquoise with a high mandarin collar that hid her scars and small black buttons up the front. She'd worn it at one of the Avro parties in the A.V. Roe Clubhouse a few months after her mother had been to visit. Crawford Gordon had made an appearance, dancing with everyone's wife, keeping the band going until they finally had to pack up and leave for another gig. Lucy kept smiling at Peter over Gordon's shoulder. Peter sat with Robert at the bar, half-heartedly drinking a beer and talking about the Fibonacci sequence. Peter had wanted to cut in, but felt he couldn't. Gordon was his boss and Peter hadn't ever learned how to dance.

"This isn't even in English," Peter looked down at the menu over his bifocals.

"Neither are menus in French restaurants," Lucy pointed out.

"I don't like French restaurants."

Lucy looked at Peter across the table. He was scanning the menu irritably. He had dark circles under his eyes and she knew that when they got home that evening he would fall asleep in an armchair reading the newspaper and she'd have to wake him and remind him to come upstairs to bed. Lucy had held great hopes for *The Great Taj Mahal of Agra Indian Restaurant*. The flyer that had come in the mail boasted exotic spices and sensual flavours. She'd even gone to Eaton's on her lunch break for a new dress that might go with the cuisine, something Peter would notice.

"This one's from Paris." The fashionable clerk had picked out a silk number. Four squares of yellow and white that hung off the hanger like a bell. "Very chic with a pair of sheer stockings."

"Very short," Lucy replied.

She'd tried on three dresses in the change room but had put them back on the racks. They needed to save their money. They'd started to put away for a college fund. Perhaps she wasn't ready to look exotic. And then Peter had said to her as they were leaving the house,

162

"you look good tonight," matter-of-factly, almost coldly, so she supposed she was glad that she hadn't spent the money.

"They have curry," she said, "with prawns."

"I can read the descriptions, Lucille. The descriptions are in English."

Lucy looked out again at the miniature Taj. The menu told the story of the building. "Set in formal gardens, the spectacular white marble mausoleum built by the Mogul Emperor Shah Jahan in memory of his favourite wife is reflected in a calm pool flanked by cypress." The cypress in the restaurant's replica garden were plastic house plants and the pool was a large roasting pan that someone had sprayed with blue paint.

"Do you think the Tandoori Chicken is sort of like Tex-Mex barbeque?"

A mausoleum. The Taj Mahal was a mausoleum. Lucy had always imagined it as a palace. A place where Indian princesses whispered behind colourful scarves and chased each other in pointed slippers around ornamental hedges. It was the poor lady's grave. And not the grave of the Mogul Emperor Shah Jahan's only wife either, simply his favourite one. Lucy spoke. "The priest called the other day, Peter."

Peter looked up over the top of the menu at her. He looked down again. "I think I'm going with this Tandoori."

"I don't know if it's the priest that found me after the accident, but he sounded reassuring somehow."

"I figure you can't do much wrong to chicken." He straightened his knife and fork. "And what about this Naan? It is listed under the heading of Bread. Is it meant to be like a dinner roll?"

"His name is Jeremiah."

"I beg your pardon?"

"Jeremiah. That's the priest's name."

Peter didn't say anything.

"And the whole way to work on the bus after speaking with him, I looked out the window."

Lucy could see that Peter's gaze rested slightly beyond her face, as if a painting on the wall of the restaurant behind her was crooked.

"There was this song playing in my mind as the city came into view. The Royal York. The harbour. All the people rushing on the sidewalks. I kept hearing Louis Armstrong's *West End Blues*. Do you remember that one, Peter? The record Claire gave to Kier and Andy."

Peter didn't respond. Lucy wasn't even sure if he had heard her.

"I didn't know what to do that morning. I was hungry. I had forgotten breakfast. There'd been that moment with the kids in the car, Andy on the side of the road, and everything felt tilted somehow. And then the song came, and it was like the entire city was moving to Louis Armstrong's horn." Lucy pressed her fingertip into the wax of the candle on their table. "And I started to pray. Well at least I think it was praying. Meditating? Quietly, you know. I didn't say anything out loud on the bus, but I started thinking of things, looking out the window."

"That's enough, Lu. I don't want to talk about this priest anymore." Peter didn't change his expression or shift his gaze back to Lucy. She looked directly at him, but his gaze pierced at something beyond her.

"I just thought of things at first. Oranges. The taste of oranges. The waxed tips of my father's moustache. Irises. Those silver buckles on Rose's overalls. Dandelions. How everyone thinks they're weeds, except children. The satisfying shuuck of opening the lid on a jar of crabapple jelly made the autumn before. The colour of one red umbrella I once saw amongst all the black ones walking down Bay Street." Lucy tested the seal of wax on her finger to see if it had hardened. "Then I thought of the men, like you, who still haven't found good work since the Arrow. I thought about our children. Our marriage." Lucy peeled the soft wax and inside was her fingerprint. "Connie Romano and her smoky laugh. How we only keep in touch with the old neighbours at Christmas. Cards filled with photos of children growing up. And, before that, all those young families that lived on College with us after the war. The window across the alleyway with all those boys. I thought of the colour of cantaloupe melons. And Claire. Who I miss, even though I feel like she abandoned me. But then, maybe I abandoned her." Lucy rolled the wax between her fingers and her fingerprint disappeared. "I thought about Laika." Lucy looked up at Peter across the table. "And it hurt. Like not being home in a long while."

"Please stop."

The waiter came by. "Can I get you two a drink to start?"

"I'll have a whiskey." Peter looked at Lucy. She looked up at the waiter.

"I'll be fine with water. Maybe wine with dinner?"

"You can take our dinner order too," Peter said. "Chicken." He pointed at the item on the menu. "Tandoori Chicken."

Lucy hadn't decided yet. "The prawns?" Lucy paused and looked quickly over the menu, "with saffron rice. Do you have a garden salad?"

"Vinaigrette?" And then the waiter was gone, and no one had ordered the wine and Peter looked down at the table setting and played with the edge of his cloth napkin and said nothing.

Lucy looked at him. She looked long and hard at the top of his head where the grey hairs were beginning to come in. She looked at his hands, how old they looked, how different from the hands that touched her when they were first married twenty years ago, the hands that held out a cup of punch for her in the stuffy basement of Saint James' church. And his forehead, irreversible creases formed across the smooth palate of his face. She looked at how he breathed as if every breath was a sigh. She looked at his shoulders sloping down in defeat. We are one of those couples who sit and say nothing, Lucy thought. She held her gaze, looked at him looking away from her. His whiskey came. She sipped her water.

When Lucy had seen Andy shaving at the sink in the upstairs bathroom, she decided about the camping trip. Kier would be starting college in the fall. Rose was moving up to middle school. The sign of Andy holding taut the tender skin of his neck, the upward glide of the razor, the shlook of shaving foam into the sink, caused a clenched pain of attachment in Lucy's throat. They would all leave her, she thought, and we haven't even gone camping.

"We could go somewhere in Algonquin, take the car up," Lucy

brought two blueberry scones and the percolator of coffee to the table. "It'll only take us a day to get there."

Peter had spread out newspapers on the tabletop of the nook. On the newspapers he had spread out the internal parts of the transistor radio. The red plastic shell of the radio lay discarded on its side like a garment, like how the wolf might untie Little Red Riding Hood's cloak and fling it over the back of granny's rocking chair before setting about to devour her.

"Rose is big enough to handle paddling. She could go in a canoe with you. I think they may have even paddled at Girl Guide camp."

Peter pulled at a round speaker to reveal a tangle of wires.

"That's something she'll remember. Canoeing with her dad in Algonquin Park."

"Now why would they have attached the speaker in such an illogical configuration to the chassis? I'm either going to have to unsolder these speaker wires or remove the speaker completely with a hex nut driver. Who was on that committee at ..." Peter turned over the hulk of radio. "... General Electric?"

"I was thinking the first week of August. Can you book it off?"

"What?"

"The first week of August."

"The first week of August what?"

"Can you book it off work?"

"I suppose. What is it that we're doing?"

"Going canoeing."

"Where?"

"In Algonquin Park."

Peter poured himself some coffee into his empty cup. "Do we have a canoe?"

¶ Lucy watched out of the passenger window of the Fairlane as Peter and Andy tied the borrowed canoes onto the roof with a blue plastic cord. Would two even fit? Lucy rolled down her window. "Are the gunnels too wide, Pete?"

"It'll be fine, Mum," Andy said, whipping a length of cord in an arc across the roof of the car.

166

"We'll tie them down through the frames of the windows at the back," Peter instructed.

"Did you hear your father? Roll the windows down, you two," Lucy told Kier and Rose in the back seat.

Kier had dug out an old Etch-A-Sketch from the basement and was drawing Rose's portrait in tiny magnetic filigree lines. Rose read a Nancy Drew. Andy stood on the pavement of the driveway with the end of the blue cord in his hand.

"But Dad, if we tie 'em down through the windows we won't be able to get out the back doors," Andy pointed out.

"Climb through on your mother's side."

"Where are we going again?" Kier asked to the front seat.

"Algonquin Park," Lucy said, turning around to face him. She was looking over the road map. "You'll love it. I went once with my father when I was a little girl. He could mimic the call of loons."

¶ Rose was sick an hour into the trip. Peter had to pull over the car. Lucy unbuckled herself from the front seat so Rose could climb through. Peter flicked on the hazards. Lucy held Rose's hair while she leaned over some ragweed at the side of the road. When she'd climbed back in Kier gave her a stick of Wrigley's Doublemint and Andy switched spots with her so that she was by the window and could look out. Rose didn't read any more of her Nancy Drew while they drove.

The Fairlane pulled through the gates of the park around four in the afternoon. The ranger directed them to their launch point on the west side of Canoe Lake. Peter drove in on the main road past Whiskey Rapids, a sign for Hardwood Lookout Trail, and the portage store.

They loaded up the two canoes with all the camping equipment: backpacks, tents, cooking pots, a Coleman stove and lantern, a cooler and a duffle bag of food.

"Lu, what are you expecting us to do with this?" Peter held up a heavy rectangular box.

Lucy had packed the croquet set. "I thought it might be fun at the campsite."

"Hon, we'll be right on the lake. Probably at an angle. I don't know if croquet is the best idea."

"Fine. I just thought it would make a good activity, that's all."

"We'll leave it in the trunk, okay?"

¶ After the supplies were loaded, Lucy and Rose climbed into a canoe. Lucy sat straight in the bow eagerly looking forward over the lake. Rose nestled into the bottom of the boat with the provisions. Kier checked that the car doors were locked and pushed the boat forward, hopping into the back. Andy and Peter were a little ways off shore perfecting their strokes.

"Andy, you keep veering us off course." Peter turned around to face the stern of their canoe. "You have to pick a point on the horizon and stick to it. Otherwise it's going to take us hours to get there."

"Dad, I *am* aiming at a point on the horizon. That white dot."

"Then why is our wake all zigzagged. Look out behind you there at those zigzags."

"Does it really matter if we go in an exact straight line?"

"We can switch whenever you want, Andrew. Just so you know, we can switch."

¶ Rose read *The Message in the Hollow Oak* while Kier and Lucy paddled. She occasionally looked up from her book to the shore they were approaching. Her thoughts drifted from her mystery to the shoreline. Rose held the book open in her lap, her hand pressing along the spine to stop the pages flapping in the wind off the lake. At first she pretended she was Pocahontas. Then she pretended that she was Nancy Drew solving a mystery for Pocahontas.

Was that a light blinking from shore? It must be a signal. Two long. One short. Rose counted the patterns of the blinking lights by tapping them out on the gunnel of the canoe. Long long short short. Morse code! What was A again? Short then long, wasn't it? She knew that question mark was short short long long short short.

"Rose, keep your hands in. I'm going to hit you with my paddle," Kier said from the stern.

Rose pulled in her hand. She tapped out the code on her knee. Maybe it was Captain Samuel Argall. He was giving his ransom.

"Give us. The arms. You have stolen. Give us. The English prisoners. Give us. Corn."

Rose knew that they needed to get to shore quickly. Pocahontas was in grave danger. Japazaws would surely have tied her up by now. Maybe they were going to burn her at the stake. Pocahontas' father was counting on her to bring his daughter home. Powhatan, that brave Algonquian chief, had tears in his eyes as he told of the kidnapping. "Please Nancy Drew, you must help get my daughter back. I think they've taken her to the shores of Petawawa." Rose wasn't actually sure where Petawawa was, but she'd seen a sign for it on the side of the highway. "Don't worry Powhatan, I'll have your beautiful daughter back in your hands as soon as I can."

They were almost at the shore. Rose looked across the horizon of trees to see if she could catch any more Morse code before they disembarked.

¶ Lucy and Peter pulled the canoes up to shore, emptied all of the backpacks and equipment onto a sandy patch of beach and turned the canoes over onto some boulders at the water's edge. As soon as they had readied the equipment to carry up to their campsite, the stove tied onto Kier's backpack, Rose carrying the lantern out in front of her like a Victorian heroine, it began to rain. It was a drizzle at first. Then the drops became louder and louder on the sheet of lake behind them. By the time they got the gear from the canoes to the campsite almost everything was soaked.

"Okay, Ando. You help me set up the tents." Peter unfurled a sheet of canvas.

"I don't want to help you set up the tents."

"Don't talk back to me."

"Don't talk to him like that Peter, he's almost a grown man."

"Mum, don't call me a grown man, okay? It sounds weird."

"Look." Peter began putting the tent poles up. "I'm just trying to get everything together as soon as possible so we can stay dry."

"I'll look for some dry wood." Kier said, slung his backpack to the ground under a tree and took off into the bush.

"What can I do?" Rose asked.

"So helpful, Rosie. Thank you." Lucy said. "Why don't you and

Andy hang this food bag in the trees after I've taken out the dinner stuff." Lucy unzipped the duffel bag and set a package of squished hotdog buns onto a log by the unlit fire grate. She opened the cooler and took out a tiny yellow squeeze bottle of mustard and a matching red squeeze bottle of ketchup along with a package of wieners, a container of ranch dip, a bag of ripple potato chips and a Ziploc of celery and carrot sticks. "Dad and I can do the tents."

The rain didn't let up.

Rose and Andy tied the duffel to a cedar tree but both of them got splinters from the bark. They tried to bite out the pieces of wood from their fingertips as they sat around the still unlit fire grate. Kier came back to the site with an armful of wood. Andy noticed that his brother's hair smelled faintly of marijuana. Peter made tiny teepees of wood around a damp piece of newspaper. Lucy tried to screw the gas tank into the Coleman stove and finally asked Kier to do it. It took him a long time to figure out which way was 'open' to let the gas through. "Open," he said. "That's the thing, we're all just so closed."

Eventually they ate their hot dogs. The kids huddled beneath a plastic red and white checked tablecloth, rivulets of rainwater collecting in the folds. Lucy pointed into the dimming forest around them and named trees. "That one's a white spruce," she said. "The white spruce is found all over Canada. From Newfoundland to the Rocky Mountains." She turned to look at a different part of the forest, her left hand holding the hood of her raincoat, her right hand holding her hot dog. "Oh look! A trembling aspen! Most people mistake those for a white birch, but their bark isn't as papery. If you see a trembling aspen it means there's been a major disturbance. Like a fire or a windstorm." She held her gaze at the tree. "But aren't they pretty?"

After cups of weak, powdery hot chocolate, fresh mosquito bites and Lucy expounding on the beauty of the balsam fir, sugar maple and Jack pine, everyone went to bed. All three kids in the biggest tent, Peter and Lucy in another.

"Mama, what time is it?" Rose asked from her sleeping bag, her shoulder pressed into one wet side of the canvas, her brothers on the other side of her.

Lucy looked at her wristwatch with her flashlight. It read 7:30 p.m. "Ten" she said.

¶ "This coffee is terrible."

Lucy looked up at Peter from where she stood with one leg on a thick birch branch that she'd placed over one of the log benches by the fire. She was trying to break the branch down for firewood. The sun had come up the next morning and things were starting to dry out a bit. "I beg your pardon?"

"The coffee. It tastes terrible."

Lucy held onto the birch and stared at Peter. "When, over the last twenty years, have you made yourself a cup of coffee?"

"I make myself coffee all the time. At work. And I can tell you that it tastes nothing like this."

"We're camping!" Lucy shouted at Peter. "The coffee will not taste as good!" She stomped down on the piece of wood with a snap.

Kier, Andy and Rose all sat together along the log farthest from their parents. Lucy had given them Tupperware bowls of instant oatmeal and tinned peaches when they had stepped out of their tent. The plastic bowls sat untouched in their hands. Cereal slowly congealed around their spoons. They were all still groggy from sleep interrupted by chipmunk chirrups and bird calls. Rose watched as her mother and father screamed at each other over the fire grate. Against her legs she felt the clammy weight of her damp jeans.

"Maybe if you'd stop worrying so much about activities and food and what sort of tree this is and what sort of tree that is."

"I care about what trees are called!"

"Maybe if we had thought to bring some more tarps this would be going a lot more smoothly."

"I care that my children know what trees are called. It's sad they don't know what a trembling aspen is. I bet they couldn't tell a conifer from a deciduous."

Andy looked at Rose.

"Conifers are evergreens," she said.

"Right." Andy moved his spoon around in his porridge. A mosquito was caught in the peachy sludge.

"It is so sad that we have spent our entire lives in the city. Not even a city, where there would be a little culture, but the suburbs, where there's nothing. We have to drive the car for five hours just to find a beaver dam." Lucy bundled herself in the sleeves of her raincoat and faced away from her family toward the lake. Why was Peter being so difficult? Why couldn't this be just one singularly good day? This was why she'd dragged them all out here in the first place. To drift a little, away from their lives.

"Maybe if our sleeping bags were a little less drenched we wouldn't be having this conversation," Peter added.

Lucy turned to face Peter. "No, Pete. You're wrong." She was so sick of his voice. She had been wanting him to speak to her more, to end his moping silences around the house, but now here he was, speaking, and all she wanted was for him to stop.

"Oh tell me! Tell me where I'm wrong!"

"You're wrong because it isn't the sleeping bags that are the problem." She let her arms hang down, weary of the argument. She lowered her voice so that it came out in a straight thin line. "The mosquitoes and the black flies and the fact that you forgot the fly for our tent and wouldn't let me bring the croquet set, none of these things are the problem," Lucy paused. "It's your attitude, Peter. Your attitude is the problem."

"Oh, come on, Lucille."

"Your attitude has been terrible for a long time."

"I'm just trying to talk about coffee here."

"Oh just shut up. You'd still be mad about something even if I'd somehow made you Italian espresso in the middle of the bush." Lucy sighed. "You've been an asshole since you lost your job, Pete." There. She'd said it.

Kier, Rose and Andy looked at each other. Asshole. Had their mother really just said asshole?

Peter picked up a rock and walked toward the canoes. He threw the rock in the water. It landed closer to shore than he'd wanted it to. Not even a satisfying splash. He had two weeks off for the entire year, and this week was one of them. This week was all he had before he had to crawl back into that dark office and hang on for another six months. "Please stop, Lucille," he said, looking out at the lake. "Please just stop."

Lucy picked up the birch branch she had broken in half and threw it onto the fire. Sparks flew up. She picked up the aluminium percolator and poured out all of the coffee onto a bush.

¶ The thing about Pocahontas, Rose realized on the canoe trip home, was what did Captain John Smith ever do for her? He didn't even send her a letter telling her he was alive. She had no idea that her dear friend hadn't been murdered or frozen to death during a harsh winter until after she'd arrived in England herself, after being rescued from kidnappers. After she had married another English guy, John Rolfe, who made her convert to Christianity and have children. Pocahontas met the King of England before Captain Smith happened to run into her at a party in London. He didn't even send her a postcard saying, "Dear Pocahontas, I suspect you might think I'm dead. And I suspect you might have been in love with me. I am well. I am living in England. Please come visit. I will send a royal ship and you can live in a palace and sleep on soft sheets and eat grapes and I will teach you what cardamom is and cinnamon."

The lake was placid after the weekend storms. Rose paddled with Peter at the stern, reaching her arm out in front of her, scooping the water and watching as it made little swirls. Peter was silent in the back of the boat. He didn't say a thing to correct Rose's stroke. Only at one point did he say, "Rosie. Look." And out in front of them, flying in tandem, were two rare harlequin ducks, beating their wings fiercely, a trail of water falling behind them as they flew toward the sky from the lake.

INTO THAT GOOD NIGHT

Andy leaned against the counter of the donut shop. The pattern of raindrops splattering above the painted Go Nuts sign looked a little like coconut sprinkles against chocolate frosting. He had got the job at Go Nuts Donuts two weeks after his high-school graduation and already he recognized the regulars. The man who sometimes held out his spoon and talked to it. "Whatcha got there?" Andy had once asked the man while he wiped down tables. "A flea," the man said, and held the spoon toward Andy for inspection.

There was a woman who came in every afternoon wearing an elaborate floral scarf wrapped around her head like a turban. She carried a large purse and an Easter basket planted with fake pink flowers and moss. She ordered one cup of Earl Grey tea each visit and asked for more hot water until her tea bag ran clear.

"Is she a fortune teller or something?" Andy asked the dark-haired girl he worked with. He had seen the woman laying cards down on the tabletop of her corner booth. No one sat down across the table from her.

"Let me tell you about her later," his co-worker said. "After she's left."

Andy couldn't remember the girl's name. Mary something. Mary-Beth? Mary-Eve? The next time the girl came by, mopping up a spilled carafe of coffee, coloured donut sprinkles streaked through the tendrils of the mop, he looked at her name tag: Maryanne. When Maryanne's bangs fell into her eyes she blew them out of the way and Andy watched the pink pout of her lips as she did this. He had noticed earlier that week that her lip gloss smelled like mint and cherries.

Andy went through the swinging doors into the back of the shop. He stood at a counter across from the Hobart dishwasher and the deep-fry vats. He took donuts drying on the dip-tray and carefully lined them up in rows on waxed paper in the silver display baskets. He had just finished chocolate dips and was on to maple. "She has a tumour."

Andy jumped. Maryanne had come up right behind him and he hadn't noticed. "What?"

"The lady. Her name's Alma. She has a brain tumour. That's why she wears those scarves."

"Oh." Andy said.

"She plays solitaire. They aren't tarot cards."

"I didn't know."

"It's grown since I've worked here. It's gotten bigger and bigger and she uses more scarves to wrap. She used to be a dance instructor." The metal bell on the counter dinged and Maryanne turned back through the kitchen doors to help a customer. Maryanne's dark hair swung in a long ponytail down her back. She wore a yellow t-shirt that rose a bit above her belted corduroy pants and the tie of Maryanne's apron pressed against her skin.

¶ Kier and Ricky Amery flipped through records downtown in *Sam the Record Man*. Ricky was a friend Kier had met in his first year of college. They'd ended up in three of the same classes together and were lab partners in Chemistry. They both pretended they weren't interested in school even though they competed for the highest marks in the class. "We're drifters, man," Ricky had said to Kier one afternoon when they'd skipped Ancient Civilizations to grab a burger. Kier nodded in agreement, but was thinking about the lecture they'd missed. He'd wanted to hear Professor Kostalis' discussion of Attic urns and forgotten it was that afternoon. Ricky, Kier had noticed, never missed Calculus with Dr. Bornstein. When they skipped class Ricky did a lot of talking about how his band was going to be noticed outside of their garage gigs and how he was thinking of moving to the Bronx.

Kier was in *Sam the Record Man* because he was looking for the new James Brown *Sex Machine* LP. Ricky was wandering around the aisles just flipping the records, not really looking at anything, holding *The Grateful Dead* under his arm.

"Hey man, what are you doing tonight?" Ricky said over the rows of records. "Cause I got these hits." Rick stuck out his tongue at Kier.

Kier looked at him across the records. "What?"

"You know, tabs." Ricky waited until a sales clerk went by. "LSD."

"Oh yeah. Sure." Kier pulled out a Bob Dylan album and tried to look casual. He scanned the tracks and put it back again. He'd never done acid before. Pot he smoked all the time. He'd done shrooms once with his friend Penny whom he'd known since elementary school and they'd spent the night on the swing set in the park sucking on dessert spoons from Penny's mother's silverware drawer. No dessert. Just the spoons. "Sounds cool," Kier said to Ricky. "On Beverley?" He looked out the front window of *Sam's* onto Yonge. He could barely see the street because of the rain. Just the red and white lights of cars.

¶ The outdoor pool was still closed. The one with the tallest diving board. Last summer Rose and her friends Rachel and Trina took turns walking slowly onto the wobbling plank. Rose stood with her toes curled around the edges, her red hair wet and auburn, slicked and dripping down her back. Her blue suit with the white straps criss-crossed at the back, the spot where she always needed more Coppertone. The rough surface of the diving board scratched into the soles of her feet. She could see the pool below like a big blue map. In the fast lane, the sleek black Speedos moved back and forth like lines drawn in ink. The tiny coloured swimsuits of the babies in the wading pool looked like petals. Straight below her there was nothing but the blue water. Then that tuck, that last look at all of the world, knees bent, chin down, arms up, hands clasped together, and then the fall. It was just a second of flight, the air around her and her eyes tightly shut, and, never when she expected, the water like a heavy liquid parachute around her, until her arms pushed back and her head broke through the surface.

But the pool was closed and Rachel was already at horse camp.

Everything Rose had imagined about her summer was not coming true.

She had thought, sitting in Math class, staring out the window at the new green grass of the soccer field, that she, Rachel, and Trina would spend their whole days at the pool. And that Tomas Nitsa would show up for some reason. Well, to swim. Maybe he'd come with Jason Levi and they'd have packed lunches to eat on the pool deck and Tomas would come over to where she and Rachel and Trina were sitting on their towels, drying out their hair, and he'd hold out a little wax paper bag, offering her some of his Swedish Berry candies. She would die if she saw him in a swimming suit. His shaggy blonde hair hanging in his eyes. His bare chest. The waistband of his shorts digging into his slim hips. But for the first whole week of summer it had rained.

Out of desperation and boredom, Rose had built a blanket fort that morning and was reading *Wuthering Heights* which she had taken from her mother's bookshelves in the living room. Numerous pieces of the living room's furniture had been employed in the fort's construction and now Rose was sprawled out under quilts and blankets with one of the reading lamps on, illuminating her patchwork cave.

Rose was too old for forts. Too old for *Cherry Aimes: War Nurse* and the yellow stack of Nancy Drews on the shelf in her bedroom. But also too lazy to get her bike out of the garage and go to the library in the rain. And the story of Heathcliff and Catherine had gripped her: poor mister Earnshaw dying and the terrible Hindley brutalizing Heathcliff, that little gypsy waif. Catherine telling Nelly the housekeeper of her acceptance of Linton's proposal. But then Heathcliff overhearing the conversation, and Catherine saying that it would be "degrading" to marry Heathcliff and then Heathcliff leaving Wuthering Heights before he hears the second part of the conversation: Catherine's confession of her love for Heathcliff. How she couldn't live without him. Why had no one ever told Rose to read this book? If it's because Catherine actually marries Edgar Linton she might puke. She wished she'd read it last year, so that she might have behaved more aloof and fiery like Catherine

Earnshaw when Tomas had walked into homeroom. Then she would have known how to speak to Tomas Alexander Nitsa all through seventh grade: "Tomas Alexander, saddle my horse and then let us ride together over the Yorkshire Moors."

Tomas Alexander Nitsa was written three hundred and forty-eight times in Rose's diary. She had found out his middle name by looking at the roll call on the teacher's desk. Alexander. Four strong syllables. Rose loved syllables. She counted them out while people spoke. She made haiku from conversation. There were only a few conversation-haikus in Rose's diary that were inspired by conversations with (or about) Tomas Alexander Nitsa. She hadn't really talked with him more than twice. Some of the conversations she'd overheard. Her favourite haiku was also the one that made her the saddest. She thought that might be the way with poetry.

Said to Jasmine Frick:
(stomach caves into my chest)
"I like your hair band."

The problem was that Tomas Alexander Nitsa didn't notice Rose. He would never hold out a paper bag of Swedish Berries for her even though once she'd helped him on a math exam. Cheated really, when the teacher was out of the room.

"Hey, Rose," he'd whispered.

Rose swallowed funny as he'd said her name and had almost choked.

"I can't remember the order. What's that thing again?"

She tried not to cough. "BEDMAS."

"What?" He leaned toward her, across the space between their rows. She could smell the fresh meadow smell of his laundry soap.

"BEDMAS. Brackets, Exponentials, Division, Multiplication, Addition, Subtraction." She whispered it fiercely, quickly, her eyes on the door at the front of the classroom.

"Right. Thanks."

"Yeah, no big deal," she'd wanted to say to him. "No prob, Tom." But instead she just held up her hand to him in a little wave and went back to her exam.

Maybe it's because I volunteer as a library monitor, Rose thought, as she read to the part where Catherine is struck by a fever after Heathcliff leaves, and, in her illness, is moved to Thrushcross Grange to be cared for by the stupid Lintons. Maybe my intelligence is quashing my sex appeal. She tried out the new phrase Rachel had shown her in *Cosmopolitan* magazine, but she didn't really care about sex appeal. Rose liked being a library monitor.

¶ Earlier that day Lucy had asked Rose if she wanted to go downtown to the Hudson's Bay and buy a bra.

"Already have one," Rose had said from the kitchen table, her shoulders hunched over the horoscopes in the newspaper.

"Oh," Lucy said.

"Do you want to hear your horoscope, Mama?"

"When did you get a bra?"

"I went with Rache and Trina two weeks ago. We all bought one."

"Okay," Lucy said.

"Gemini, right?"

"I would have gone with you."

"Small objects and machinery could break down today. You might have to stop and repair them. Anything that was weak or limping along could collapse now. Remember: all is not lost."

"Did you get the right size?"

"Yeah, the saleslady helped us find the right sizes. Mama, this does not bode well."

"Good," Lucy said. "The salesladies are good at that."

Eventually, Lucy thought, there will be no point to my existence.

¶ That afternoon, rather than sleeping upstairs for the day, Peter left after a brief nap. "I'm going to run a few errands," he said to Lucy on the way out. No kiss or gesture of affection. The slam of the screen door.

Peter drove the Fairlane down the streets of Toronto. The classified section of the newspaper was sprawled beside him on the passenger seat. The windows were fogged up because of the rain. He kept having to look from the addresses in the classifieds to the road through a small patch of his side window that he'd rubbed clear with his sleeve. Peter had circled a number of ads in tidy blue ballpoint and was now cruising slowly down a street looking for the turnoff to Carleton Mews.

He'd seen some dives. There was a bachelor that had been painted orange and was streaked with mould, like living inside a rotting pumpkin. Another had a leak in the roof that dripped into an old Folgers coffee tin. Tink. Tink. Tink. "We'll be getting that leak fixed up real soon," the man showing the place had assured him. Tink. Tink. Tink. The last one he'd seen was hardly an apartment at all. An elderly lady had taken him down some steps into what appeared to be the cellar of her house. There was one window that had a board across it. Near the front door there was an old ringer washing machine, a wooden box of potatoes, and a shelf lined with empty canning jars covered in cobwebs.

"Sometimes I may come down here to use the laundry. I'd prefer if you didn't use any of my soap flakes." She gestured to a dusty mint-coloured box with the faded picture of a cowboy.

Peter could see dirt between the cracks of wood flooring and linoleum. No subfloor beneath them. No foundation. God, imagine the winter.

If I were superstitious, Peter thought, I would take these dumps as a sign. Go back to Maple Avenue. Keep moving through time. Peter looked down again at the last ad he'd circled that morning: *Ring Buzz 17. 1898 Carleton Mews*. A narrow service street. Peter recalled the list of street names the children had tacked to the wall. Whatever had happened to that map?

He looked up at the apartment building as he turned onto Carlton Mews. It was at least sixteen-storeys tall. Not what he'd imagined on a Mews. He imagined a Mews to have a garden and a gate. He imagined sparrows at a feeder and trees in bloom. Maybe a small stone apartment with a front desk clerk who read the newspaper from editorial to obituary each day with a magnifying glass and knew all of the tenants' names. "Morning, Mister Jacobs. Best to bring an umbrella wid' you." Peter wanted an unobserved experiment. He wanted to know what life was like without the opacity of

181

other human beings. What it was like to fall asleep and wake up alone. Peter knew that to Lucy this apartment would be worse than infidelity. He parked the car and got out into the rain to take a look.

¶ Andy contemplated the metaphysics of the donut hole. What exactly was the physical property of a hole when you really thought about it? A hole consisted, presumably, of nothing. Or was the hole the material of the something that had been cut out to form the nothing? Really, donut holes were a complicated example. Andy liked that to the customers it appeared they were using every last piece of cake they could, but the donut holes were not in fact cut out of the donuts. Donuts were rolled into donut shapes and the holes were rolled from a separate piece of dough. But which was the hole: the ball of dough, or the nothing at the centre of the donut? Were the holes the nothing, or were the holes the little pieces of cake? Hole had been his favourite pick for twenty questions when he was a kid.

"Is it bigger than a breadbox?"

"It can be."

"Is it a colour?"

"Not really."

It always took twenty guesses.

Andy and Maryanne Wren had the same work schedule. That was her last name. Wren. Andy had seen it on the timetable on the back of the mop closet door. In a little circle on that night the manager had written: *Wren and Jacobs close*. He read it as 'close' the first time—as in close enough to smell the camomile conditioner in her straight dark hair—and then realized it meant he would have to learn how to do cash-out and lock up the store.

"The big thing is you have to remember to lock the door." They stood behind the counter double-checking the float for the next day. The others had gone home and it was just the two of them. "That may sound really stupid. But after you've put everything in the fridges and put the day-olds in the charity box at the back and done the tills, you might forget about the door. I've left the shop open at least four times." She paused. "Don't tell anyone though."

"I wouldn't do that."

182

"No, I didn't think you would." She turned the main light switch off by the cash registers and they walked together through the dark store.

"Hey, I didn't mean to freak you out earlier about Alma. Her tumour. I just thought you should know."

"No, no. That's good." He almost tripped on the leg of a chair and pushed it under a table. "I want to know."

"She's probably going to die soon."

Andy flipped the sign on the door to CLOSED.

It was still raining. Maryanne held a raincoat over their heads. "So this is the thing." She was always surprising him with her voice in his ear.

"There's this film playing tonight at this art place in Kensington and I think you should take me."

He turned around to look at her. Her eyes were like a photograph he'd seen when he was a kid in a Time Life book of the Grindelwald Glacier in Switzerland. He'd taken that book out from the library at least eight times. He could still find that book in the Dogwood Terrace branch without looking up the call number if he wanted. Her eyes were the exact blue of that glacial lake formed at the basin of a cirque; the minerals of the ice age mixed with algae.

The raincoat she was holding over them wasn't really helping. They were getting soaked. "You want me to come to a movie with you?"

"It's not like *Escape from Planet of the Apes* or something. It's a short-film festival. It's okay if you're not into it."

"No, no. I'm into it."

They walked toward the parking lot.

"Did you lock the door?" he asked her.

"Shit."

Andy waited in the rain while Maryanne ran back.

¶ The Bev's porch was littered with second-hand floral couches. There were hanging plants and crystals on strands of beads. Ivy and caladium spilled out of pots and down the pillars of the porch. Someone had planted herbs in window boxes. Kier could smell oregano. The rain had let up for a moment. Kier hadn't noticed at first, and then he realized the drips of water on his cheeks were coming from his long hair and not from the sky. He dried his face and the beard he was trying to grow with the hem of his worn checked shirt. Now that the sun was out and Ricky and he were standing on the porch, Kier could smell the oregano and it surprised him. Rainbows were shimmering and moving through the hanging crystals. The air felt clear.

Ricky walked through the beaded curtains in the front entranceway without ringing the doorbell. Kier had never seen anyone ring the doorbell at the Bev. He wasn't even sure the doorbell worked. He'd only been to the house a few times. Alice lived there. Alice who was older than he was and kissed him once while they were passing around a joint. She blew smoke into his mouth so that he choked and coughed in front of everyone in the circle. But no one laughed, they just sort of grinned their relaxed grins and leaned against the couches and cushions in the living room that were covered in fabrics from India. Posters of Dylan and Che and *Travel Cuba* plastered the walls.

"Hey Man."

"Hey Bro."

Kier watched as Ricky high-fived a guy in the kitchen. Al, Kier thought. He remembered the guy's name being Al. The kitchen was Kier's favourite part of the house. The cupboards were a rainbow. Each door had been painted a different colour. The counters were lined with mason jars full of beans and chick peas and seeds and barley. It smelled of freshly baked bread. More plants hung in the kitchen's small bay window above a round wooden table. On the table rested a Chianti-bottle candle-holder covered in wax and a clay bowl of brown sugar. Alice was sitting at the table in a long blue cotton caftan. She had her knees up. Her toes poked out under her hem and grabbed the edge of the chair slightly. Her blonde hair glowed almost white with the light from the window. She was holding a mug of tea in one hand and a copy of *Siddhartha* in the other.

"Hi Alice," Kier said.

She looked up from her book. "Hi," she said and smiled. "Sorry. I forget your name."

"Kier," Kier said, shoving his hands into the pockets of his jeans.

"Right," she said and took a sip of her tea.

"Do you guys want to trip?" Ricky asked, and pulled out a tiny pouch of tinfoil from his pocket.

"Whatcha got, Ricky?" Alice asked, still reading her book.

"Lucy."

She looked up. "Oh, goodie."

¶ It was eight o'clock at night. Not quite dark yet, but it would be shortly, and Peter was due at work to manage the late shift. Peter and Lucy were in the kitchen trying to keep their voices down. Neither of the boys was home. Kier was out downtown at a show, or at a friend's house, Peter wasn't sure. Sometimes he came home to sleep in his room in the basement, but since the semester had let out he'd spent the nights at friends' houses in the city. "It's fine, Dad. They have lots of room. Tons of people crash. I'm going to chip in for a big tub of peanut butter anyway, so it'll be cool." Andy was at a movie with someone from work. Mary Eve? Is that what he'd said as he'd run for the bus to downtown? Rose was upstairs. She'd come home early from a birthday party and gone up to her room. Peter and Lucy had both been aware of Rose being upstairs when the argument had begun. They didn't want to upset her. But now that the situation was becoming clearer, Peter standing there in his work clothes, holding onto a suitcase, they had stopped thinking about Rose being upstairs entirely.

"You have an apartment?" Lucy asked.

"Yes," Peter said. He watched her as he spoke.

She was standing on his shoes at the threshold of the side kitchen door, her elbows and hands hard against the door frame. She looked at Peter, concentrated, as if he was a cryptic crossword clue she was trying to figure out.

Peter could see that the balls of Lucy's feet were digging into his best pair of black shoes. Creases formed across the polished leather as her weight pressed down. He had other shoes he could wear to work if he needed. Despite Lucy standing with her arms against the frame of the kitchen door, Peter could walk out the front if he wanted to. It surprised him that in the end the decision was no more complicated than a suitcase.

"You have rented an apartment?" Lucy asked again, incredulous.

"Yes. A bachelor apartment. It's two hundred a month. I'll still support you and the kids. I'll come over for Sunday dinner. They're hardly children any more, Lu."

"Why didn't you talk about this with me? Why didn't you let me know you were thinking about this? Why, if one of us is leaving, does it get to be you?"

"Rose needs a mother."

"Bullshit. She needs a father too."

"I'm still Rose's father."

"What about the house?"

"What do you mean, 'What about the house?'"

"What about our house?"

"I'll make sure you're taken care of. I'm not abandoning you." Peter bent down toward Lucy's feet to collect his shoes. She kicked at him.

"Lu, stop this."

"Peter." The way she said his name. So plainly. Like a fact.

He looked up at her from where he was crouched near her feet. "Please, Lu. I need to go."

"Well then, take some of that lemon marmalade you like."

"What?" He looked at her.

"I won't be making any more until next winter."

He couldn't tell if this was a trick. Was she being passive-aggressive, or strangely serene. "Well, do you want to talk about this?" Peter tried. And which was worse?

"Here," she kicked his shoes to him. "You'll be late for work."

Peter looked at her. Was this it?

Lucy slid down onto the floor so that her legs were out in front of her beneath the green checks of her skirt.

Peter tied one shoe up and then the next. As he was bent over the thought occurred to him that he would never again see his wife in her underwear. In that pink lace pair with the small black bow at the hip. He wouldn't rest his hand on her stomach, her breath rising and falling inside her body, and taste her, and feel her body breathing all around him. He stayed there for a moment, bent over, his shoes on, his forearm resting on his knees. Then he pressed himself up off

186

the floor and lifted his suitcase. The same suitcase he had taken to Buffalo all those years ago. He stepped over Lucy's legs, out toward the evening, without taking any marmalade.

The screen door snapped closed.

Lucy leaned back against the door frame. "One thing, Peter."

He turned to look at her.

Her voice was calm but reedy. "I'm throwing the space-nook in the basement as soon as you're gone." Her face looked like a shadow behind the screen door.

He put the suitcase in the trunk and opened the driver's-side door.

"I hate that table," she said more sternly. Defiantly. Her breath came out short, sudden. "I hate it." Her shoulders were shuddering against the door frame. She didn't want to be crying. "I hated it the day you gave it to me, and I hate it now."

Peter sat with the car door open, one foot still on the driveway, the other foot near the pedals of the car, listening to Lucy, partly wanting to go back to her and partly, longingly, wanting the dim anonymity of his room at work. He pictured his new furnished bachelor apartment on Carlton Mews, the clean lines of the bed and blinds, the bland pastel painting of seagulls, the noiselessness.

The street lights came on over Peter's head. He was late for work. He shut the car door, turned the key in the ignition and drove away.

¶ When Lucy could no longer see the red tail lights of the car she sat for a long time. She sat and stared at the frame of the door, the knots in the wood that the paint couldn't cover up. She looked out the screen door and realized it was dark. Lucy took the hem of her dress and wiped at her tears. Two black moons of mascara on green gingham. She stood up. She straightened her sleeves and collar, tucked a stray strand of hair behind her ear, pulled open the utensil drawer and took out the rolling pin. She looked at the nook, took three lunging steps and swung. A booming thud echoed throughout the house. The rolling pin did nothing, only dented the chrome plating.

Lucy threw the rolling pin onto the kitchen counter and walked out the side door, across the pavement, where Peter's car had just been, to the garage. She pulled open the garage door, putting all her weight into heaving up the clanking roll of metal. She did not turn on the light. She stood in the dark, the street lights sending her shadow over the oil drips on the concrete floor, and spotted the small axe they used when camping. She took it off the wall.

The axe head buried itself into the chrome plating. When she yanked it out, Lucy could see the bare flesh of the wood beneath the polished surface. She raised the axe again and smashed it down onto the surface of the tabletop. She slammed the blade into the benches, foam stuffing bleeding out from the opened vinyl surfaces like wounds. She struck the side shelving units, the blade going straight through the flimsy panelling into the kitchen wall. Lucy was sweating. Her bobby pins were dropping to the floor. She picked up a piece of jagged chrome plating and tore it away from the wood. The flash of silver metal cut into her hands, but she kept tearing, wanting to get back at the wood with the axe.

¶ Rose sat motionless at her desk and listened to the noise downstairs. Her mother had just yelled something at her father, and then the car left and there were two loud slams, and now it was quiet again. What was happening? She heard the screen door of the kitchen. Silence. She heard it slam again. Then hurried, repetitive thumping echoed up the stairs to her bedroom. It sounded loud and violent, even with her door shut tight. She listened, trying to figure out what was happening. She heard a crash, something being broken. Then another crash. Finally everything was completely silent for a long while and that's when Rose got scared. She folded the letter she'd been writing to Rachel and tucked it into an envelope. She wrote Equestrian Adventure Summer Camp and the address that Rache had left her, licked the back of the envelope and then stuck a sticker over top. Banana Split. Rose held the letter in her hand as she slowly walked down the stairs, an excuse if Lucy got upset for interrupting whatever was going on, "I was just going to mail this letter to Rachel," but she didn't need to say anything. Before she was at the bottom step, Rose could see that Lucy was lying on the kitchen floor, crying, surrounded by the splintered, obliterated remains of the breakfast nook.

"Mama." Rose sat down on the floor next to Lucy and softly patted her mother's hair. "What happened?"

Lucy sobbed.

"It's okay, Mama. Shhhh. It'll be alright. Just tell me what happened. What happened to the nook? Your hands are bleeding."

¶ "Kier! Look!" Alice and Kier were in one of the upstairs rooms of the Bev. The others were in the living room downstairs and someone had put on a record of Dylan Thomas reading "Do Not Go Gentle Into That Good Night." They kept playing the poem over, Al picking the needle of the record player up and moving it back again. "Rage, rage against the dying of the light."

"That's it, man. That's so fucking it," Ricky kept saying.

"Come and get us when you put on Howl," Alice had said. "We're going exploring." She took Kier by the hand and led him up the stairs.

It looked like it might be someone's office, but Kier couldn't figure out what the person's work might be. There were books all along one wall. The closet door was open and there were more papers and more books. Two worn cardigan sweaters hung on hangers: one blue, one grey.

"Look!" Alice tugged at Kier's sleeve. "This was absolutely left here for us to play with."

Kier looked down at the desk: a thick stack of typed pages; a pottery mug missing a handle that held pens and pencils, two pairs of scissors, and a small metal stapler. "This?" he asked her.

"Yes." She grabbed both of his hands and whispered excitedly, "Snowflakes!"

"Snowflakes," Kier said meaningfully, although not quite sure what Alice meant.

"Clearly this has been left here for us to make snowflakes."

Kier looked down again at the office supplies and the pile of neatly stacked paper riddled with type and red pencil marks. It seemed probable. Yes. There were scissors and a pile of paper. There were two pairs of scissors and they were two.

"Here." She put a pair of scissors in his hand and moved the entire stack of paper onto the rug on the floor. She sat down cross-legged in front of the pile and began to fold the pages and cut out triangles of paper snow. Kier sat down beside her and began to cut tiny diamonds and squares. Confetti with letters and words sprinkled onto the floor: *ice shield, Labrador, salinity,* the snow-confetti read.

"Howl!" He heard them calling up the stairs. Alice and Kier looked up from their work. How long had they been upstairs? There were tiny flakes all over the floor. Alice had taken the stapler and stapled the snowflakes all over after they were cut out. "Sparkles," she'd said, and the snowflakes did sparkle.

Alice looked at Kier and howled. "Awooowwoo."

He took her hands and helped her stand up.

"Just a minute!" She yelled back down the stairs. "We're decorating."

They picked up the snowflakes they had made and rested them on the shelves of the bookcase. Thirty-two snowflakes. They stood back, their bare feet in the confetti. Alice put her arm around Kier's waist.

"I told you," she said softly. She kissed him on the cheek and howled down the stairs.

¶ Rose didn't know what to do. "Mama," she said softly. Lucy's head was in her lap. Rose could feel the wetness of her mother's tears on one pant leg. Rose's right foot was starting to fall asleep, but she didn't want to move Lucy. Rose had finally gotten her to calm down. She might even have been asleep. "Mama, are you okay if I move you?" Lucy didn't answer. "I'm going to put you to bed, okay?" Rose had no idea how she'd get her up the stairs. Where was Andy? Where the hell was Kier?

Rose slowly eased her lap from beneath Lucy. She held her mother's head gently in her hands. She reached her arm out and grabbed a tea towel hanging from the handle of the fridge door and put it beneath Lucy's head. "Come on," she said. Lucy looked up at her daughter. "Come on, Mum," Rose said, and motioned for Lucy to get up.

Lucy stared at Rose.

"Mama, I need you to get up."

"Okay," Lucy breathed. "Okay," as if reassuring herself of something absolutely impossible.

"Okay," Rose said.

Lucy pushed herself up. She sat, her skirt spread all around her, lines of makeup in streaks down her face. "Could I have a glass of water?"

"Of course."

"And can you get me some pills from the medicine cabinet, Rosie?"

"Pills?"

"Near the back of the second shelf. Behind the Tylenol and Solarcaine. My name is on them."

¶ Lucy took two Valium with Rose's glass of water, still sitting on the floor.

Rose watched that it was only two.

"Valium is how I fell in love with this daisy wallpaper," she said to Rose.

Rose didn't say anything. She sat with her back resting against the refrigerator. She had never had a conversation like this with her mother.

"I would go to the paint stores and get sheets of their wallpaper samples and I'd take them home and touch them in the afternoons when Kier was down for his naps. The textures. All those gorgeous colours. It felt decadent to think of putting such things on a wall. To have a whole wall that beautiful." Lucy finished drinking her glass of water. They sat in silence for a moment.

"Do you want me to put you to bed, Mama?" Rose asked.

Lucy sat for a moment, holding her empty glass of water. "I would like to be in my nightgown, yes."

¶ "Your film was incredible," Andy said. "Why didn't you tell me?"

"I don't know. I just wanted to show you."

Andy and Maryanne were sitting in Twiggy's, an all-night diner downtown. Andy had gone home quickly to change out of his yellow Go-Nuts T-shirt, into a crisp blue dress shirt and his brown corduroy coat. He hadn't had time to shower and the sweet greasy smell of donuts clung to his hair and collar. When he'd met Maryanne outside the gallery-café in Kensington Market she was wearing an embroidered dress under a jean jacket with a pin that said *Food*

Not Bombs. She had on a pair of worn cowboy boots. Her hair was down and her blue eyes shone. She'd been standing on Augusta talking to a short bald guy with round-framed glasses, but when Andy crossed the street to stand by them she took his hand and lead him inside the room.

Maryanne had shot her short film on Super-8 in Alma's booth of Go Nuts before Andy began working there. Sunlight shone on Alma through the window. The entire film consisted of Alma sitting quietly, drinking her Earl Grey tea and playing solitaire. Maryanne had set the film to music. A piece, she'd told Andy after, that Alma had danced to when she was younger. Erik Satie's *Gnossienne*. There was nothing really special about the action of the movie. Alma just played cards with herself like Andy had already seen her do each afternoon. She sipped at her tea, adjusted the scarves wrapped around her head, moved her flower basket to one side of the laminate table and looked out the window into what Andy knew was the parking lot. But somehow in the film everything about her movements was sharp and regal.

"I can't believe Alma let you film her."

"Why not? She's beautiful."

"I wouldn't have noticed her."

"She carries around a basket of fake flowers, Andy. Everyone notices her."

The waitress came with their fries.

"Ketchup?" Maryanne asked Andy. She squeezed a small pool of ketchup into the corner of the basket.

"No, I mean I wouldn't have noticed that she was beautiful."

"You would have eventually."

"She scares me." Andy took a fry. "I can't help it. The thought of her tumour scares me."

"Everyone's beautiful if you look at them long enough."

Andy looked over Maryanne's shoulder to a man wearing a crooked black toupée who had sloppy joe sauce on his face. Andy gave Maryanne a look. "What about that guy?"

Maryanne looked over her shoulder and laughed. "Yes, Andy. Even him."

"What about that guy at the store who talks to the flea?"

"Bolero?"

"You know his name?"

"I've filmed him too." Maryanne blew her bangs out of her eyes and ate another French fry. She had ordered a coffee and it was almost ten o'clock. Andy had noticed this. That she had ordered a coffee. Also that she smoked. The two actions in combination somehow seemed sophisticated. Andy played with her package of cigarettes that she'd put on the table next to a purse that was from Mexico or someplace. There was a bird on it. A phoenix. "What are you doing now?" he asked her.

"I'm here. With you."

"Yes, but after that?"

"What do you have in mind?"

"Do you want to come to my house?" He'd never brought a girl into his house before. "I've never even had a girl at my house before." He said it out loud to her without thinking.

She smiled at him.

"There are records we could listen to. My mum has every jazz album ever produced, I swear."

Maryanne licked the salt from her fingers. "I'd like that."

He looked again at the stitched bird on her purse. The flames taking over the feathers. Andy imagined falling asleep next to Maryanne while they listened to records on the living-room carpet, the carpet he'd spilled cereal on when he was a kid.

¶ Rose took a bus to the subway station and then a subway downtown after she had watched Lucy fall asleep. She had grabbed the spare house key from the key-shaped hook by the back kitchen door and had taken forty dollars from the safety money that Lucy kept in a Danish Butter Cookie tin on top of the fridge. She remembered Kier saying something about Penny's house and Alice's house and that Ricky and he had been to this great place called the Bev. Beverley Street. She knew almost every street name in Toronto because of the map that had been pinned to the kitchen wall. She brought that too, which she found folded up and stored in a kitchen drawer. She had no idea how she would find Kier, but she felt like she could find him. If Heathcliff and Catherine's ghosts could be together after death, she could surely find her brother. Besides, she'd read almost every Nancy Drew.

The subway felt desolate at ten o'clock on a Friday even though there were loads of people in the cars. The blue light made everyone's face look pale. Rose sat in a double seat by the window and pulled her knees up to her chest. She thought about how she might be getting the seat dirty with her sneakers. She decided not to care. She looked at the window. When they weren't at a station the window became a mirror to the subway car. She could look at everyone around her without them knowing she was looking. A man read a newspaper, the shine of a flask as he quickly moved it from his pocket, spun the lid between his fingers and put it to his mouth. A group of three women with lipsticked lips looked ready for dancing. A small Chinese girl sat with her grandmother. The grandmother had torn her transfer into the shape of a dog and put it on the floor of the car. At first the grandmother flapped at the dog with her hand. Then the doors opened at Landsdowne and as the passengers got on and off the dog moved with the currents of the wind from the train. Back and forth by people's shoes. The little girl was smiling, pointing at the dog, slapping at her grandmother's lap.

At Saint Patrick Station Rose got off the car and took out the street map. She decided to walk to Beverley Street. Beverley was only eight blocks long between Queen and College, and then after that it became St. George. Kier had never mentioned a St. George. After she had passed the Art Gallery of Ontario and the rush of streetcars along Dundas, Rose turned north onto Beverley. She shut her eyes for a few steps and kept walking. She opened them. A straight line. She shut them again. Walked. Opened them. Crooked, almost into someone's front garden. The street lights buzzed faintly. She had no idea what she was doing. She was on her own in downtown Toronto. She needed to find Kier.

Rose shut her eyes. Opened them. When she saw the porch Rose knew she had found the house. The crystals hanging. The plants. The front door was wide open and when Rose climbed to the second step of the porch she could see straight into the kitchen through the beaded curtains. She could see her brother's long legs and the blue skirt of a girl. She could hear her brother's laugh coming out onto the street from the kitchen. He hardly ever laughed at home. Rose stood still for a moment, watching her brother's bare feet shift on the kitchen floor as he leaned against the counter. She listened again for his laugh, thick but slightly sad, like an oboe.

¶ "Holy shit." Kier blinked, holding a piece of homemade bread with jam. "Rose," Was this her, his sister, here in Alice's kitchen? "What are you doing here?"

Alice reached out and hugged her. "Rose," she said, like she knew her.

"Hi," Rose said awkwardly, her head somehow resting on this woman's shoulder.

"Toast?" Alice offered.

"No thanks," Rose said.

"Sit down," Kier said, and pulled out a chair from the table where earlier, so much earlier it seemed, Alice had been reading *Siddhartha* and drinking tea. "How did you get here?"

"I took the subway. Listen. Mama chopped up the kitchen table."

"What?"

"Dad left."

"What?"

Alice looked from brother to sister and picked up her slice of toast and the jar of blackberry jam. "I'm just going to be in the other room," Alice said. "Get me if you need anything, okay?" She paused at the entranceway. "There's tea." She pointed with her chin to the cupboard door that was painted purple.

Neither Kier nor Rose looked up at her.

"Kier. Dad's gone and Mama hurt herself trying to cut up the kitchen table and I gave her Valium, I didn't know if I should do that, but she only took two, and then I got her up the stairs and she fell asleep, I stroked her hair until she fell asleep, and then I washed the cuts on her hand and put pieces of gauze on them, but there wasn't any of that first-aid tape, so I used the Scotch tape from the kitchen drawer, and now there's wood everywhere and I didn't know what to do and I remembered Beverley and I couldn't have stayed in that house and, Andy, I don't know where Andy is and," Rose took a deep breath, "I needed you."

Kier looked at Rose. "Oh, Rosie." He stared deeply at her: her freckles, her eyelashes, her sweet swooping nose. "You have the most beautiful face."

"What?"

"Your face Rosie. You are so beautiful."

"Kier," she said. "Did you even hear me?" She took the half-eaten piece of bread from out of her brother's hands and put it on the counter. "We have to go home."

¶ Andy and Maryanne heard the cab pull up and looked through the living-room curtains. Cabs never pulled up in front of their house. Andy didn't think he'd ever seen his parents take a cab. But there it was, and Kier was getting out. And then, wait, Rose. What the hell was going on? He'd brought Maryanne home and they'd found the intergalactic breakfast nook smashed to pieces and no one at home.

"Who's that?" Maryanne asked.

"My brother," Andy paused, looked back out the window, "and my little sister, Rose."

"What were they doing tonight?"

"I have no idea."

¶ Andy opened the door and Rose hit him hard in the solar plexus. "Where were you?"

"I was out. Geez, Rose, manners. This is Maryanne. Maryanne, Rose."

Rose waved in Maryanne's direction and slung her arm through the crook of Kier's elbow, directing him toward the kitchen. "Kier's high on acid, Mama cut open both of her hands on the table, Dad left, and I didn't know where either of you were."

"*Mama* did that to the table?" said Andy.

"Yes," Rose said. "With the camping axe."

"Jesus," Maryanne said.

¶ The four of them stood in the kitchen. Kier leaned against the door of the fridge, holding a mug of mint tea. He watched the mint leaves move in the water. Andy sat on the counter. Maryanne stood next to Rose by the sink. "You okay?"

Rose noticed the thick black eyeliner around Maryanne's blue eyes. How did she get the lines so straight? She smelled like cigarette smoke and bergamot, wildflowers after a forest fire. "I don't know," Rose finally said, so long since the question was asked she almost forgot what she was answering.

"What's it like?" Andy asked Kier.

"Rage," Kier said.

"What?" Andy said.

"Rage, rage against the dying of the light."

"Oh," Andy said, as if that were an answer.

¶ Andy began cleaning up the pieces of the table. Maryanne helped him pick up the wood and metal and take them to the basement. Kier finished his tea, came down from his trip a bit and found the old Formica table in the garage. He and Rose moved it into the kitchen together, chairs and table legs and tabletop. Rose wet a cloth, cleaned the dust off the tabletop and chairs and sat down. She could hear the birds starting to sing through the kitchen window. She put her cheek against the cool surface of the table. Dad will be getting off work soon, Rose thought, the first morning of not coming home.

"Pancakes?" Kier asked.

"Sure," Rose said, looking at Kier but with her face still resting against the table.

"I'd be into pancakes," Maryanne offered from the kitchen door. She stood smoking a cigarette, exhaling her smoke behind her into the lightening driveway.

Andy took out a mixing bowl and moved the flour container forward on the counter. Kier opened the drawer beneath the oven and took out the cast-iron pan.

"Sorry you had to come get me," Kier said as he poured oil into the pan and set it on low.

Kier passed Andy the baking soda. Maryanne came in and sat down next to Rose.

Kier looked over at Rose. "Sorry I was fucked up and you had to come get me and no one was here with you."

She didn't say anything.

"Rose?" Kier looked at her from the stove.

"Don't." Rose said. She watched her brothers move around the kitchen. Andy had put on Lucy's apron. Kier held up a spatula.

"I'm sorry too," Andy said and cracked an egg into the bowl.

Rose felt like she was going to cry, she was so tired.

"How about a Mickey Mouse one?" Kier asked, "Or Minnie? I'll do the bow."

"It's okay." Rose said.

"No bow?"

"No, I'll have the bow. It's okay though. Don't worry about not being here." Rose lifted her head and looked out the window. "That's the thing." She said it calmly, not accusing, but just that it was a fact. "You're not always going to be here."

Andy and Kier looked at one another.

"Sure we are," Kier said.

"No. You're not."

¶ Lucy came downstairs in her nightgown just as they began to eat the pancakes. "You're all up early." She looked around the table at her three children, then at Maryanne sitting beside Andy. "You must be Mary Eve."

"Maryanne."

"Good morning."

Kier went into the dining room and brought in an extra chair to sit on. Andy stood up and took another plate from the cupboard, a fork and knife from the cutlery drawer. He poured Lucy a glass of orange juice.

"Thanks for making breakfast," Lucy said.

"No problem," Kier said.

"If I wasn't your mother," Lucy started. She hadn't even mentioned the table or the broken nook they'd just spent an hour cleaning up. Keir couldn't tell if she was still stoned on Valium. Although he was probably still high on acid. Not the best judge. "If I wasn't your mother," Lucy said again, "I would go to church today." She drizzled some maple syrup onto her pancakes.

Kier looked across the table to Rose. Rose shrugged.

"After church, I would go downtown to a club I once knew and listen to some jazz. I'd drink gin juleps all day long and hang out with the girl who works the coat check." Her hair was brushed but her eyes were glassy.

"How are your hands, Mama?" Rose asked.

"I'd stare at the man playing drums, because the drummer's always the one that looks farthest away when he plays."

Rose could see that the tape on her bandages hadn't stuck.

"I'd request *Can't Take That Away from Me* because that's how I'm feeling." The fork in Lucy's hand shook. "I'm feeling a little 'the way you sip your tea' today."

"Rose asked you a question, Mama," Kier said. "Are your hands okay?"

She looked down at her hands and then slowly up at Kier again. "They'll be fine, Bean." She hadn't called him that in a long time.

¶ The first night asleep in his own apartment, Peter dreamt that he was on a boat. The boat drifted down a river, a bayou. Alongside the boat there were lush trees. The branches stood tall against the line of the sky, huge purple blossoms. The water before him was brown and murky, flowing softly, but deep, so that Peter worried about what was hiding in the muddy tides.

Peter stood on the bow deck with his hand over his eyes to keep them from the sun. Beside him stood an interpreter wearing a beige safari hat and coat. What was being interpreted? Peter wondered.

All along the shore there were herons. A flock of five beautiful blue herons, except that their legs were as long as stilts, and their bodies and beaks were so high up they were grazing in the leaves of the trees. Standing on the uppermost deck, staring at the herons, Peter leaned toward the interpreter.

"Tell me about those birds," Peter asked and pointed out across the water.

All the interpreter said was "They are very fragile."

AMBROSIA

Lucy sat with the cactus before she went across the street to see the priest. Our Lady of the Night Cactus, a new plaque read. Lucy had not been to the gardens since the boys were young, but she'd remembered the crooked cactus pressing its spines and hidden blooms against the ceiling of the conservatory, and so she sat with this cactus before she crossed the street, knowing that behind her the cactus stood unceasing, green arms held up against the sky in the glass house.

A secretary of the church showed Lucy into Jeremiah Bulmer's office. The rectory she had called it, and Lucy realized she hadn't learned the word when she was confirmed.

"Would you like some tea?" the woman asked, her head adorned with a pillbox ribbon hat like a confectionary, so that Lucy felt underdressed without her hat and gloves.

"No thank you, I won't be staying long."

"Coffee, then?" his voice came from the hall, and Lucy turned. He came to the door where Lucy and the secretary were standing and he smiled kindly. The Reverend Jeremiah Bulmer had a smooth dark face, tight dark curls, and a radiant smile that immediately made Lucy feel disarmed. The Reverend was a black man. Lucy had not realized this when she had spoken with his voice on the phone.

"Coffee. Sure I'd have a coffee."

"Would you mind fetching us two cups of coffee, Francine?"

"Certainly, Reverend Bulmer," and the secretary left Lucy in the rectory of the one kind priest in Toronto who had returned her telephone call.

Lucy sat down in a chair. She looked around the small office. The Reverend Bulmer had shelves of books along one wall: a New Jerusalem Bible, the Bhagavad Gita, a number of sacred texts in languages Lucy could not read, and the entire Chronicles of Narnia by C.S. Lewis. On the wall behind Jeremiah Bulmer's desk, next to a plain wooden cross, was a black and white photograph of a woman laughing. Lucy leaned toward the photograph. It was slightly blurred, out of focus. The woman was wearing a white pinafore over a plain dark dress and behind her was a garden. She was standing in front of an azalea tree that was in full bloom.

"Who is that?" Lucy asked.

The Reverend sat down at the desk across from Lucy. "My mother," he said, without turning around. "She died in a car accident around the time you left your message with Francine." He leaned on the green surface of the ink blotter on his desk. "I was on my way to Sylvania, Georgia, to see about her funeral."

"I'm so sorry," Lucy said.

The secretary came in and set down a tray with two cups of coffee with saucers, spoons, a small creamer and a sugar bowl. "Let me know if either of you need anything else," and Francine in her ribboned hat was gone.

"Do you believe in God?" Jeremiah asked as he poured cream into Lucy's coffee and gave it a stir and passed it to her. He was younger than his voice sounded on the phone as well. No older than forty, Lucy thought. She had noticed that he was wearing bell-bottomed trousers like Kier might.

"I beg your pardon?"

"Actually, let me phrase this a different way. Do you think that things happen in our lives for reasons that are beyond us? Do you think there is some kind of guiding force out there? Fate, the ancients might have called it?"

This was not the conversation Lucy was expecting. No priest had ever asked Lucy such a question before: Do you believe in God? What a question! In matter of fact, no man had engaged Lucy in a theological discussion of any kind. Lucy sipped at her coffee. What had this Jeremiah Bulmer asked her again? Fate? Was there a guiding force to the actions of her life? Lucy thought of Peter's tail lights as he drove away from the house. "Not lately," Lucy said. Lucy looked again at the photograph of Jeremiah's mother on the wall. Lucy's own mother was dead now too. Her father in a home somewhere. And she hadn't had a chance to visit them in Berkshire. "I know I used to believe in God." Why was she having this conversation? "It was just that ... God ... God wasn't particularly a question I even needed to ask, you know? I just believed, well, I don't know, I guess I believed like a child." There. She had answered. Lucy would go after her coffee was finished. This really was far too personal.

"The poet William Blake believed that children were more holy because they had more recently come from God. He believed children were, spiritually speaking, the most knowledgeable about our creator."

The man was not behaving as a priest should. The man was making her feel like she, Lucy Jacobs, might be able to help answer a question they had both been asking.

"I ask," Jeremiah said, "because you sounded as if you were having trouble with your belief when I was talking to you on the phone."

"No one had called me back. I had called down to Saint Xavier and no one had called me back."

"About the priest?"

"Yes."

"The one who you say found a body in a field."

"Yes. A woman in a field. Almost twelve years ago now."

"Would you like to tell me about this woman?"

Lucy paused. She scanned the bookshelf with her eyes for something to look to. What was it she wanted to know? "My husband left me," Lucy said. She had not at all meant to say it, and then there it was in the room, like a moth had gotten in and was battering against a light.

"I am sorry, Mrs. Jacobs."

"He left in the car and he didn't tell me much of anything. Just that he'd found an apartment and that we would be taken care of and that he would come over for dinner on Sundays, but—" Lucy's coffee cup shook in its saucer. "—But I don't really know what that means."

"I see, Ma'am. I really am so very sorry."

"And I still have the children. The boys are almost gone from the house. I can see it in them, their leaving is in them. But Rose is still just a girl, and I can't imagine what it would be like not to have a father ... to not have a father around." Why was Lucy saying all this? Who did she think she was, sitting in this office, just saying everything. This poor fellow. She was talking his ear off. Lucy looked down at her coffee cup. She'd hardly touched it. "I must go," Lucy said and stood up.

"But," Jeremiah put down his cup and stood as well. "We have just begun ..."

"I shouldn't have bothered you. You aren't the person I'm looking for."

"I was so enjoying our conversation."

"I'm sorry about your mother," Lucy picked up her purse from beneath her chair. "She had a beautiful smile," Lucy said, and then left the rectory office of Jeremiah Bulmer.

When Lucy arrived home from the church there was a letter in the mailbox from Doctor Sousa. They had not been in contact for a number of years; only occasionally meeting in the hallways of the hospital during checkups with the cardiologist about Rose's heart. Lucy put the letter on the kitchen table and left the room. That afternoon she swept and mopped the floors of the house incessantly. She alphabetized the books on the shelf in the living room; contemplated a recipe for thatched Bing-cherry tarts that had come in last weekend's newspaper but didn't bake them.

Lucy sat at the kitchen table holding the envelope. Kier came in reading a book.

"I didn't realize you were home, hon."

"I'm going out." He opened the fridge and poured himself a glass of milk.

Lucy picked up Kier's copy of *Beautiful Losers* that he had set down on the edge of the table beside her: *we leaned out to watch the Danish Vibrator move down the marble stories of the hotel.*

Kier grabbed it from her hand, "Thanks, Mom," he said, and not in a mean way, but she'd felt guilty, guilty enough that, by way of distraction, she had taken up the letter-opener and ripped the envelope of Sousa's letter open. She wasn't spying on Kier, she just wanted to know what the book was about. After all, if Doctor Sousa's letter said that Rose needed more tests, she would have to ask this son who had taken to reading erotic literature to come with her to the hospital. She couldn't sit in Sousa's office alone. Should she phone Peter? He'd left a phone number for emergency situations. But instead of tests the opened envelope revealed a professional looking pamphlet and registration package for the North American Lightning Strike Survivors' Conference to be held in Oshawa at the end of the month. Sousa had scribbled a note on a prescription slip that Lucy couldn't read at first, but which she finally, after a number of attempts at the inky script, understood as: *Group discussion proven to aid long-term recovery. Best to the family. Sousa.*

¶ Lucy sat on the edge of Rose's bed and watched her daughter put on lip gloss that made the room smell like strawberries. Kier had promised Rose a ride downtown in an MG he'd borrowed from his friend Ricky.

"It's not normally the type of event I would attend," Lucy explained to Rose. "But it could answer some questions."

Rose smacked her lips together and looked at her mom in the mirror. "It'll be good. Like a vacation. Rachel can stay with me overnight."

"You could even come with me," Lucy offered.

Rose turned from the mirror. "Mom. Seriously."

"You were there too you know."

"As if I would remember."

"The muscles of the body can sometimes recall our histories better than our minds. I read that in one of your dad's science journals." Peter had forgotten to cancel the subscription.

"You should go. Oshawa's like an hour away." Rose stood up and slung an army canteen bag over the shoulder of her flowered blouse. She'd sewn patches on the army bag. She has made an army bag somehow look feminine, Lucy thought, although she still didn't understand the clothes her daughter decided to wear. "Okay Mom, I gotta go. I'll be back after dinner."

"Where are you going again?"

"I have to get a book from one of the downtown libraries."

"Can't the Dogwood Terrace branch get it in?"

"It's part of some special collection," Rose said. "On Reserve. Yeah. That's what it's called."

"So it's just me for dinner?" Lucy looked at the registration package in her hand. She should go to the conference. It was an excuse to go somewhere she hadn't been before. Oshawa, for instance. Lucy had never been to Oshawa.

R ose was the first of the kids to visit Peter in his new apartment. She found the address by searching through some papers Peter had left behind in a cabinet by his workbench in the basement. She didn't ring the apartment intercom but waited. Kier had dropped her off at the library down the street—she hadn't told him where she was going—and had waited until a woman walked out of her dad's building with a dog. Rose pretended she was searching in her bag for a key, held the door open for the lady and her dog, and slipped into the building without having to ring the buzzer. It was five o'clock, on a Tuesday, so unless her dad had seriously altered his lifestyle, that meant he was awake and most likely getting some dinner ready before he had to head off to work.

Rose took the elevator to the fifth floor and followed the signs indicating the different suite numbers off the long corridor. One of the florescent hall lights at the entrance to Peter's apartment was flickering. Apartment 508. Rose looked down at her piece of notepaper to double-check. On the door there was a peephole and a simple brass knocker in the shape of an anchor. Rose knocked. Behind the door she heard cutlery clinking against a plate and then footsteps coming toward her.

Peter looked through the peephole to see his daughter standing as if in a fishbowl, the crown of her head large and round and softly out of focus. For a moment he mistook Rose for a younger Lucy. Lucy from when they'd first lived in the apartment on College Street. But then he recognized his daughter's brown flowered blouse and worn blue jeans and unlatched the door to let her in.

"Hi, Dad," Rose said, and took her army bag with the smiley-face patch off her shoulder and put it on the ground.

"Hi, kiddo."

They stood for a moment looking awkwardly at one another, and then Rose opened her arms and leaned toward her dad and gave him a hug.

¶ Peter and Rose sat across from one another at his tiny two-person dining table. Her dad looked slightly older somehow in his own space, but also more rested. The bags beneath his eyes were not so dark. His greying hair needed to be cut, and she noticed that a button was missing from his shirt and hadn't been sewn back on. There was no television in Peter's apartment, and no books.

Peter was eating a Swanson Salisbury steak dinner that he had heated up in the oven in its rectangular tin serving plate, and then transferred to a proper dinner plate, so that it had the look of a real dinner. Without asking, he sliced the rubbery piece of meat in two, brought over another plate for his daughter and placed half his carrots, potatoes and steak onto the dish for her. They had never eaten dinner together, just the two of them. "How's your mom?" he asked after they had both chewed in silence for a while.

"Not bad. Not good," Rose said.

They were silent again.

"How are you, Dad?"

"Alright ... calm."

"Good," she said, and looked around the room. There was no sign of anyone else living in the tiny apartment except her father. No women's clothing or cosmetics anywhere. A few of Peter's collared shirts hung from wire hangers over the shower rod. Black socks dried on the window ledge at the back of the main room, past the bed and single armchair. The curtains were open, letting in a breeze and the early evening light. Rose noticed that there was a bland watercolour of seagulls and a beach above her dad's bed and she wondered if it came with the place or if he'd actually gone to the bother of picking up such boring art at a garage sale somewhere.

"How's your summer going?" Peter asked.

"You know. Not bad."

"What have you been doing?"

"Swimming a little. Playing soccer."

"That's good."

Rose ate the last of her carrots, rested her knife and fork together on her plate and leaned back in her chair looking at her father. He took a swig of milk from his glass. No, she thought, he did look tired. No, maybe not tired, but sad. Or is that just what she'd wanted to see when she came here, her father sad and desolate without them? When really he seemed honestly to be fine. She couldn't tell which idea hurt more. Him really needing them and being alone, or him not needing them after all.

"I'm going to go now, Dad," she said.

"Okay, sweetie," he put his glass down, moved to take his paper napkin off his lap. "I'm glad you stopped by."

Rose motioned for him to stay seated. "No, Dad. Finish up. The lights will be coming on soon." She leaned over and gave him a kiss on the cheek.

"Come over again," he said, half sitting, half standing, waving to her.

"Alright," she said, and moved toward the door.

The signs in the lobby of the hotel were less discreet than Lucy would have liked: large poster boards with a man being struck, his body hovering above the air and a terrifying black cloud above him shooting out sparks of light. Lucy checked in to the hotel and was given a name tag at the conference registration table with a tiny cartoon cloud and lightning bolt above her name. *Lucille Jacobs*, it read, *survivor.*

Lucy put her overnight bag down on the carpeted floor of the elevator. She disliked elevators, ever since the iron-barred clunker on College, but she made an exception. Her room was on the fifteenth floor. A man in a cowboy hat stood next to her.

"You're a survivor too," the man said and stuck out a meaty hand for Lucy to shake. "Now I hope for your sake this elevator don't stop on us."

Lucy looked down at his crocodile-skin boots.

"Ever since the strike I have the tendency to stop electrical objects from working proper." He laughed a deep laugh. "Christmas lights, street lights. Toasters." He grinned and his teeth shone like the metal tips on the toes of his boots.

Lucy looked up at the floor numbers to make sure they were still moving upwards.

"Now for instance, I see you're wearing a wristwatch," he leaned toward her. "I cannot wear a wristwatch without it stopping. Give it half an hour. Dead on the wrist."

The doors opened at Lucy's floor and she got out. "See you downstairs," she said politely.

"Wish me luck," he said and looked up as the elevator doors closed.

¶ Lucy turned on the lights in her room. A king-sized bed. A desk. An armchair. A framed picture of two girls lighting paper-lanterns in a garden. In the bathroom: tiny shampoos and wrapped soaps; a sewing kit; a miniature shoeshine cloth. The last time Lucy stayed in a hotel was on her honeymoon. She still had a lavender-scented soap bar that said Royal York in the back of her sock drawer at home. Lucy opened her bag and hung up the dress she had picked out for the next day. She unpacked her nightgown and placed it, folded, beneath the pillows. She took out her toothbrush, toothpaste and floss and lined them up on the bathroom counter. Then she sat on the edge of the bed. Still half an hour before the conference started. She opened her curtains to a view of the car lots of Oshawa in the distance with their shining banners and flags. She turned on the television and turned it off again. She sat on the edge of the bed and polished her shoes with the miniature shoeshine cloth until her wristwatch read four o'clock, when she went back down to the lobby, this time by the stairs.

The poster-boards of the electrocuted man pointed Lucy in the direction of the Emerald Lake Room, a ballroom two times the size of her house filled with people who, for a split second in their lives, had been exposed to enough electricity to each power billions of light bulbs. Lucy sat down in a chair and smoothed the fabric of her peach-coloured skirt. It appeared that the keynote address was going to be delivered by that woman at the front with the short blonde bob and very large glasses. One of the organizers was coaching her on how to use the microphone. Lucy flipped through her programme. Ruby Newmeyer, the programme said her name was. A woman struck by lightning on four separate occasions over the past twenty-seven years.

"This conference is the only place I have found," Ruby confessed in a loud voice, holding a hand to her left ear, "where, when someone asks me how I am doing, I can answer honestly." The first time Ruby Newmeyer was struck she was standing outside a post office unleashing her dog. The second time she had been on the phone in her Florida home, talking to a daughter living in Cincinnati, when the current ran through the wiring in the wall up to the receiver and into the orifice of her left ear causing significant hearing loss and temporarily paralyzing the respiratory centre in her brain stem. The third time she was struck she'd been doing dishes and the current had travelled from the water in the sink to her arms. The last time she awoke in a hospital room not remembering how she had arrived there, her husband telling her that witnesses had seen her car veer off the road and had found her unconscious at the wheel with her window rolled down. The sky, the last time she had been struck was a pure blue. There had been no signs of a strike except for her stopped heart. The lightning had left no trace on her, but Ruby Newmeyer knew that it had been hit number four.

At the break, sticky cherry Danishes and carafes of stale coffee were served. Lucy chewed at her rubbery pastry and feigned interest in an array of medical textbooks and articles displayed on a banquet table near the entrance. When she turned back to the ballroom the chairs had been rearranged into tight circular formations. Holding her cold cup of coffee and her Danish crumbs scrunched into an oily napkin, Lucy sat with seven other attendees for what the programme had described as disclosure groups.

"I have had a constant craving for tropical fruit," a sporty woman in her mid-forties claimed. "Particularly mangosteens." A fruit she ate as a girl when her father was stationed as a diplomat in Bangkok.

"They're the shape of a tomato and the colour of a plum and the fruit inside is like a cloud," she said. "But they're impossible to find in my hometown of Juno, Alaska."

An older lady with a grey bouffant sitting next to Lucy went next. Lucy could smell the thick floral scent of her hairspray. This woman had been struck through her open living-room window while reading a newspaper when the current leapt first to a hanging birdcage and then to a copper hoop earring she'd been wearing in her right ear. "I felt like a jackhammer had hit me in the teeth, and then, when I had good sense enough to do so," the woman paused and played with the elasticized string of her name tag, "I looked up to the cage where Renaldo, my Brazilian scarlet macaw, had spent the better part of twelve years teaching me how to speak Portuguese, to find him dead at the bottom of the cage, lying in his own pellets."

A tall man wearing a pinstriped suit jacket had been golfing the eighth hole one moment and then awoke to find he could play all thirty-two of Beethoven's piano sonatas, including the difficult twenty-third, "Appassionata," at concert-level proficiency. Upon urging from the sporty woman, the man went over to a baby grand in the corner of the conference room, lifted the green quilted protective cloth from the keys, and proceeded to demonstrate.

Lucy mentioned, when it was her turn, that she had been pregnant when she was struck and was surprised to learn that many of the members of her disclosure group had heard of her strike, either through research into their own conditions, or through doctors and friends. "I was found in a field," Lucy said to them and paused. "The nurses at the hospital saved my life. Nurses are miracles in white dresses," Lucy said and laughed nervously. The faces around her looked on supportively, earnestly, and this made Lucy blush. Even at the time she had not spoken much to Peter about the accident. It had always been something to get through, not dwell on. "A man found me," Lucy continued. "Although I don't know who he is, so I haven't been able to thank him." She rolled the program into a baton and clenched it in her fist. "I think that's about it...."

"And your husband? Has he been supportive?" the older woman next to her asked.

"My children are wonderful," Lucy said.

By dinner time, Lucy couldn't tell if she felt at home with these people, or as if she'd walked unexpectedly into the backstage of a carnival tent—women who can tame pythons; men like giants; Medusa, the bearded woman, who can read your dreams. At dinner the man Lucy had met in the elevator sat next to her.

"I'm Hank," Hank said.

"I'm Lucy."

A woman named Renee sat on Lucy's right.

"Renee's a new name for me." She reached across the table for a dinner roll. "I renamed myself after the mood swings hit. One Christmas I fell into such a rage I lit the tree on fire." She bit into her buttered roll and continued to talk with her mouth full. "But the worst is the depression; that absence of texture. Isn't that how hell was once described? Any place where God is not?"

Lucy chewed on an ice cube, not answering. She was grateful when the trout was served.

"You have scars!" Renee exclaimed from beside her.

Lucy turned, a forkful of trout.

Renee reached out and pulled at the flowered collar of Lucy's blouse before Lucy could put her fork down and reach up to stop her.

Hank looked over. "You're lucky."

"Isn't she?" Renee said.

Lucy clutched her collar and looked back and forth between her dinner companions.

"Only five percent of victims show," Renee said in a nasally teacher-voice.

"*Survivors* please, Miss Renee," Hank said, "not victims."

"Deeper burns occur in less than five percent is all," Renee said again, looking at Lucy's neck, vampiric for another glimpse of her scars.

"Why would you think I'm lucky?" Lucy said.

"Because people believe in your injury," Hank said quietly.

Renee nodded fervently, more buttered dinner roll in her mouth.

"Most people do not believe that I have been struck by lightning, ma'am," Hank said to Lucy. "Friends do not believe it even after we have walked down the brightest street in Miami at night and I have turned off every street lamp one by one just by touching them."

"My husband didn't believe me at first," Renee said. "Even when he would wake me up in the middle of the night because the sheets were soaked in sweat but my body was cold as an icebox."

"I've never encountered.... I've never had anyone disbelieve," Lucy said.

"I told you," Renee said, "you're lucky."

¶ Without eating her blueberry cheesecake, Lucy excused herself to go to her room. She took off her name tag and put it in the front pocket of her blouse as she climbed the fifteen flights of stairs to her room. She brushed and flossed her teeth and got into her nightgown. She propped herself up on the enormous bed with three pillows and opened her copy of Ovid's *Metamorphoses*. When she took off her wristwatch and put it on the bedside table she noticed that the hands had stopped moving and she wondered if the battery had run low or if it was Hank's arm resting next to hers on the table throughout dinner.

Lucy looked down at her scars beneath the gauzy nylon of her nightgown. She'd never thought of the scarred scrawl worming itself across her skin as a blessing; as a marking. Marking that day in the field. That day like a hinge.

¶ The next morning Lucy did not go down to the Emerald Lake ballroom to hear the panel of doctors discuss methods of coping with long-term physiological defects. She did not attend the plenary lecture on anxieties and phobias. She avoided completely the second round of disclosure group sessions. In fact, Lucy threw the conference's schedule of events into the bathroom garbage, ordered poached eggs for breakfast from room service and stayed in bed, preferring to spend the rest of her weekend with Arachne, Apollo, and Daphne, than with Renee and the bouffanted scarlet macaw Lady downstairs. Philomela and Procne, followed by Daedalus and Icarus, followed by lunch, followed by Medea.

¶ Lucy stayed in bed and read ancient stories of humans distorted by gods. Philomela's tongue had been cut out. Medea had been so tormented by her husband she'd taken the lives of her children with her own hands. Arachne's body had become trapped in the eight-legged scuttling shell of a spider. Lucy thought about the room full of people downstairs. People of every race and age and culture. There were eleven-year-old children downstairs who had been struck while canoeing at summer camp. There were eighty-year-old women who had been struck while hanging clothes on the line. This was the first time she could remember having a morning in bed all to herself. So she felt the clean sheets against her legs, opened the blinds to the light, and had room service delivered.

¶ Lucy took a hot shower, packed her overnight bag, returned her room key and asked the front desk clerk to order her a taxi to take her to the bus depot.

Under the hotel awning Hank was smoking a cigarette.

"You off?" he said to Lucy.

"Yes. My family needs me," Lucy lied as her taxi pulled into the drive.

"Take care," he said.

"You too, Hank," she said, feeling the pleasure of escape, the reminiscent guilt of grade school sick-days, the dead wristwatch lying silent in her purse.

Peter swung open his front door. Robert held a bottle of red wine and a chess set. He was wearing a houndstooth coat and his hat with the quail feather. Peter hadn't made anything fancy: Hamburger Helper, Instant Rice, steamed carrots. His friend's naturally dapper appearance made Peter already feel disappointed in the meal he would serve. Halfway through the grocery aisles he remembered that Robert liked dessert and he'd put a lemon-pudding cake mix into the basket. He wished Robert hadn't brought the wine. He would have to serve it in the juice glasses he had got free in his laundry soap that were embossed with tiny golden hockey players. Robert was the first guest Peter had asked to dinner. He'd hoped Rose would come again, but she hadn't yet that month.

Peter made a gesture with his arm to indicate to Robert the apartment.

Robert nodded and took off his hat, coat and brown patent leather shoes.

Peter hung up the coat in a small closet by the door and put the hat on the top shelf. Robert sat down at the table while Peter stirred the hamburger and got down two plates.

"Nous, les ingénieurs, les constructeur-méchaniciens, on va faire un autre avion," Robert said from the table.

"What?"

"Une reproduction."

"Why?" Peter put a plate down in front of Robert. "What would be the purpose in that?"

"Mais, the plane won't fly."

Peter put his plate down. "They're making an Arrow that won't fly?" There was a pause. A pop as Peter opened the wine.

"Pour un musée ... the Toronto Museum of Flight."

Peter laughed. "Have we gotten that old?" He dished out the hamburger, rice and a spoonful of carrots onto the plates. He hadn't prepared enough carrots. He was used to cooking only for himself.

"To preserve the fact of the plane. Pour s'en souvenir," Robert said pouring wine into the hockey-player glasses.

Peter sat down. He looked at their plates. "Do you want me to make more carrots?"

"Non, c'est parfait." Robert put the paper towel that was the dinner serviette onto his lap. They ate in silence.

"How can you possibly move straight into construction?" Peter asked. "With what plans?"

"They've found blueprints that were secreted. Some of ours, Pierre. I have seen them. The rest we will have to invent."

"Do they need help?"

"I need help. I am in charge of the wings."

Peter looked at Robert. "You're asking me to do my old job, for which I used to get paid, work for which there used to be a purpose, all in my spare time, on weekends presumably, after I have finished working my real job for the week, and I will do this with you just for fun?"

"For fun," Robert explained.

Peter ate a forkful of rice. It was overcooked. How did he manage to overcook Instant Rice? "I have to say your plan sounds ludicrous."

"Good." Robert said and poured himself more wine. "You will join me Saturday."

"I said the plan sounds crazy."

"Yes, but I can see the gladness in the eye corners, Pierre. I told the others. Pierre, I know him. He will join us on Saturday."

¶ After dinner Robert and Peter played chess. Peter made coffee. The dishes sat in the sink. He leaned back in his chair as Robert chose his move and he watched for the street lights to turn on outside the window. "What do you think of my apartment?"

Robert moved a bishop blocking Peter's queen.

Peter moved a pawn.

Robert looked around the tiny carpeted room. "It is agreeable."

Peter could tell Robert didn't like it. "I have a bathtub. It's not just one of those shower stalls."

"Yes," Robert said, not even looking toward the washroom.

"You don't like it."

Robert stared at the chessboard and then up at his friend. "How is Lucille?"

"It's your turn," Peter said.

"Did she want you resting in this apartment also?"

"Your knight's in trouble."

"This was your choice?"

"I don't want to hear you tell me that I should have stayed with Lucille, okay Robert? Can we agree to that? I just want to have a relaxing evening."

"Why did you leave her?" Robert's fingers rested on the battlement of his rook.

"You're not going to do anything about that knight?"

"Was she...infidèle?"

"No. Nothing like that," Peter said. He paused. "This is a better life. This place is a better place for me. The kids can come visit. There's an open invitation. I'm having dinner with all three of them and Lucy next Sunday night at the house. Rose came over. Rose came over the first week I was gone."

"Non, Pierre," Robert said. In a swift move of his rook he put Peter in check. "I don't think the choice is good."

"What's not good? You said it was agreeable." Peter looked at his cornered king.

Robert was silent for a moment. He looked around the apartment, appraising the sparse furnishings: the carefully made bed with its thin grey blanket and folded hospital corners; the curtains sighing in and out with the breeze. "You will be sad here."

Peter realized the more he stared at the black and white squares surrounding his king that Robert hadn't just put him in check but in checkmate. He looked at his friend. "You've never been married, Robert. You wouldn't know."

"You are correct. I don't know what it is to wake up with a wife."

¶ Robert put the chess pieces and board back in their leather case. Peter took down Robert's hat and held out his coat to him.

"Come over again. I'll watch out for your rook next time."

"I will telephone you about Saturday."

"For the remaking of the doomed plane."

"Non," Robert said, "the reborn plane." He surrounded Peter with the arms of his houndstooth coat and clapped him hard on the back, "comme un phénix," he said, and walked out of Peter's apartment into the flickering florescent light of the corridor.

It was a slow day at the donut shop. Lisa Heinrich went home with a headache after honey-dipping the crullers and now it was just Maryanne and Andy. Alma was the only customer and the sound of her cards slapped against the corner table as she played solitaire. Andy was hunched over a spiral-bound notebook in his position at cash. Maryanne scooped coffee grounds into a floppy paper filter.

The owner had introduced new flavoured coffees. Andy couldn't stand coffee to begin with, but maple walnut? That was an ice cream flavour. Coffee, Andy believed, should remain coffee flavoured.

"What are you drawing?" Maryanne asked over her shoulder.

"Nothing."

She dumped the used maple walnut grounds into the garbage and manoeuvred a freshly-filled coffee filter into the machine.

Andy looked down at the images in his notebook: three spherical shapes proportionately drawn in the square grid of the graph pages: the Segmentor from the side; the Segmentor from below; the Segmentor from above, with special detail given to the ergonomics of the handle and the angle of curvature for the blades.

"I didn't even know that you drew." Maryanne turned on a red switch and the maple walnut began to brew. "Can I see?"

"I don't draw. Kier was the one to draw. At least he took lessons when we were younger."

Maryanne came over and stood next to Andy at the cash. She looked down at his notebook.

"I'm working on a mechanical device that segments grapefruits for a quick and healthy breakfast," Andy said.

Maryanne laughed.

Andy wrinkled his brow and continued. "You start with a grapefruit already cut in half width-wise." He pointed to the figures drawn in his book with the eraser tip of his pencil. "The ring of blades that you see here in figure two presses downward when you gently put pressure on the ergonomic handle in figure three." Next to him Maryanne smelled metallic and sweet and the scent reminded him of the Ferris wheel at the Canadian National Exhibition when he was younger. "The slight curve to the blades is modeled after samurai swords known as Tachi." The Ferris wheel safety bar and a new-spun cloud of pink cotton candy and suddenly Toronto and the harbour beneath his dangling feet. "The tip of the knife-blades, the Kissaki, is what impales the grapefruit on first impact. The angle allows for perfect segmentation and," Andy demonstrated with a movement of his wrist, "if you give a slight twist to the handle once the Segmentor is fully plunged, the entire meat of the fruit is separated from the pith and the skin acts as a natural bowl."

"You've always been like this, haven't you?" Maryanne asked. "Since you were a kid?"

"I'm applying the principles of samurai sword fighting to breakfast knives."

"You built models and robots didn't you?"

"It works on oranges too."

"I bet you had a chemistry set."

Andy looked from the lines of the Segmentor to Maryanne. "No. We never had a chemistry set. My dad always wanted to get us one, but Mum thought we'd obliterate the upstairs rooms."

The door chimed and Andy put his notebook under the counter. He served a man in a ball cap a cup of regular flavoured coffee and a Berliner and the man took a seat by the front window. Maryanne went into the back.

"I think you need a mascot," Maryanne said holding a stack of clean trays at her hip. "You know, like Tony the Tiger or Toucan Sam. Breakfast items seem to have mascots."

"Do you have something in mind?" Andy asked.

"I'm thinking like a stegosaurus mixed with the Minotaur." Maryanne put down the stack of trays. She grabbed a pen resting on the cash register and a paper napkin from a dispenser. She drew a fiercesome grapefruit-slashing mascot in samurai-inspired workout gear. A band across the grapefruit-monster's forehead shone with the rays of a great eastern sun.

"My mom wants you to come for dinner on Sunday," Andy said as he looked down at Maryanne's design.

"Seriously?"

"Well, I asked if you could come for dinner and she said wouldn't that be lovely."

Maryanne slid her drawing across the counter to Andy.

"I think it's going to be weird though. My dad's coming. So if you don't want to come, I'll understand."

The man with the ball cap balled up his waxy paper donut slip with a loud crinkle, tossed it into the garbage and left with another chime of the door. Alma shuffled her deck and looked out the window to the parking lot.

"Count me in," Maryanne said.

Andy took Maryanne's napkin-drawing and pressed it between the pages of his notebook.

"You should patent the Segmentor," she said.

"Can I use your mascot?" Andy asked.

They leaned against the counter.

"Yes," Maryanne said, "but when you make it big you have to share the profits so we can both stop working here."

A click behind them indicated that the maple walnut had brewed.

"Do me a favour?" Maryanne opened her hand, palm up on the counter. "Put your hand right here?"

Andy put his hand in hers.

"Better," Maryanne said and, holding hands with Andy, they leaned against the counter.

Rose read a *Seventeen* magazine, her legs slung sideways in Peter's reading chair. Maryanne flipped through a photo album on the settee. Lucy had made more food than they could possibly eat. There was a stuffed roast chicken in the oven, mashed potatoes, steamed carrots, a green salad, and a mini rainbow-coloured marshmallow salad that the recipe book had called *Ambrosia: Food of the Gods.* They were snacking on crab dip and Sociables crackers. The family never had hors d'oeuvres in the living room together. Lucy never bought Sociables crackers. She'd asked Andy to make everyone cocktails except for Rose, and Kier was reading out drink names from the Savoy Cocktail Book: *Magnolia Blossom, Tuxedo, Zanzibar.*

"You boys are too cute." Maryanne had found a photograph of Kier and Andy waiting for the school bus in matching plaid coats. They held lunch boxes in one hand and green canvas satchels in the other. A magnifying glass was sticking out from Kier's coat pocket and a toy rubber snake coiled around Andy's wrist.

Andy looked over from the hutch where the liquor was kept. "We always had to wear these stupid matching coats."

"They weren't stupid," Lucy said from the swinging kitchen doors, "you two looked darling."

Kier rolled his eyes at Andy.

They were waiting for Peter. It was the first Sunday dinner since he'd left. Dinner was supposed to be simple, but then Rose noticed that Lucy started to freak out halfway into the afternoon and made Andy rush out and get more eggs so she could make an angel food cake instead of serving the half-eaten tub of pistachio ice cream from the freezer. "It's just Dad," Rose kept saying. "He doesn't need all this."

¶ "Hi there." Peter stood at the screen door where Lucy had last seen him leave.

"Hi," she said from the stepstool, startled. She was taking down the windmill-patterned plates. "You've had your hair cut."

He opened the screen door and put a paper bag with a bottle of wine down on the floor and leaned over to unlace his shoes. The nook was gone. He stared at the steel legs of the resurrected Formica table.

Lucy stepped down off the stool. "Let me take your coat."

"Relax, will you? I know where the closet it." He walked out of the kitchen and into the hall.

"I am relaxed," Lucy said after him, holding the china plates against her chest.

Lucy handed Kier the stack of plates to put around the mahogany dining table that she had already set with six linen napkins and the good silver. She'd covered the table with a lilac cloth that she'd found in the upstairs linen closet, an unopened wedding gift. She had looked at the packaging and knew that she had tucked it in the closet decades ago to save it for a special occasion. When Lucy saw that unopened tablecloth in the closet she had the thought that there was no point in saving anything for a special occasion, that *now* was a special occasion, or at least it ought to be if one was paying attention.

Kier thought that the table looked like the cover of a Victorian novel. He had been noticing aesthetics more after the acid. He remembered washing his face that morning, after the pancakes, before he went to sleep, and how good the washcloth had felt as he looked out the open bathroom window at the sun through the leaves. He wanted to feel that good about a washcloth every morning.

He'd seen Alice that week to tell her about a scholarship cheque for continued university studies. "They just sent me the cheque made out to Kier Jacobs. This has to be a mistake." It was more money than he'd ever had to himself. He hadn't told Ricky or his family. "Don't they know that if I was completely irresponsible I could cash this and leave the country?"

"People who get scholarship cheques aren't irresponsible." Alice flopped down on a couch beneath the poster of Che Guevara and lit a bidi. "What about that statue with the human eyes you were telling me about? You said you wanted to be an archaeologist."

"The charioteer of Delphi?" asked Kier. He'd forgotten that he'd told Alice about the statue. One of the few bronzes in the Early Classical style to retain its glass inlaid eyes. Had he mentioned the bronze votive horse from the Geometric period? When Professor Kostalis had shown the slide to Kier's class he had stared, enraptured, at the horse's long snout and sad eyes caught in thought, as if the artist had poured the bronze into the wax-coated mud moulding just as the horse was trying to say something, and, realizing the new steadfastness of his position, became resigned never to speak again.

Kier had wanted Alice to convince him to use his scholarship cheque for something other than school. He'd wanted her to say, "Let's go then. Mexico? Greece? Where are you going to take me?" Instead she'd said, "Hey, listen to this," and picked up the book of Rumi she'd been reading. "Today, like every other day, we wake up empty and frightened." He stood there and shut his eyes. He had wanted just her voice to exist, to become a room. "Don't open the door to the study and begin reading. Take down a musical instrument. Let the beauty we love be what we do. There are a hundred ways to kneel and kiss the ground." Alice's voice sounded like a bell.

Laying out the plates Kier could see the beauty in the dinner table Lucy had set. Like Renoir's painting *Luncheon of the Boating Party*. The crispness of the linen napkins in the silver rings. The round repetition of the plates. Kier wondered if this was some sort of secret he had never realized before: that the repetition of plates and the roughness of a washcloth were actually just beautiful on their own, without hallucinogens. "Let the beauty we love be what we do." The thought felt expansive. Almost too much for his mind. Like the universe was, for a brief moment, inside the cave of his skull.

The set table and the blue plates and the sound of Rose's voice reading an article to Maryanne from her magazine. Kier looked into the blue china hills and windmills he had set down and realized he would not stay in Malton or Toronto. Wherever he went he would ask Alice to come along.

¶ "Do you want me to get the corkscrew?" Lucy asked as she brought out the first of many dishes of food.

"I know where the corkscrew is," Peter said.

"And glasses?" Lucy asked behind her into the kitchen where Peter had gone.

"You didn't have to go to this much trouble, Lucille."

"Andy, will you get the other salad?"

"I don't want this to be a chore for you," Peter said in a raised voice from the kitchen. "I know you're busy. Let's just keep these meals casual, okay? Hamburger Helper is all I need. Instant Rice."

"Instant Rice has no nutrients, you know that, right Peter?" Lucy shouted to the swinging kitchen doors. "Those packaged foods have the nutritional equivalent of paste."

Peter came back with two glasses and the uncorked wine and sat down, deliberately ignoring her.

"Kier," Lucy said, "could you bring the pepper to the table?" He retrieved the crystal salt and pepper shakers on the sideboard. "Andy, have you introduced Maryanne?"

"I was getting the salad."

"Peter, this is Maryanne," Lucy gestured to Maryanne at the other end of the table. "Andrew's new girlfriend."

"Mum, please."

Maryanne unfolded her cloth napkin from its silver ring and smoothed it over her lap.

"Well she is, isn't she Andrew? Your girlfriend?" Lucy turned to Rose. "You'll eat some carrots, Rosie. I read that they're good for eyesight." Lucy surveyed the table and then joined her hands together. "Let's say grace then, shall we?"

Everyone stared at her. They never had Sociables crackers and they never said grace.

"Who would like to say it?"

Peter clinked his fork down in disbelief. "Lucille ..." Peter warned.

"Peter, just stop it, you don't know." She kept her hands together. "Kier? Would you say grace for us?"

"I don't know how ..."

"I'll start," Maryanne said. She bowed her head.

Andy looked over at her.

"I am thankful for the hands that prepared this food. I'm thankful for Alma and I hope that she'll be okay. And I'm thankful for my boyfriend, Andrew, the inventor. If anyone else has anything they'd like to say...?"

"I am *so* thankful that Rachel is back from horse camp," Rose said.

"I hope for peace," Kier said.

There was silence. Peter didn't say anything. Andy didn't say anything.

"I'm thankful for the priest who took me from the field, wherever he may be," Lucy said. Kier and Andy looked up at one another from across the table. She had never mentioned that.

"Okay," Maryanne said.

"Amen," Lucy said.

"I'm going." Peter stood up.

"What?" Lucy gaped at him.

"I'm going. This isn't what we talked about."

"Sit down."

Peter stayed standing.

"Dad," Rose finally said. "I think you should sit down."

Peter looked at his daughter. Then at Lucy. "We'll talk about this later," he said and sat.

"Don't speak to me like I'm a child," Lucy said.

"I said we'll talk about this later."

Lucy adjusted her silverware so her fork and knife were square with her plate. "Please, everyone," she said, "help yourselves or it will get cold." She took the serving spoon in front of her and scooped up a spoonful of Ambrosia.

"I wanted this to be a casual dinner," Peter said.

She held the serving spoon above her plate, the tiny multi-coloured marshmallows wobbling. "I mean it," Lucy said, her voice stretched and piercing, "dig in."

"I wanted this all to be simple," Peter went on.

Lucy dumped the spoonful of salad onto her plate with a thwack and looked fiercely across the table at Peter. "Stop it," she said, holding the sticky spoon up like a gavel, tiny marshmallows and yogurt slicking its surface. "Seriously, just stop it with your high and mighty attitude."

He grimaced at her.

"I don't believe I need to be the one to tell you the obvious, Peter." She spoke with the spoon still in her hand. "You have left your family." She held her frame upright like a statue of blind Athena holding the scales of justice. "I know you live in some fashionable high-rise in Yorkville or Yorkdale or Yorktown or whatever, and that it must be hard for you to comprehend that when you aren't here life goes on without you," she took a breath and continued, "but you no longer get to say what's for dinner. You don't get to tell me that you just want something simple—Instant Rice for godsake—because you. Don't." She spoke with the same rhythmic hammering as the axe slamming into the chrome-topped table, "Live. Here."

She stared at her husband sitting smugly, and, then, as if a doctor had hit her wrist with a patellar hammer, Lucy's hand flicked in uncontrollable reflex and the salad that remained on the spoon flew through the air above the table, past Maryanne, Andy, Rose and Kier. The sticky parabola hovered, ever so briefly, in a rainbow of movement between them all, before its arc ended directly at Peter's forehead; a mini marshmallow stuck to his eyebrow, coconut and mandarin orange slices sliding down the edge of the tablecloth and onto his lap.

Peter sat silently for a moment. He leaned forward on his chair. He leaned back. He took the cloth napkin out of its ring.

Rose, Kier, Maryanne and Andy stared. Lucy sat as still as a vase, watching her husband from across the table, the spoon still held upward, yogurt dripping onto her wrist.

Peter unfurled the linen napkin and lowered his head. He

carefully blotted the glob of salad from his forehead. He dabbed at the splotches of ambrosia that had landed in his lap. He put the napkin down beside his dinner plate and looked up but did not meet Lucy's gaze. Peter opened his mouth as if he was about to say something but then closed it and just shook his head slightly from side to side. Finally, he leaned forward toward the centre of the table, slow and deliberate, still not looking at Lucy. He picked up the serving dish of mashed potatoes and brought it toward him. He placed a spoonful delicately onto the side of his dish. His entire body was rigid. Peter passed the bowl of potatoes to Maryanne on his right.

This movement of Peter's arm and Maryanne's acceptance of the dish without incident signalled to Kier that he should say something, anything, to relieve the unbearable weight of silence, particularly before he laughed, a sensation he could feel at the base of his belly like a pressurized bottle of Orange Crush.

"The snowflakes," Kier said to no one in particular, "were Al's PhD thesis."

Silence.

"Al?" Rose asked, reaching cautiously for the carrots. "The short guy with black hair?"

"No, that's Ricky. Al's tall and lanky. He was playing records when you came to the Bev."

A taut bow of silence remained where the marshmallow had flown, flexing in the air between Lucy and Peter.

"This girl," Kier continued, "Alice and I. We were making snowflakes in this room together." He took a piece of chicken onto his plate. "We found two pairs of scissors ..." but before Kier could finish his story another spoonful of food sprayed itself across the table. Peter, it turned out, had not resigned himself to sit silently after all and a sweep of greens followed by stuffing followed by carrots rained itself across the table toward Lucy.

¶ Kier was pretty certain the table didn't look like *Luncheon of the Boating Party* anymore. He, Andy, Rose and Maryanne had slowly slipped beneath the lilac tablecloth as Peter and Lucy began to throw their entire dinners at one another.

226

"You will never," they heard Peter say, "speak to me like that again."

More food hit the surface of the table like the dump of a snowplough.

"Not toward the record player!"

The children were crouched down by the table legs. Maryanne had stretched her bangled arm up into the crossfire for the rest of the red wine Peter had brought.

"Here," she passed the bottle to Rose.

Rose liked it under the table. It felt like her blanket fort. She'd always gotten into trouble as a kid for slipping under the booths if ever they went to a restaurant, but now she remembered why she liked it. It felt dark and quiet and she could look at everyone's legs detached from their heads and not have to pay attention to what they were saying to each other.

"Now what?" Kier asked, leaning against a table leg.

"I am seriously liking coming over to your house," Maryanne said to Andy.

¶ They passed the bottle of wine around in a slow circle and when the bottle was finished the fighting above seemed to have stopped. "Dessert?" they could hear Lucy asking from above the table.

"What?" Andy said. "She can't be serious."

They slowly slid back into their seats.

"I'd love some," Maryanne said. She used her napkin to wipe a section of table free from potatoes and greens.

Lucy served the angel food cake on the blue windmill dessert plates with a silver serving dish of raspberry coulis. Peter refused to eat. He sat at the table with his hands loose and defeated in his lap. Then, without excusing himself, he went upstairs to the washroom to clean his shirt in the sink.

"A lovely cake," Maryanne offered. The purple tablecloth was covered in a thick slick of chicken, carrot and marshmallow slime.

Rose stayed behind to help Lucy clean up. Peter took the others to the A&W for teen burgers.

¶ Alice had told Kier about Al's thesis after she'd read him the passage from Rumi. Kier had been leaving, standing at the beaded curtain door that led to the porch. "You know the snowflakes," she'd said, almost as an afterthought.

"Yeah?" Kier asked.

"Al woke up that afternoon, after your sister came. He made Ricky and me a coffee, and Ricky was going on and on about lucid dreaming and this unconsciousness stuff, and then Samantha came over." Alice paused. "Have you met Sam? She's this really hip chick I met at the café down the street. She plays at the open mic, and she's performing in *Hair* next week. Samantha's getting naked on stage. I can't wait." Alice put out her hand-rolled cigarette in a mermaid-shaped ashtray on a shelf by the door.

"And the snowflakes?"

"Right. So Ricky and Samantha and I are all having coffee, right? And Al says he's gotta get to work and takes his coffee upstairs and then, like a minute later, I hear this cry from the top of the stairs. It was a cry too, not a scream. Like someone gulping." Alice twisted the blonde strands of her hair. "And so I go to see what's going on, and Al's at the top of the stairs holding a snowflake, man."

"How many did we make again?"

"It's like an entire chapter of his thesis."

"We made snowflakes out of a chapter of his thesis?"

"Yeah, but get this. The best part is that he's studying the glacial formations in northern Labrador."

"I don't get it."

"Like, he's basically studying snow."

"Was he mad?" Kier bumped into the beaded curtain behind him and it made a shushing sound.

"He said he'd try to read through the snowflake-holes and retype."

NOBODY WRITES HOME

L ucy sat at the counter in the Zellers restaurant with her grocery bags on the brown vinyl seats to either side of her. Packets of green Jell-O and canned peaches peeked out of the bag to her left. Lucy planned on setting a Jell-O salad in the copper rooster dessert mould when she got home, the peaches fanning out like feathers.

She knew she shouldn't put the grocery bags on the chairs to either side of her like this, that other patrons might want to sit at the counter. But Lucy didn't want to make idle chit-chat with the older ladies who'd gotten their perms done—all they talked about was *General Hospital* and rainy weather—and the small cafeteria was mostly empty, so Lucy kept the bags where they were, a fortress to either side of her while the background shopping music played light and twinkly, making you forget about the prices of things.

Lucy swivelled on her stool sipping a chocolate milkshake. She could feel the coldness of the ice cream at the back of her throat, a slight ache in her jawbone, like breathing in winter. She stared ahead at the shine off the milkshake machine, the smart-looking eight-slot toaster, the mini boxes of Raisin Bran lined up on a shelf above the counter. She kept her lips on her straw and swivelled back and forth in her seat, hovering over her life, observing distantly, sipping her milkshake.

¶ Mr. Miller was a retired man who had moved into the Romanos' house next door when Connie and the kids had left after the cancellation. He collected antique licence plates and talked to Kier about a Mustang convertible that sat under a tarpaulin in his driveway. Mr.

Miller's wife was the best gardener on the street. She would some-times send him out into the yard to do the weeding. When Ms. Not-tingham drove up, Mr. Miller was resting his knees on an old floral cushion, leaning over the front bed trying to determine which were weeds and which were flowers. He wore comfortable green suede gardening gloves that made him feel like he might be able to fig-ure out what he was meant to be doing without going inside to ask his wife. He knelt facing this task when the school secretary drove hurriedly down the street and stopped outside the Jacobs' house. Through the slats in the fence all he could see was her brown skirt and her blonde bob moving up the path to the front door.

Ms. Nottingham knocked repeatedly on the front door and then began to panic. She had already tried phoning, but had left her desk, gotten in her car and driven to the Jacobs' house in the end, because she had been instructed to try everything. She remembered seeing Rose once before when the girl had felt dizzy and had to sleep in the infirmary—a small white room where the nurse worked, behind Ms. Nottingham's desk.

"Hello? Mrs. Jacobs?" She peered into the windows, moved back to the front door, knocked again, louder than politeness would nor-mally allow. "Hello?"

Mr. Miller stood and brushed off his knees. He moved to the fence that separated the properties. He saw Ms. Nottingham more com-pletely now, her hands twisting a torn piece of tissue, worried lines at the corners of her squinting brown eyes.

Ms. Nottingham moved backwards, almost to the edge of the sidewalk, with a hand at her brow, looking towards the upstairs window. "Hello? Mrs. Jacobs?"

"Hello." Mr. Miller spoke across the fence to her.

Ms. Nottingham jumped.

"Could I be of some help?"

"I'm looking for Mrs. Lucille Jacobs. Rose Jacobs' mother."

Mr. Miller knew Rose; she'd once knocked on their door to retrieve a soccer ball she'd kicked into their backyard. His own daughter had moved out a long time ago down to Chicago.

"She's not in, Ma'am. She's gone to the shopping plaza I believe. Goes most Thursdays."

Ms. Nottingham looked as if she were about to cry.

"Let me fetch her for you." He took off his gloves. "Here, you just sit on the front step and I'll fetch her."

Ms. Nottingham did as she was told. She was relieved to sit down and raised the torn tissue by way of a thank you, her other hand nervously at her throat, but Mr. Miller had already left, jogging quickly down the street. Ms. Nottingham sat with her knees at her chin, just like a girl might. She smoothed the wales of her corduroy skirt and tried to breathe normally, holding in a sob.

Mr. Miller ran to the street lights, through the tiny strip mall's parking lot and into the closest doors of the Zellers. He happened to see Lucy on his way through to the grocery store. He could see her staring off at nothing, the half-drunk chocolate milkshake, a lipstick mark on her straw. He didn't even have to page her on the intercom. The twinkly music in the background continued to twinkle, and his disruption of her solitude was as unobtrusive as possible, no loud shouting, no panic. Instead, he said four words to her, put a dollar bill on the counter and grabbed onto her wrist. Then they both ran out of Zellers, the grocery bags with the green Jell-O and canned peaches forgotten on the brown swivel chairs.

Maybe it would have been different if Lucy had been at home. If she had answered the door herself, to Ms. Nottingham's first rapid knocks. Maybe Lucy would have been all right if she'd answered the door drying off her hands with a dishtowel, looking gracious, as if she'd been expecting someone. Maybe, when the school secretary said the speech she'd practised over and over in the car—"Your daughter fell down on the school playing field. She's in the hospital. I'll take you to her."—Lucy would have said calmly, "It will be all right," to Ms. Nottingham, and taken the house keys from the key-shaped key hook from the kitchen door, picked up her purse from the handle on the hallway closet, gotten into the secretary's car, and still been okay afterward. But that's not the way it happened. Lucy knew as soon as she heard Mr. Miller say, "I think it's Rose." She knew with immediate utter certainty that her daughter was dead. And by the time Lucy was standing on the lawn with Ms. Nottingham; by the time Ms. Nottingham tearfully tried to talk to Lucy and take her to the hospital; by the time she was seated in the passenger seat of Ms. Nottingham's car, something in Lucy's brain had already clicked, had switched over, almost like turning off a light. Lucy's brain went to that place where the twinkly shopping music played all the time. So that when she finally found herself beside Rose's dead body, and when Peter arrived, and Andy, and then Kier, Lucy was hovering over the entire scene like she had been hovering over her milkshake: detached and alone; the ache of winter in her clenched teeth and jawbone.

Rose was playing soccer and ooohhh what a kick! What a soar. What a sail. What a fly over the clouds, up and over, above it all. Thick white fluff like Mama's marshmallow s'mores. What a day! Standing tall in her green soccer socks pulled up tight to her knees. Here, over here, the one with the red braids! The girl who looks strong and fast in her green and yellow T-shirt, in her shiny soccer shorts. Look at those tiny blonde hairs on her tanned arms, look at the freckles on her nose, her sharp green eyes taking it all in: the field and the sun and the smell of the freshly mown lawn. And now she's gone, the rest of them still planted firmly on the earth's soft grasses, and not grateful enough for a moment of it. None of them enjoying the air, how it feels to breathe, what it means to ache slightly in the hip, or scratch absent-mindedly at an itch, or feel their eardrums throbbing from music loud in their headphones. All those great bands Kier would play for her when he was home: *The White Album*, Lou Reed, The Brubeck Quartet. Nobody buys ice cream enough. (Oh strawberry! Just to have one frozen strawberry!) Nobody lies down on their backs and looks at the shapes of clouds enough. Nobody writes home enough. Letters with real stationary and pens and *sincerely* and *yours truly* and *love*!

And she died right before summer holidays. Right on June 19, 1971. What a dumb day to die on. Three sleeps from summer vacation and hanging out at the pool with her friends and having the tip of her nose burn the way it did. If only she could have died on September 1st and had one more summer, had the chance to wear her new red bathing suit. If only she could have had the feeling of the sun on her shoulders at her suit straps one last time. The taste of warm lemonade out of her tartan Thermos. Salmon sandwiches how Lucy made them on thick brown bread with English salad dressing. Hostess salt and vinegar potato chips in those little silver bags.

But oooohhh what a kick! What a perfect kick! The ball hitting the side arch of her foot. Her muscles so strong like that. Pushing under the ball and up and up and up it flew to the sky. Her T-shirt sweaty from all that running and all that kicking. Her throat sore from shouting at her teammates, "Rachel, hey Rache! Go left!" or "Sue, Sue, over here! I'm open!" And then that perfect kick. Up and up and up and all of the other Phys. Ed. classes on the field just standing there looking toward the sun, the ball still going, higher and higher and higher. And Rose, feeling her heart so big in her chest, so full and thumping against each rib, so expansive like the green field. And then an eclipse—the black and white circle of the soccer ball covering up the sun. And Rose, face down on the earth. Each perfect blade of grass. Each tiny beetle and little black ant in the blades of it. That rich smell of mud and dirt and grass-stained shirts. And then that last deep gulping breath and all those smells and her classmates yelling at each other and the teacher's whistle, and the sun so faint now off in that distance.

Lucy chose the photograph of Rose from the top of the piano to place on the small altar with flowers, on the hill of the graveyard, where her daughter's coffin would come. In the photo Rose is wearing her favourite pair of bell-bottomed jeans and a green T-shirt with three blue stripes up the arms. On her feet are sandals and you can even see the pink polish on her toes. Rose's soccer team and their families had come back to the house the night the photo was taken, after a league match at the end of the previous summer; after the girls had changed out of their uniforms and called each other on the phone to decide where they were going to put their medals. Upstairs, as the photo was taken, Rose's medal hung on the bedpost in her bedroom. It's still there, where Lucy rests now in the afternoons. The red and blue of the ribbon faded, the medal's shine dulled.

That evening, Peter had come over and, although reticent, flipped burgers in the backyard and drank beer with the other dads. Earlier, before the game, Rose and Lucy had sat together on the vinyl rocking chaise in the backyard with a big silver mixing bowl between their feet. They shucked two dozen cobs of sweet summer corn which were then wrapped in tinfoil to be roasted over coals next to the hamburger patties. Rose is laughing in the photograph. She's leaning forward slightly toward the camera, toward Lucy. She has freckles on her nose. The sun is to Rose's left, just above the roof of the house, and in the viewfinder Lucy saw a rainbow crystal of sunlight above Rose's head. Lucy snapped the photograph just then, the sun moving through the lens of the Kodachrome, and with a click of the shutter the image of her daughter burned itself permanently laughing, permanently leaning-forward, onto the film.

¶ And now, as quick as the click of the Kodachrome, she was gone.

¶ She was not sleeping. She was not breathing. She was not waving a leaflet in front of her face like a fan. She could not sit next to Lucy on a folding metal chair. She did not just whisper into her mama's ear. She did not dig the heels of her good shoes into the sod to form two moons of dark earth while she waited for the men to come up from the hearse with her casket on their shoulders. She could not smell the syrupy scent of the flowers her classmates had brought; petals of white roses, pink lilies, purple irises wilting in the sun. She couldn't see that Rachel held a parasol over Trina's head or notice that Rachel's fingertips were raw from where she'd bitten her fingernails to the quick. Rose couldn't see that the girls clutched their grief into their handkerchiefs like Girl Guide knots. She did not wave to her friends. They could not wave back. She was not coming out. She was nailed shut. Her heart had given up.

¶ Kier breathed in and bent his knees. Andy mirrored the movement on the casket's other side. Peter and a cousin were stationed behind. Kier bore the weight, gripping the brass handle, into the ridge of his shoulder, down his spine, through his back and into his feet, pushing against the ground. He couldn't think about what was inside the box.

They climbed the graveyard's slope and the people stood around the open rectangle of earth. They moved together, the four men, up the hill, and they put the casket down.

Andy sat on one side of Lucy and Kier sat on the other. Peter sat behind them, leaning forward and resting his hands on his sons' shoulders. Maryanne had come and had seated herself in a row at the back. She did not wear the eyeliner Rose had liked because she did not want black streaks across her face when she squeezed Andy's shoulder goodbye that night.

Andy and Kier both held Lucy's hands so they would stop shaking in her lap. "I want to feel something!" she had shouted at Kier in the grocery store parking lot and then slammed her left hand in the car door on purpose. Lucy had sobbed as Kier ran around the car, frantically undoing the lock through the open passenger window and released her from the door. She screamed and he held her, half in and half out of the car, his hand over her mouth, Lucy's spit on his palm, the people returning their shopping carts in the parking lot staring.

She was bruised, and now, at Rose's service, Kier touched his thumb to his mother's hand, delicately, how he would touch a ripe plum.

¶ After the service they drove back to the house in silence. Peter drove. Lucy sat in the seat beside him. Andy and Kier looked out opposite windows in the back.

The neighbours had brought over cakes and squares and sausage rolls and platters of cut-up carrot sticks. Robert had baked two tourtière from his mother's recipe. No one ate.

¶ For weeks afterward, Lucy sat as slow as a flower until she was a wilted stem. Kier brought her books from the library but she didn't read. Unfinished scarves she had knit and purled onto needles lay at her side. She occasionally reached for her diary that sat beside her on the settee, but she didn't write. Sometimes she walked up the stairs to fall asleep, sometimes she curled up in her clothes in the living room. Andy phoned Janice, Lucy's boss at the phone company, and requested a long-term sick leave for his mother. For two months she was relieved of her duties as operator and the hands of the blank-faced clock moved round and round.

To Lucy in her stillness the hours felt like a blur of movement: Kier with a cup of herbal tea that she let sit until it was cold; Andy with a blanket and more yarn he had picked up at a shop on his way home. Lucy's hands held her knitting needles but nothing moved. The clock hands ticked. The boys came and went. Kier read to Lucy out loud from his Ancient Civilizations textbook. Andy talked about films he'd seen with Maryanne. The moon hands moved round and round. But then, after a month of stillness and wilting, Lucy submersed herself in a warm bath. Her hands buttoned up a clean shirt, a black skirt. Her hands picked up the diary, picked up the pen, and scratched out, line by line, every single entry she had written. The pen pushed so hard that the pages tore:

January 27th ~~Early Morn. It is three. No one else is up. Had to say that the snow flurries and then the snowplows made the street look like a ladder to the horizon.~~

February 15th ~~Six years old is our Canadian flag, for in 1965 on this date the first time the Canadian flag flew on the parliament buildings in Ottawa. Gordon Sinclair says this day may be called Heritage Day. This afternoon, read more Virginia Woolf. Mrs. Dalloway and her party. Thought there were lilacs. There were no lilacs.~~

March 17th ~~Went to see cactus again. Slight problem with the garage door being frozen to the ground. Three kettles of hot water got the door free. Left around 9:30am. Also, got a new licence plate on my own first car. N34 496. "What things soever ye desire, when ye pray, believe that ye receive them, and ye shall have them." St. Mark 11:24.~~

April 27th ~~Would have been Duke Ellington's 72nd Birthday. Peter never liked The Duke.~~

May 4th ~~Full moon in the North West sky. Seems a little closer to Earth. Read that new book Kier bought me: Saint Urbain's Horsemen. Liked the sounds of Montréal. Should go to Montréal.~~

June 16th ~~Found Wrigley had a double wrapper on a single piece of gum. Andy taking aptitude test. Went downtown. Got a buy of foam treads slippers. Tried the new Crackling Bran cereal. A new taste in cereal. Watched "Misty" a horse on T.V.~~

June 17th ~~There is a rat in the compost and nobody to take it away.~~

June 18th ~~Chicken Hawk flying west. Read somewhere today that Gold was for victory, Frankincense was for prayer and Myrrh was for death. Why would you ever give a baby Myrrh? Bought Boy Scout apples.~~

June 19th

A blankness left on June 19:

And then Lucy standing up, making two phone calls and leaving the house wearing one black pump and one navy pump and only noticing once she'd already taken her seat on the bus.

Kier was unaware that Lucy had risen, dressed herself, and left the house for the first time since Rose's funeral the morning that he cashed his scholarship cheque and got on a plane to Vancouver. He packed a backpack full of clothes, two books, and one jar of Lucy's rhubarb strawberry jam. He left a note on the kitchen table: *Needed to get away for a while. Want some distance. Sending a postcard soon.* By the time he arrived in Vancouver he was hungry and it was night.

¶ The taxi descended toward English Bay from the slopes of Fairview. Kier could see the lights of the downtown office towers like vertical columns of constellations. Above the buildings were ribbons of light in the sky that Kier didn't understand.

Kier pointed out the front window. "What are those?" he asked the cabbie when they had reached a stop light.

"Ski hills. Seymour, Cypress, and then you've got Grouse."

"Those are mountains?"

A pool of darkness where the ocean was.

The cabbie took him to a hostel on Jericho Beach, driving through a neighbourhood he called Kitsilano, places named after Spanish explorers with gold in the holds of their galleons hundreds of years ago. There were people out on every street. Kier could smell fried meat, bananas. A blur of coloured Christmas lights hung from the trees along Fourth Avenue. Tables and an assortment of kitchen chairs huddled on patios and decks. Children played with a new puppy on the corner of Fourth and Larch while two Nordic-looking couples wearing lose cotton caftans and colourful saris sat on a set of stairs laughing and drinking beer from the bottle. Kier could hear the chime of one of the women's bangles through the open taxi window as she pushed her hair back from her face.

Kier had told Alice that he loved her the morning he left. He had cashed his scholarship cheque and thought she might come with him out west. He told her about how pods of orcas come right into the harbour of downtown, breaching in the waters of English Bay. He told her he would find her a house with a porch and a view of the ocean where she could plant another herb garden and play the guitar like Joni Mitchell. They had stayed up talking late into the night on the porch of the Bev until the sun began to rise. When he'd said I love you, Alice had laughed.

He looked at her. "No, Alice. I love you."

She stopped laughing.

"Please come with me."

Alice pulled her hair into her fist and twisted it. A cloud moved and the sun got brighter. A wind chime made a hollow metal sound that made Kier feel empty and dull.

"I don't know what to say," Alice finally answered.

They sat quietly on the old couch on the porch and watched a woman push a shopping cart down Beverley Street. The cans and bottles she was collecting from people's garbage bins rattled and sounded how icicles sound in winter when they crash down from the eaves. The woman stopped to inspect a rusted hibachi barbeque that someone had put out. She poked at it with a branch she'd found and the branch went right through the rust. The woman threw away the stick and pushed her cart again, moving on.

"I should go," Kier said.

"Okay," Alice said and let go of her hair. She sat up on her knees on the couch. "I'm sorry," she said. "I'm just not…" and trailed off.

"Look," Kier said and then didn't finish. He kissed her cheek, grabbed his backpack and climbed down the wooden steps of the porch without looking back. He walked toward the woman's sound of falling icicles.

At home, Kier wrote the note, took the jar of jam, and, not yet having slept, not checking to see if either Lucy or Andy were home, left to wait at the airport for a standby seat on the next available flight. In Vancouver, he checked into his hostel by the beach, made the bed with clean sheets and, for the first time, heard the crashing of waves as he fell asleep.

A ndy was standing in his striped pyjamas, groggy from sleep, holding a bowl of cereal in one hand and a spoon in the other, when he saw Kier's note on the kitchen table. All he could think at first was, "Bastard." He looked at the pad of paper. Kier hadn't even bothered to use a normal piece of paper. He'd written in ballpoint on a skinny notepad printed with the face of a real estate agent who was smiling with false white teeth and a comb-over: *Needed to get away for a while. Want some distance.* Andy stared at his brother's quick scrawl. He looked out the window of the kitchen, holding onto his bowl, the flakes slowly getting soggy in the milk. A hovering group of crows in the backyard elm lifted off the branches and settled back down. Andy looked again at Kier's note. *Sending a postcard soon.*

¶ Andy took the bus to Maryanne's apartment. When he came in she was curled up on the couch. A cigarette and a stick of incense burned from the coffee table. She was looking at film reels in the light from her living room window. She was holding up the cells in a long line to see what shots she'd gotten. Silver circular cases were stacked in towers on the beige shag carpet just beside her. A curator had seen Maryanne's work at the Ontario College of Art grad show and had asked to exhibit the piece at a new gallery on Queen Street. Andy had gone down to the space with Maryanne just the week before. The front of the gallery had glass doors that rolled up into the ceiling like a mechanic's shop. There had been a wooden boat on display when they'd walked in, and all around the gallery were huge glass jars of water. "It's actual sea water," the gallery woman with the thick glasses had said. Andy watched a lonely minnow swim around in a jar while Maryanne went in the back to speak to the curator.

¶ Andy had come into Maryanne's apartment still wearing his pyjamas with a coat tied around his waist. "He needs to get away for a while," he said, quoting the note by heart. "He wants some distance. He's sending a postcard soon."

"Who?" Maryanne asked, putting the film reel down.

"Seriously, can you believe this shit?"

She motioned to the couch. "Come here."

"He wants some distance," Andy repeated.

"Who wants distance?" Maryanne tried again.

"... I totally understand needing a bit of perspective right about now, but couldn't he have gotten distance by, I don't know, like reading a book or something? Starting therapy?" Andy sat down next to Maryanne.

"Kier? Your dad?"

He picked up a magazine from the coffee table and put it back down again. "Kier. He's gone."

"Here," Maryanne motioned for Andy to put his feet onto her lap.

Andy turned and lay down on the couch. "You know what this means, right?"

Maryanne took his stockinged feet in her hands and began to massage them.

"This means I'm the only one left."

The apartment was silent except for a radio coming from the other room. Leonard Cohen's gravely voice from beyond the wall: *All the sisters of mercy, they are not departed or gone. They were waiting for me when I thought that I just can't go on.*

Maryanne pushed her thumbs deep into the soles of Andy's feet. "Be still, Andy."

He looked at her eyes the colour of glacial waters. *And they brought me their comfort and later they brought me this song.* Andy put his head back. He closed his eyes. *Oh I hope you run into them, you who've been travelling so long.*

Maryanne moved her hands to his heels. She held each of them in turn and rubbed deep into every place that Andy had ever walked. She put her palms against the soles of his feet and pushed and her hand became the backyard grass of his childhood house, and the beach sand of the Great Lakes, and the sidewalk, hot on summer days, when he and Kier would walk barefoot to the corner store to get Popsicles. *You who must leave everything that you cannot control.* Andy could feel the pressure of Maryanne's touch and then the release. He felt dizzy lying on the couch. He was suddenly flushed. He untied his coat. *It begins with your family, but soon it comes round to your soul.* He put a hand to his cheek and his cheek was wet. He was crying. When had he started crying? He sat up. "It's okay," Maryanne said. He looked at her. She slid her thumbs up his arches and massaged deeply. Andy leaned back and stared at the ceiling. His shoulders shook. "It's okay," Maryanne said again. And the room was silent and shushing and behind the music Andy could hear the faint clicking of pipes moving water through the wall.

J eremiah Bulmer sat beneath the Lady of the Night cactus with a plastic bag next to him. He held two paper cups of coffee. "You know, I have never had the pleasure of coming across the street into this Arid House until you suggested it on the phone," he said as Lucy sat down beside him.

"I have a fondness for this cactus," Lucy said.

Jeremiah gave Lucy one of the cups of coffee. "Just a touch of cream if I recall." Jeremiah gestured to the plastic bag between them. Inside was a plain white baker's box tied with string. "And sitting there are two of the best chocolatines this city has to offer."

"Thank you," Lucy managed, hardly noticing the presence of the box. The thought of any food in the month after Rose's death had made her just feel more hollow. "You are too kind."

"I'm so glad that you called again. I didn't mean to scare you away with my questions about your beliefs and going on as I did about Blake and all that. It was too forward of me. I often ask questions when I am not certain what else to say. It is a bad habit of mine. I need to learn how to listen."

"Why wouldn't you know what to say to me?"

"Well," Jeremiah untied the string and opened the box of pastries. He offered one to Lucy who shook her head. "I know you are looking for something, but I am just certain that it is not in me that you will find what it is you are seeking." He closed the box without taking one himself.

"My daughter has died," Lucy said without looking at the priest. She could feel Jeremiah's sleeve move against her arm as his posture changed and he leaned forward.

Jeremiah placed his coffee on the flagstones. He leaned forward as if in prayer but did not clasp his hands together. "You have already been through so much, Mrs. Jacobs."

"You mean my husband?"

"Yes, with your husband," Jeremiah said. "I cannot imagine—" he said and looked up at Lucy. "I am so terribly sorry," he said again.

"I was thinking about what you had asked me in your office the last time I came to visit. I was thinking of whether or not I believe in God," Lucy said. "And I told you at the time, I think, that I wasn't certain. That I might not believe. And I suppose I don't exactly believe because of the problem of suffering." Lucy had never spoken to anyone about this. It was as if inside of her a dollhouse was being opened on its hinge so that all of the furniture was revealed. "I don't understand how a god can exist if there is suffering. And I don't believe that my daughter is in heaven."

"You don't believe she's in heaven?" Jeremiah asked, still leaning forward.

"I don't believe in heaven," Lucy said. How far she had travelled since being that girl in a church pew in Saint James' Cathedral less than twenty blocks away. "I don't believe we should be relying on a great place of splendour if we live our lives a certain way."

Jeremiah leaned back against the bench again. "What if heaven wasn't a place exactly?" he finally said, almost not to Lucy but to the arms of the cactus. "What if it was like a clarity. Like piercing through a cloud. An assurance about the path of the world that is impossible for most humans to comprehend from our infinitesimal position in the universe."

"There is no assurance," Lucy said. "There is no assurance that our lives will work out a certain way."

"But that's exactly it. Not the way we had planned. But yet believing uninhibitedly. Trusting that both the good and the bad are God's will, despite what we have done or left undone."

"I don't believe in God's will. My child has died. There is no explanation."

"But your child lived. This is a miracle." Jeremiah made a tent out of the fingers of his hands while he was thinking. "Think of it another way. You never had that child. That child was never yours. And you got to spend ... how old was she?—"

"Twelve. Nearly thirteen."

"You got to spend thirteen years with her instead of not having any of that time."

Lucy stood up to go. "I'm sorry, but I actually don't think I should have come here," Lucy said. "You've been right all along. You aren't the person I'm looking for."

"What can I say to you?"

"Tell me the truth," Lucy picked up her coat. "No one has ever told me the truth."

"I am trying to."

Lucy picked up her bag and walked toward the glass doors of the Arid House. "Ma'am," she heard him say behind her and she stopped. For a brief moment hope guttered against her like the rain on the conservatory's roof. He would tell her what she had been waiting by the cactus to hear. He would say, Lucille, I have been meaning to tell you, and he would recall to her the field and the burning apple tree and the sticking right windshield wiper on his blue truck, and would tell her, years ago, that girl on an errand to get a cake had been her in his arms.

"Please take these," Jeremiah said. He was holding out the plastic bag with the baker's box in his hand. "They really are the best pastries in the city. And although you might not feel like them now, they might be what you're looking for a bit later. A little bit of sweet my mother always called them."

Lucy took the bag from Jeremiah's hand. "I am sorry that I've bothered you."

"You have been no bother to me whatsoever. It has been a pleasure meeting you."

"You as well, Reverend."

¶ Lucy walked to her streetcar stop and boarded amongst elbowing passengers. The streetcar clanged toward an area of the waterfront that Lucy hadn't visited in a long while. Her second phone call that morning had been unanswered so Lucy did not expect, standing on the sidewalk, that the door to the bar would be unlocked. From the exterior's chipped paint and the rusting bolts of the neon sign, the establishment looked as though it hadn't been opened for business in over a decade.

Lucy walked through the unlatched door to The Swan and up the stairs to the old entrance and the counter where the coat check stood. The shoulders of a few forgotten raincoats were covered in dust. Inside there was only one light on, above the stage, and Lucy could hear the music of an accordion before she could see anyone. A woman began to sing. The soloist breathing in time to her instrument's breath. The voice sounded out a lament. A ragged-sounding song. Lucy knew that in the billows of the accordion was the sound that had shunted back and forth in the chambers of Rose's heart.

Lucy leaned against the entrance to the dance hall of her youth and saw that the furniture had been covered in white sheets so that the room looked as though it were filled with children pretending that they were ghosts. Maybe Peter had been right. Maybe they should have been married in this bar. How different their whole marriage might have been if begun in a dance hall. But now there was no liquor on the shelves. The train car looked smaller than Lucy remembered, hunkered in darkness against the back wall. There was no noise from the kitchen and no cigarette smoke.

Lucy realized the song was finished only when she heard the

metal click of the accordion case and the sound of a stool scraping backward against the wooden floor of the stage as the musician stood.

"Hello?" Lucy said into the room.

"We're closed," the woman said.

Lucy walked further into the bar. "I'm looking for the address of a friend," she said walking between ghost chairs and tables toward the stage. "Claire Tilley France," Lucy said, and looking up to the slim woman in the stage light, her wild hair untied, realized that she had found her.

¶ When they sat down at a table in the back of The Swan with two glasses of straight gin that Claire had scrounged from the kitchen shelves, Lucy did not feel, as the neighbour-women like Linda Stewanakie or Connie Romano might have exclaimed of rekindled friendships from their youth, that "time had ceased to pass since their last meeting," or, that in seeing Claire again, "it was as if they could pick up where they left off." Instead, Lucy recalled a stanza from an Emily Dickinson poem she and Claire had been taught in the same high-school English class: *This is the Hour of Lead— Remembered, if outlived, As Freezing persons, recollect the Snow— First—Chill—then Stupor—then the letting go—*Over twenty winters lay between them across the table. The warehouse ceiling of the room made their silence high-roofed and immense.

"Pops is dead," Claire finally said in a gasping voice from taking too large a sip from her glass.

"So is Rose."

"Rose?"

"My daughter."

"Right."

Lucy looked around the room and then back at Claire. The empty shelves and booths. Claire's hair frizzed in unkempt strands. She wore a polka-dot dress that was too tight at the waist, as though she hadn't worn it since much younger days when Lucy could imagine the lace hem being crisp. One of Claire's heeled boots rested on her accordion case. She was wearing men's wool socks rather than stockings and this, the red and grey wool of Claire's socks, made Lucy think of Mimì's song from *La Bohème* and the woman's voice who sung to her in the apartment on College Street.

"I've come back," Claire said to Lucy's silence, "to see about the club. Charlie wants it sold, but me, I'm sentimental about this place."

"Why didn't you call me when you got in?"

Claire looked at Lucy. "Come on, Lu, what would I have said?"

"Hello? It's Claire?"

"It's been twenty-five years. What do we even have in common?"

Lucy turned her glass of gin on the table making circles in the dust. "Well, really?"

"When I thought of you in Paris I could picture your view of the Cathedral."

Claire knocked back the rest of her gin and put her glass down on the table too hard so that Lucy's spilled.

"I could hear a piano through the wall from another room and birds from a park; green tree light at breakfast falling across a newspaper, and a coffee with steamed milk; us winding our way along the canals on bikes in the afternoons."

"That's all very romantic, Lu, but I didn't stay in the apartment by Notre Dame. The woman was a drunk."

"But you sang with Duke Ellington."

"Ellington?"

"You sang in bars with Duke Ellington, Claire. Who gets to do that in their lifetime? Think of how lucky you are."

"I never sung with The Duke."

"You didn't?"

"I've been a burlesque dancer. I've taken my clothes off for businessmen. I have a large collection of feathered fans. But that's not something you write in a postcard, is it? Especially to your perfect housewife friend."

Lucy turned her glass again and then finally took a sip of the untouched gin. "Peter and I are getting a divorce."

There was a noise in the rafters. A struggling against a cracked pane of glass. Feathers floating down in the dusty shaft of light the window gave off.

"There are goddamn pigeons in the bar," Claire said.

Lucy looked up.

Claire reached her hand across the table so that her fingertips barely touched the sleeve of Lucy's blouse. "I'm sorry to hear about you and Peter."

Lucy looked at Claire. "I'm sorry to hear about your dad." She stared at her friend, dark circles beneath her eyes. Lucy shifted her chair back. "You're tired." Lucy took her purse off the shoulder of the chair and put it onto her own. "I was just trying to get an address. Your postcard didn't have a return address." Lucy paused, she picked up the plastic bag of pastries. "You were the only person I wanted to talk to."

"How old was Rose?"

"Almost thirteen," Lucy said, half standing, half sitting. Ready to leave but not certain she wanted to.

"God," Claire said.

"Just a month ago."

"I'm so sorry, Lu."

Lucy didn't know what to say. Any detail spoken would be trivial. Rose liked rock and roll. Rose could paddle a canoe. And she could run. Her head back and her ponytail and her face gleaming. Nothing spoken would be adequate. Nothing ever spoken would be adequate. Lucy stood. "I'm going to go." She touched Claire's shoulder. "Phone me if you want. When you get settled. Or stop by."

¶ When Lucy left the bar the asphalt streets with their streetcar tracks and subway vents were cobblestone. Down the harbourfront, the sugar factory had become the Tour d'Eiffel and its refining room the glass dome of the menagerie at the Jardin des Plantes. Algonquin and Ward Islands in the distance of boats and wild swans became the Île de la Cité with the Cathédral de Notre Dame, and the Île St-Louis where lovers strolled at sunset with their cones of crème-glacée. While Lucy crossed King Street and headed north, pigeons strutted in Place de la Bastille and the setting sun cast the shadow of a winged statue across Lucy's path. Lucy imagined looking up and finding Claire in an upstairs balcony, the shutter doors open and the lace curtains gusting out with the breeze. Her accordion sitting like a happy baby on her lap. Claire, spying Lucy, would take a magnolia blossom from her hair and throw it down to the street, waving wildly, "Bienvenue ma petite cherie!" After the blossom, a key on a red silk ribbon would arc down to Lucy's feet so that she could ascend the wrought-iron stairway to the apartment of her minstrel friend and stay for awhile and eat bread with cheese, and drink wine, and sleep in the same bed under a chenille blanket with the windows left open to the sounds of Parisian streets.

A hundred Parises that never happened.

"What are you doing here? You never come over here."

"The last time I came over I got food thrown at me."

"So you came to argue?"

Peter was standing in the backyard when Lucy got home. He wore work gloves on his hands. He had on a pair of gumboots. He was holding a rake.

"You came over to garden?"

"I needed something to do."

She looked at him standing in the backyard. At his feet was a fan of metal gardening supplies he'd taken out of the garage: a hoe, a pitchfork, a shovel, several trowels and a hose neatly coiled.

"I don't have anything to do where I live."

"Phone first next time," she said and went into the house.

¶ Peter's grief felt like a tired gripping weed. Like the tendrils of Virginia creeper on the back fence on Maple Avenue. And so he decided that's where he would go. Well, not decided exactly. He got into his car and drove to the house and found himself standing in the middle of the backyard of his past life. He found himself with gumboots on, from the garage. And tools on the ground beside him. He found himself standing there holding onto a rake and then Lucy coming and speaking with him and now he found himself facing the Virginia creeper and tearing at the vines. He tore and tore at the vines with the rake, with the pitchfork, with his hands, and still, the vines clung, their roots deep in the earth, their suckers choking the boards of the fence, trapping moisture in, rotting the wood.

Lucy came out again. "There's a note. Kier's gone."

"What?"

"Kier has left."

"I heard you."

Lucy turned to go back inside.

"What does that mean?" asked Peter.

"My guess is that it means Kier isn't here anymore. That he's gone. That eventually everyone will go, and that no one will have the decency to write me a proper letter." She paused, "Except for you apparently. You will remain. Gardening." She walked back through the kitchen door. Lucy put water into the kettle for a cup of tea and watched Peter out the kitchen window.

The vines clung and Peter tore at them and slowly the fence was revealed: split, ugly, knotted. The vines at least faded to a purple in summer and then a red over the autumn. The fence was a mess.

Peter didn't really understand what Lucy had meant by "Kier isn't here." Was this what she had meant? That Kier was gone? Kier had left for some place else? What was Kier doing there? Peter picked up the defeated vines and piled them together. He found a garbage bag in the garage and put the torn-off branches on the front curb. The fence looked uglier, Peter thought, than when he'd arrived. He went into the garage again and found some sandpaper. He made an attempt to sand at some of the fence, but then his arms felt tired and he had to head to work. He stood looking at what he had done.

Lucy came out holding a cup of tea for Peter.

They stood together in the yard staring at the ugly fence.

"It looks worse," Lucy said.

"It will grow back by next summer." He took a long gulp of Darjeeling and handed her his empty cup. "Kier is actually gone?"

"So it would seem," Lucy said.

¶ Lucy went back into the kitchen and sat down at the table. She had dropped her purse and house keys and the plastic bag Jeremiah Bulmer had given to her with the chocolatines onto the Formica table. She could hear Peter's car pulling out of the driveway. She would have one of these pastries alone in her kitchen. She would have one of the chocolatines with her own cup of tea. Lucy untied the knot in the handles of the plastic bag and pulled out the pastry box. *Hawthorn's Fine Cakes and Pastries* the box read, in silver script.

Robert had phoned Peter every week since Rose's death urging him to come down to the flight museum and see the work they had begun on the replica Arrow. "It will be good for you, Pierre, to take off your mind, non?"

Peter had resisted. The disappointment he would feel if this project was somehow a joke, a preserved and historicized might-have-been, he couldn't manage. He could barely get himself into work at the lighting company. He'd taken five sick days in the past month. "I'm busy, Robert," he lied.

He found himself just sitting on the side of the bed in his empty apartment. His joints sore, his shoulders heavy. Watching the light from the window slide down the painting of the seagulls until the entire wall was in shadow. Take-out containers of Chinese food were scattered on the kitchen counter. A pile of dry cleaning from weeks before stayed slumped over a kitchen chair, shirts gauzed in thin plastic. He continually had the urge to phone Lucy, but resisted.

Robert finally showed up at Peter's door on a Saturday morning in late July and woke him up with old-fashioned glazed donuts and a coffee, his Datsun parked in a no-parking zone at the end of the mews. To Peter's protests, Robert simply said, "Tabernac, Pierre, trust me. Juste viens ici already. Dépêche toi."

When Peter walked through the industrial doors into the echoing hangar of the Toronto Flight Museum, the first thing he saw was the suspended cockpit and nose piece that Robert's group of rogue engineers, designers, and aficionados had already managed to draft and build.

Despite himself, Peter smiled.

By the end of August Peter came to the museum with Robert every weekend. "Pouvez-vous me passer la règle, s'il te plait?" He and Robert once again had desks facing each other, this time right on the hangar floor next to a wall of corrugated metal doors that in the summer were opened so that the breeze and the light pooled over their papers and half-assembled plane parts.

The wing that they had begun to construct stretched toward the other galleries and corridors of the museum. Peter waited for his coffee to brew and watched visitors walk beneath a de Havilland Beaver, a bush plane suspended from the ceiling. Two little girls looked and pointed up at the belly of the aircraft. On the wall opposite Peter was a portrait of Punch Dickins, Northern Explorer, wearing furs and an aviator's cap.

The project was a second-hand jigsaw puzzle left at someone's cottage. A musty gathering. There were pieces missing. They were trying to put together a full puzzle out of a box with missing parts.

Peter poured milk into two mugs of coffee. Robert peered over the rims of his bifocals at a partial drawing of the wings that someone had snuck out. He rolled out the yellowed scroll etched with Peter's blue lines. When Robert had first shown Peter the salvaged slip of paper, the prototype in Peter's tidy draftsman's hand—before the notch was put in, before they'd even reached Mach 1—Peter couldn't speak. A part of him had escaped. A tiny handwritten part of his younger self—before disappointment had set in, before working in the dark—had made it out. He had been secreted, as Robert would have said, and was meeting himself again fifteen years later in a museum.

Peter set down the coffees on their table beneath the risen piece of broken plane.

"Why can't we fly this one?" Peter asked Robert across their shared drafting table.

"We are making the wings partially out of wood for one 'ting," Robert said, sipping at his coffee.

"Okay, but after we've fiddled around with this test model. Why not make one to fly?"

"What is this, Pierre?" Robert looked slyly at him. "You are 'aving fun? You are 'appy?"

Bent over the figures of flight once again—no corridors of draftsmen, no machinists, no hiss of the welder's torches and pneumatic rifle-crack of the riveters, no snow yet over the runways' paths, just the familiar sounds of Radio Canada emanating a reassuring lilt from the portable radio Robert had brought along; *Peter Jacobs and Robert Lambert, Wing Development*, not written on any door—in this utter act of futility, Peter was, yes Robert.

CRASH LANDINGS
& LIFE JACKETS

The phone call from Andy that Kier received in his bed-sit apartment on Commercial Drive had come as a surprise. Since Kier had moved out west that summer, the brothers had not spoken. They'd sent a few letters back and forth, but Kier drifted at first, not knowing what he was doing. He hadn't given his family his phone number yet, even though he'd found the apartment in September. His initial postcard home, a sailboat tacking beneath the Lion's Gate bridge, had read:

July 12th, 1971
In Vancouver for the summer. Might stay longer if something comes along. Forgot to leave the house key—I've got it here. Somebody please tell Dad where I am. Didn't have a chance to call before I left. I'm fine. I would have told you about leaving, but I didn't want you to convince me to stay. Needed a change of scene. Hope you understand. Kier.

And then, almost as an afterthought, scrawled after his name:

xo.

The call came in mid-October, Andy's voice awkwardly formal on the end of the line. "Could I please speak to Kier Jacobs?"

"Ando, is that you?"

"Kier. Sorry. I had to get Mama to pull some operator magic to even get this number."

"So good to hear from you. Apologies, bro—" Kier paced back and forth across his bedroom floor and Andy could hear his brother's footsteps "—You know. Sorry I haven't been in very good touch. I've been meaning to call with the number, but ..."

Andy cut him off. "Look, this is expensive and I'm calling from Maryanne's. I have a favour to ask you."

"Sure."

"We just got married."

"Who got married?"

"What do you mean who? Maryanne and I."

Andy heard Kier's pacing stop for a moment and then heard his footsteps resume. "Of course, of course. It's just. Wow. Congratulations? When did this even happen?"

"We decided to elope. I kept thinking what am I waiting for, and then I just proposed to her, and then she said yes. We're moving into a place on the Danforth in November." Andy was speaking quickly. Kier looked out of his kitchen window at the bowling ally across the street. The sign had just lit up pink. A ball crashing into a full set of pins. A perfect strike. "But that's actually not why I'm calling."

"What's up?"

"It's Mama." Andy took a breath. "She's sold the place on Maple Avenue and I need you to come home and help her pack everything up."

Kier was silent. Andy could hear the springs of a chair as his brother sat down.

Kier listened as Andy told the story of how he and Maryanne were married at City Hall. "Just the marriage commissioner and two friends," Andy said. He'd asked Maryanne again and again if such a small ceremony was all right with her. He didn't have the energy to manage Lucy and Peter and where they would stand and if they would be speaking to each other and whether it was likely that they would throw food. "I just want to look at you and make a promise," he'd said to Maryanne one morning in bed—the blue blinds casting their colour over the bed, her blue shape beneath the covers, her blue wave of hair against the pillow making her look like a Picasso.

On the day of the ceremony one massive cumulus cloud hung black over an otherwise perfect blue sky. Maryanne and Andy's

friends signed the registry. Lisa Heinrich, the honey-dipper of Crullers, was Andy's bridesmaid. Simon Lee, a friend of Maryanne's
from the Art College, was her best man. After the ceremony the four
stood on the steps and held unopened umbrellas deciding where to
take photographs. Cars driving by honked their horns at Maryanne
in her veil, white mini-dress, and cowboy boots. In the courtyard of
City Hall, in Nathan Philips Square, a magician performed tricks.
He placed a glass of milk onto a small folding table, held a black
handkerchief over the glass of milk, turned it upside down, and two
white doves emerged from the cloth. The glass of milk was gone.
The birds flew into the sky and then landed on the steps near Andy
and Maryanne.

Simon took the photographs in High Park and just as the last
shots were taken a crack of thunder and the rain came down in great
sheets. Andy scooped Maryanne up close to him beneath the cover
of a pine tree and kissed her hard on the mouth. They were soaked.
They were beaming. One of Maryanne's films had been accepted to
a show in Stockholm; Maryanne would be flying at the beginning of
the month and Andy would follow for their honeymoon.

"I wouldn't normally leave Mama with all this packing to do, Kier.
But this is a big break for Maryanne. It's our honeymoon. You know
I would only call if I had to."

"Sure," Kier had said, "I'll have to rearrange a few things with
my professors—"

"Professors?"

"Yeah. I'm trying out school. UBC."

"Good. So you can come. All told it will take about a month, I
think." Andy sounded relieved, but uncertain. "Can you try for all
of November? The title on the house transfers December first and
Maryanne and I will be moving our stuff into the new place and then
we'll be away until after the new year."

"I'll work something out."

"Yes?" Andy said, making sure.

"Yes, Ando." Kier hated his brother doubting him. "I helped when
Mama smashed up the table, didn't I?"

"You were high on acid, Kier."

"Sure," Kier said, "but I helped."

"Call back when you have the flight booked, okay?" Andy said. "I should go."

"Andy?"

"Yeah, Kier?"

"Seriously. About you and Maryanne. Congratulations."

¶ Kier returned home on a red-eye flight landing in Toronto at 4:48 a.m. on November first. The luggage turnstile lazily circled without any luggage. A woman mopped the floors. Aside from bleary-eyed passengers, cleaning personnel and security guards were the only people present in the terminal when Kier debarked from the plane.

After his luggage came down the chute, Kier flagged a taxi, told the driver Maple Avenue and closed his eyes. When he opened them again, they had driven beyond the highways, past Finch Avenue with its gas stations and drive-thru restaurants, and the car had turned into the maze of culs-de-sacs that made up Malton, now a glorified suburb of Greater Toronto.

The maple trees planted in front of each yard when the houses had been built bent over Maple Avenue as if Kier's bedraggled early-morning homecoming was a parade. Their leaves having turned colour fell into the gutters of the street.

From the back of the taxi Kier could see the house midway up the street. For a brief moment the strangest thought occurred to him: Kier helping the cabby pull two carboys of gasoline from the back of the trunk rather than his newly-purchased suitcase and his backpack of books. Kier unscrewing the carboy's plastic lids, unlocking the door to the house and yelling "Get out!" He imagined Peter, Andy and Lucy still there together, all three of them, rushing out to stand in the sandy pit of the swing set across the street. Kier pouring gasoline over Lucy's records and her yarn, over their photographs. Kier walking up the stairs, spilling gasoline behind him onto each step, past bookshelves, past piles of mail on the wooden steps, past Rose's Minnie Mouse doll still standing google-eyed on the stairs. Kier glugging gasoline onto the beds and quilts and over every pillow in the house, and then Kier going down to the basement and pouring gasoline over Peter's unfinished electrical projects at the workbench, over the final remains of the intergalactic nook that, years

256

ago now, they had moved, piece by piece, downstairs. Kier standing on the street. Behind him the squeaking sound of the swings' chains: his mother, father, and brother swinging on the swing set. A box of wooden matches rattling as Kier takes them out of his pocket, strikes a match and lets it burn for a moment in his hand.

"That'll be twelve-fifty." The taxi was in front of the house. Kier opened the back door of the cab to the cold autumn air.

"Mama?" Kier said when he entered through the kitchen door. A light was on in the living room. "In here." She sat on the settee next to the coral wall and looked up from *The Feminine Mystique* to see her first-born son.

O n the day of Andy's flight, both Claire and Peter had come over. Claire to help Lucy with the packing, Peter to say goodbye to his son. They were in the kitchen, arguing about Christmas coffee porter.

"Claire. Seriously. That's got to stay on the menu," Peter was practically shouting, as Lucy stood on a stepstool, passing plates down from the cupboards to Claire's hands, a gold tennis bracelet dangling at Claire's wrist.

"But are the kids these days drinking porter, Peter? Are they? No. They're drinking their highballs. The disco kids love their highballs." Claire herself, never to be one out of fashion, was wearing chandelier earrings and, hands hovering up to Lucy waiting for the next stack of dishes to be passed down, had rolled up the gold lamé sleeves of her disco blouse.

"Your dad's porter was the benchmark of beer."

"How would you know?" Lucy cut in, a martini shaker clasped in both hands, "that was the only beer you drank."

"That's because nothing else compared."

Claire had bought her brother Charlie out of his share of The Swan and was refurbishing the sprung floors and train car seats to open it up again in time for New Year's.

"Do you think you're going to be able to manage," Lucy asked from the sink, "operating a dance club?"

"The best club owners of history have been women," Claire said emphatically. "Helen Oakley was the one to convince Benny Goodman he should play live with his famous trio at the Rhythm Club. Goodman had refused at first, on account of his piano player, Teddy Wilson, being black, and not wanting to upset the fans with an integrated number." Claire took the teapot from Lucy and began to wrap it in newspaper. "But Helen Oakley said something like, 'Benny, don't be a bigot. You know full well that Teddy's the best there is and that music, and music's fans, don't give a damn about colour.' Everyone thinks Benny was convinced by his producer, John Hammond, but it was a woman, and without her the trio would never have played live. She even paid for Wilson's bus fare from New York to Chicago so he would make it to the show on time."

Peter had driven Andy out from downtown, his suitcase for Stockholm meticulously packed days before, to say goodbye to the family and meet up with Kier who would drive Andy to the airport in Claire's Pop's vintage Mustang. "One must always start a trip to Europe in style," she had said, and offered the boys the use of the car.

The two brothers sat at the kitchen table listening to the banter from another era, to their estranged godmother who, long ago, Claire revelled in telling them, had brought over Armstrong's *West End Blues* when they were both small enough for a playpen.

¶ Andy and Kier had built model planes when they were younger. The planes had flown over their beds on strings; winged shadows cast on their bedspreads while they slept. A fleet of tiny wings and tiny wheels and sometimes tiny pilots protecting them while they dreamt: Spitfires, Blue Angels, Hornets, Peacemakers. Now real planes flew the skies above the house on Maple Avenue continually, landing at the nearby International Airport Terminal that had been built up over the years where the old Malton airport had been: old lines of hangars and straight-forward parking lots replaced with confusing concrete garages and terminals and sliding glass doors and warbling announcements that no one could ever comprehend, like a badly wired circuit board. Andy could recognize many makes of planes before they landed simply by looking at their undercarriages.

The closest he'd been to a plane was seventeen years ago at the rollout of the Arrow, when, after the speeches had been made and before they'd realized their mama had gone missing, the silk rope was taken away and both he and Kier had put their hands against the huge tandem wheels. The entire plane had loomed above them like an unanswered question, like trying to think about infinity. But, at the age of twenty-six, Andy had never flown.

"In 1929, Jan Zurakowski won the Polish national competition for model plane building," Peter said. This speech, Andy knew, was his father's way of saying goodbye. And although he hadn't been over to the house on Maple Avenue since he pulled the Virginia creeper from the fence half a year ago—which had, thankfully, grown back, filling in thick with reds and purples—Peter seemed to feel comfortable there, sitting at the old kitchen table by the back door where Andy was nervously double-checking for his passport.

Peter had given Andy a gift: a plain black-covered draftsman's notebook. The pages alternated between green sheets of graph paper and plain lined notepaper. On the front cover beside *Subject* Peter had written for Andy in his tidy draftsman's hand: *Trip to Sweden.* "The prize for the model plane building competition was a ride in an airplane," Peter continued. "That was the first time Janusz ever flew." Peter paused and looked at Andy standing by the door.

"Thank you, Dad," Andy held up the book, "Very thoughtful." He didn't want to check-in late. He was supposed to be there two hours before his flight. "No one actually goes two hours before their flight," Kier had told him.

"So I thought, don't worry that this is your first flight, your maiden voyage." It looked as though Peter would keep talking. It looked as though Peter wanted to get on the plane with Andy. Andy was pretty sure that if he suggested it, "Dad, why don't you come along? You've never been to Sweden, have you?" Peter would have said "Right-O, I'll get a few things packed up then."

"—Okay, Dad. Thanks." Andy held up the notebook again. "I really should get going now."

"Be quiet, Peter. Let me say goodbye to him." Lucy got off the stepstool and gave Andy a hug. "I'll miss you," she said into his ear. "You have the address of the condo for when you get back into town?" She and Claire had bought condo suites in the same complex near High Park, less than five blocks from their old high school.

"Yes, Mum. And you said you've managed to keep the same telephone number?"

"Janice pulled a few strings for me at work."

"Okay then, Maryanne and I will give you a call when we get back in January."

"Take lots of pictures," Claire said from the sink.

"Remember to chew some gum," Peter added.

"Okay, okay," Kier said, ushering Andy toward the door. "He'll be fine."

"For your ears. Remember to chew some gum." Peter repeated behind them.

"Alright, Dad," both Kier and Andy said at once on their way to the car.

"Safe travels," Lucy said, and waved to her sons as they drove away.

"Do you remember how we used to pretend we were the ones to rescue her from the field?" Andy asked. They had turned at the on-ramp and were on the highway to the airport.

"I don't remember that. I remember us looking at her, but not rescuing her." Kier said.

"Really?" Andy played with the clasp of the glove compartment. He opened it and closed it nervously. "I remember rescuing her." His suitcase and carry-on were neatly stacked in the trunk.

Kier clicked the turn signal and then merged into the next lane. "I thought we just looked for clues."

"The clock. Remember we used to pretend that the clock was stopped?"

Kier looked out the front window of the car. "And the burnt tree. I remember pointing at the burnt tree." The windshield wipers were on and it felt as though Andy and Kier were in a vessel at sea, not in a car, not driving.

"I thought we were actually there," Andy said. "I remember us imagining that day so fiercely that I recalled it as if it was a memory."

Kier steered carefully. "I remember being there too."

The brothers were silent. The flick of the windshield wiper blades, the drumming of the rain against the car roof. Lucy's blue chiffon scarf that sat on the white vinyl seat of the DeSoto like a pool of water.

¶ Andy walked slowly down the aisle of the plane behind a woman who smelled like eucalyptus cough drops. She'd offered him one while they waited to board.

"No thank you. I'm not sick."

"Neither am I," she said.

Andy looked down at his boarding pass and up at the illuminated rows of numbers and letters that indicated seating. He matched his number with the corresponding row and noticed he was by the wing. He took off his jacket and put it in the overhead bin. Other passengers pushed past. Andy had the window seat. Through the tiny portal he could see men on the tarmac below loading luggage using a portable conveyer belt.

Everyone was seated. The seat-belt sign came on. Andy already had his done up. The plane rolled backward and Andy felt a lurch in his stomach. He watched another plane taxi on a distant runway, build up speed and take off.

Along the length of the aisle flight attendants stood in formation and waved safety booklets above their heads like semaphore. A soothing female voice came over the loudspeakers, instructing passengers. "Please follow along with the safety demonstration by locating the laminated card in the seat pocket in front of you." She repeated herself in Swedish. "This will outline the safety features of our aircraft. If you have any questions, our in-flight agents will be happy to assist you." Andy took the laminated brochure out and examined the cartoon figures of passengers blowing into inflatable life jackets and putting air masks onto the elderly. He looked up at the stewardess closest to him who was clicking a seat belt above her head and pointing to the illuminated strip along the cabin floor.

Andy noticed that no one in the seats around him was looking at the safety pamphlet or the safety demonstration. A boy in the seat next to him was blowing huge pink bubbles with his chewing gum. The woman who had offered the cough drop was ahead of Andy in a row to his left. She had an inflatable travel neck pillow on and it looked like she was already asleep. Andy read every word of the safety pamphlet in English and Swedish: Kraschlandning, Crash Landing; Flyväst, Life Jacket.

It happened suddenly. The flight attendants were gone from the aisle and the patches of grass to the side of the runway sped up outside Andy's window. The acceleration pushed his weight into the back of the seat and the world was at an angle and the world was below him and Andy couldn't take his eyes from the window as the suburbs, the light from the city, the CN Tower, the lit pinwheel of a Ferris wheel, and the wide-mouthed basin of Toronto Harbour were all far beneath him. In one ascent, rows of train cars, lines of transport trucks, stadiums, schools, hospitals, backyard pools and the marked rows of graveyards unfurled themselves simultaneously, as if the entire scope of life was being revealed from a great height. A white cloud and then an endless pitch of blue.

If Lucy had decided to see Jeremiah Bulmer again at the parish of Saint Mary's he would have told her. He would still have claimed that he was not the man she was looking for, and that what she was seeking would never be found in a singular person. After all, does it matter whether the Samaritan in the proverb ever lived in flesh and blood? Is it not the truth in the story that most matters? But, if Lucy had come to see him again, he would have told her what she wanted to hear: that it had been the most beautiful morning for a wedding.

¶ It was the first wedding Jeremiah Bulmer was to perform on his own. He was twenty-five years old, had just been ordained a priest a month and a half earlier, at the end of August 1957, and had sent a postcard photograph down to his mother in Georgia of him standing in his clerical robes outside of his new parish church in Toronto. His mother had saved up to give him the truck that had driven him north through Nashville, Louisville, Dayton, Detroit and across into Ontario. "Now it ain't new or anything, but it run good and the mechanic told me she's got a good number of miles left on her." She had set aside enough money for a truck by cleaning other people's houses so that Jeremiah could attend Saint Michael's theological college at the University of Toronto, and Jeremiah hadn't the faintest idea of how he would be able to thank her.

The wedding was to be out in a farmhouse off the Peel Regional Road. The bride was in an upstairs bedroom with all her women. Her mother and her grandmother had just helped her with her veil. The men were in the kitchen, smoking cigars in their shirt sleeves. They'd got the windows propped wide open because of the humidity from a storm that had come up. The groom was acting like he wasn't nervous, watching the clock, expecting for the priest to come. And the priest, on his way to the wedding, his cleric's gown hung in the back window, slowing down in his truck to see if there'd been a flat, a car pulled over in the rain that had just started and would surely pour down by the look of those dark clouds.

The priest slowed down to see a woman in the field, looking as though she'd been sick with something, and then the flash of lightning right there, illuminating everything like the strike of a bomb, like heaven itself had opened up, and he could feel the electricity himself in the hairs of his arms. Out the splattered windshield of his truck window, the right windshield wiper stuck, he saw the woman in the field caught in that light, a blue arc, and then down, her skirt flung up and her hair coming loose and a fire in the tree right above her like something out of that priest's picture Bible that his mother handed him as a child to shush him up on the kitchen floor. He slowed the truck down to a stop on the gravel beside this woman's car. The rain was coming down heavy now, he could hardly see her anymore from out the windshield, whether she was moving, whether there was another vehicle that would come and take care of this. He was to be at the wedding any moment. The men had shut the windows. The bride had sat down on the bed and taken off her shoes. She had sent one of her sisters down to see about whether that priest had come.

This was a stranger. He was meant to be at the wedding. This was his first wedding and he had a duty to perform. Was he to keep driving to where he was supposed to be that afternoon? To a celebration that would cause him no harm? Or was he to stop here? The priest sat silently in his truck, the current of electricity still palpable in the air, like a filament of metal in the mouth.

His mother had sent a card back to Jeremiah after receiving his postcard with the picture of him dressed in his cleric's gowns. It was a picture of herself that she sent back to him. Slightly out of focus. It was the last shot of film on her neighbour's camera, and she had been in a hurry to get to work, so couldn't have taken another one. The photograph of Jeremiah's mother standing by the azalea tree in the front yard in Georgia. She had on her work clothes, a maid's clothes, and she was smiling her smile just for him, her son. On the back she had written a quote from the Old Testament: *Before I created you in the womb, I selected you; Before you were born, I consecrated you; I appointed you a prophet concerning the nations. See, I appoint you this day Over nations and kingdoms: to uproot and pull down, To destroy and overthrow, To build and to plant.—Jeremiah, chapter 1, verses 1 through 10. I'm right proud of you. Mom*

Despite feeling like a child, despite resisting the call even as he pulled open the heaving metal door of the beat-up blue truck—finding himself in his dress clothes, in his one pair of good shoes, getting soaked through to the skin in the rain—Jeremiah descended into the field off the highway road. He slid through the gravel and mud and at one point fell down so that there was a rip on the knee of his pants and grass stained onto the skin of his palms. He righted himself, swam forward toward the woman in the field. He knelt down beside her and put his face close to her face to see if he couldn't feel her breath in his ear. Jeremiah put his arms awkwardly around the woman's limp body. One arm beneath her knees and the other beneath her back and neck, and he leaned into the lifting, pushed down against the slick field of grass with all the strength in his back and in his knees, hoping he wouldn't slip again, hoping he could make it back to the cab of his truck.

At the door to the truck Jeremiah had to put her down again. He had to put the stranger's body on the ground. He laid her down on the white side-line on the tarmac of the highway while he swung open the passenger door to the cab, heaved her up again and rested her head as delicately as possible against the seat back, tucking Lucy's legs and her right arm, and the tulle fabric of her dress into the dry space of the truck before he slammed the door. He then walked the eight paces down the highway to the car, opened the passenger side door of the DeSoto, and unclasped the gold snap on Lucy's navy purse that was resting beside a piece of notepaper that read *Hawthorn's Fine Cakes and Pastries, Queen Street West. Near Dovercourt. North Side,* and a blue scarf. Jeremiah removed her wallet with her identification before getting into the driver's side door of his truck and revving the engine.

The bride at this point had given up. She had her mother downstairs calling furiously to the church trying to get hold of where the priest had gotten to. The men had lit more cigars and the groom had opened the windows again, the storm having passed through. The groom fiddled with the carnation in his buttonhole, trying to get the red wilted petals to stand straight again. He nearly pricked his finger on the pin. He was anxious to see his bride's face and to get through the ceremony so that he could get into the car with her—decorated earlier that day by the groomsmen with tins attached and strings and a *Just Married* sign—to finally take her beautiful body home.

At the Emergency, Jeremiah dropped Lucy off at the nurses' station. He gently slung Lucy's body in a black leather wheelchair, carefully placed her feet onto the metal footrests—one stocking singed, that foot missing its shoe—and wheeled her into the long corridor past the sliding glass doors. The nurses saw his collar and asked after him as he ran out the door. He mentioned the lightning strike and where Lucy's car was along the highway. He said he had a wedding to get to. He forgot to mention his name, or the name of his parish, "Her wallet is on her lap, her identification should be in there," and like the unnamed Samaritan he was gone.

By the time Jeremiah arrived to the house the sun was out again as if the storm had never happened. The groom and the bride and all of their friends and family were sitting at a long table in the covered sun porch eating potato salad and sandwiches and coleslaw and boiled pieces of sweet autumn corn with thick slabs of butter. It was as if the woman in that field had hardly existed. As if that time was the time of a different man. When Jeremiah came up the path of the house to the screen door of the porch the groomsmen cheered. They had been chugging back beers with their cigars in the kitchen for two hours.

The wedding takes place right there on the sun porch. The torn knee of Jeremiah's pants covered by his robes. The aunts and uncles and cousins and grandparents are all gathered in the one room as Jeremiah performs his first marriage ceremony. The young couple face each other in front of their families and, holding onto each other's hands, make the promise to give each other their lives.

Many books, archival materials and museum exhibitions have proven invaluable to my research including, but not limited to: fonds from the National Library and Archives of Canada; The Arrowheads' *Avro Arrow: The Story of the Avro Arrow from its Evolution to its Extinction* (ed. Richard Organ et al. 1980); James Dow's *Arrow* (1979); Palmiro Campagna's *Storms of Controversy: The Secret Avro Arrow Files Revealed* (1992); Chris Gainor's *Who Killed the Avro Arrow?* (2007); E.K. Shaw's *There Never Was An Arrow* (1981); Greig Stewart's *Shutting Down the National Dream* (1988); Bill Zuk's *Avro Arrow Story* (2004) and Peter Zuuring's *Arrow Scrapbook* (1999). My visit in August of 2004 to see the Barry's Bay Janusz Zurakowski Memorial Park, built with neighbourhood donations to honour the first Arrow test pilot, as well as museum visits to *Avro Arrow: A Dream Denied*, exhibited at the West Vancouver Museum in May 2004, and to the Toronto Aerospace Museum in July 2004 to see the reconstruction of the Arrow, gave me visual and tactile inspiration impossible to access otherwise. The volunteers at these museums went beyond the bounds of duty to answer questions. I am grateful for their spirited assistance.

    Throughout this book many characters are reading or being read to. Lieutenant Briggs recites from Christopher Marlowe's "The Passionate Shepherd to His Love" (1600). Lucy reads to Peter from Virgina Woolf's *The Waves* (1931). Lucy's desire to walk into her patterned plates is inspired by Anne Simpson's poem "Willow Pattern" from *Quick* (2007). Lucy's orange is dedicated to my literature students at Saint Mary's and Dalhousie Universities, and is inspired by our thinking about odes. Lucy sings lyrics to Rose from the blues classic *Muddy Water* (1926), lyrics written by Jo Trent with music by Peter DeRose & Harry Richman. Kier is reading Leonard Cohen's *Beautiful Losers* (1966). Upon seeing Claire again, Lucy recalls the Emily Dickinson poem which begins "After great pain, a formal feeling comes—" numbered 341 by editor Thomas H. Johnson. Maryanne and Andy are listening to Leonard Cohen's "Sisters of Mercy": Sony/ATV Songs LLC (BMI)/ Sony/ATV Music Publishing Canada (SOCAN); all rights reserved; used by permission.

Thank you to the Canada Council of the Arts, the Nova Scotia Department of Tourism and Culture, and the Banff Centre for the Arts for their financial support, without which this project would not have been possible. Thank you to the Elizabeth Bishop House. Thank you to the editors of *PRISM International* for publishing an early excerpt from this manuscript. Thank you to Chris Hand at Zeke's Gallery in Montréal; Alison and Mira at Pete's Candy Store in Brooklyn; and the Banff Centre for the Arts for hosting and recording readings of this work while it was in progress. Thank you to my inspiring colleagues and mentors at the University of Victoria, Concordia University, and the 2006 Banff Writing Studio.

Thank you to Frank Jessup, David and Jo Marshall, and Mario Pesando for their insightful interviews about working on the Avro Arrow and the Orenda Engine.

For cheering me along the way; furthering in me a questioning and discerning love of language; or compelling me to Rilke's imperative that I must change my life: thank you John Beach, Stephanie Bolster, Annie Bray, Lorna Crozier, Diane Faulkner, Bill Gaston, Katia Grubisic, Vesla Haley, Ami Harbin, Marika Hudz, Sheila Kier, Patrick Lane, the Lunch Group, Massey College, Don McKay, Anne Simpson, Vanessa Lee Sorenson, Allison Sullings, the ladies of the Toronto Salon, Derk Wynand and Patricia Young. For also reading and commenting on early drafts and excerpts of this manuscript, extra-special thanks to Scott Fotheringham, Judith Herz, Mikhail Iossel, Colin McAdam, Lisa Moore, Kate Stearns, Peter Such, Megan Switzer, and Heidi Wightman. Thank you Trina Grant Adam, publicist-extraordinaire in high-top sneakers.

For your exacting eye and your expansive heart, thank you Jack Hodgins. Thank you Michael Winter for your mentorship, concision and kindness. Thank you Sarah Selecky, writing genie. Sheryda Warrener, you are my international pen pal of the heart, thank you. For keeping my mind full of poems and for the joy and delirium of Delirium Press, thank you Kate Hall. Fiona Foster, for your editorship and friendship, infinite mermaid thanks. Jacquie Jessup and Bart Jessup, thank you for your unconditional and unfailing love. I am unspeakably grateful. Best friend in the universe, without whom I would be like Laika, orbiting without enough air or light to survive, thank you Jocelyn Parr, you come to the rescue dressed like a fiery rocket-ship every time. What would I do without you? For sealing our friendship with your grandmother's bread recipe, for the Atlantic Ocean, and for every single letter, thank you Warren Heiti. Thank you Andrew Steeves, Gary Dunfield, and everyone at Gaspereau Press for making the most beautiful books in the world. I am endlessly proud to work with you. And thank you, dear reader, for trusting in this inexplicable alchemy.

¶ The types used in this book are new designs by Rod McDonald of Lake Echo, Nova Scotia, used here in trial form in advance of their commercial release. The main type is GOLUSKA, designed in homage to the typographer and letterpress printer Glenn Goluska (1947–2011).

ABCDEFGHIJKLMNOPQURSTVWXYZ
abcdefghijklmnopqurstvwxyz & 1234567890
ABCDEFGHIJKLMNOPQURSTVWXYZ

ABCDEFGHIJKLMNOPQURSTVWXYZ
abcdefghijklmnopqurstvwxyz & 1234567890
ABCDEFGHIJKLMNOPQURSTVWXYZ

The sans serif type is CLASSIC GROTESQUE, an extensive digital revival of a German grotesque which McDonald completed in seven weights for Monotype Imaging. Monotype's F.H. Pierpont originally adapted this type for machine composition in 1926 from grotesques pioneered by the German type foundries of H. Berthold and Wagner & Schimdt.

GGGGG**GGROTESQUE**

ABCDEFGHIJKLMNOPQURSTVWXYZ
abcdefghijklmnopqurstvwxyz & 1234567890
ABCDEFGHIJKLMNOPQURSTVWXYZ

ABCDEFGHIJKLMNOPQURSTVWXYZ
abcdefghijklmnopqurstvwxyz & 1234567890
ABCDEFGHIJKLMNOPQURSTVWXYZ

Also making brief appearances are Courier New and Adobe's Garamond Premier Pro.

Typeset in Goluska and Classic Grotesque by
Andrew Steeves and printed offset and bound under
the direction of Gary Dunfield at Gaspereau Press,
Kentville, Nova Scotia.

1   3   5   7   6   4   2

National Library of Canada Cataloguing in Publication

Jessup, Heather
The lightning field / Heather Jessup.

ISBN 978-1-55447-106-5

1. Avro Arrow (Jet fighter plane)—Fiction.   I. Title.

PS8619.E795L55 2011   C813'.6   C2011-906347-6

GASPEREAU PRESS LIMITED
Gary Dunfield & Andrew Steeves—Printers & Publishers
47 CHURCH AVENUE KENTVILLE NS B4N 2M7
WWW.GASPEREAU.COM